MW00513422

Praise for Under the Table

"A snappy heist novel, set during the production of an out-of-control television comedy in 1989 Toronto, *Under the Table* is a clever noir that will keep 'em guessing. Wickedly funny, you'll laugh even though you know you shouldn't. Much like the sketch show that it portrays, *Under the Table* entertains with dark humor, quirky characters, and celebrity appearances, while poking fun at the absurdity of societal constructs. Quippy and smart, Smith's prose is electric and crackles across the page."—Meagan Lucas, author of *Songbirds and Stray Dogs*, editor of *Reckon Review*

"A drag queen Cher sings 'If I Could Turn Back Time'. . . Vern Smith does. *Under the Table* is a magician's conjuring of 1989, an era of more innocent dangers, nuclear annihilation, say, or Billy Idol's later output. With a plot as tight as a cock-rocker's perm and dialogue so sharp you'll be looking over your shoulder to see who's talking, this is a novel of sass, heart, and the bemusement of being dealt a hand that looked so good you made the mistake of checking. Vern Smith is a rare combination of a true craftsman and a genuine entertainer."
—Tom McCulloch, author of *The Accidental Recluse*

"Combine a handful of offbeat characters-with-pasts, a television studio, too many drugs and a vulnerable payroll, and you have Vern Smith's new noir novel, *Under the Table*. Set in 1989, with a distinctly Canadian vibe, the novel well captures the era's unique flavor and electric-cocaine madness. The plotting and personalities are unpredictable, right up to and beyond an explosive climax."—Karl Wenclas, *New Pop Lit*

"You're new in town and you're watching this bunch of sluggards, chancers and grifters, wagering on who's okay and who ain't. But it's all just a shadow play of their own making and you ain't sure if you can see beyond the silhouettes. By the time you do, your money is all gone."—u.v.ray, author of *Drug Story*

"*Under the Table* is a high-voltage satire of life behind the scenes of Toronto's 'Hollywood North' in the last days of the analog era—when the smartest phone looked like a brick with buttons, and digital communication tended to involve the raising of a finger. The frenetic misadventures of its amped-up underdogs, outsiders, antiheroes, and tarnished glitterati play out through an atmosphere of steamy summer-in-the-city languor. Readers who like dangerous good fun are sure to get a charge off this latest from Vern Smith. It is, in short, a blast!"—Steve Venright, author of *The Least You Can Do Is Be Magnificent*

"Triggered by the Hollywood power structure corrupting a Toronto TV studio, the well-mannered Canadian stereotype proves to be the perfect ski-mask when an inside-job crime is hashed. Vern Smith offers an informed perspective into entertainment hierarchies, how they tempt the bottom rung into mimicking the top elite right under their noses—the same ruthless inner voice that asks, 'How much can I get away with?' Sprinkled with erudite snark and late '80s pop-culture gemstones, *Under the Table* is a lively, refreshing take on the heist drama."
—Gabriel Hart, author of *A Return to Spring*

Praise for Vern Smith's Fiction

"Reading Vern Smith is to be reminded that urban America is more than the sum of its con jobs; it is a texture built of rips and stitches, a circus tent under which some of its wackiest animators hold forth . . . *The Green Ghetto* is electric, eccentric, extracellular madness."—Michael Turner, author of *Hard Core Logo*

"Wilderness meets the city in 'The Great Salmon Hunt,' Vern Smith's delightful, wicked tall tale. Men fish for monster-size salmon on Lake Ontario while in the distance, 'The city core, the SkyDome, the CN Tower, and the Gardiner Expressway were enveloped in a green plume of smog, as if a lime rainbow had wrapped itself around downtown.' . . . The city is wilderness."
—Zsuzsi Gartner, *Quill & Quire*

Copyright © Vern Smith, 2021

All rights reserved. No part of this publication may be reproduced, distributed, or transmitted in any form or by any means, including photocopying, recording, or other electronic or mechanical methods, without the prior written permission of the publisher, except in the case of brief quotations embodied in critical reviews and certain other noncommercial uses permitted by copyright law.

Book design by Gary Anderson
Cover design by Gretchen Jankowski
Cover photo by Garth Jackson
Cover model Lua of Windsor

ISBN: 978-1-7333526-7-3
Run Amok Books, 2021
First Edition

Run Amok

Printed in the USA

Under the Table

A novel by
Vern Smith

For Vi

1

Friday, July 7, 1989

Arlene Marion was fucking back. Abel Otto himself—star of his own show now—declared as much when they finished shooting season one last night. Of course, he also said working with her was like pissing in the wind. That, and he liked her better on painkillers.

Arlene tried to forget those last two parts. She shook them off as backhanded compliments, telling herself Abel was cocky, cheeky, and a little too keen to get TV trash talking about him as a water-cooler kind of guy.

"Fucking back," she said, sticking to message. "You heard Abel Otto. 'Arlene Marion is fucking back.'"

Veronica Williams wasn't around when Abel made said proclamation. But, sitting at her desk and counting money, she knew enough to nod anyway, and say, "Back."

Hovering, Arlene sipped Earl Grey Traditional from a plain Wedgwood cup.

After 18 days of rehearsal and shooting, the first 10 episodes of *The Otto Show*—a made-in-Canada American comedy sketch program—were in the can. Studio audiences agreed that it was a little like *Kids in the Hall* meets *Saturday Night Live*, albeit more willing to risk offense. Trouble was, Arlene wanted to hear the word "palatable," for this thing was supposed to appeal to as many people as possible—another Arlene Marion confection. Regardless, agreements were in place to start shooting season two next week. Arlene had met all obligations thus far, meaning she was out of Cherry Beach Studios, back at her Queen Street East headquarters.

Outside, against a clay-brick wall, a skinny hippie sat cross-legged with a ferret wrapped around her shoulders like a live low-rent mink, sparing for change. Above her head, an egg-shaped brass sign marked the official territory.

Arlene Marion and Associates (AMA)
Production Company

Inside Veronica's cubicle looking out, Arlene stood on her toes, pressing her face against the window. "It is like she knows when we have money. That does not make you nervous?"

Veronica rolled her shoulders. "Not my money."

Arlene did not care for either the tone or remark. Condescending, she thought, stepping closer, watching Veronica count. Now came the time for money to exchange hands, and Arlene always hated this part, time wasted. As per routine, she didn't meet payroll until the end of shooting, ensuring her peeps, as she called them, would be too scared to quit, too scared to refuse free overtime. And well, that's just how it worked in Hollywood North, often enough anyway.

"That production assistant, Kiwi." Arlene sipped, swallowed. "Looks up with these sad bloodhound eyes every time I catch him not doing something. The piss-tank—letting people steal walkie-talkies, three, from us."

"The indifference," Veronica said. Recounting to $1,800, she placed the stack in a security envelope, handing it to Arlene who stood there doing her own math. Slowly pulling a face, sour, she said, "This is for the new parking guy, the one you girls have been flirting with?"

Veronica gasped. "I don't flirt with the help, ma'am."

Ma'am—Arlene could see it, the girl getting flippant again. Deeming it time to nip that in the bud, Arlene lined her up, spreading the cash in her fist. "You are the help. Now help me, is this Lawn Boy's remuneration?"

Veronica nodded at the envelope. "Read the label."

"I am asking you."

"Yes." Veronica smirked. "It's Nathan's pay."

"Then it is heavy. Fishhooks, I swear you do this on purpose, or are you distracted?"

As a matter of fact, Veronica wanted to say she was distracted, what the hovering, that she hadn't made this mistake before, that she worked 14-hour days. But it all screamed victim, so early '80s. Instead, she just said, "You pull rank more often than CBC finds gigs for the *Street Legal* players. Why did it have to be that way? Why did everything have to be personal?"

Personal? Arlene had paid for the VHS tapes on the shelves, printed boxes of her shows. The leopard couch near reception was a *Buy & Sell* bargain, sure, but she paid cash for it. Same with the frames wallpapering the place with autographed eight-by-tens. She paid for everything. And until the investors said differently, this was still her house, so you bet it was personal.

"Just make me another Traditional, talking to me like that. You should know the drill by now. Dip three times—not four—quickly." Arlene dipped an imaginary teabag into the cup as if swatting at something swimming on top. "Do not allow the bag to linger, barely stain the water. And use the correct cup this time, mine."

Veronica turned, muttering OCD on her way to the kitchen.

"Pardon me, Little Arlene. What was that?"

Failing to elicit a response, Arlene sat in Veronica's chair, locating the envelope marked Kiwi, clearly an illegal, removing a hundred-dollar bill. Smiling, removing another, she thought, yes, she would make him responsible for the stolen walkies, financially.

***

Veronica flicked on the burner, placed the kettle upon it, then looked into a mirror mounted next to the stove, thinking how the old beastie had clever nicknames for everyone. Veronica, for instance, had been dubbed Little Arlene because she looked like the lady in charge, in her youth. At least that's what the grunts said after seeing the faded studio photos near reception.

Veronica didn't think so, even if she was 5'5", a pinch shorter. And so what if they dressed a little alike, always wearing dueling linen jackets over T-shirts tucked into high-waist jeans. Each owned upwards of a dozen tennis shoes, too. Today, Arlene wore red, Veronica tan.

Clad comfortably, sensibly, they would have both been what mousy women like to call sandy blonde without product. With it,

Veronica's first distinction was that she'd given up the hassle of straightening her curls. She looked all the better for it. Felt better, too, relaxed.

Another distinction was the thin, angular scar running through the thick part of her right brow. Rueben, Veronica's stylist, taught her how to camouflage the wound. Half dab of mascara mixed with equal parts cigarette ash would do the trick, but Veronica didn't have time, what with a job like hers. Time—she liked the way the scar brought attention away from her nose. She'd seen her photographs. The least bit of shadow and her nose disappeared like she'd been shot through a Vaseline lens.

Looks aside, Veronica's moniker also had something to do with the gossips saying she'd been handpicked to take over the production company, eventually, and her abilities were tested when Arlene out and admitted she had the problem in April. That she'd been addicted to those little Percodans ever since the-slip-and-fall at last year's film fest.

Veronica, as the (acting) executive producer, filled in admirably while the head lady was six weeks at some secret Vancouver rehab, finalizing details on *The Otto Show* while juggling post-production on a Chris Farley special for HBO.

At worst, her work was deemed solid, stable. Then she went above and beyond, lining up an international one-nighter with impressionist André-Philippe Gagnon. He'd been dining out on his ability to do every voice on "We Are the World," and seemed to have a special place in Johnny Carson's heart. More importantly, nobody expected that deal, not even Arlene, who was forced to admit that Veronica had been a dream stop-gap.

But again, Arlene Marion was fucking back, making Veronica Williams the director of development all over again. That would have still meant something at any other production company. At AMA, it meant she was in the kitchen, waiting on a whistle.

***

Arlene looked off to a photo of stand-up Ellen DeGeneres, the inscription saying something about a blind lesbian in a sushi bar. Then Bill Murray, telling Arlene she was *Scrooged*, nice. She was trying to decipher Sam Kinison's screaming scribble when the kettle went off.

Wishing one of them could have been more gracious and less glib, she went back to business. Counting and recounting the rent-a-cop's pay until Veronica returned, Arlene reached for the cup with her name on it, old English type. Dunking a pinky, testing it, okay, she took a sip, puckered, warm inside. In the next instant, she was thinking about how she never could get her hair pin straight. Ah, if it wasn't for those tedious side bits curving around her face in the style of Gidget hitting middle-age. For years, Arlene had tried a layered pixie brushed forward, but those fricking side bits would not take. That's why she was tugging at them, trying in vain to train them, to straighten them, multi-tasking as she checked Veronica's math.

Over the next few minutes she found an extra hundred in one envelope, a fifty in another. She thought she should have been getting angrier, saying something, but it didn't matter, not really, not anymore. Whatever happened next, she was over the worst part of coming back, feeling good again, proud, almost euphoric. Fishhooks, she was a survivor, akin to an older Madonna that way, redefining herself.

But then what the frick was that? Her stomach was growling, yet she already had a peanut-butter energy bar and a juice box. While she felt a tad bloated, cramps, she wasn't due, so maybe it was the antibiotics, Clindamycin, upsetting her stomach. The head rush was probably just a by-product of the trauma of change. That, and she had been working hard, putting out fires.

In between, she allowed the girl to become a distraction, so Arlene was thinking about trying a new tact, apologizing. She was going to do it, too, right before Veronica said she was going for a double-double, and was that alright with Arlene? Always going for a Tim Hortons, more time wasted, when they had a $600 espresso machine in the office kitchen.

"I will thank you to pick this up while you are out." From her inside jacket pocket, Arlene removed a dry-cleaning chit and held it out, thinking go ahead, be nice, see what Little Arlene does with a curve. "And hey, I am sorry about before."

"It's okay" Veronica took the chit, looking at it. "I'm used to it." Then making eye contact. "How are you doing? You don't seem yourself."

"I'm fine." Arlene blinked, a darker line of shadow on the right eye. Tracing a picture of local stand-up Mike Bullard through the cubicle's open side, she thought how the guy signed everything the same—I love it here, Mike Bullard. "The tea, Ronnie." Of all the Earl Greys, Traditional was the best, well-rounded and as-sertive enough to engage the citrus oil, as one critic put it. Also, it was imported from Philadelphia, somewhat expensive, so the girl had better be figuring it out. "I think you finally got it right this time, soothing."

Veronica said thanks, then thank you, watching Arlene put the cup down and hold her palms out, blotchy. At that, she looked up, doing that thing with her lower jaw, moving it back and forth. Here we go, mood swing.

"When you are scared, that is when you get caught."

Arlene was just testing at first, but then Veronica tightened, asking what? Arlene couldn't put her finger on it, saying only that something was different. Something vague, yet tangible.

"Must be my shoes." Veronica touched her collarbone with an open palm, doing her own little test. "Naughty little T-strap with a hidden lift. Makes me tall as you, maybe taller. And my legs." Turning her back. "Will you just look at my—"

"You are wearing tennis shoes, as always." Dry, Arlene took an-other pull on her tea. "And you are using a sarcastic tone, more and more." Forehead creasing the bridge of her nose, concerned, she gripped the corners of Veronica's oxblood desk, pulling herself up, looking a photo of John Candy in the eyes. Both seemed sur-prised as she fell ass-backwards into the chair.

Veronica could see the warning signs—the bruise-blue tint of Arlene's face, same color as her eye shadow, especially around the lips and nostrils. The slight jaundice in her eyes, the shivering, the sweating. Breathing increasingly labored as her eyes shifted up to

Eugene Levy, sideways to Howie Mandel, who's notation asked Arlene if she could give him a hand with a crate of fake testicles being held at the Windsor-Detroit border. Her mouth turned down when it occurred to her. It was the young bravery plain in Dan Aykroyd's Ray-Ban glare, circa *The Blues Brothers*, as much as what he'd inscribed.

To Arlene:
One day, somebody's going to put
something in your drink.
xo Elwood Blues

2

Thursday, June 22

Fifteen days earlier, Nathan Collins attached a walkie-talkie to his hip pocket, headset over his hat, Oakland Hills Country Club, and took to outlining the parking lot with orange pylons at 8 am sharp. For the fourth day in a row, he'd arrived early for vanilla yogurt, nuts and twigs and stuff, *avec* fresh OJ, at the craft services table. He thought it was like making money. Inside Cherry Beach Studios, AMA was scheduled to start taping the first episode of *The Otto Show* at 9:30. Nathan figured that wouldn't happen until after lunch, but he had to be on time, just had to, something about the insurance.

Didn't matter, he was going to be punctual, professional, and diplomatic, as always. Do whatever it took to run a tight lot, impress that high-strung Arlene flake. Maybe he'd even stick for the next block of shooting she'd dangled, saying she'd do a little something for Nathan if he worked out. Another block? Hell, another block would see him through until his usual company got well, end of summer anyway. Plus, not 15 minutes ago, Charlie Murphy reported in a leased Jag, so this prodco had a line on some loot. And Goddammit if they didn't hire a fine-looking piece of white woman for a rent-a-cop, something nice to look at.

Tall, almost six-feet, Nathan thought, big, strong *derrière*, 159 pounds, maybe more, substantial. Dark hair tied tightly behind a blue cop baseball cap and headset, she wore cop shades, standard boots, tens from where Nathan stood.

The girl's getup also included navy Bermudas that seemed to be issued as opposed to purchased. Her pastel-blue cop shirt was heavier in places where crests had been removed. On her belt, dozens of keys jingled against handcuffs and a nightstick that doubled as an emergency flasher on one hip, a white cellular telephone—the brick, they called it—on the other.

"Woman in love with her own uniform," Nathan said under his breath. "Must be a made-in-Canada American comedy."

8

After three days of rehearsal, this was the first day of shooting. That's why AMA had a cop on the case, looking out for folks a step or three away from stardom as much as those on the way down. She was looking out for Nathan Collins, too, smiling, touching the visor on her cap as if to say, yes, him.

Nathan looked down at himself, the word entrapment floating about his head. It turned out warmer than late-night radio forecast, so he wound up wearing green overalls, unzipped far enough to show the orange lettering of a PING T-shirt. Sure, that university-educated white girl was looking out for a guy like him alright. Pylons, he told him himself. Just keep dropping orange cones every three yards, you'll be fine—pylons.

In his youth, Nathan worked as a caddy at The Royal Montreal Golf Club. Went from recruit to captain, the top spot below caddy master, in less than two summers. Did eight years on the Canadian tour and another four-plus on the PGA circuit, mostly for Richard Zokol. Disco Dick they called him by reason of he wore a Walkman in between shots.

For now, the important thing was that Nathan knew how to pace yardage, professionally. It was a handy skill by reason of the painted lines at Cherry Beach Studios had been thinned out to faint speckles among the rag weeds, thistles, and dandelions coming up through cracks.

The only intentional shrubbery was a browning evergreen outgrowing a fractured pebble-concrete planter near the main doors. Nathan thought it didn't help that folks were emptying coffee and cigarettes into the soil. All jacked up on caffeine, nicotine, not enough room to grow—why didn't they just set the poor tree on fire? Yeah, it was a good class of people in this business, killing a living thing slowly like that.

Outlining spot 38, he ticked another one off. Seven more, he said to himself, looking past a few-hundred yards of brush to the west, Lake Ontario. Breathing in deeply, he thought it smelled, hmm, sea-weedy. Wondering why just about every beach was closed when he heard the now familiar roar of a 1960 Chevrolet

Impala four-door hardtop accelerating, bearing down on him like a blue-assed fly.

Standing near the center of the lot, alone, Nathan saw left or right as equally bad options—he didn't know which way the asshole was going today—holding his spot as the blue-assed fly grew larger. The driver gunned hard, mowing over rows of pylons. Fifteen or 20 feet away, Nathan heard Billy Idol singing that he almost died on a blue highway. The Impala swerved in a zigzag skid—left, then right—pulling into spot five near the set-design door with a screech.

Hands at his sides, Nathan thought he should do something, or at least say something. But like yesterday and the day before he found himself stiff, almost paralyzed. Watching that rent-a-cop this time, Claire Something, her first day on the job. She brought the headset down over her neck like one of those toilet-seat neck braces football linemen wear, heading for the Impala, almost marching, shaking her ass a little.

Was that for Nathan, too?

The driver, still inside, was gathering an electric toothbrush, paste, and some toiletries into a navy Adidas shaving bag when the nightstick tapped his window. He didn't bother hurrying, so she did it again, flicking on the flashing red light on her nightstick. She hauled back and belted the window a third and fourth time before the door exploded open, knocking her a few stumble steps back.

Quickly, the driver was outside, standing upright. Big, beautiful man wearing a lemon Polo with the collar popped, vanilla trousers tight at the ankles, checkerboard shoes. Pointing to his car, he said, "This is vintage, mint, just back from the shop." Smiling like he wanted her to say something else, try something, when the snap of a nightstick to the dimple made him pliable. Turned around, spread-eagled across the driver-side door, he tried to regroup, speaking over his shoulder, telling the big girl this was truly irregular. She was a security guard, and was she even supposed to have cuffs? He didn't think so. What about the electric truncheon? He didn't think she was supposed to have one of those, either.

Twisting her lips, she said, "First, you ran at the parking guy, using a vehicle for intent."

"Intent of what?"

"I'll think of something, but then you made your second mistake, your real mistake, assault an officer."

Breath heavy, he said, "Assault an officer—you're so fired." Gave her a backwards head butt, real nice move, knocking her down. Turning, saying Arlene Marion was in love with his shit, he looked down at her, smirking, teeth so free of mercury they all had to be capped. He was laughing at how he'd truly knocked her headset off when she noticed his eyes were the same hue as the sky, bringing the flashing nightstick back again.

"And now that's a second assault an officer."

3

After the regular parking guy didn't show—some poor old man on disability who drank too much because his fused spine prevented him from turning sideways—Veronica Williams seconded Nathan Collins from William Arie Productions. And yes, while Nathan also had back issues, the Arie people said it was mild scoliosis, a slight curvature of his spine from carrying golf bags all those years. Then, that's how they knew he was punctual, profession, and diplomatic—a former tour caddy, used to getting up early, used to etiquette. Better, Nathan could turn sideways, and he had a knack for striking a balance between keeping riff-raff out and addressing stars properly in both English and French.

For 17 of 18 days, the possible exception being what they called a dark day, his shifts were to be eight in the morning to 10 at night. Nathan had done his accounting, and the pay was decent, all things considered. But it was the catered lunches and dinners that made the gig good. Aside from the odd Rita MacNeil special and made-in-Canada American comedy sketches, that was about the only thing AMA was known for—big food—so he would eat well, like everyone else on crew, off the same menu as Abel Otto. Wouldn't have to buy groceries for that whole stretch, socking money away until maybe things turned around with his regular company.

Plus, he'd have use of a cellular telephone, just like the rent-a-cop. And even if the Motorola DynaTAC 8000M was bulky, it was a novelty as much as a guilty pleasure. Who had a cellular telephone? No one, pretty much, and so what if Arlene said it was for AMA business only? If Nathan wanted, he could call in a request to the part-time jazz station from his kiosk and no one would be the wiser. Now there was a convenience.

It was just that Hollywood North was a brand-new industry, almost. The Canada-U.S. Free Trade Agreement was six months old, and slowly American productions were trickling into Canada. Toronto mostly, but Vancouver, too. While Nathan wasn't sure of the precise connection between a phonebook size trade agreement and the Canadian film and TV industry, he knew the value of the American dollar, having made most of his money in the States, so the currency advantage was obvious. Plus there were enough grants, tax credits, write-offs, and border-opening loopholes to make it attractive for American companies to farm out productions here. So yes, Nathan was finding work that basically required him to sit on his *derrière*.

But even as the industry was born, there were as many stops as starts. For instance, the show Nathan was supposed to be working on, *Moonlighting*, was made in the States. Earlier this year, with the advantages of free trade, ABC decided to up and move production to Toronto. As it was explained to Nathan, the crew packed entire contents of set and wardrobe into trucks, preparing detailed manifests for Customs. Getting it all together, documented, and moved took months, after which ABC decided to cancel the show. Now trucks filled with this *Moonlighting* material were sitting in Toronto. Even then, the Arie people were hoping another network would pick up the show, in which case ABC would, ideally, just sell the gear along with the rights.

Nathan thought that was optimistic by reason of nobody gave a fuck about Bruce Willis and Cybill Shepherd anymore. Everyone just wanted to see them play kissy-kissy. Once they did, their ratings tanked, no more show. So, while work was emerging here, it was still scarce enough for those in the star system, let alone people who earned their money. And now, on the first day of shooting at his plan-C job, Nathan already had trouble.

Along with the rent-a-cop and the Impala-driving man, he sat jittery as a boy bracing for the principal's strap in one of five black leather chairs. Brought into the studio from AMA headquarters, the furniture was supposed to make Arlene feel calmer, at home. But it was having the opposite effect, given that Kiwi managed to scratch three legs during the move. She told the New Zealander, use bubble wrap, told him thrice, and now she was thinking about him, again.

Oh frick, the time, Arlene never could get it back, and she was wasting more of it. Shuffling through pink paperwork passing for employment contracts, thinking about something else she did not want to think about, getting madder. Blast it, why were they always taking her away from the creative part?

Finding the contract she was looking for, studying it, she rounded her desk and sat on the corner, clasping a hand in front of her left knee. "Claire Malik?"

The rent-a-cop stood, crossing her arms. "Arlene Marion?"

Standing, throwing her name back like that—now Arlene had to break this new bitch, too. What did they call women like that anyway, amazons? Maybe way back, but Arlene was sure the new word was bodacious, and she feared using it would make her sound like a thespian, that the cop would take it as a come-on. "Please help me out. How is it my set designer ended up in handcuffs after a sharp blow to his cranium, then another to his, shall we say, tender bits?"

Claire told Arlene the same thing she told Cyrus. First, he took a run at the parking attendant, using a vehicle for intent. Moving along before anyone could ask intent of what, she said Cyrus was coming on fast, aggressive, knocking down rows of pylons, that he could have killed the parking guy here.

"Then, he assaulted me, an officer, twice. Knocked me back with his door, then a reverse coco butt. That's right, a coco butt. Put me on the ground." Taking her headset off, holding it out as evidence. "Hit me so hard he knocked this off. Bad enough, then he starts talking, laughing at how he gave me a coco butt. That's confessional malice. I'm contracted out to you by the union as a paid-duty officer, and he assaulted me. That's assault an officer. Pretty serious crime, assault an officer, especially when malicious circumstances are considered."

"And yes, let us consider circumstance, Ms. Malik. You hit my set designer . . . Twice. I mean, this is not exactly Kensington Market at night, a little restraint, please."

"Man assaults an officer, he gets a wood shampoo. Standard procedure."

Arlene looked at the parking guy, deciding to slather the blame around. "William Arie, his people said you were punctual, professional, and diplomatic. That is what Veronica was told, at least what she told me. Point is, we have not even started shooting in here and you mean to tell me there is already trouble out there?"

Nathan said wait a minute, pointing at Claire. "Happened just like the security lady said."

"Paid-duty officer."

Nathan ignored Claire, went on. "I haven't kicked about it by reason of I don't want to cause dissention. See, I know my role—keep the lot like a new Cadillac and my mouth shut." Pointing at the set-design guy. "But that *homme*'s coming at me faster than a boozy teenager just got his license, playing the Billy Idol too loud." Holding up the appropriate number of digits. "Three days in a row. All due respect, *Madame* Marion, he didn't exactly get the club from Angie Dickinson here for driving below the speed limit. There's a pattern here, recklessness."

"Maliciousness," Claire added.

"They want to split hairs, fine." Cyrus Dagan massaged his temples, the ringing still there. "But she hit me with her electric truncheon twice, truly an order of business unto itself."

Arlene put the pink paper on her desk and closed her eyes. Truncheon—where did the pretentious prick pick it up? Giving her head a shake, she sat there wishing she listened to dad when acting was over. That she went to school for something normal, prepared herself for a job-job, something less stressful. Now here she was getting tired. Tired of what she did, of the excuses, all the excuses, and today the new guy with another one. Oh fishhooks, who wanted it? The horror of the things she had to do to hang on. And the time, more time wasted when she could have been doing something else, anything.

Cyrus was going on about a conspiracy of grunts when Arlene silenced him, putting a hand up, pointing at Nathan. "Your job is in the lot. Unless you are eating or defecating, you are in trouble if you find yourself inside the studio." Pointing at Claire then out the window. "Your job is also out there, and to be invisible while you are at it." Now pointing at Cyrus. "Second, that man is the best set designer in all of Hollywood North."

"Tell them how much you pay me," Cyrus said. "Tell them why."

"That man makes $300 a day. Do you know what that means?"

"That it's okay to run down your parking man?" Claire leaned forward. "Give the paid-duty officer a coco butt? That what it means, a man makes $300 a day?"

"It means that a man who makes $300 a day is an irreplaceable man." Arlene stood, still looking up at Claire. "Nobody else can do that job, understand?"

Irreplaceable, Claire thought, if he was so irreplaceable, he'd be in the States, and that much about the business she already knew. "He's a glorified furniture picker-outer guilty of at least three things—reckless driving, assault an officer, and another assault an officer."

"As I understand it." Arlene paused, running her tongue over her teeth. "You are a glorified security guard, suspended."

"On leave pending," Claire said, just like the union guy told her. "Standard procedure."

"No, no." Arlene waggled a finger. "Standard procedure is to be on leave with pay. You are on leave without pay. I have sources— what was it I heard about insubordination charges?"

Claire said Arlene's sources didn't know Goobers from Raisinets, adding that insubordination was a whole lot less serious than assault an officer—a felonious matter, highly.

Cyrus pointed in stabs. "Overzealous bitch with a record of overzealousness. We can't have it, her talking this way. Truly a dangerous situation in this business."

Oh frick, Arlene wished Cyrus wasn't always cornering her, forcing her into another unified front against the poor grunts over something he shouldn't have done. But then what was she supposed to do? For all the dookie he caused—the insults, the arguments, the fights—Cyrus was pretty good, maybe even the most prolific of Arlene's peeps, considering his ability to get things. This rent-a-cop, Arlene could replace her in exactly one phone call.

Turning, Arlene said, "I will have you know that I have fired people for less, Ms. Malik, much less."

Shoulders slumping as he stood, Nathan took off his Oakland Hills hat. "*Pardon*, but if you fire her for helping me, I'm swearing out a complaint against the *homme* makes $300 a day myself. I don't care if he's the last gallon of gas for 60 miles, you have to be kidding, it's okay to run me down by reason of money."

Arlene didn't want to fire anyone. It would have meant hiring new people, more time lost. She just wanted to scare them, simmer them down. But where did this parking peon get his nerve? Coming in here dressed like he's working the tarmac for Air Abu Dhabi, talking French. What was he? Some kind of decaf Haitian? From now on his secret name was going to be Lawn Boy, the way he just stood out there. Or sat, rather, the fricking guy was getting paid to sit, and this was the hill he wanted to die on? Fine. "Didn't I tell you we would do a little something for you if this all worked out? I thought you were interested in sticking with AMA."

Nathan looked down, damn hat in hand. "I'm happy to run a tight lot. Be punctual, professional, and diplomatic. But that's a two-way street, *Madame*."

That did it, this Lawn Boy orating on two-way streets like a Jane Jacobs groupie. Arlene had heard enough, calling it a wrap, telling Cyrus to stop running down the help. When he said something else about a conspiracy of grunts, she told him to just cut the damn stunt out. He was going to kill somebody and that would only serve as a distraction from the making of a quality television program. Also, she told him to stop forcing Billy Idol on everyone, that Billy Idol was on the decline. False, Cyrus said Billy was currently playing Cousin Kevin in *Tommy*, that he had a new album dropping next year, as well as a leading role in a movie about The Doors. Arlene told Cyrus *Tommy* was the shlock of has-beens, and that crack was going to kill Billy Idol before any of that other nonsense came to fruition. It was time for Cyrus to find a another starfuck, perhaps those new guys, Milli Vanilli. Arlene said they were on the rise.

Cyrus said he had it from a reliable source that the Milli Vanilli guys didn't sing their own songs, that they were models, lipsynching, that homely guys with sweet voices did the actual singing. When Arlene asked for Cyrus' source, he said he protected his peeps. Arlene told Cyrus to stop promoting conspiracy conjecture within the business. Also, Cyrus was to refrain from making Arlene wrong. Then she motioned to Claire. "Go to work, Ms. Malik, and try not to cuff any more senior staffers."

"Junior staffers okay?"

Fishhooks, Arlene was letting them all off, and they were still sassing. Looking down at her hands, she thought, frick, they were blotchy again. What was this, a Raynaud's attack? Stress? Something else? Arms spread, veiny, she looked up at Claire, said, "And if you're not allowed to wear all of your uniform, please do not wear any of it. Uniforms give creative people the creeps. We like to be casual, comfortable. You have never worked with creative people before, have you, Ms. Malik?"

4

Abel Otto looked in his dressing-room mirror, talking to himself. "Are you as good as the best?" Waiting a beat. "No, you're better. Better than John fucking Belushi." Smiling, taking himself a pinch less seriously. "Better than Jim fucking Belushi anyway."

Psyched, he took a last look at his hair pushed over to one side, oversize glasses, saying now he was Larry fucking King. Then he wandered on set, kissing Charlie Murphy's ass, kibitzing, shucking and jiving with people he hadn't seen in a while, introducing himself to those he didn't know, pleasing everybody. He'd made a mental note, warning himself against getting a head. Just look at Dan Aykroyd, the poor guy, squeezing his *Ghostbusters II* lemon for every drop. And was that right about Aykroyd talking up the possibility of a *Blues Brothers* tour with Jim Belushi? Jesus, none of them knew when to quit, not even John's nearest and dearest.

Seeing his own name on a temporary sign hung from the rafters, Abel made certain to drink in as much of the moment as he could. Feeling it, all eyes following his chance to be a water-cooler guy. Only get one shot, he said inwardly, thinking he should enjoy his summer in the sun, that it might never get this good again.

"Looking good, Abel," the director, Dan Meckler, said, thumbs up. "Your day, man."

Abel smiled, running fingers along the lapel of his two-button grey suit. The pants showed a hint of cuff and the shoulders fit comfortably. Wardrobe had done the job in a single fitting, nice. After, the girl who wears her G-string above her pants tied his tie into a perfect Windsor knot. She brought him a sunflower bud boutonniere, too, and who wore a sunflower bud boutonniere? No one. Maybe Abel would make it his thing. But he still didn't see what it had to do with the skit. Abel was going in jacket off, suspenders showing, sleeves rolled.

He was the man now, suited up like the man. That's why he took the high road with Meckler. Said thanks, Dan, left it at that, thinking how Meckler didn't know him on that Richard Lewis spot for one of the new cellular telephone companies last year, a riff on the drag race scene from *Rebel Without a Cause*; Richard as the James Dean character, Abel as the guy who goes over the cliff. Yeah, thanks Danny, like they were *amigos* now.

Whatever, Abel wasn't going to let personalities get in the way. Last night, he was up more often than not, babbling into his bed-side tape recorder, just like Jerry Seinfeld.

Now that it was all really happening, Abel was here, man, and he was trying to keep it in perspective. But dammit, he couldn't stop from getting glassy-eyed, thinking of all those cameos and grimy clubs before he made Second City, coming up through the open-mike circuit, just like Jerry. And did anyone hear of Jerry before he signed with NBC to make a pilot for a show with his name on it? Abel didn't think so.

Sure, they were contemporaries. And sure, Abel wished Jerry well. In fact, Abel was even happy for Jerry that his pilot was airing first—next month, July 5th, if memory served—and that Jerry would get his own time in the sun, because, really, how long could a show about nothing last? Not very. By the time The Comedy Channel debuted in November, Abel would be charging out of the gate with 10 whole episodes. Then, it would only be a matter of time before people saw that Abel was about something and forgot all about Jerry. That would probably be it for NBC, too. Who was going to watch antenna TV when they could catch *The Otto Show* on pirate cable?

***

Headphones in hand, Nathan snailed out of the studio after Claire, meeting her on the steps near the maroon canopy. Up close, she could see where a line of stitches had sewn up a two-inch cut on the left side of his chin. Dark hair closely cropped, receding on the sides, eyes so brown they were almost black. Pretty boy, she thought, exotic, and she liked the touches of salt in his widow's peak. What was he? Part Hawaiian? Eskimo? A little of both?

"Thanks." She pulled the mouthpiece on her headset down. "You didn't have to do that."

He flashed a conspiratorial smile. "Thanks nothing, you're tougher than Angie Dickinson. Spread-eagle that *grande dame*, slap his package with, what'd he call it? Oh yeah, your electric truncheon."

"*Grande dame?*" Claire tilted her head, crinkling a mist of freckles across her cheeks. "That doesn't sound very nice. Tell me you're not a homophobe. That's just so like 1984."

Nathan closed his eyes, opened them slowly, thinking here we go, the university-educated white girl getting political. Oh well, it was better than being called *sexiste*. Once these university-educated white bitches called you *sexiste*, that was it, no cho-cho.

"I only use it against them if they are uncool. Freddy Mercury, now there's a cool *grande dame*," he said, showing a thumb then an index. "Scott Thompson, tall blond from *Kids in the Hall*, my other company did a one-hour special with him. Anyone with enough foresight to tap Shadowy Men on a Shadowy Planet to do their theme song is alright with me, no matter." Flashing a third finger. "And the chick sang 'High School Confidential'?"

"Carole Pope, Rough Trade."

"Right, proud gay lady sings about a girl makes her body twitch. I was reading a list of the top-50 Canadian bands, no mention of Rough Trade. That's homophobic, but this Tyrus—"

"Cyrus."

Nathan brought his headphones over his head, resting them on his neck. "He's been playing *poulet* with me through rehearsals, twice on the second day. Sooner or later one of us is going to turn the wrong way, and then everyone's going to wonder why Nathan's stain is on the concrete. That makes him uncool, and I'll use anything against a man who's got to be the lot bully behind the wheel of his big, bad car by reason of money. Why? You're not . . ."

"My partner." Claire held a laugh. "On the force."

"Doesn't matter." Nathan put up his hands, turning sideways. "Look, I didn't mean—"

"It's okay. He's a cool one."

Nathan, laughing sadly at himself, his explanations, said, "Anyway, I've got a run to make for Arlene. Means you've got to oversee the lot while I'm gone."

"I'm a paid duty officer. Don't do parking detail, union rules."

"No reason to get all work-to-rule," Nathan said. "I just give you my list." Opening his clipboard, flashing a page of names and assigned spots on a map he'd drawn up. "Don't let people in unless they're on my list, all there is to it. If they're here, you assign them their spot number and see to it they use the right one. Sneaky buggers, some of them always trying to steal a better spot. Especially that Mr. Meckler, and he's Born Again, should know better." Closing his clipboard, pulling it against the wire running between his walkie and headset. "Asides, parking is a security issue. Your problem as much as mine."

Eyes wide, Claire took off her headset, pulling the clipboard away from Nathan's chest, pointing at the wire. "I could hear you just then on the phones, had your talk button jammed."

Nathan looked down. "Sorry." Back at Claire. "Put your headset back on." When she did, he said, "Okay now?"

"Yeah, clear."

"Did I say anything?"

Claire softened her eyes. "You were just giving me some valuable policing guidance."

Nathan nodded self-consciously, re-opening his clipboard. "Everything's here." Pointing at Arlene's tan Jeep Cherokee parked in spot two. "Now I have got to go, make that run."

"What is it?"

He shook his head, turned away, his body language saying she didn't want to know.

"C'mon."

Out of the corner of Nathan's eye, he picked up Veronica emerging from the canopy, jogging towards them. "Good." Catching her breath. "I was afraid you'd left. Now Arlene says she wants anything but OB."

Claire said, "You've got to be joking."

Veronica rolled her shoulders. "She's punishing him."

"But he didn't do anything."

"If there's trouble in the lot, it's his fault. Same for you. If some loon sneaks in and puts a gun on Abel Otto, you're to blame."

"But there are six ways in and I can only see two." Claire threw her hands up. "Six ways, I can't guarantee anything. You need more paid-duty officers, you want six ways guaranteed."

"It's not me." Veronica said. "But as Arlene sees it, that's the way of your job."

***

Abel was ready, on the right path, and that's probably why shooting started earlier than Nathan figured. Somewhere around 9:40, the main man stepped onto set one. Snapping his suspenders, pushing his glasses to the top of his nose, in that moment he really was CNN anchor Larry King. The spoof had Abel, as King, interviewing Charlie Murphy playing Laurent Kabila, the ousted dictator of a breakaway Congolese state who was widely reported dead. Together, they sat on foldable lawn chairs in front of a beach backdrop, caricatures of large breasted women in skimpy bathing suits behind them.

> King: "So, you're 49, finished with public life but very much alive. What's next for the former dictator of a Marxist state in the Congo?"

> Kabila, *wearing a San Diego Padres cap, Bob Marley T-shirt, army shorts, Birkenstocks*: "I basically live with my mother now. She's very supportive. It's been tough. I'm unemployed, without a car, but coping. And I wouldn't say I'm done with public life."

> King: "But you fled, man. You disappeared yourself. We here at CNN thought you were dead until you contacted us."

> Kabila: "And that is why I am here, Larry. I want people to know I am well, planning for a return, any return. If not the Congo, I am also thinking globally, getting my irons in the fires."

King: "Irons, you say? Fires?"

Kabila, *nodding*: "Things are happening. The USSR, East Germany, and Romania could fall any day. You know this, Larry. Afghanistan, no matter what Mr. Gorbachev would have you believe, could also be up for grabs. Volatile. After that, I've got Cuba."

King: "Not yet, Laurent. What makes you think the Cubans want you?"

Kabila: "I'm young with lots of experience. Castro, he's 63 or something. He got old, man. And if there's one thing I've learned about being a dictator, it's not a job for life anymore. Things are opening up, and I just don't see young people with experience filling the leadership void."

The sketch was sending up a round of bizarre print interviews Kabila had given weeks earlier in Uganda. He hadn't mentioned Castro by name, but Kabila genuinely thought he might get another chance, somewhere. Until then, the deadpan schtick seemed to be carrying well enough, a decent start.

Standing behind Meckler on camera one, Veronica stopped paying attention when she noticed the studio audience. Although they weren't pounding their knees, they were at least amused, laughing a half-beat before the prompts. Veronica had approved this one, so she was scanning the metal bleachers, gauging reaction, most everyone happy. High atop, however, Arlene seemed to be splitting her attention between her headset and the contents of her purse.

***

Nathan spent a good 45 minutes tooling around, listening to a Freddie Hubbard special on the part-time jazz station, CJRT 91.1 FM. He counter-clockwised the volume when Freddie faded into BBC World News, the lead item pegging the number of civilians killed at Tiananmen Square less than three weeks ago at anywhere from a hundred to several thousand. After breaking news about a ruling allowing Americans to burn their own flag, and other stories, Nathan clockwised the volume when CJRT cut back to the special, the DJ saying Freddie had two new albums due out this year before the man's trumpet returned.

In the process, Nathan ran the tank down to a quarter, returning Arlene's Jeep to spot number two, stepping out, a box shaping the Shoppers Drug Mart bag under his arm. He made a playful face at Claire. She smiled, lighting a fancy brown cigarette while he headed into the studio. Before she finished smoking, Nathan was on his way back, holding the same bagged box.

"Already shooting inside," he said. "Never seen this before. On schedule, day one."

Claire crinkled her nose. "I think I saw Eddie Murphy in there."

"Uh-uh, no. That's Charlie, Eddie's brother. No way this production could afford Eddie."

"Figures." Claire pointed at the bag. "Why do you still have that?"

Nathan took a breath. "These here are unacceptable, wrong brand." Letting it out.

Claire laughed, shocked and appalled. "I heard that lady's girl Friday—Little Arlene?"

"You probably shouldn't call her that. She's Veronica, director of development, to us."

"Everyone else, Kiwi anyway, calls her Little Arlene. They dress alike, look alike."

"We aren't everybody else. Besides, she's on our side. Why? Why are you down on her?"

"Just don't like her," Claire said, sneering.

"Yeah, that's the impression that I get."

Claire couldn't help herself, elbowing Nathan, winking. "Treat her right, I bet she'd bake you muffins, every day."

Nathan looked at the building, said Veronica was a little out of his league.

"Point is," Claire said, "I specifically heard her tell you anything but OB."

Head down, Nathan said not to turn a molehill into a mountain, but yeah, he was being punished, passive aggressive. Yesterday, last day of rehearsals, Veronica was the one punished for pulling Nathan inside by reason of a sheet metal fire at the nearby Babylon plant.

"Sky the color of shit soup," Claire said. "I saw it, smelled it. Led the news every hour."

That's right, Nathan said. Veronica was worried about him breathing *toxines* and ordered him in the building. Five minutes later, Arlene sent him out, only Veronica called him right back. That's when the part-time jazz station reported that officials were determining whether the smoke was toxic. Arlene wanted to know what the frick Nathan was doing inside, so he told her about that, *la toxicité*. She told him to speak English. Sent him out by reason of the part-time jazz station was volunteer-run, saying a lot of ripping-and-reading went on there, so who knew where they were getting their information? By then, Nathan was a little concerned, so he repeated that, according to the best info he had, officials were in the process of determining whether toxic matter was hanging over his work station. While it was later determined nontoxic, things were still up in the air, so to speak, and Nathan tried to stress that.

Same thing would never happen at the Arie company. That's how Nathan knew Veronica was on his side. By reason of, after all that, she crossed Arlene and called him in a third time, took him to the dining room. Arlene, she was telling Veronica to pick the beans out of her chili, until the caterer, Toledo Marseilles, volunteered. Then, Arlene, gracious as she could, said no Toledo, it's just that a man who makes $100 a day has to be out there rain, sleet, and snow.

"And, apparently," Claire added, "poisonous fumes."

"Apparently." Nathan looked up to see that Arlene wasn't watching from her window. "Today, it's me being punished by reason I was somehow involved with upsetting the furniture picker-outer. *Grande dame* gets $300 a day for picking out shit looks like it came from Leon's. I've seen his sets, every Goddamn thing a pastel."

There. Nathan wasn't sure if he was done, but thought he better stop, seeing Claire trying not to smile, saying, "This is my fault."

No, no. If Claire didn't rough that big man up, Nathan said he would've brought in the Pittsburgh Persimmon golf club he kept behind his door and done it himself. If he did that, called upon the Pittsburgh Persimmon, Cyrus would've cried that it was *prémédité.* Nathan would be fired, in trouble with his usual company, and he was still hoping against hope that another network would pick up *Moonlighting.* So what? He spends the day buying the university-educated white lady hygiene products. It got him out of there, playing her stereo, stressing her woofers. It was all the same by reason of someone else would take care of her. That's what Dan Aykroyd said—and did Claire see how Aykroyd signed his picture back at Arlene's full-time office?

Claire held the clipboard against her chest, wires sticking out. She made a twirling motion as if to hand-wind a projector, saying let's roll it back and get this straight. "So Arlene wants you to return those, get a refund, and then buy her another box, different brand?"

"Yeah, Tampax."

"Tampax," Claire said, impressed. "Buy that bitch a douche bag while you're out."

Nathan chuckled quietly, blushing for the first time since Craig Stadler—the tour's chief temper-head—exploded after four-putting at the Kemper Open back in '86.

Claire brought a hand over her mouth, talking through her fingers. "Let me buy you a beer after work, standing up for me like that. Let me make it up."

"Nothing to make up, but I'd like that just the same, *merci.*" Nathan looked sideways as Arlene stormed out wearing her headset, pointing back and forth at them.

"One of you lovebirds has your talk button on, stuck," Arlene said, focusing on Claire. "Buy me a douche bag—say that again and I will have your badge, personally. Do you know how many people I know?"

5

Wrapping the unemployed dictator skit, Dan Meckler kept ahead of schedule. He had something about Robin Givens (played outrageously by Shirley Hemphill) force-feeding anti-depressants to Mike Tyson (Charlie Murphy again) in the can by two. By nine, Meckler was shooting the last of *The Untouchables* send up, which revolved around an allegedly deleted scene Brian De Palma had re-inserted into the director's cut for a special VHS edition.

Abel, as Robert De Niro playing Al Capone, was attending a sensitivity retreat with seven other men, played entirely by unknowns through the guild. Out in the bush wearing loincloths, they were lathering mud on their chests when a banker walked into the scene strumming a guitar. Saying it was time to get in touch with their acoustic sides, he broke into song.

I dreamed I saw Joe Hill last night
Alive as you or me
Says I, but Joe, you're ten years dead

"See this?" Abel pulled a chromed-up handgun from his loincloth. "Says I, Al Capone, this is a Smith & Wesson 629 Trail Boss with a Hogue grip. Fires six rounds." Putting the hardware on acoustic guy, firing, putting him down. "Means I got five more bullets, any more of you pansies wanna get in touch with your acoustic sides."

"What happens to the sixth?" the one in front asked, still rubbing mud onto his round belly. "What happens if all of us get in touch with our acoustic sides? Then what'd you do?"

Abel aimed, shot him—blam. "Sixth gets strangled, so fuhgedaboutit."

With that, the only thing left was a step-by-stop instructional on how to get rid of bodies.

"Large aquatic environment's always good, dilutes the smell." Abel pointed west. "And we've got the lake not a half-mile away.

No one finds them, how do you have a trial? You don't. You just fuhgedaboutit."

As instructed at gunpoint, the others started tying stones to lifeless limbs, fastening them down with several knots. This, Abel told them, tapping his temple with his pistol, would guard against gasses carrying the body to the lake's surface. Said several times over, Meckler called it a day well before 10, told Abel all was going swimmingly, made a beeline for the exit.

Abel thought he better get going, too, have drinks back at his hotel. Come down, call Nora back in Chicago, maybe get off over the phone, try to get some sleep. But he was lingering like he didn't want to wake up from his dream, feeling good, steering forward. Comfortable in the loin cloth and mud, he was thinking how he'd stood firm on the changes and made people laugh all day. Tomorrow, it was going to be more of the same, calling his own shot. That's why he was walking over to Cyrus, putting an arm around him and pressing buttons.

"You're getting that shit on my shirt," Cyrus said, looking at his shoulder, mud flakes.

Abel kept his arm where it was. "New skit tomorrow morning. We're working out beats, fixing it. Still not very good, but it's Arlene's baby. Damndest thing though. The way I see it, we need a chicken if we're going to save this thing. A big-assed rubber chicken to distract from the fact that the joke isn't very funny. Can do?"

Cyrus bit his lip. "Of course." Nodding cautiously. "Only how big a rubber chicken?"

"Big." Abel spanned his arms out like wings. "Very, very big."

"Specs, Abel. A vague measurement, please."

"Has to be 10-feet. I'd prefer more, but no less than 10."

Cyrus nodded, then shook his head, no. "I'm sorry, Abel. I truly don't want to let you down on day one, you know, but I truly can't do that. Not by morning."

"Thought you were the can-do guy, Cyrus. A guy who does what it takes. Irreplaceable, Arlene says, 300 bucks a day. I mean, that's as much as I make."

"Not quite."

"Almost, Cyrus, almost. Either way, this here is my vehicle, and Arlene told me you'd be at my disposal to get things." Abel looked up and away. "I wonder what I'll tell her."

Feeling the pinch, Cyrus strived for compromise. "Give me an hour on the phone first thing and I can maybe get you something by afternoon, if it's crucial. This moment, I truly don't know." Shrugging. "Just never had a call for it, so let me dig, talk to my peeps, some of whom I only have day numbers for. See if one of my sources has a source, so on. Hopefully, I find another source who carries an extremely large item I don't see a lot of industry demand for. After that, I need to find an efficient way of getting it here. If that doesn't pan—like, if they're asking a stupid amount of money—I have to find alternative sources, so on." Then he stopped, something clicking. "Forget everything I just said, cancel it." Running fingers through the part in the middle of his hair, feathering, he looked at Abel. "You'll owe me."

"Yeah, yeah. I'll owe. But I absolutely, positively have to have it overnight. Can do?"

Cyrus, clenching his teeth, said, "Can do."

***

Toni Jo's was located five minutes from set, a few blocks west of Arlene's production office on Queen Street East. It was supposed to be an Australian roadhouse, but Nathan thought it looked like any given British pub that sprouted up in any given strip mall. It had all the usual brands—Guinness, Rickards Red, Keith's. Other than Men at Work, Midnight Oil, and The Hoodoo Gurus, TJ's had mostly the same music, too—The Pogues, Proclaimers, Morrissey, Van Morrison, plus domestic acts like Frozen Ghost, Blue Rodeo, and The Tragically Hip. Nathan's selection was on the juke now, the sad part of "Summer Wind" from the new album by Shadowy Men on a Shadowy Planet, Brian Connelly's guitar singing softer than a piper man.

It was Kiwi, one of the production assistants, who had most everyone on set going here. He was sitting with Nathan and Claire at a table near the bar, discussing the finer links between British and Australian culture. "Indirectly, we drink English beer because they threw all the Ozzies out of the bloody country."

Claire looked at him, drawing her chin in. "But I thought you were a New Zealander."

"Same region." Kiwi pointed his pint of stout at a framed map. "Only our people are worse still, thrown out of Australia after being thrown out of England. Unwelcome anywhere but New Zealand. Some aren't even welcome there, the worst possible gene pool on one little island. Thing is, we were all British at some point, so I reckon we all inherited a taste for British beer."

"At least your people had the chance to leave," Nathan said. "Motherland is a hole."

"You been?"

Nathan held up three fingers, said London was that many days of rain, substandard coffee, and when you blew your nose black *merde* came out. Plus, he stayed at this B&B, a cold-water flat that reserved the right to evict anyone at any time should an ex-Polish service man come needing a roof in a no-vacancy situation. No kidding, that was their policy, framed. Also, Nathan had to sleep with bumf in his ears by reason of the loudspeakers from Victoria Station across the street.

Soon, he got himself a plane to France. No playing around with that boat to Calais, then a train to Paris. No, Nathan spent good money to buy a plane ticket off that cold, miserable little island. Rest of the six weeks he spent in France. Civilized, crepe vendors on the street where we have them selling expired hot dogs, lips and bums.

Kiwi said he spent time doing charcoals of tombstones at that famous graveyard in Paris, graffiti everywhere—even on Édith Piaf's stone, like it's no worries—arrows saying this way to the Jesus Lizard, Jim Morrison. Then he leaned toward Nathan. "Let me ask you something." Tentative, looking around to make sure no one was listening. "Personal."

Nathan nodded, said careful.

"You're not black, are you? Mulatto?"

"No," Nathan said. "At least not that I know of."

Claire tilted her head. "What do you mean, not that you know of?"

"I'm adopted. No clue about my ethnicity. Always saw myself as dark, like maybe part Sicilian, Arab, Cambodian, Latin, a combination, something else. I don't know, is what I mean."

"I thought they pass that information on," Kiwi said. "Don't you get papers, genealogy?"

"Sometimes, sometimes not." Nathan said. "Why? What made you go right to black?"

"I think it was what you said about how at least Kiwi's people had the chance to leave," Claire said. "Like yours didn't."

No, Nathan didn't mean it like that. All he was saying was that at least New Zealanders had a chance to seek out a more desirable climate, that England was shite. Now, again, why did the Kiwi go right to black?

"It's just what I heard Arlene say." Kiwi stopped, letting Nathan know these were her words. "Calling you Lawn Boy."

"I saw her here earlier." Nathan stood, shoulders bobbing left and right, scanning the large room, the booths. "I see her again, I'll call her butt-fucked—Lawn Boy?"

"No worries, mate." Kiwi put a hand on Nathan's shoulder. "But you didn't hear it from me." Guiding him down to his seat. "They call me Kiwi. Same difference, I reckon."

Nathan said he didn't think so. Kiwi was nicknamed after an ugly, hairy fruit tastes sweet. Some might see that as wrong. Personally, Nathan wouldn't appreciate it. That said, he needed Kiwi to understand the ramifications of calling a man who doesn't know his own background Lawn Boy. That was another matter entirely, a matter of degrees, yardage.

"Could've sworn you were part Hawaiian." Claire frowned. "At least a little Eskimo."

"Sorry to disappoint."

"Whoa." Claire raised both hands, a little insulted herself. "Just thought you were an interesting person."

"More like a person of interest," Nathan said.

Kiwi waved, saying no worries, Arlene was the common enemy here.

Nathan figured Kiwi was saying no worries more often than Crocodile Dundee, getting off on being the Kiwi, dishing insider info, telling them only a few of the investors were said to get on with Arlene. Most everyone on set, save for Cyrus, Kiwi reckoned, hated her, even if they didn't let it be known.

Today, for instance, Kiwi did a count on the walkie-talkies, coming up three short. He's charged with doling out the two-ways, no worries, right? But then he's charged with other things, too, things that take him off set. Means he's not always with the walkies. You know what she does when he tells her three are missing? Calls him a bloody bastard. No reason to drag Kiwi's poor dead daddy into it. Tells him he'll have to pay for the walkies if they don't turn up.

"That's like telling cops to pay for repairs when drunks ram our cruisers." Claire stuck out her tongue. "You don't make your people pay, your operatives."

"Oh, you wait. I reckon she finds a way to dock just about everyone. You'll get most of your money, no worries there. She always pays. Just her little taxes she gets you with, penalties."

***

Less than two miles east of Toni Jo's—a few streetcar stops further east of Arlene's production office on Queen Street East—the Impala pulled onto the clean asphalt parking lot of Heathcliffe Wilson's Fried Chicken. Cyrus parked behind the dumpster, killed the engine. He stepped out, followed by two production assistants, Sundance and Freak, the three of them sharing a joint. Cyrus ran fingers on one hand through the part in his hair, pointing up with the other.

"There she is."

Above them hovered a 15-foot chicken, big feral eyes, sagging in the middle, with red and yellow feathering. It wore a uniform with the chain's name printed across the chest. Like when you pulled up to the window there would be a big rubber chicken smiling, trading chicken parts that had been pressed together to make bigger chicken parts for money. Yeah, Cyrus was going to eat at a place that had a cheery animal selling its own kind. How twisted was that?

"You sure we can do this?" Sundance sucked on the spliff, handing it to Freak.

"Don't you worry." Cyrus intercepted, inhaling, pointing the burning ember at the restaurant, a retro-fit Ponderosa. "It's dark inside, boys, means no one's home. Also means we have ourselves a can-do situation, a must-do situation."

Sundance let his smoke escape, saying, "But Cyrus, Heathcliffe Wilson's going miss this right away. And have you seen Heathcliffe? He's huge, played for the old Montreal Concordes in the CFL before they folded in '85."

Freak looked up at the sky, stars. "Was he on the original roster in '82?"

"Pretty sure," Sundance said. "Second string kicker behind Don Sweet. He's only four years retired, young enough to kick all our asses when he finds out we stole from him." Thinking about it, cracking up. "And he'll probably bring Lyall Woznesensky. What's he, 270?"

"Woznesensky's more like 240, and Heathcliffe won't be bringing him," Cyrus said. "We're just borrowing the bird. I mean, I'll see he gets it back and it's not as if he's going to take this personally. He'll be insured up the cornhole. Probably happens all the time. And hey, he was second-string. Kickers, even first-stringers, are little, same size as jockeys. You ever see that old Super Bowl replay of Garo Yepremian? He's like 5'7", 160, and the ball ends up in his hands after a blocked kick. They manhandled him. So what's this Wilson going to do? Kick us, all three of us?"

"If we're talking the same guy . . ." Sundance caressed his lips. "Seem to think I saw Heathcliffe Wilson on the French sports channel replaying classic games—the one where he misses four field goals in a row—and he's a little bigger than Garo."

"Besides." It was Freak's turn, nervously tugging at his *Superman IV* cap. "What happens when Five-O gets here? Sundance is right. This is stealing—theft over something-something, jail."

"Please." Cyrus brought his hands together in a praying position. "Abel Otto isn't just the star of his own show. No, he's the head writer and show runner, and he asked me to do this special. That's why I'm now directing you to do it. We are something between frat brothers and peacekeepers following orders, doing what we're told. Anything happens, we're taken care of, believe me. Arlene Marion stands behind her peeps. I stand behind my peeps. It's only going to take a few minutes anyway. It's just a chicken air-balloon. All we have to do is deflate it, roll it up, and we're gone." Again, he reassured them, they were just borrowing it. Coming through for Abel Otto in the clutch, crucial. "This is the kind of thing that makes me irreplaceable." Pointing to Sundance then Freak. "Makes you irreplaceable, too."

6

The tequila took some sorting. Nathan wanted Cuervo light, Claire Cuervo gold. Kiwi wanted the brand that had the worm, but not the worm itself.

"You know, authentic Mexican tequila, there's no worm," Claire said. "It's actually mezcal, for the Americans—that's why they're putting worms in." Simulating male masturbation with her right fist. "Jerking-off the gringos. You can eat it, they say, protein. Won't hurt you. Funny though, eating the worm doesn't get you higher."

"And." Nathan turned to the New Zealander. "Why would you want to eat a little pickled *insecte* lives in a cocoon doesn't get you higher?"

Kiwi waited, mouth hanging open, exposing a gold tooth, bottom row. "You two done?"

Nathan and Claire looked at he each other, back at Kiwi, yeah.

"Again, I want the brand the worm comes in—it's smokier—not the worm itself."

When everyone had the correct shot, Kiwi raised his glass. "To Arlene, who should have her own nickname as well."

"I've noticed." Claire paused, something fitting. "She's given everyone a bitch handle."

Nathan said, "I'm the one called you Angie Dickinson."

"And yet I didn't get around to thanking you."

"You like it. At least Angie Dickinson's hot."

Claire flashed her eyes at Nathan. Alright, she liked it a little. "Other than that. Kiwi, Sundance, Freak—you call each other by snide aliases she's assigned to you."

"That's right." Kiwi said, still holding up his glass, a toast. "So let's get on with it then. From now on, we shall call her Attila the Hen. Back home, that's what we call Thatcher."

Nathan and Claire looked at each other, nodding. "To Attila the Hen." The three of them went through the ritual of clinking glasses, licking hands, salting, licking again. Throwing his shot back, Kiwi bit the lemon, pursing, standing. "Little lady's waiting on me, her birthday."

Claire exposed teeth she'd been grinding in her sleep. "But you're smashed, got here before us."

"No worries, Angie. She will be as well by the time I get home. Lives to drink, that one."

"Kiwi?"

"Yeah."

"What's your real name?"

He looked at her like she had to be daft. "Not bloody well telling you, a cop, no reason."

With that, he was on his way.

Huh, Nathan turned to Claire, looking her up and down, smiling, the tequila already making him brave. "What do you call that what you got on?"

"Claire is wearing a streamlined, candy-striped tankini featuring a long tank top and tear-away skirt," she said, speaking of herself like a runway MC. "Beneath." Standing, tearing away. "She's wearing boy-cut shorts."

"*Oui.*" Nathan scanned the bar, heads turning. "And most of the crew is looking at those boy-cut shorts. What'd you do, go home to change? You didn't have time."

"I always keep a spare set of clothes in the trunk."

"Practical." He pointed at a sheer black band high on her right thigh, hot. "And that?"

"Lipstick garter." She reached down for the hidden tube, opening it slowly, catching the bartender's eye, motioning for two shots of tequila. "Dark for me and light for darky."

Nathan shot her a look. Classy girl doing touch-up at the table, calling him darky. Yeah, he was about to get clever, then decided it might bugger up his chances for some cho-cho and changed the subject. "So what's Arlene on about, you being suspended, insubordination?"

Insubordination—he cut through the crap, had that going for him. "What's it to you?"

"It's okay. I'm subletting a bachelor until I don't know when, not going to judge."

"Let me ask something first." Claire waited for him to nod, go ahead. "I appreciate you standing up for me. Other times, why let Arlene get away with it? Sending you twice for pads."

"I told you, don't make too much of that," Nathan said. "Last year, I had to buy one of the *Kids in the Hall* a cock ring. Had his size traced out on a piece of paper and everything. Then, when I get to the place he sends me—a bar called The Barn, has its own sex shop—the clerk thinks it's for me. He's concerned the size is too small, wants to measure. And you know the *Kids in the Hall* guy is doing this for his own jollies, probably has the whole thing on VHS."

Claire reached across the table, pushed his shoulder. "Which one sent you?"

"Would be unprofessional to say." Nathan glared at a kid walking away from the jukebox, making a note to intervene if he played Glass Tiger again. "Point is, we're working for half-people in a half-world, people who need their *derrières* wiped, so just color me lucky that *Madame* thought she was going to shock me."

"I wouldn't do it for her." Claire shook her head in jerks. "Bitch can buy her own."

"Meaning what about me?"

"Just that you seem smarter than you act on set, saying due respect, hat-in-hand."

Nathan looked at her, touchy. "Arlene wants to underestimate me, that's just what I'll let her do, her tragic flaw. A consummate pro wouldn't make that mistake, but so be it. She's the kind of person—you notice how Dan Aykroyd signed his picture back at her shop on Queen?"

No, Claire just remembered the wall covered in photos inscribed by people she mostly hadn't heard of. Why? What'd Aykroyd say?

"He wrote, 'To Arlene: One day somebody's going to put something in your drink.' And somebody really will, only Arlene's too smart to know by reason of she's neither professional nor diplomatic. Now tell me what happened, how you ended up in the lot with me."

Claire brought her right hand next to her ear, pointing at him, dainty. "You first."

Now that he'd chit-chatted in this direction, Nathan wasn't sure he wanted to go there. Asides from it being impolite to answer a question with a question, nine-to-fivers generally didn't understand, like it was a little boy's job. "I was a caddy, golf."

She made a face, willing to be impressed. "Professional?"

"Yes, professional," he said. Thinking *tabernac*, it was the same thing every time, Nathan trotting out Disco Dicks's mediocre tour record to justify his own existence. "Would you call caddying for the 54-hole leader of the 1987 Canadian Open professional?"

"Fifty-four? Don't they play 72?"

Nathan held his breath, nodding.

"Well then, what happened Sunday?"

"Dick bogeyed the first three holes, shot 75, finished six back of Curtis Strange in a national championship, not awful. That professional enough?"

"Oh, I suppose." Claire smiled nice, trying to let him know she was playing. "Sounds like a decent gig, travelling to Hawaii, Puerto Rico, Myrtle Beach."

"Weather asides, Myrtle's an armpit, but I've been to those places, including." Nathan brought a hand up to his Oakland Hills hat. "Bloomfield Hills, Michigan, my favorite by reason of there's this great seafood joint, Charley's Crab, not too far from the caddy hotel."

Claire shook her head. "What happened?"

"It was my man and my back. Just came to the point where I had enough, walked.

"What? Like, you off the course?"

Nathan smiled as he spoke. Yeah, this part made him proud. Working his ass off, scoliosis and all, thinking every week was his last chance for a big pay day. And here's Richard, gifted with more natural talent than a snake tamer, hamming it up, listening to "Dancing Queen" on his headphones. Shots worth thousands on the line and Richard's getting down. What a waste.

The papers had been calling him Disco Dick for a while. To this day, he was still the great Canadian hope, so it was a bit of a situation when Nathan bailed during the second round of last year's Phoenix Open. The way the Canadian papers wrote it, they blamed Nathan when Dick missed the cut. Unnerved, they reported, by his standby caddy. Forget about winning. Now Dick was struggling to keep his tour card. Some said it might've turned out different if Nathan stayed by reason of knowing the man's game so well. That Nathan saved him a shot or two each round, a big difference on the PGA circuit.

"Disco Dick, look at him now, a sideshow, 181st on the money list." Nathan pointed at the table. "After travel, hotels, meals, taxes, caddy fees—it takes a lot of money to be on tour—I bet I make what he does, almost, and I work in parking lots."

"Yeah, but you do work in parking lots and he's on a golf course. Isn't that a drag?"

Nathan thought about it, said, "It's not so bad, work a few weeks, take a few off, go somewhere. After caddying, I just never really wanted to do anything else, never wanted to be anything else." Looking up at the ceiling. "And please Lord, strike me down before I have to learn computer." Eyes back on Claire. "Besides, you get up and go to work every day, that's unnatural, counterproductive to your own private pursuit of happiness. Becomes who you are, defines you. Gig like this, I stay on top of news, music, read my paperbacks—that's my real escape, reading—while I get three squares a day. Means I'm not spending while I'm working, and I like that. Plus, it's cash, pretty much under the table."

"Cash?" Claire drew back. "Fuck around, you mean she pays us cash money?"

Nathan looked at her oddly. "You didn't know?"

"Uh-uh." She was surprised, interested. Said she couldn't remember being paid cash since working at Buddy's Bait & Tackle the summer her dad, an efficiency expert, did a contract downsizing Heinz in Leamington. That was half a lifetime ago, almost. "Why cash?"

Nathan didn't know, didn't care. "Beat the government, the unions, us." He sipped his beer, scanning the room. "Could be any of those things, all of those things. Could be *Madame*'s spending government money meant for one thing on another. Some kind of angle. I don't know what it is, in particular. But if someone's paying cash in 1989, they have a particular angle."

"So pay day is the day after shooting finishes, right? That's what I was told, dodgy."

Oui. For instance, Nathan would go to AMA at an assigned time and collect an envelope containing $1,800. That was the arrangement. After, he'd take a cab to the bank by reason it scared the hell out of him to carry that amount of cash money. He didn't like having it at his sublet bachelor in St. Jamestown any better. It seemed like once a month someone was killed in those towers, and money was usually involved. That being the case, he wanted his cash in the bank. And hey, when did they start charging fees instead of paying interest?

Fees were new, Claire said, but who all was getting paid cash, everyone? They didn't pay actors cash, right? Claire already figured that much out. They got cheques, right? Probably because their bean counters needed to make visual contact with the raw numbers, the decimals, the deductions.

Nathan played with the zipper on his coveralls and went off somewhere in his mind, swinging one of those newfangled drivers in development, sure to make old golf courses obsolete. Thinking your average weekend hacker would belt it 300 yards once these war clubs hit pro shops, he saw himself twirling a Cobra model, clubhead the size of an infant's skull, shuffling down a fairway like a natural walking man. Then he came out of it, saying, "Aside from actors, the director, people like that, most everyone gets cash. Me, you, PAs, the designers—set, lighting, hair, make-up, costume— audio people, audience assistants, caterers, the grip."

"The fuck's a grip anyway?"

Now that she mentioned it, Nathan wasn't sure. Never thought to ask. He imagined it'd be hard to respect yourself, being a grip.

Here *homme*, could you grip this? But yes, everyone who worked for their money got paid cash at AMA.

"My regular outfit, William Arie Productions, uses a payroll company," Nathan said, "fairly standard. But there are always cash jobs, plus petty cash flying everywhere. In this case, it's just most of the shoot is a cash operation, not exactly unheard of, this business."

Claire made a curious frown. "How many people we talkin'?"

Nathan paused to do some quick math. "Twenty, I'd say, 25, maybe 40 once you start counting people being called in for a day here, a few days there."

"All different amounts?"

Oui. Nathan was at the bottom making $100 a day. PAs like Kiwi made $120. After that, you had people at various daily wage scales, depending on their job, all the way up to Cyrus at $300. Then he looked at Claire, saying, "And how much you make?"

"Flat rate, $225 a day."

Pressing his tongue against his cheek, he thought that was so much *merde*, the two of them doing a comparable gig, Nathan getting a whole $125 less.

"That's what it's like in this business," he said. "People make a lot in a short time, get paid a lump sum, often cash, then we don't work for a month or three."

Claire crunched invisible numbers on the table. "You haven't thought about it?"

Nathan looked into the corner, people playing pool, shook his head.

Facing the wall, elbows on the table, hands folded beneath her chin, she let him take a good look at her long fingers, cinnamon nails. "When I was interviewed at Arlene's office, I didn't see cameras, security, nothing. Depending on what she's paying, she might have $60,000, maybe more, cash, in one place at one time. At least 35 people know, and seven years police service says that's not a secure situation."

Nathan rolled his right hand, pushing her along.

"They're telling people how they're getting paid, where and when." Excited, she caught herself, looking about, hushing her voice. "Husbands, wives, mistresses, girlfriends, boyfriends, buddies. By the time those people pick up their wad, they've shot their mouths off. Means, when we get paid, a hundred people will know AMA has that kind of money lying around on July 7th."

"So what are you saying?"

"I'm not saying, I'm just saying. Why? What do you think I'm saying?"

Nathan made big innocent eyes. "What you're talking about is stealing Kiwi's stipend so as he won't have enough money to keep Mrs. Kiwi good and tight."

Claire said, "I'm talking about stealing everybody's pay."

"Well I'm saying you used to be a *policière*. And I want to state, for the record, I'm the least bit surprised, trying to look like that anyway."

"Technically, I'm still a *policière*, so you want me to say it first?"

He was tired of playing. "Look, ever since I said we're getting cash, you've been casing the place for a good, old-fashioned payroll heist. And due respect, this is our first date."

Date? Claire wrung her hands. If this was a date they could dish. "How would you do it?"

"Theoretically?"

"Theoretically."

"Theoretically, I'd keep it simple as a three-man band." Nathan readjusted, crossing his legs. "Theoretically, if I was that kind of man, I'd grab that *pistolet* from props—good looking piece they used in *The Untouchables* skit today—hold her up bright and early on pay day."

Claire held up an index, something missing. "Where's our tequila?" Catching the bartender's eye, waving. He hit his forehead with the heel of his hand, indicating he forgot. Claire nodded, turned back to Nathan, told him, "Never use a toy gun."

"Pretty sure it's real," Nathan said. "Saw some of the sketch when I was inside. Smith & Wesson 629 Trail Boss. Shoots six rounds, Abel Otto said, blanks in this case."

"Smith & Wesson 629 Trail Boss—that's more gun than Toronto cops carry," Claire said. "I own the same piece, personal use, solid, reliable." Making a six-shooter with her hand. "But you draw a gun, you might need to back it up. Gun with blanks is a toy, caveat being robbery with a toy is armed robbery. Wouldn't get far, either. That's the glass in the ass—you can't be seen doing it—and how do you do it without being seen?"

"Can't," Nathan said. "Anyway, like you, I'm not saying. I'm just saying. Theoretically, somebody could pilfer petty cash, too. I bet they have five K lying around in petty alone. Everything's in cash here, almost. Example: Second day, rehearsals, *Madame* comes waving hundred-dollar bills. Says run to Chinatown, pick up a soft blue sofa cover at Pong's Furniture, pre-selected, bring back a receipt. Standard with small prodcos. Even big ones work that way, lots of cash on hand."

"And you never thought about it?"

Nathan contained his smile, saying okay, she was just saying, so he was just saying. And if she wasn't just saying, she was trying to trick him. That was entrapment. Same time, it didn't matter. He'd been working these gigs more than a year and it had never been done. If it had never been done—like, he'd never heard of it—that meant it couldn't be done.

"Asides, *stupide* and *stupide* as I am, I'm not confessing a crime before I do it to Angie Dickinson herself, even if she is suspended, by reason of what again?"

She looked at him. "You honestly don't know who I am?"

7

It was taking Cyrus and the boys longer than expected, a hell of a lot longer. Finally, after 40 minutes or more, they had the 15-foot rubber bird almost deflated. Rolling it up, they managed to stuff most of it into the Impala's trunk. There was still some air in the chicken's head, so Cyrus had his hands around the throat, trying to force it out.

"You're choking it." Sundance giggled, poking Freak in the ribs. "Get it?"

Cyrus looked over his shoulder, unamused. "Just you two infuriating heterosexual yum-yums please load the compressor."

"The compressor?" Sundance said. "You want the compressor, too? The fuck're we going to put the compressor?"

"Next to you in the back."

"But it's still hot, man. I'm not getting physically burnt for this."

"Unless you want to keep that bird filled the old-fashioned way, blowing it, you'll be curled up in the back with the compressor."

Sundance looked at him, then the compressor. Fucking thing really was hot. Cyrus had to be off his rocker if he thought Sundance was sidling up to that. "Let's put it in the back on its own then I'll ride up front with you and Freak."

"Deal," Cyrus said. "Now put your gloves on, get the compressor, then get it in yourselves, pronto." Looking around. "We've truly been here too long."

Freak rubbed his soul patch, looking at Cyrus, the Impala, then the gear. "Still going to take some doing, some angling."

"So let's see a little more doing and angling." Cyrus watched a squad car pass. "And a little less pissing and moaning."

"I just don't want to have to do it twice." Freak removed his *Superman IV* cap, rolling the visor. "Let's just take our time figuring out how to get it inside the car. Take our time to do it right rather than buggering it up and having to start over, is all I'm trying to say."

Cyrus had heard enough. "Just you do it, Freak. You, too, Sundance. It's time for us to be getting. A little bit of help, please."

"Sure, sure, I get that." Freak stepped forward, holding up a hand. "But let me ask a question first."

Cyrus closed his eyes, okay.

"Like, why are we doing this?"

"Like, why do you care?" Cyrus pounded his feet. "It doesn't matter."

"Answer his question," Sundance said. "Why are we doing this?"

"I don't know the details, not my end," Cyrus said. "But Abel needs it to fix a broken sketch, to make it funny."

"You know." Freak looked at the bird bunched up in the trunk. "This might actually make it worse."

***

Nathan shook his head as the bartender served two more tequilas, trimmings. Was Claire the chick from the cheese commercial gets mad when her friend asks for a bite of her Havarti-Avocado wrap then eats the entire sandwich? No? Then he didn't know. Why? Did they have a mutual friend, something like that? Or, had Nathan hit on her somewhere far, far away?

Claire pointed her eyes at the bar guy, just a sec. As he walked away from their table, they licked, salted, licked again, clinked glasses, threw the shots back, and bit lemons. She puckered when Nathan looked across at her, watching as she tilted her head forward, bangs dangling in her green-brown eyes. "At least we'll never get the scurvy."

Nathan waved to himself. "Just tell me."

"You being polite?" She took a deep breath, letting it out when he shook his head, no. "I'm the cop they want fired, posing nude."

He felt his dick twitch, bringing a hand over his open mouth. *Ooh là là.*

"Heard of me now?"

Now that she mentioned it, he'd read about her, connecting her face to a picture with bars over all the right places in *The Toronto Sun*. But when he wouldn't say as much, she said he really was being polite, telling him how it started going south late last year with the police woman calendar. Tastefully selected bikini shots of Claire and 11 other female cops. Soon as it came out, Bob Bigington, Ward 19—the girls were just raising some money for the victims of crime program—must've got the first copy. Sexist, Bigington said. Christ, he was pinching turds over how your garden-variety calendar girl was down to a six from a 10, and, somehow, police women like Claire were to blame.

"I mean, look at me." She caressed a hand up and down the outline of her pop-bottle torso. "I'm a 12, classic, and he's telling the media we're negative role models, too skinny."

"You're not skinny." Nathan saw her raising her eyes like he was going too far the other way. He opened a palm, held it to her. "Me, I was just thinking how one day . . ." Looking off. ". . . there'll be enough wholesome girls to bring back Russ Meyer films."

Wholesome—yeah, it was a decent recovery. She gave him that, thinking his ability to BS his way out of a jam was mischievously cute. Plus, if he knew Russ Meyer, he didn't mind a girl ate a sandwich. "Anyway, Bigington managed to get the calendars pulped in January, censored, so I'm thinking it's over, right? Of 50,000 printed, only 4,000 remained in circulation, stolen, and then it became a collector's item, big in the underground, aficionados paying $50 per at porn shops. That's going on, lots of talk, pressure. Then boom, out of left field, I show up in *Gallery*. I mean, I didn't sign off on that."

Nathan didn't get it. "So it was an accident, you being in the magazine *érotique*?"

Massaging a crick in her neck, she said the pictures were from a drunken session with her ex, Calvert, back when she was in the academy, before she was serious about being a career cop. It was just going to be a J-O-B for a while, and old Calvert, he'd convinced her to wear her rookie outfit. Claire, removing items as he snapped, saying this was for personal use. Then in May, seven years after the fact, six after they break up—like, Claire's just at the point where they're considering her for promotion—the pictures turn up in the girl-next-door section of *Gallery*. Again, it was all over the papers, radio, and TV, more so this time. A complete panic.

The police board was ducking the whole thing until meeting again. But it was Calvert who really PO'd her, selling her out for a hundred bucks or something. Worst part, Calvert was balls deep into someone skinnier all along.

Nathan stopped her, said, "What were you doing before May?"

"Hello." Was he that drunk? "I was a cop, just got through telling you."

"I mean what kind of cop?"

Just a regular cop in a car, she told him. Traffic, assaults, domestics, in-your-face drug deals, B&Es, C-level detective work, whatever. So, Nathan said, now the chief wanted to set the bar higher for the thin blue line by reason of bad publicity?

Something like that. First, the top cop told the papers Claire was suspended for insubordination. Then, on radio, he said conduct unbecoming. Either way, the union lawyer was calling it discrimination, plain and simple, a human rights thing.

When the bartender dropped the bill in front of them, Claire put a hand up, said, "I'll get it." She fished inside her red vinyl purse for a loose credit card, slapping it down in front of the bartender, making a charade with her hands to indicate writing, to get on with it. He nodded, said sure, sure, walking to the bar to run her card.

"So can I see it then?" Nathan said.

"What? The magazine *érotique*?"

Nathan nodded, *oui*.

Claire twirled a lock of hair with her index, pulling tight. "You can do better than that."

Nathan could do better—what the hell was he supposed to say to that? "Okay."

"So you're not going to mind I can't cook?"

Again, Nathan fumbled for a response, listening for something he could use from the song on the juke, "Good Girls Don't" by The Knack. And while he fantasized away, he thought he heard the bartender say Claire's Mastercard had been rejected.

***

Behind the wheel of his Impala, finally, Cyrus was taking Queen Street East back to the studio. He had the stereo on low, a cassette bootleg of Generation X, live in Osaka Japan, 1979. Billy Idol was singing about hair that makes people stop and stare when Cyrus' cellular phone rang. With Freak and Sundance up front, Cyrus had to squirm to reach for his brick on the backseat floor, answering, hello.

"Cyrus, hi," Abel said. "How're you doing?"

Hitting the indicator, Cyrus pulled over. "Good, Abel."

There was a pause, Abel saying, "Aren't you going to ask how I am?"

Cyrus looked at Freak next to him. "How are you doing, Abel?"

"Good Cyrus, thank you. I appreciate it."

Waiting for the hook of it, getting dead air, Cyrus said, "Is there something I can help you with?"

Yes, and it was sweet of Cyrus to ask. First, main reason Abel was calling was to see how Cyrus was doing on the bird thing. Was he able to get one? Cyrus said he didn't want to discuss it on the brick, adding only that Abel would be pleased.

"How big is it?" Abel wanted to know. "My bird?"

Resisting the temptation to call Abel's entendre, Cyrus said they'd talk first thing, that they truly couldn't discuss it at this given moment.

"Why's that?" Abel said. "Did you have to steal it? You're actively driving around with stolen rubber bird product? Is that what you're trying to say?"

Cyrus said it was late, that he'd tell Abel all about it in the morning, damndest thing. Cyrus was about to click off when Abel said it sounded promising, that he really needed the bird to cover for Arlene's writer. Without the bird, the skit wasn't going to work. Even with the bird, Abel had to pull a rabbit out of his hat, and he still hadn't found the funny bone.

"Good luck with that," Cyrus said. "See you in the ayem."

"Just one more thing."

Cyrus exhaled. He didn't like the idea of idling on Queen with the stolen chicken bulging out of the Impala's trunk. But then he truly didn't want to be having this annoying conversation in traffic, either. "What, Abel? What else can I do for you at this time of night?"

"Some cola, please. I would like to purchase a small amount of cola."

Cyrus asked Abel where he was staying, the Inn on Carlton? Yes. Well, then they for sure had pop machines right there in the hotel—look.

"I need coke, Cyrus. Arlene told me you'd be at my disposal to get things, and I'm telling you I need a line or two to get through tomorrow. I'm thinking, this one time, if I could have a bump, maybe I can make this skit funny, and that's if you got the bird thing right."

Thinking on it for all of a second, Cyrus said cocaine truly wasn't on the list of things he was required to get, not even for people like Abel, and Abel could take that straight to Arlene. When Abel argued that this was a matter of artistic performance enhancement, Cyrus said no way. Ever since Len Bias OD'd, Cyrus had retired from the cola-delivery circuit, and that was final. Meantime, if Abel wanted to score himself, there was a Whitney Houston drag queen at Club Colby's, walking distance from the Inn on Carlton, who could probably take care of him.

"Whitney Houston?" Abel said. "That supposed to be ironic?"

Cyrus closed his eyes. "How so, Abel?"

"How so? Everybody in the business knows Whitney likes to ski. So why would someone sell snow while impersonating a known skier?"

"I don't know, Abel. I truly don't." Cyrus looked at his eyes in the rearview, edgy. "Otherwise, I'm sorry to cut this short, but I've got to get off the street."

8

Outside Toni Jo's, Claire said there must've been some snafu on the other end, sure that she had $53 space on her Mastercard. Must've been interest kicking in, something like that. But thanks, Nathan, and sorry. Otherwise, she was in no shape, but Nathan swore he could drive her Dodge Daytona to her place near King and Dufferin, no problem. He opened the passenger side for her then rounded the car, climbing in, keying the ignition. When they lurched forward, he kicked the brake. "You putting me on? Why would you buy a car like this?"

"What?"

"I can't drive it. Why do they even make stick-shift anymore?"

"You, the parking guy, mean to say you can't drive standard?"

Nathan brought his index fingers into a cross. "It's not like that. I don't do valet by reason of that's not my gig. Plus, most rich folks don't want me driving their fancy cars, so I just tell them where to park. Keep them in the fairway, so to speak, between the pylons."

Claire said, "It's a black thing, they don't want you driving their cars?"

Maybe it was a class thing, but black people didn't want Nathan driving their cars, either. Nathan said it was a car hang-up, people and their cars. And hey, why did she go right to black? First Kiwi, now her. Why didn't she say maybe it was a Latin thing? Or a Cambodian thing? It was like they wanted him to be black.

"But Arlene, you drive her Jeep."

"It's not stick. And look, driving stick is not something that's ever been called on me. Not the *emploi* I specialize in."

"Sounds like you specialize in sitting on your arse." Claire looked at him, playful eyes through her bangs again. "You tell 'em—Arlene, Veronica—you can't drive standard?"

He gave it some thought, said they never asked.

"Didn't think so."

Briefly, they discussed the possibility of Nathan driving while

Claire shifted gears from the passenger side. Claire decided that would be double DWI, so Nathan hailed a Crown Taxi.

At Parliament, he saw the Impala heading south, some big contraption in the back, no doubt on their way to the studio. The windows were down and Cyrus was driving. Sundance rode bitch with Freak on the passenger side holding a rope keeping the trunk tied down, not quite shut. Nathan figured any mention of Cyrus might mess with the mood. Asides, the cabby—Jerome Leggit, according to paperwork posted on his sun visor—was playing Q107 FM a bit loud, the new Guns N' Roses, Axel singing about how he wants to see you bleed, the sick fuck.

Claire caught the driver doing a number of things contrary to code, but she didn't want to mess with the mood, either. Reaching for Nathan's thigh, pulling away when a speed bump surprised her, trying again.

By the time Guns N' Roses bled into Whitesnake which bled into Lee Aaron, they arrived at Claire's sitting close, touching, whispering warm in each other's ear.

So far as Toronto basement-style lofts go, her place was swish—12-foot-high ceiling, hardwood floors, ceramics everywhere, a dryer mounted above a washer in an open closet. Various garments, including a tangerine silk thing with blue polka dots, were strewn about, like Claire had tried on a bunch of outfits before deciding what to wear this morning. As she collected her clothes, Nathan looked at a picture taped to the paneled wall of Molly Ringwald in a similar polka-dot number. Only the color combination was different.

There were other famous women—Wendy O. Williams in transparent jeans, Markie Post as a cowgirl, Belinda Carlisle wearing nothing but an oversized Ramones T-shirt full of holes . . . Nathan wondered if Claire was going to lift those designs, too, then wondered why? It was *stupide* clothes the girls were wearing, neither practical, comfortable, or even nice to look at, just *stupide*.

Other than Claire and a parched cactus with a red head, nothing else lived there. No cats, which was good by reason of Nathan was allergic, the dander. Plus it was his experience that cats became inappropriately territorial when he was bedding their human companions.

It appeared, however, that Claire was first on her block to have one of those swanky new CD players, even though she only seemed to have about a dozen CDs.

He watched as she slid a Kenny G disc, *Duotones*, into the player on her way to the kitchen. By the time she came back with a rum and Coke, Nathan was sitting in a blue marble recliner. Reaching for the drink, he said thank you, then *merci* when she dropped the notorious edition of *Gallery* on his lap, excusing herself.

Alone, he sipped his drink. Too strong, he winced, headed to the kitchen for more mix, looked in the fridge, said *tabernac*. She was passing off RC as Coke, cheap. The can he grabbed didn't feel right, too light, so he shook it, something soft brushing the inside. Holding it up, he saw a tiny edge that didn't quite connect and pulled the can apart, finding a wad of twenties and fifties inside. No room on her credit card, but lots of cash in the fridge. Funny, but not funny ha-ha, seeing as how she hadn't sprung for a thing all night. Buy him a beer, right.

Re-connecting the can, he studied the fridge contents. The DS Salad Dressing didn't look right, so he gave it a shake, jewelry rattling. Another jar had a wrap-around graphic of salsa but felt light. Unscrewing the cap, he found something green chopped up inside, taking a whiff, pot.

He felt guilty about going through her things—guilt and something else. Like it wasn't just him by reason of there was something off-putting about a woman stocking her fridge with valuables while she doesn't have $53 dollars space on her Mastercard. Maybe that's why she was suspended, for stealing everything she was hiding in her fridge.

So she's a for-real thief, huh? That girl could be all sorts of things, but Nathan couldn't know, and the answer wasn't entirely in her fridge. Eventually, he settled on something between quirky and paranoid, almost endearing. At least that's how he was trying to look at it.

Shaking until he found a real can of cola, he flipped the tab, weakening his drink. He thought about putting it back in the fridge, then decided to take it with him, worried he'd have trouble finding the real thing later.

Back in the living room, flipping through CDs on a shelf, he wondered how any music collection could include both Taylor Dayne and AC/DC, then selected something else, hitting stop. Getting rid of Kenny G by reason of his sax tried so hard to appeal to everybody without satisfying anyone. In fact, Kenny was kind of giving Nathan a soft-on, so he'd chosen a Blue Note compilation missing liner notes, thinking, whatever it was, it had to be better, as he inserted the CD into the player and hit play. Grant Green up first, "Sookie, Sookie."

Ahh, Nathan leaned back, hands behind his head.

Claire raised her voice from the shower. Why was Nathan putting on the acid jazz? Didn't he hear about praise *The New Age Journal* had for Kenny G? No, Nathan shouted that he generally didn't consult the hippies before playing a record. He then picked a leather-bound book off the second shelf, *The Complete Works of William Shakespeare*. Looking up, through the doorway at her refrigerator, he focused on a naked *homme*, a fridge magnet. Lots of cute little magnet shorts and tank tops to dress him up like an adult Ken doll, but Claire had him natural, anatomically correct. What the hell? He looked back to the book in his hand, singing an old *Sesame Street* song. Which one of these things was different than the other? Which one didn't belong?

It seemed to be an actual book, but Nathan was stumped about how to open it until he noticed a keyhole blended into the Acme Publishers logo on the spine. Hefting it, he thought it was a smart place to hide a Smith & Wesson 629 Trail Boss. Then he figured any self-respecting thief would make the book as a safe, heft it just like him, take it, and break into the book later.

Back to the recliner, he picked up the magazine. On the cover was a throw to page 86, OUR COPS ARE TOPS. There, a slightly younger Claire unbuttoned a sky-blue police shirt. By 87, it was on the four-poster bed behind her. Eighty-eight saw her do like so with a zip-off skirt. A garment described in the cutline as a bullet-proof bra went next, before she lost a navy thong on 92. And *tabernac*, did she ever have her *minou* waxed, or maybe it was air-brushed, smooth.

What stuck out most was that the shoot seemed planned, judging by the sequence and tidiness of the room. Her green-brown eyes were relatively clear, even if the lights were harsh, like someone needed to rush that girl into the sun. Nice and flushed tonight, though, he thought. Closing the magazine, looking at the cover, a girl calling herself Charming Chantel. She wore a strapless white bra and slip, one leg up on a bed as she adjusted a rust stocking matching her hair. Another wholesome girl, he whispered, re-opening the magazine to the table of contents.

Standouts included a brunette from Sandusky named Silvia who started out wearing a black teddy, then three blondes of various shades. Now flipping past Claire's spread, he checked out the centerfold, turning the magazine sideways when it was stripped from his hands.

"Already comparison shopping." Claire dropped the magazine on the floor, stepped back.

Sheepishly, Nathan looked up. "It was the letters section I was reading."

"Bullshit, you were looking at the centerfold. How'd I rate?"

He looked her up and down. "Favorably."

"Favorably?" She stepped forward, standing over him, close, wearing the same outfit from the magazine. It was tighter now, something she attributed to declining estrogen levels. She playfully ran her hands through her wet hair, pushing it up and in front of her face. It was clear she'd just experienced the vitality of organically grown lavender and spearmint.

"You poor thing," he said.

"What?"

"You really are in love with the uniform. It's the clothes. That's why you're a *policière*."

She snickered, scanning the room, the bookshelf. "You into Shakespeare?"

"Wouldn't open." Nathan held up his cola can. "And as you can see, me and my RC."

"Bugger." She reached for her billy club, hitting her open hand with it. "You snooped."

Nathan smiled tightly, wait a minute. He went to smooth his drink out—she made it too strong, probably slipped him a mickey—and she had cash in the cola. Like he was really expecting to find money, something personal, in her fridge. If she wanted to put cash in the cola, he wouldn't judge. But did she have any actual food in there? Or was it just a big safety deposit box and she keeps her food in a fridge that looks like a bank?

Yeah, yeah, yeah—she told him it was the latest thing in home security. That the Tonawanda Crime Commission, among others, recommended diversion safes. And Tonawanda, they had real trouble—big, bad American city like Buffalo right there, not enough cops. Anyway, the commission said the average burglary takes eight minutes. That thieves don't bother with books, pop, salad dressing, salsa—stuff like that.

"Lots of thieves, professionals, reading that same article," Nathan said. "By the time you buy in, crooks already know the technology exists. Tonawanda Crime Commission probably has the Hamburglar dissecting people's Cap'n Crunch right now."

He'd made his point, and it probably would have resonated if he'd left it there. But then he could feel himself getting irritated by the complexity of living. His sublet landlord, Larry Something, was coming back, but when? Nathan didn't know by reason of the last he heard Larry was looking for a cheap flight, standby, from Amsterdam. Man, it was so much work to get laid anymore, expensive. Between the tab and the cab, he'd spent what, $75? A suck-and-a-fuck back in St. Jamestown wasn't more than that, and Nathan had never heard of a pro yet who deployed Kenny G as an aphrodisiac.

He could see himself beneath this pretty, paranoid girl smells like plants and gum, Grant Green leading that trance-like jam, and he was going off again. Saying where were rich folks going hide their goodies next? This time next year, they'd be parking their

minivans in their *derrières* complaining to his adoptive momma—
she's a game warden—how come First Nations can spearfish?
Like, they were afraid the First Nations might go stand on a bridge
and spear all the fish, live high on *le porc. Tabernac*, they were
gonna need all the experienced spearfishers they could find once
that Snakehead took over Lake Ontario.

Claire squinted, said, Snakehead?

Snakehead, the next Zebra mussel, he told her, invasive species
in the Great Lakes, fucks up the eco-system. Native to China, Snake-
heads could breathe out of water. Looked like a snake, but it was
a fish, plus it had these little legs to run up to you on the beach,
bite your ankle, run back before it starts hurting. No natural
predators, so if you catch one, they said don't throw it back—call
Natural Resources, or Nathan's adoptive momma—Snakehead.

"Snakehead." Even though Claire was pretty sure he was jerking her chain—like, this was some Sasquatch-type deal, only
smaller, right?—it was fun to say. "Snakehead, sounds like a metal
band. And yeah, I see what you're saying, about the spearfishing."

9

Friday, June 23

Caught in morning gridlock on Lake Shore Boulevard, Arlene called Nathan on her brick and told him to ensure her spot was clear, bye. If she was abrupt, it was because she was listening to CHUM 104.5 FM, the extended dance mix of the new Madonna song everyone was having a cow over, thinking about how things used to be, how she got here from there.

Arlene had been a quasi-child star. First TV commercials for Woolworths and Sears, then a recurring role on *The Forest Rangers*, an adventure series about resourceful children of the North. Cancelled in 1966, she had one more nice bounce, landing as the niece of a coroner on *Wojeck*, but that was it. She had been typecast, just like Gary Coleman, Todd Bridges, Dana Plato. . . And *The Addams Family* kids, where was Wednesday? Married to a porn star? From Dennis the Menace (bitter and broke) to Jerry Mathers (opening grocery stores with a crooked smile) to Danny Bonaduce (drugs and violence), Arlene figured she turned out better than all of them. Fishhooks, now that she thought of it, Drew Barrymore was the worst of the wrecks, going to rehab at, what, 14? And where were her guardians?

Fortunately, Arlene's parents had put everything, less expenses, into trust for the day she became too old to play a kid. When time came, they went against their better judgement, sent her to Louisiana State University for screenwriting. Graduating with honors, her marks were outstanding, top notch. But, unable to produce a sellable script, she did the next best thing and became an industry bureaucrat—production assistant, audience coordinator, production secretary, script reader, casting director, head of prints and marketing . . .

Jack of all trades, master of none, she learned every job, making it to director of development at George Taylor and Associates by the time her parents died in that Dallas-Fort Worth crash in '83, trying to land during a storm. Investigators kept saying something about windshear, and while Arlene never completely understood what that meant, she thought that was the idea. Muddy it with buzzwords so nobody could ever get to the bottom of it.

Windshear, she thought—finding an opening, hitting the gas, and turning her Jeep onto Cherry Street—however it really happened, it helped that her parents were always planning against this sort of thing, always buying extra insurance. Along with their regular policies worth a half-million each, they purchased another four-million from one of those quickie booths at Detroit Metropolitan where they caught that fateful connection to Texas.

Only child, the inheritance was enough for Arlene to buy her existing company—George Taylor was happy to sell, retire—and put her name on the shingle. With what was left, she bought a bourgie bungalow in the Beaches and moved on up in the world, keeping the firm's existing contracts and landing new ones. When she took over in '85, AMA was already producing specials for Canadian content rock stars like The Spoons, Platinum Blonde, Luba, and Gowan. Then, with a little insider information from one of her father's Tory contacts, Arlene gambled that free trade would proceed as planned and won, bringing small productions over at a loss to establish herself with the Americans years before the deal went through last January. Albeit expensive, it was perfect timing. Armed with grants, tax credits, and a choice exchange rate, Hollywood North was producing all kinds of big and small screen content. Along the way, AMA was coming to specialize in second-rate, made-in-Canada American comedies. Arlene was thinking how it was a good niche, even if it wasn't quite what she wanted, when her cellular telephone rang on the passenger seat.

She ignored it, listening to Madonna tell her she was not what she seemed, turning off Cherry Street, waving as she slowly passed Nathan in his kiosk reading an old paperback with Paul Newman and Julie Andrews on the cover, parking in spot number two. The chorus—just like a prayer, I'll take you there—stopped abruptly when Arlene killed the engine and stepped out. Walking to the canopy, inside, the brick rang again. Arlene answered without breaking stride, saying how did you get this number? Thinking she eats difficult people for breakfast when she saw the bird, her mouth dropping open. To the person on the phone, some mother—a friend of a friend who was trying to get her son a gig as a PA—yes, there probably would be an opening for season two. She had his resume. She would call him at her convenience, click.

The 15-foot bird was almost fully inflated, oscillating. Arlene pointed at it. "Heathcliffe Wilson's Fried Chicken."

"I truly promise, we'll bring it right back." Cyrus glanced up, qualifying himself. "Soon as we're done with it, it quietly turns up right where we found it."

Fishhooks, Arlene wanted to hear that arrangements had been made. So long as it was reasonable, she would have paid. When did she ever put the ixne on anything over money? But this—this was not copacetic.

"Heathcliffe Wilson and I belong to the same business improvement association," she said. "That is how I know this has happened before, our newsletter, and that is also how I know he is rightly PO'd."

Abel walked into the middle of it, hands cradling an invisible globe. "Arlene, I understand what you're saying, point taken. But I directed Cyrus to get a chicken about yay big." Spreading his arms far apart, huge. "And I absolutely, positively had to have it overnight."

"Did you say he should steal it?"

"I didn't tell him not to." Abel yawned, stretching his arms. "That's not the point anyway. But listen, it's going to work out as advertising for the guy, the way I'm doing it. When this hits cable, Heathcliffe Wilson will be able to set up shop in every state, with the possible exception of Alaska. It'll be more valuable than a Super Bowl spot, almost."

"Super Bowl—Goddamn both of you." She pointed at her windpipe. "I am the one who is going to get the call. And the time it is going to take to people-please Heathcliffe—you never get the time back, but you do not know that yet. Still too young..."

Abel watched as she trailed off, hands in his pockets. "Look Arlene, the chicken is for the fat camp skit your writer brought in. We had to rework it. It needed a thing, okay, a hook."

"What do you mean, it needed a thing? A hook?"

"Relax, we just had to bring in a prop. Show people instead of telling them."

"Show people?"

Fuck it. Abel had kissed ass long enough, and if he didn't manage to put a fix on this, he was going start leaking momentum. "Truth is I didn't want some of that shit about fat people coming out of my mouth. And well, I thought the chicken might take the edge off. My sister Ordella, she's twice my size. With the bird, we're just going a little easier. I mean, push it over, don't kick it down, you know?"

Push it over—that did it. Fricking Americans, anything they wanted, they would just take, justify it later. Not this time. No way Abel Otto was calling the shots on an AMA show. "I will thank you to know that I wrote the sketch."

Abel hesitated, stepping back. "Well, it's not funny. And Red Skelton, any time he had a routine that wasn't funny, he'd trot out a rubber chicken and everyone would laugh at that."

"The piece stands, as is. Lose the bird."

Abel looked at Cyrus, back to Arlene, holding a hand up, pinching his thumb and forefinger. "We just need to tweak it. And hey, Arlene, congratulations, by the way. Since when were you a screenwriter?" He waited for an answer. Getting none, he said, "So does this mean you're in the guild now?" Extending his right hand. "Welcome aboard, sister."

***

The sublet landlord had been clear. Nathan was not to touch the makeshift cabinet lined with rare and out-of-print spy paperbacks. Originally, Nathan agreed, then Larry Something didn't pay the cable before he went off to find himself. The record-player wasn't exactly working, either. Seeing as how the amenities he'd paid for didn't come as advertised, Nathan felt right about sampling the books as compensation. Today, he was so bold as to bring one to work, Richard Wormser's novelization of *Tom Curtain*.

The movie was sometimes referred to as Hitchcock's stinker, but Nathan hadn't seen it, so no matter. The neat part was reading from the original document promising espionage playing east against west, lover against mistress. Probably would've been worth 40 bucks if not for the stamp on the inside cover—The Book Bin, Buffalo, New York. Someone smart enough to open a bookstore yet *stupide* enough to devalue a rare gem, Nathan thought. Looking up to see Jeffrey Brewer, the PA Arlene called Sundance, take an envelope from Claire. After exchanging words, he grew larger, dragging his feet towards the kiosk.

"Discount copper told me to give you this. Now hide me. I'm one of the after-guys in the fat camp sketch, have to get high, mentally prepare."

Nathan took the envelope, ripping it open, putting up a hand as he read the note.

> Nathan,
> Meet me in the green room at 2:35 sharp for further interrogation. Knock 3 times quickly, pause, then knock 2 more times slowly.
> Constable Claire

"You going to hide me?" Sundance's eyes shifted to the exits, watching for Arlene.

"In a minute," Nathan said. "Just tell me where's the green room before you get giggly."

"Swanky dressing room reserved for the stars. Vanity, lead chick from that raunchy all-girl Prince band, Vanity 6. That's where she'll chill."

Nathan said it was impolite to be evasive. Now, he knew what a green room was. He just needed to find this one in particular.

"I eat at 1:30," Sundance said. "Relaxed patio motif. Grilled veggie and orzo salad, oriental pasta, chicken with basil sauce. I'll show you the green room then." Looking at Claire, back to Nathan. "How come you suddenly need to know where's the green room?"

"Just show me."

As Sundance ducked behind the kiosk, Nathan turned over

Claire's note. It had been written on the back of a computer-printed news brief from *Variety*, October 22, 1982.

BANDITS BILK BARRIS

LOS ANGELES—Armed robbers made off with more than $35,000 in a payroll heist last week at Chuck Barris' downtown prodco.

Shortly after 8:30 a.m. Friday, two men ransacked Barris Industries, firing warning shots into the floor. That afternoon, Barris told KQLZ 100.3 FM the gunplay was an "attention-getter" for three employees to turn over the cash and lie on the floor, as instructed.

Asked why employees were being paid cash, Barris said: "I just deal with talent, the creative end. Other people handle payroll." Although police are not commenting, a source with connections to Barris' house says the caper is being investigated as an inside job.

Below was a notation in Claire's handwriting.

Can it be done?
It HAS been done.

"You spanking that Angie Dickinson or what?" It was Sundance, making a crude noise with his tongue. "Are you?"

Only now aware of the sticky-sweet smell, Nathan folded the note into the envelope, shoving it into the back pocket of his khakis as he spoke through the door. "Now I hide you every day so you can get your little reefer fix, right?"

"I guess," Sundance said.

"I guess nothing. I do it for you."

"You hide me, fine."

"Well, you've got to cover for me at 2:35 until 2:55," Nathan said. "Twenty minutes, a little more, a little less. Can you get away, do that for me?"

"Sure. Meckler doesn't want me until later. For now, they got me watching the walkies."

"I thought Kiwi's watching walkies."

"They need somebody can lift more than me, like a lot. Plus Kiwi lost some walkies. He's been reassigned, you could say, to hard labor. So yeah, I can sneak away, cover." Taking another toke, Sundance peaked around the kiosk, stealing a look at Claire. "Security's got good hind parts, thick." Jerking back when she caught him. "Now are you spanking her or what?"

"Sundance, that's none of your Goddamn business."

"Who are you talking to mister?"

That right there was a third voice.

Nathan looked up, a puffy-faced girl, 15 or 16, thereabouts, peering in at him. A woman appearing to be mom stood behind, asking, "Did you just say Goddamn?"

"No ma'am."

"I heard you."

"I mean, yes." Nathan smiled. "Practicing to win a wee part in this here *Otto Show*."

"I thought this set was supposed to be profanity free." She looked at him suspiciously, pointing at the building. "They say Goddamn?" Like the daughter, she was a plus, dark hair and freckles everywhere. Pretty, Nathan thought, but uptight.

"Your daughter," he said. "She's an extra?"

"Background performer. This may be her first role, but she's a background performer. That much entertainment lingo I know. A man in your position ought to know that much as well. You're a welcomer, God sakes. Part of your job is to welcome people with the right lingo."

Nathan forced a smile, unfolding his clipboard. "May I have your daughter's last name?"

"Cavellerie, and what's that smell? Skunk?"

Nathan ignored the question by reason of he wasn't going to do Sundance's explaining, scanning the call sheet. Yes, she was in the 1:45 skit. Normally, Nathan would contact Kiwi, Freak, or Sundance—now snickering and dabbing the heater on his joint with a wet finger behind the kiosk—or one of the other PAs. Let them know a background performer—*merde*, nobody called them that, no matter what the extras said—was here for their bit. But a note here said for Nathan to contact Arlene as soon as this girl arrived, so he pressed the talk button on the wire running between his headset and walkie, and said, "Nathan for *Madame* Marion."

There was static, then Arlene's voice. "Go for Arlene, and I told you, speak English."

"Silvie Cavellerie, here for the 1:45. Call sheet says call you, personally."

"Nathan, go to 10."

Unlike eight—the production channel Nathan and Claire regularly tuned to—10 was the so-called private channel. Nathan switched to it, wondering if he was the only one who listened in from time to time when he heard his boss again. "Arlene for Nathan."

He hit his talk button. "Go for Nathan."

"This Cavellerie girl, does she get a lot of dairy?"

Nathan adjusted his headphones. "Come again?"

"Look, we already had to re-shoot a bit from another series because the Tufte Agency sent us the wrong type of girl. This thing Abel is doing revolves around a girl of ample proportions, so I need a yes or no. Is she plump enough to be at the center of a fat camp sketch?"

"Is there a problem?" the mother said.

Nathan shook his head, a non-verbal wait a minute.

"Last time," Arlene said, "does she have a great big money-maker she can shake?"

Nathan tentatively said yes, trying to smile at the woman and her daughter.

"Then just please send her directly to me," Arlene said. "Can you manage that?"

Could Nathan manage that? Oh, if someone didn't put something in Arlene's drink soon, he was going to explode the place, see what she had to say then. "Copy," he said into the mouthpiece. Then he pointed to the canopy, talking to the mother. "Tell them you're here to see Arlene Marion, personally. Contact Nathan if someone questions that."

As the mother and daughter started to the door, he tuned back into Arlene on his headset, still talking at him, something about that ex-cop. Arlene could see Claire from the window, headphones around her neck, again. Fishhooks, they did not do any good if one did not wear them properly, on the ears. And what did she call that get-up she was she wearing today? Nathan pressed the talk button, said he believed you called it a tankini, Ms. Marion, this one with retro floral printing and a matching tear-away skirt. He thought about saying something about how Arlene told Claire not to wear her uniform, then thought better of it.

10

Veronica checked her grey Swatch, past 2:30, strolling through the set department, noticing Cyrus' keys on his desk. Out in the hall, she saw Claire walk into the green room like a boss. Knowing what that might be about, Veronica returned to Cyrus' desk, grabbed his keys and hightailed it up to Arlene's office. She watched Nathan through the window, shuffling across the lot. No doubt proceeding to the green room, Veronica thought, smiling, opening Arlene's drawer then the locked safe inside, removing cash, stuffing it in an envelope, locking up.

Veronica made her next move after confirming the state of security. Other than Sundance vegetating behind Nathan's kiosk and singing along to his radio about a plan to get out of here, there was no one in the lot, so she went ahead and used Cyrus' keys to open the Impala's trunk. Noticing a brown envelope, leaving it undisturbed, she slid the envelope containing the cash under the spare, clicking the trunk shut while Sundance wailed about driving in someone's car. Back inside, returning Cyrus' keys, Veronica walked into the studio, standing behind Dan Meckler—who, as a Christian, was already offended by the act of humiliation television about to commence, but nonetheless going along with it—watching Abel get to the fat camp sketch. They were having trouble keeping the bird inflated, behind schedule, the studio audience testy.

Abel was portraying a psychologist from the Pentecostal Charismatic Movement, counseling a girl who'd escaped the church's rural Ohio weight loss retreat. While there, she said she only gained weight, that she lived on rubber chicken. Abel, waiting a beat, asked how she kept herself from falling off? The laugh sign flashed, but nobody bit. Instead, they quietly watched Abel place his hands on the Cavellerie girl's scalp, massaging it as if to heal her, make her skinny. Eyes closed, she shuddered when Abel pushed her back.

"Open your eyes."

The girl did so, a fine crying job to boot. "I'm still fat, and I still see it."

"What—what do you see?"

She pointed, up to the 15-foot bird bouncing like a greasy wet dream with the pressure of wind fans off-camera. "Heathcliffe Wilson's rubber chicken."

A hush washed over the audience. Abel could see that he hadn't pulled it off, even with a wink and a prop and a bump. He could feel the failure. Most folks in the bleachers looked too embarrassed to laugh, while those who did seemed nervous. Bad enough, then an old man, heavyset himself, stood up wearing an upside-down visor, shouting "product placement" from the third row. By the time Rupert the audience coordinator came for him, the guy was going on about how it was okay for Red Skelton to make rubber chicken jokes because he didn't use the device to denigrate people of size. Also, Red was funny, and try as he might, Abel was never going to fill out Red's Jockeys no matter whose schlong he sucked.

Shit the bed, why hadn't Abel just told Arlene this was a non-starter? How did she stop herself from falling off—it was so stupid. Why did he even try to fix it? He should have told Arlene, no, because now he really was losing momentum, loyalties. Letting the old junkie put words in his mouth—this was beneath Abel. Now look at the audience. Everyone was mad.

"And hey," Abel shouted, looking around. "Has anyone said cut?"

Still standing behind Meckler's director chair when he finally put an end to it, "cut," Veronica watched Arlene in the last row of bleachers. Going for her purse, working her hands inside, she came up with something, plopping it into her mouth, throwing it back with a swish of tea when Veronica stepped away from Meckler and hit the talk button.

"Veronica for Arlene."

"Go for Arlene."

"You okay?"

Feeling the bite, Arlene scanned the floor, finding Veronica. "What?"

"I just wanted to tell you not to worry about the laughs. Meckler can dub 'em in later."

Arlene snapped her purse shut, starting down the bleachers as she told Veronica to tell Meckler to lose the bird, and do it again. Fricking Abel, Arlene had told him how many times, no bird, and what did the Pentecostal Charismatics have to do with it? The Comedy Channel was not going to dig this religious dookie. Why couldn't Abel just do it the way it was written? Arlene would thank Veronica to tell Meckler to see to it that Abel did more rehearsing and less improvising. That would be good, Veronica was to tell Meckler to tell Abel, like that.

***

Claire watched herself in the mirror, standing in her tankini, boy-cut shorts, and boots. Her flanks were smooth, thick, but not overly defined, and some men still preferred a girl who was a girl, even if the sports sections didn't. Take Bonnie Blair, the speed-skater. The papers never showed her below the waist, like they were doing her a favor hiding her great big, beautiful ass. Didn't anyone else pick up on that?

Claire turned to look at her own can, running a hand over the muscle going into her back. Sturdy, she thought, reaching into her purse for a condom sealed in a gold coin, setting it atop of the couch, flinching at three quick knocks. After a pause then two slow taps, she opened the door a crack. Nathan stood there in his dull navy T-shirt, Oakwood Country Club, home of the 1985 Lite Quad Cities Open.

"What?" she said. "You soliciting?"

Nathan looked left, right, saying the dead brown dog barks wildly at the dark side of the moon, code. Now let him in, and she did.

Inside, she asked what took him? He said he went to the facilities first so as he had an alibi for being inside. Then, seeing her tear-away skirt bunched up on a cushion, he asked if she started without him? As a matter of fact, she had, she said, putting a hand behind his head, and he had some catching up to do. Nathan said he didn't need a fluffer, kissing her softly, harder as he undid her tankini from the back, forcing her boy-cut shorts down to her knees with a free hand, doing the rest with an oil-stained desert boot. He made her turn to face the mirror, moving against his hand, watching. Then *tabernac*, just when she lost sight of herself, he couldn't get the condom out of the coin with just one hand and his teeth. What was this? Money in the cola, pot in the salsa, a gun in a book, and now a condom in a coin? Did everything have to come in some fake package? And hey, why did she want him to vulcanize now when she didn't last night?

***

Through the kitchen, Arlene scooped up a slice of melon on her way past craft services, eating, spitting seeds as she started up another set of stairs, the building's east wing. At the top, she took a right, then a left, dropping into a chair at her desk in her temporary office.

She went for her purse, looking inside, a half dozen pills left. She knew the bottle in her desk was empty, so she reached for the landline, punching digits, calling Dr. Platt's office, and yes, she would hold, thanks. Just tell him it's Arlene Marion, she said, hearing a Muzak version of "Start Me Up," thinking how she'd spun the rehab thing better than a rock star.

Her first instinct had been to hide and quietly get well, say she had been off on a whirlwind romance. That's why she chose a secret narc center out west, BC. Then, that picture of her on all fours at the film fest wound up in *Frank*, a satirical magazine, the talk bubble saying Hollywood North cough syrup connoisseur Arlene Marion searches for pocket change outside the Uptown Theatre.

They were making fun of her, mocking her. That just made her mad, determined to come back the right way. She would stick it up all their rectal cavities. Save for making a list of people she had harmed, that's what got her through the 12 steps. She spent that whole time planning in her hospital-yellow room, thinking, reading dated industry rags, taking notes—until it came to her while reading *Rolling Stone*. Sure, Boy George had been doing two grams of heroin a day, openly referring to himself as everyone's favorite drug addict. But he was simply trying to feel better, and that was a good thing, a human thing. The way they did Boy, however, Arlene thought, no way. Instead of groveling, sorry over time owing to opiates, she would go the other way and surprise them all, particularly her detractors among the investors.

She may have looked a bit like Mary Tyler Moore during that rough patch. Yes, Arlene knew. But she had been to places the rest of them never heard of—which was why, by the way, they called it a trip. Trip, get it?

And that's pretty much what she told the round table, highlighting key phrases with her fingers. It was all about "exploration," making her "a better comedy bureaucrat." The comedians were "dark bastards all," only now she knew where they were "coming from." Did the investors know where they were "coming from?" No, she didn't think so.

Of course, what with the slip-and-fall, Dr. Platt was partly to blame, the way he was doling out those little Percodans like Sammy Davis Jr. singing "The Candyman," tossing Kraft caramels all over the place. Dr. Platt, he was the dark master who turned her on, she thought, hearing the Muzak cut out, then Platt himself. "Arlene?"

"Hi Dr. Platt. Sorry—so sorry to bother you, but I need a refill called in, can't get away."

"Fine." He sounded scared. "Go to Rankin Pharmacy this time, Wellesley near Jarvis."

Arlene looked at her hands, blotchy again. "Also, a round of antibiotics, Clindamycin."

"Clinda—that's a pretty radical antibiotic, for what?"

"My hands, they are red like beets—eczema, again. Maybe that is causing the Raynaud's, the attacks. My hands just start pulsing, veins sticking out everywhere."

"More like stress, like John Hinckley Jr., who also sought treatment for red hands."

"More like chemicals, is what I heard. That Hinckley was plotting to mail chemicals to Reagan before deciding to shoot him, that he acquired an infection from handling chemicals."

"I heard it was stress over how he was going to shoot the president," Platt said. "Stress, or in your case, could be the Peres, but you don't have eczema or even Raynaud's. We've been through this. You don't need antibiotics. Just let your system—"

"My system—you do not even know what it is, so just you call in the antibiotics."

"Fine," he said, hanging up before she could demand something else she didn't need.

Arlene placed the phone on its cradle. Sitting back, she remembered the rest of it, how she told the investors, sure, she aged five years in one, but that was only because she went cold turkey on Oil of Olay. She should not have done that—once you start you have to stay with it—but that, too, was a metaphor for something or other about suffering.

Anyway, it was time to come back and see who she could be. Arlene was a new woman now, a survivor. Akin to an older Madonna, redefining herself. Arlene laughed, thinking how that part that part always pissed Veronica off.

In her purse, Arlene found her wallet light. She forgot to hit the ATM, so she decided to borrow from petty cash, pay it back. No, find a way to expense the meds, she told herself, keying her desk drawer. It wasn't like she could use benefits to buy Percs at this point, red flag, so she made a mental note to find a receipt on the floor somewhere, opening the little desk safe.

***

Nathan checked the Casio on his wrist, 2:57 pm, emerging from the green room. He was hoping to find the hallway empty and mosey on to his kiosk like he was coming back from the facilities. But *tabernac*, the Cavellerie girl was out there, crying. Nathan considered what that might be about, awkwardly stepping around her, the waterworks continuing.

"I can't believe what they did to me."

He turned, seeing her rocking back and forth, face in her hands.

"Nathan, did you do something to that little girl?" It was Arlene, stepping into the hallway. "Answer me . . . ANSWER ME."

Nathan held his hands high, said nothing, watching Arlene kneel behind the girl, arms around her shoulders. Arlene was looking at Nathan as if to protect the girl from him when the girl bit Arlene's hand. Sitting cross-legged, the girl twisted on the floor, eyes swollen, pointing at Arlene. "You did this, you."

Arlene wrung her hand, rubbing the pain away, looking to Nathan. "Get this trash out of my studio, bringing everybody down." Back to the girl. "What was your name again, honey?"

"Why? Why do you care?"

"Because you just got yourself on the blacklist, double." Out of the corner of her eye, Arlene noticed Claire walk out of the green room adjusting her tear-away skirt. Looking to Nathan, back to Claire, Arlene said, "No wonder you are not answering on eight."

"What?" Claire took a step forward, proud. "You need a suppository?"

Arlene pointed her headset at Claire, then the open door. "While you were doing something you are not supposed to be doing in a place you are not supposed to be doing it, petty cash was robbed—robbed to the tune of $4,800." Then to Veronica who was just walking into the scene. "Get one of the PAs in here to clean this up." Back to Nathan, Claire. "What are you now, part of some special club? Doing it in the green room, just like the stars."

11

Claire stood outside beneath the canopy and slid her thumbs through her tankini's straps, half-thinking she was going to be fired, again, if she didn't find out who made off with petty cash. Same time, Arlene was more worked up about rooting out the audacity of disloyalty, as she put it, and didn't think Claire was stupid enough to get caught shagging and stealing the same day. The good part was that Claire appeared to have an alibi, however compromising.

As per instructions, she started working the case, paging her former partner Morton McNab. A few minutes later, he called Claire's brick from a payphone, en route.

Although the *Gallery* spread affected her relationships on the force, Morton had been her constant. He took the trouble to involve her socially, even if just for beers and smokes. True, he thought he was finding himself doing shitty jobs because they'd been partners. Then, sometimes, he thought they'd found out about him, sure the higher-ups were talking, making inside jokes.

Pulling his white, blue, and red Chevy Caprice up to the kiosk where Claire said she'd be waiting, he said, "You look like a scoop of mango gelato in cop boots. That retro floral print, I could see you from the overpass, no question." Nodding to Nathan inside, a battery-operated fan blowing on his face, smiling nice, turning back to Claire. "What's the gig like?"

"A little bizarro." Claire, headset around her neck, held a hand out. "Nathan here calls it a half-world. Creative people, they fancy themselves. More like people who don't have their feet on the ground. People who maybe got a taste of Hollywood proper, only Hollywood didn't call back, so they're mad, precious. I mean, look at this place." Motioning to the lot, cracked concrete, weeds. "If you left it alone for a month, it'd be an industrial drug squat. As is, people fuzzy their eyes when they pull in, act like they're arriving at Universal Studios." Looking directly at Morton. "What about you? I saw Jojo Chintoh reporting on CityTV where you got the pepper spray."

Morton reached for his belt, extracting a black and red cannister, admiring it, holding it up. "New alternative to deadly force, replaces chemical mace. Thing I like, it puts the fucker down without hassle. Guy mouths off, you give him the spice. They say it's like being able to shoot without worrying about Internal."

"They say." Claire waved to herself. "Gimme."

Morton handed the cannister over. "G'head."

She rolled the weapon side to side. "Looks like common household product."

Morton nodded, recalling points from the presser. "It's all-natural agents, organic. You get a guy square, he's all fucked up. His eyes—he can't see, can't breathe, and man does it burn. Takes a guy's coordination, debilitates him. But he'll recover. It's non-lethal. Should've seen the press conference, reporters lining up to do first-persons, getting blasted, writhing around like tormented worms. After that, it's the coppers lining up to blast each other, research purposes. Everyone pouring milk into each other's eyes. Community."

"So." Claire cracked her gum as she handed the cannister back, wishing she'd been at the presser with the others, the camaraderie. "Still chasing baseheads?"

"Better—you're going to love this." Morton stretched out the window, looking at the new dent above the front tire. "Craziest thing. Heathcliffe Wilson's Fried Chicken, they've got a huge inflatable bird out front, right? Thing keeps getting stolen. Three times in two months."

"Unsolved killings all over 51 Division, home invasions, in your face drug-deals, hos in skirts don't cover their heinies working playgrounds—they got you tracking balloons?"

Morton rubbed his tightly trimmed goatee. He couldn't believe it, either. "Turns out Heathcliffe is Deputy Chief Walsh's brother in law. Heathcliffe, he's tired of his birds being bagged, being made the fool. Apparently, they run like seven grand each, plus compressor, so the deputy chief sent word up to the chief, who sent it down to the captain, who assigned it to me."

"Calling all cars, whydonchya."

"Is what is," Morton said. "Probably frat boys, initiation, something like that. Just found the remains of a joint—a roach wrapped in grape papers, expensive taste—at the scene. Anyway, you said something about they have a petty cash deficit here. How much?"

"Forty-eight hundred."

"Thought you said petty." Morton swiveled his head and made a sucking sound. "People leave that much cash around, there's little you can do. What kind of safe? A combo? Cause if it's a combo, we find out who has it, then find out who's their friends, say hey, buddy—"

Claire cut him off. "Standard desk-drawer key job, something from Home Hardware."

"How many keys?"

"Three. She says she has them all, two copies at home, one on her chain."

"And who is she?"

"Arlene Marion, her production company, Arlene Marion and Associates."

"And you don't think she's stealing from herself, insurance purposes?"

"Can't see it." Claire held her palms out. "But who knows, these times."

"Where were you, you don't mind my asking?"

Claire licked her lips. "Actually, I kinda' do."

"The fuck you mean, you kinda' do?"

Nathan stood in his kiosk, checking the wire running between his walkie and headset, shooting Morton a look. "She was indisposed, is all."

Morton looked at Nathan. "And you?"

"Also indisposed."

Eyes back on Claire, Morton winked, said okay.

"Why ask anyway?"

"Cause you always ask the guy called it in, Claire, standard procedure. You'd disrespect me, I didn't ask the guy called it in."

Claire fanned a hand over her tankini. "I look like a guy to you?"

"You know what I mean."

Nathan kept his mouth shut, smiling nice while the two of them went through some bonding ritual dating back to the fall of anarchy. Thinking, last night he mentions petty cash to Claire and it goes poof the next day. On top of that, where did she get the news clipping about Chuck Barris' joint being robbed? It's not like she could've dropped by the library, looked it up on the computer, printed it, picked up her car, and made it to work on time. She probably would've had to wait in line just to use the computer. Nice-looking university-educated white girl, what would she see in him anyway? A has-been caddy in a parking lot, what could she see in him? Aside from her ex-partner grilling her, it was all just suspicious, and it didn't help that she had money issues. Same time, Nathan had been with Claire since she arrived an hour after him, so when did she have a chance to pilfer petty? She didn't.

As for Morton McNab, he couldn't bother concealing his smile, Claire getting caught with her skirt hiked, again—go girl. "So you need me to do what?"

"Meet a few people, ask around, get someone running scared. You know the drill, keep hitting until someone twitches, sweats."

"Let you follow up?"

"Would be good. Give me something to do, keep me sharp." Claire adjusted her tear-away skirt at the waist. "And when you meet a guy, Cyrus, make it special."

"This guy, Cyrus, you think it was him?"

"Not particularly, just a worm I want squirmed. Had some trouble with him."

"Trouble? What kind?"

"My first day, he races in here playing Billy Idol too loud, almost runs down Nathan." She hesitated. "Then he hits me opening his door and gives me a coco butt."

"A coco butt?" Morton pointed at the ground. "This guy, Cyrus, gives a paid duty officer a coco butt, that's assault an officer for fuck sakes."

"I know. That's what I told them, serious crime, especially when malicious."

"Malicious assault an officer, the worst. Why didn't you have 'em charged two times?"

"I gave him the wood shampoo, then a shot to the groinal area." Claire raised her brow. "Think I caught a nut. They seem to be overlooking that, so..."

Morton held the wheel, flexing fingers. "Still assault an officer." Pulling away.

Parking in spot one next to Arlene's Jeep, he cut the engine, stepped out and took off his hat, revealing a No. 2 soldier shave and wiping the fuzz with a handkerchief.

"What's that mean again?" Claire said, catching up. "The white hanky?"

"Means beat my meat."

"So it's hand jobs you're seeking?"

"That's right." Morton returned the hanky to his left back pocket, top exposed. "Safe."

"And what if you wore it in your right? Like, there's a difference?"

"Absolutely." Morton positioned his hat. "White hanky in your back right pocket means I'll do both, hardcore." Next, he bummed a ciggy, a light. "Still smoking Mores, eh?" Looking at the brown wrap, returning the cigarette to his mouth. "May as well not smoke at all, this brand."

Claire said, "How many's that today?"

"Today?" Morton struck a match, lighting up, exhaling. "This is like my seventh in about a week. Same as not smoking, this city. Best part." Molding his lips around the filter, sucking hard—head rush. "Each one's good this way."

A few drags later, Claire tossed her butt into the concrete box containing the browning evergreen. Morton was about to do the same, then stopped, just a sec, watching a clique of wind surfers as he took another hit. "At least you've got a nice view."

"I have to remind myself," Claire said. "Sometimes, when I look out there, everything in my head is clear—clear as the best part of the day."

"I can see that, and we could all use a little more water," Morton said. "Open water."

A puff later, he flicked his butt into the planter, said let's book, following Claire inside.

12

Word of the petty cash caper ran through the studio like a breaking CNN circle jerk. By the time it reached the floor, the minions were whispering that something like 10-grand was missing. Morton met a dozen or so, handing out business cards, jotting down names. He'd just finished with Janet Boroski, the production co-ordinator, going through the motions until he met Cyrus, slowing down. "Cyrus, you say?" Morton opened his spiral notebook, poising his pen.

"That's right, Cyrus Dagan."

"Cyrus." Morton scribbled. "Last name double A, double G?"

"Two As, one G," Cyrus said, spelling it out. "D-A-G-A-N."

Morton wrote it down, motioning to some chairs and telling Cyrus to sit, that this might take a while. Still standing himself, Morton waited for Cyrus to be seated and said, "Know anyone needs $4,800 fast, Mr. Dagan?"

Mister, Cyrus thought. "Don't look at me. I make $300 a day."

Morton looked him square in the forehead anyway, thinking how this always works—looking through them like an X-ray above the eyes, detaching himself. "That a no, captain?"

First mister, now captain, and why was the cop looking at Cyrus like that? Was he spaced? And why did he tell Cyrus to sit when he was going to stand? "Course it's a no."

"It's just, a man makes $300 a day is a man with expensive tastes, sometimes too expensive." Morton noticed Cyrus' checker-board shoes. "Your car, for instance, make?"

"Impala."

"Year?"

"Old, 1960."

"Ahh." Morton nodded, humble. "I bet a man needs a lot of money for hard-to-find parts, he drives a 29-year-old car."

"Let's just say I know how to get things." Cyrus felt himself stickhandling, explaining how it was his job to hunt down every weird thing they needed for set, sometimes wardrobe. That he was good at it, important.

"Important?" Morton frowned. "G'head, tell me how you mean, important?"

"What would you call a man who can track the same gun Chuck Connors used in *The Rifleman*? That an important man? A man who can get a patent-leather mini Nancy Sinatra wore in 1969, important? Or how about a man that can acquire a great big giant rubber bird on short notice?" Cyrus stopped, backpedaling. "Let's just say I know how to get things."

"No question, no question." Bird, Morton hadn't missed it. This guy, Cyrus, could've listed off all the curios these dweebs made him source, but he stopped abruptly at bird, when it just so happened Morton was looking for a bird. "That is an important man, can get all that."

Revisiting Cyrus' checkerboard twelves, Morton said he was thinking about getting a pair himself. "Reminds me of Madness, ska band does 'One Step Beyond.' Something I'd wear to my high school reunion. Only now, a shoe like that's a specialty item. Vans Corp. has itself a copyright, and that makes a $20 item $59.99."

"A man who makes $300 a day can afford $59.99, thanks." Cyrus nodded assuredly. "I wear $30 socks, so why not move on to the next guy already?"

"It's just..." Morton paused. "You seem a little unstrung." Chuckling to Claire, pointing at Cyrus' feet. "Unstrung, get it? His shoes have no laces." Turning to Cyrus. "And, no question, an unstrung man is always an interesting man."

"More like a fag is always interesting," Cyrus said. "At least to a cop."

"Is that right?" Morton looked concerned. "It's on account of you like the San Francisco treat makes you suspect, my eyes?"

"That's right. You, calling me mister, captain, intimidating a fag in his own workplace. Like, it must be the fag because of that Air Canada flight attendant, Gaëtan Dugas. Ever since *The American Journal of Medicine* named him patient zero, conspiracy one, saying he gave AIDS to like 2,500 guys, conspiracy two, gays are bad news, again, conspiracy three, profiled so smart cops like you can relate one gay's behavior to the next."

Fuck around, Claire couldn't believe Cyrus was going down this rabbit hole. Didn't these people have gaydar? And how could they get laid if they couldn't spot their own kind? Maybe that's why they have hankies, she thought while Morton finally pulled up a chair, sitting backwards. Moving closer, crowding Cyrus, getting a whiff of his rainwater shampoo, Morton looked at the big, bad, rich butch who gave a paid-duty officer—a female paid-duty officer—a coco butt, and said, yes, as it happened, Cyrus was exhibiting certain behavioral gesticulations. But they had more to do with a man with something to hide and less about how he gets through the night.

"And those are?" Cyrus cleared his throat. "Gesticulations of guys hiding things?"

"First, they start off helpful, polite, like you, making sure we have your name spelled correctly, sundry details, doing your civic duty." Morton held a hand over his heart. "Then, sensing they're cornered, they get flippant, also like you. Showing off your car, shoes, your socks, like why would you steal when you can pay? After that, it's just plain unstrung—you again—doing something stupid like playing the queer card when it's uncalled for."

"Uncalled for?" Cyrus held his smile. But inside, he was thinking bird, why had he said that? Didn't matter. This McNab couldn't know anything about a bird, so it wouldn't hurt to push back. "How is it that you, a cop, know my gesticulations so well? Just being a fag was only decriminalized like 20 years ago, and half of being queer is still illegal, at least the good half. So how do you know I'm not just a-scared of cops?"

"Experience," Morton said, motioning to the set.

Cyrus looked at the pile of sheets draped over the rubber chicken no more than 30 feet away, thinking no, that still couldn't be it. The cop was motioning to open space, that's all. Besides, he was here about the money, and Cyrus truly didn't know anything about that.

Morton followed Cyrus' line-of-sight. "What are you looking at?"

Cyrus' eyes shot back. "Just off into the direction of your gesticulations. And look, I don't know anything about a bird."

Goddammit, he said it again.

Thinking he might be home, Morton suppressed a smile, careful. See, he didn't say anything about a bird, but now that Cyrus mentioned it twice, Morton was following up. "Is that the thing you're going to tell me about?"

"What thing?"

"The thing that you're hiding with your gesticulations, the bird you keep mentioning."

"Bird means cash in this business," Cyrus said. "When I say I don't know anything about a bird, it means I don't know anything about $4,800 cash. Bird means cash, get it?"

"Bird." Morton looked to Claire. "He was bragging about acquiring a bird, wasn't he?"

"Affirmative." Dead-eyed, Claire held contact with Cyrus, holding him down in her world. "Said it makes him important, how he can get a big bird on short notice. Now he says bird means cash. Story's changing already, and that's on top of the suspicious gesticulations."

That's how Morton was reading it out, too, looking over at the pile of sheets again. "Bird, it's no big thing, you stole a bird. No more serious than your garden-variety hazing ritual. It's just, if I know you're truthing about the bird, you're probably truthing about the 48-hundred. Look at it as a way of clearing yourself, so far as the money is concerned."

Cyrus glanced around the studio. Next to a column of bleachers, he saw Freak whispering to Janet Boroski. Another stupid white girl with dreadlocks, Cyrus thought, how boring. And what was with the G-string past her waistline? When did that become acceptable? Club Colby's drag queens weren't even doing it.

"Like I told you." Cyrus reached, touched Morton's arm. "In this business, bird truly means cash, man."

Morton looked at Cyrus' hand, withdrew his arm, said he'd never heard of a bird being cash in any business, man. Yes, he'd heard of it as paper, girl, and mundi. Traditionally, bacon, bread, and dough. Sour dough and queer for counterfeit. He'd also heard cabbage, lettuce, green, rhino, jack, and lizard. There were more, no question. But he'd never heard bird to mean cash. Not once. Did Cyrus ever hear bad guys in the movies say, this is a hold-up, give us your bird?"

Cyrus sighed, annoyed. No, he'd never heard movie bad guys say give us your bird.

"Well," Morton said, voice rising. "Then nobody ever said bird is cash, man."

"It's fresh. They just started saying it on the street."

Claire held her nose. "It's fresh all right." Thinking it was sweet the way she had Cyrus arsed, she watched Abel walk by wearing a high fallutin' sunflower bud boutonniere on his lapel. Claire thought Abel knew what was going on, making himself scarce when he heard enough. And what was that on his nose? Fuck around, was everyone here on some kind of shit?

"Where's Heathcliffe Wilson's chicken?" Morton said. It was here, he told himself, likely that bulge in the sheets not 30 feet away. He could feel it.

Hearing Morton nail the chain name, Cyrus' shoulders slumped. "You know where it is already." Blinking at the sheets. "So why drag this out?"

"I want you to show me, mostly because you were so vehement about how I was getting all homophobe in your workplace." Morton stood, hands on his hips. "G'head. Show me."

Arlene knew nothing when Morton called her over. Claiming she never thought to ask about the bird, she took one step back, distancing herself. "Well," she said, flashing her eyes at Cyrus. "We're all waiting for a plausible explanation."

Cyrus looked back and forth at Arlene and Morton. "I truly didn't steal anything."

"Did you borrow something?" Arlene widened her eyes. "Something you were going to return as soon as you were done with it?"

"Abel made me do it." Cyrus sat awkwardly, pumping his right knee over the left, pointing at the door he saw Abel go through.

"I know he didn't say you should steal one."

"May as well. How else am I going to get a 15-foot chicken for this morning when he asks late last night?"

Going through his notes, Morton looked up at Arlene. "Man can't pack away a 15-foot bird and a compressor alone. Must've had help."

Cyrus looked at Freak, who mouthed "Shut-up," then back at Morton. "Even if there was, it would be against code."

"What code?" Arlene said.

Cyrus looked at her. "The one that says you protect your peeps, so lawyer me already."

Arlene told Cyrus to zip it, turning to Morton. She tried to deal with the bird matter under the table, too, promising to call Heathcliffe Wilson herself and apologize, pledging to pay cash for any and all damages, as well as costs of inconvenience, pain and suffering.

Morton couldn't have cared whether she was willing to go down on the Attorney General. This was a little feather in Morton's cap, and he thought it best not to mention Deputy Chief Walsh's interest as an explanation of why this bird caper was being taken seriously. That if he did, no question, someone might start throwing around the term conflict-of-interest.

Best way to get off shitty cases is to solve them, he told himself, cuffing Cyrus, pushing him outside where the parking lot guy, that Nathan, was shouting *tabernac, tabernac* . . . Training a fire extinguisher on a blackened evergreen tree, smoke coming off it . . . Recalling that he and Claire tossed cigarettes into that planter, Morton averted his eyes, directing Cyrus to the cruiser, opening the back, holding his head down, locking him in.

Rounding the car, Morton opened his trunk for Kiwi and Freak, who threw the deflated bird in, pounding it down, forcing the trunk shut.

"I reckon you'll want the compressor as well," Kiwi said.

"Could you be a little more helpful?" Cyrus shouted from the back of the car.

Kiwi walked to the side of cruiser, said, "No worries there."

Cyrus shouted something about Kiwi being here illegally. Ignoring Cyrus—like, Morton didn't work for Immigration—Morton said he didn't have room for the compressor. But it was evidence, so thanks for mentioning it. No one should touch it until he sent someone to pick it up.

As for the rest, Morton told himself to keep his mouth shut, climbing inside his ride. Just zip it—like that cocksure lady in charge said—and bring this coco-butting, checkerboard-shoe-affording, vintage-Impala-driving prick away in cuffs. Charge him with theft over a thousand, anything else he could think of. And on the way to 51 Division, Morton did come up with something, stopping in an alley behind a defunct Total Station.

"The fuck's this?" Cyrus said.

Morton spoke over his shoulder, saying this was about evidence collection. As in, he needed to collect additional evidence to convict Cyrus of something they both know he was guilty of, something indisputable.

"I cooperated." Cyrus watched Morton through the waffle screen. "And now you have the bird. You're a regular Sam Spade, truly. Should have your own show."

Morton was out of the car, opening Cyrus' door. "May as well come out and take a shot. G'head, I'm going to say you did anyway."

"Sure." Cyrus gave himself a shake, avoiding Morton's eyes. "I've got hands behind my back, truly fair. How am I going to take a shot?"

"I figured you'd give me a coco butt," Morton said, waving fingers at himself. "G'head."

Cyrus pulled to the middle of the back bench.

"Fine." Morton stepped to within inches of a spray-painted wall. Eye level with some commie mural—a topless green woman, Lenin's profile over her shoulder—tagged DAMMIT! "Suit yourself." Morton slammed his forehead against Lenin, two quick blows. Getting back in the car, turning, giving Cyrus a look at his abrasions. "Just figured a man like you'd take his shot. Either way, they see me, it'll be, 'What happened, Morty?' I'll say, 'Assault an officer.'"

"Fuck you, pig."

"Fuck me?" Morton stepped out again, going for his belt and showing the cannister to Cyrus pushing himself up against the far door. "And pig? Really?"

"You going to shoot potpourri at me? What is that? What does it do?"

"First time on a civilian, so we're both going to see, at least I will." Morton looked at the cannister, putting it in Cyrus' face and opening the spout as he'd been trained. A cloud appeared and Cyrus convulsed, screaming his eyes, his eyes—this was beneath an officer of the law. Then Cyrus was getting another round of spice, Morton keeping the spout open, watching Cyrus flail about, doing the worm like those coppers at the press conference.

"You like that? Assault an officer, huh? A female officer?" Morton looked at the cannister, shaking it, empty. Wishing he had another when he slammed the back door and dropped into the front. Putting the car into drive, he looked in the rearview, offering Cyrus advice on how to act on the inside, to make friends fast. Pretty boy like Cyrus, it shouldn't be difficult. He just needed to be careful of which pocket he kept his hanky, and to mind the colors.

Thirty minutes later, Morton had the man who made $300 a day fingerprinted, photographed, caged, and otherwise defiled.

13

In all, Cyrus spent three hours at 51 Division before Orest F. Jefferies, Arlene's big shot lawyer, worked himself in front of a friendly judge. Kicking ass, taking names, and making noises about civil liberties. In between claims of brutality and half-truths, he seasoned everything with the term conflict-of-interest and managed to bail Cyrus out at a cost of 10,000 AMA dollars.

Albeit with resignation, Arlene was again saying no one else could do Cyrus' job, hardly anyway, and that she had to look out for her peeps, even when they did wrong.

After arriving in time for surf-and-turf-and-surf—lobster, lamb, and calamari—Cyrus was back in the studio micro-managing his crew, scrambling, and trying to make everything right all at once.

Outside, things were more relaxed. Claire was by the canopy, smoking. Sundance and Kiwi shared a spliff behind the kiosk. Inside, Nathan, was catching the CKLN jazz hour, nothing but old school instrumentals, facedown in his book when a bike courier pulled up.

"Hey chief, what're you reading there?"

Chief? Nathan thought he better give the guy a break, that he probably didn't mean it like that. "*Torn Curtain.*"

"Saw the movie a couple weeks back," the courier said, pulling his dust mask down, revealing a messy no-style moustache, blinking through big, clunky 1950s-style glasses. "Part of a Paul Newman mini-festival on my pirate cable."

Finally, Nathan thought, a fellow geek. "You into Hitchcock or spooks?"

Hitchcock mostly, the courier was a McMuffin hunter. Didn't he mean MacGuffin? Yeah, only this guy liked to call them McMuffins—by reason of Nathan didn't catch—but that was his thing. He liked to try to pick the crazy diversions out from what was really going on. Take *Notorious*: Story's about radio-active diamonds, right, but it's not really about radio-active diamonds. That's just what ropes you in. Yes, same type of device in *Torn Curtain*, Nathan said, holding up the paperback. Professor

Armstrong—the Newman character—had defected from the States to work for East Berlin, but by reason of what?

"I know," the courier said. "And did you get to the part where the fiancée, Julie Andrews, sticks with Newman even when she finds out the defection is bogus. That he really wants to get the key to some new rocket gun—that's the real McMuffin—and bring it back to the Americans."

Nathan's smile dropped. No, he hadn't read that far. Thanks for saving him the trouble. Sliding the book into its plastic, he rolled a hand, a non-verbal state-your-business.

"For Claire Malik." He produced a letter-size security envelope.

Nathan waited to be prompted. When he wasn't, he said, "I have to sign somewhere?"

The courier shook his head. "Uh-uh. Not like that. It's personal."

"Personal?" Nathan reached for the package, taking it. What was this? Accepting personal packages for Claire now? What did that mean? And what did it make him?

As the courier pedaled off, Nathan opened the back door of his kiosk and started across the lot. "This just in," he said to Claire. "Courier fresh off the set of *Mad Max Four*—road warrior works for a living—brought it." He stopped, looking at her cold. "Said it was personal."

"Personal?"

"That's right, personal."

Claire looked at Nathan curiously, same way at her name on the envelope. "You want to stay while I open it?" Nathan said only if she wanted. "It's okay," she said, slitting the envelope with a key, withdrawing a piece of paper, unfolding it, angling it so that Nathan could read the typed message along with her.

$omething mi$$ing? Get lucky in the Impala.

Love, Deepthroat

Claire was all smiles, telling Nathan, "Go back to your teepee, and watch—"

"Teepee?" Nathan was pissed. First the courier calling him chief, then Claire with this *merde*. "It's a kiosk, white trash skank rent-a-cop bitch."

"Christ, I'm playing," Claire said, trying not to laugh. "I think this is a gift to us. Just go back there and watch and learn, baby. And tell those guys smoking pot to clear out." Hitting the talk button on her walkie. "Claire for Arlene."

Inside, at her perch high atop the bleachers, Arlene hit her button. "Go for Arlene."

"Something you'll want to see out here."

"Go to 10," Arlene said, doing likewise. "Claire?"

"Yeah, Arlene. I'm telling you, you need to get out here."

"Tell me here. This is a private channel."

"Look," Claire said, "just get out here, okay?"

Thinking this had better be fricking good, Arlene galloped down, passing Kiwi and Sundance near craft services, smelling pot, meeting Claire outside near the canopy, more pot. She was worried when she took the note, thinking Heathcliffe Wilson's people were already suing. But then she read it, read it twice. "Where did this come from?"

"Courier dropped it off." Claire motioned to the kiosk. "Nathan took delivery."

Arlene crossed the lot waving the note, and yes, she was still smelling that fucking reefer everywhere. "Nathan, this courier, what did he look like?"

"Black guy, white helmet." Nathan looked out of his kiosk north on Cherry Street, remembering. "Wearing skintight Lycra grape-smuggling shorts. Messy moustache under his dust mask."

Arlene thought she had him there, caught. "How do you know his moustache was messy under his dust mask?"

"By reason of he took the mask off to talk, taking the time ruin my book, giving the Paul Newman character's intentions away." *Merde*, Nathan was tired of providing evidence every time Arlene asked a question, catching himself getting lippy, letting it fly anyway. "That's right. Guy rode up, took off his mask, and ruined my book by telling me how Paul Newman was screwing over Julie Andrews, then put his mask back on and left. Also, he called me chief. Why? What's the deal about the mask? And which part do you think I'm fibbing about?"

Ignoring him, Arlene hit her talk button. "Arlene for Cyrus."

"Go for Cyrus."

"Get out here, now."

"Here? What's your twenty?"

"Parking lot. And bring your keys."

Cyrus said he was in the middle of getting the Amoral Crusade set together. What? Did Arlene want to go for a ride? He had to make this place look like Abel's boyhood church within an hour. Meckler would go truly crazy if Cyrus walked. Abel, too.

"July 7th, who pays you? Abel Otto? Dan Meckler?"

"Copy, Arlene," Cyrus said tightly. "Be right there."

Do I want to go for a ride, Arlene thought, getting madder, testing Nathan some more while she waited. "What company did you say this courier was from?"

Nathan gave her an I'm-not-sure eyeroll. Courier didn't say and Nathan didn't ask. Didn't he have to sign something? Nathan shook that off. "He said it wasn't like that. I said okay and took the envelope, *merci*, like that. He said it was personal."

"You are either a bad liar or a nervous person, Nathan, and if it is the former, you are going to get scared. When you are scared, that is when you get caught. Now, if I catch you—"

"And he had big, clunky glasses," Nathan added, cutting the old flake off. "1950s style."

"Oh," Arlene said. "I didn't believe you until you mentioned the big, clunky glasses, 1950s style. You say that, it must be so. Who could make that up?"

"*Pardon moi, Madame*, but please don't shoot the messenger by reason that you don't want to hear bad news. I'll tell you the same thing I told Disco Dick. If I say something's so, it's so." There, she could kiss Nathan's vaguely ethnic ass, making him provide more evidence. First the guy spoils his book, nothing else to read except *The Globe and Mail*, no store in sight. Now here he is, Arlene's own private Bob Woodward—and she's still giving him hell.

"What?" It was Cyrus walking out, holding his keys, jangling them.

"Note here asks, missing something? It spells missing with dollar signs. Then it says get lucky in the Impala." Arlene held up the paper. "Do you know a Deepthroat?"

As Cyrus snatched the note, Arlene went for the keys in his other hand, throwing them to Claire. "See if you can finally do a little police work for me, personally."

"No, no." Cyrus cut Claire off at the Cutlass parked in front of his Impala. She held out her electric nightstick. "I don't want her in my car and this isn't legal, truly."

"Sure is," Claire said. "Law says I can search your vehicle if I suspect inside there's drugs." Leaning closer, taking a whiff. "And I can smell it on you, pot." Turning, facing Arlene. "Also, his eyes are red. And if his eyes are red and I can smell it on him, means it's reasonable to suspect he's got drugs in the vehicle. Means I have reasonable grounds to search said vehicle."

"My eyes are red from the pepper-spray, and you, you're not even a cop anymore." Cyrus looked to Arlene for help. "She's suspended, right? Doesn't have active powers?"

"I'm a paid duty officer," Claire said. "Same rights and privileges as any cop."

Cyrus smiled, making light. "Then where's your gun?"

Arlene told Claire to just do the search. She did not care if it was legal. This was a loyalty matter, and Arlene would be the first to apologize if this was some big misunderstanding—truly. Besides, Arlene also smelled pot, so Claire should absolutely proceed.

Quickly, Claire was in the Impala leafing through the glove box, producing a Ziplock baggie containing the original owner's manual. Inside was a second, smaller Ziplock containing about a quarter ounce of weed and a book of grape papers. "Well, we know for sure he's on drugs. Aside from the fact Constable McNab found evidence of similar drug use at the scene of the rubber bird robbery—you guessed it, grape papers—a man on drugs is always a man looking for money to buy more drugs, seven years of police work says."

For the first time, Arlene thought Claire was making sense, saying so while giving Cyrus a stern once-over. He looked back, thinking come on.

Back inside, Claire checked the visors, between seats, beneath seats, floor mats, the ashtray. Other than a plastic box appearing to contain cassettes of all Generation X and Billy Idol albums up to *Rebel Yell*, plus what would appear to be some live bootlegs, given the photocopied liners, it seemed clean. Arlene said to seize the unsanctioned recordings. Claire called Nathan out of his kiosk, handed the box to him since he seemed to know so much about music. While he was separating the boots from the store-boughts, Cyrus quizzed Arlene on why she was seizing his tapes. Arlene said it was a copyright infringement issue, a matter of artists getting paid. Cyrus said Billy Idol was doing fine, money-wise. Arlene said that wasn't the point. Claire, meanwhile, studied the carpet for small tears. Finding none, she stepped out, saying she had some gloves in the Daytona, maybe she ought to go get 'em, conduct a cavity search.

"How about it?" Arlene crossed her arms. "Is my money up your patootie?"

"This is how you know it's truly a conspiracy. If it was up my ass, that McNab would've found it." Cyrus looked at Claire. "And he hasn't come out, right? Another jerk-off closet case with a white hanky in his left back pocket."

Arlene said McNab's sexuality had nothing to do with it, that there were lots of men-loving-men around. Toledo had to be a ho-mophile. Rupert, too. And talk about dykes, Janet Boroski was turning everyone on, hiking her gitch like that. Yes sir, Hollywood North was pretty tubular, and if Cyrus thought he was some pro-tected species, he had overplayed his card.

"It's somebody else, truly, jealous because you are in love with my shit." Cyrus whirled around, pointing at Nathan and Claire. "Them, I bet."

Arlene brushed that off, saying Nathan and Claire didn't have the initiative. That's why they were working in the lot. Besides, they had been getting some stankie—is that how you say it now?—in the green room, and probably would not have had the courage to get said stankie if they were stealing. Blocking the unpleasant imagery, Lawn Boy humping, she blinked, saying check the trunk. As instructed, Claire keyed the hole, popping the hatch.

"Empty." Cyrus laughed, coughing.

"Not quite." Claire produced a large rectangular brown envelope, holding it up for Cyrus to see. "What fresh hell am I going to find in here?"

"That's personal."

Cyrus took a step forward, but Arlene grabbed his polo and pulled him back, chin-nodding to Claire, the envelope. "See what is inside."

Claire pulled the flap and removed a file folder. Opening it, she glanced at Cyrus, flipping through photos. "Looks like he's got naked pictures of a very young Billy Idol."

Tentatively walking over, Arlene looked on wide-eyed as Claire turned the black-and-whites. "Jesus, this must be pre-Generation X." Arlene, glaring at Cyrus. "What is he, a child?"

"Those pictures are from when Billy was in the band Chelsea, 1976," Cyrus said. "He's 21 at that point, perfectly legal."

"And what are you?" Arlene said. "Thirty-two?"

"Thirty-three, same age as Billy now."

Arlene was disgusted. "You are still a 33-year-old man looking at a 21-year-old boy. That makes you a chickenhawk."

Nathan sniffed, said, "Him like the *poulet*."

Turning to Claire, Arlene told her to seize the contraband pornography as well.

Cyrus held a hand out, said those were art shots.

"Art shots?" Now Claire was disgusted. "His officer is at attention in every picture. And as someone who had her own intimate photos published without permission, I'm guessing Billy Idol never signed off on you receiving them. That makes this probably all kinds of illegal. Also opens you up to civil litigation." Pointing to the Impala. "And any litigation will be informed by the fact that you have bootlegs of Billy Idol shows, also unauthorized."

"Billy Idol is truly not going to sue me," Cyrus said.

"Let's get on with it." Arlene waved at the trunk. "Keep checking."

Lifting the carpet away, Claire removed the spare with one arm, looking down, removing a security letter envelope with her free-hand. Replacing the tire, she opened the mailer, fighting off a grin, counting money. If there was any doubt, she had him arsed now. Dammit, maybe she really was supposed to be a cop after all. "Yeah, Arlene, Cyrus is holding your bank alright."

"I'm telling you someone put that there," Cyrus said, protesting further about a great conspiracy of grunts, truly dangerous.

Claire finished her tally, asking, to be sure, how much should be there? Arlene said $4,800.

"Then he's already spent some of it," Claire said. "Sixty-five dollars short—the cost of pot and a pack of grape rolling papers."

"Look Arlene," Cyrus said. "You pay me good money. I don't need to steal. Besides, I truly didn't have time to spend any. I haven't been in my car since the money went missing."

"How do you know when it went missing?" Arlene was pleased with herself, like maybe she should have been a cop, too. "Because I don't quite know myself."

Claire watched Cyrus make a face like a man at a urinal when a lady walks in, saying he didn't know exactly, either. He tried to say generally speaking, coughing again.

"Please." Arlene held a hand up. "Over the last week alone, you have run down the parking attendant thrice, assaulted our paid-duty officer twice, stole from my business neighbor, stole from me, procured inappropriate photos of a very young Billy Idol and unauthorized Billy Idol recordings, cheating the artist, and done drugs on my dime. All that makes you a bully, a thief, a druggie, a bootlegger, a dirty old man, and a time-stealer. It also makes a man who was once irreplaceable replaceable. A beautiful man, distracting us from the task at hand. I don't know how, but you got hooked on pot and porn. I can see it in your eyes, crazed, paranoid."

"Crazed?" Cyrus said. "Paranoid? In the last 24 hours, I've been directed to steal, arrested for doing so, pepper-sprayed— I keep saying, that's why my eyes are red, you bitches—then deloused. You bet I'm fucked-up. As for the pot, you want to go after me for that, you'll have to fire everyone. Nobody's going to work with you if you're uptight about grass. That's why the place smells like skunk. We're creative people." He stopped to cough, pointing. "You, of anyone, should understand that. A survivor, isn't that what you told them? Akin to an older Madonna?"

Arlene turned to Claire. "Take him inside, see that he returns his brick, and watch while he clears out." Back to Cyrus, pointing at him, then herself. "You stole from me." Moving her lower jaw back and forth. "And it's not the first time, now is it, Cyrus?"

14

Saturday, June 24

Claire was second to arrive at Cherry Beach Studios the next morning, waving from her Daytona on her way past Nathan's kiosk, a white gerbera daisy in her hair. Freak followed, buzzing by on a motorized scooter. His white T-shirt said BRING BACK BOOMERANGS in fat black type.

Nathan smiled at both, easy. It felt good, little things that amused him, moments that made the day worth getting up for. Although not too outwardly, he, like all of Arlene's peeps, was a little too de-fucking-lighted over Cyrus' predicament. Relaxed, outside himself, Nathan watched Claire get out of her car and walk over. Yes, he'd recalled that this was St. Jean Baptiste Day, but hadn't given it another thought until she turned up like that.

Her white tank top was plain enough, a hint of respectful *décolletage*, her *Fête nationale* sarong another matter entirely. He loved it, laughing like he was home celebrating with the pepsies. The French didn't like Nathan calling them pepsies because of all the sugar they consumed, but he figured it was alright by reason of recent blood shed over a golf course built on ancient burial grounds, the disrespect.

He touched Claire's hair, the flower. She was never more beautiful than right now. She even smelled like home, peppery. He wanted to tell her, but they didn't know each other well enough. Instead, he asked, "Where did you get a wraparound *Fleur-de-Lis* skirt comes to your ankles?"

"Quebec City," Claire said. "I get the gist of it—a day to celebrate the language—I go every year, almost. Great parties, parades, fireworks, concerts. Last year, we saw the French Madonna, the girl sings 'Bye Bye Mon Cowboy.' Great show, but she needs a sandwich."

"Mitsou," Nathan said. He thought of some earnest reasons to celebrate, tidbits of history about St. Jean, before admitting he used to go for pretty much the same reasons, and so what? Immigrants shot off cannons in 1638 to celebrate the season, exactly what the pepsies were celebrating today—summer. "So, you're French now, *Vive le Québec libre?*"

Claire struck a pose, looping thumbs into her waistline, flexing her bare stomach. "When it suits me. Figured it'd suit you today, too. Something that tastes like home."

And Goddammit if he didn't think she would, peppery.

For a while there, he thought he could love her and heard himself say the words in his head *à la française*, doing a little internal immersion, practicing. It didn't matter that the day dragged otherwise. Inside the studio, with delays and confusion caused by Cyrus' debacles, the AMA machine wasn't running on all cylinders. Although *merde* like that had a way of rolling downhill, Nathan let it slide. All day, he was getting paid for hanging out with Claire, reading her little notes. And even if she didn't like good music, for the most part, she seemed willing to learn.

Yeah, Nathan was having a time, getting laid at night and playing around in the lot all day. It wasn't much of a job, but he had a 6in1 Radio Lantern, a girl, more spy paperbacks than he could read, all the food he could eat, a cellular telephone, and a little bit of money coming in. It was enough for the here and now, and he could have done worse than Claire.

Worse—he'd been stroking the light fantastic so much he'd been coming around to Ike Turner's way of thinking, wishing he had a longer neck so as he could do his own self.

In a way, all the action, along with Claire's cute outfits and even cuter theories on how to rob the place, made him feel what it was like out on the tour again. Hanging with the other caddies, talking shop, creating banter.

At one point, "Bizarre Love Triangle" by New Order came on the 6in1 Radio Lantern, Bernard Sumner on lead. Claire pointed at the speaker and said, "Did that guy just sing 'Every time I think of you, I feel a shock right through a boat of poo'?"

"Bolt of blue," Nathan said. "He feels a shot right through with a bolt of blue."

Yeah, well, Claire was dancing, sort of, having fun with an overly dramatic song about the guy lives a life he can't leave behind, but she was pretty sure he sang boat of poo.

Whatever, work was getting to be fun, and it helped that everyone was quietly snickering about Cyrus. About the only thing they disagreed on was whether he actually stole the cash.

Claire insisted she'd found the smoking gun, and most of Arlene's peeps thought likewise. But not Nathan. No. While he was happy about it, he thought Cyrus had a good thing going with AMA, so why bugger it? Claire said Nathan would be surprised. As a civilian, he didn't realize how sloppy the average criminal was, especially workplace criminals, the worst, because they stole from people they worked for. Cyrus, he'd probably been doing it all along, bragging, maybe to someone he slept with. Claire knew about gays from Morton, and Morton implied that gays tend to sleep with a lot of other gays, even just for a hand release, safe. And did Nathan know that? That most gay sex was just a handy. No? Well, whatever they did, the more men gays sleep with, the greater the chance of a gay telling another gay something he shouldn't.

Nathan noted that the Soviets used the same mindset to entrap American spies, then raised an index. "But isn't that making a man more suspect by reason of he takes it like a bitch?"

"Thought you'd use anything against him," Claire said.

***

The Amoral Crusade skit was almost 24 hours behind schedule by the time Dan Meckler had the stage set to Abel's satisfaction. Star of his own show now, Meckler thought Abel was getting uppity the way he was sweating the details on this, his so-called "signature sketch."

As a result, Meckler had to stay late last night and missed this morning's shower, face grizzled. Dingy hair parted down the middle, oily, hanging near his creased brown eyes. With Cyrus gone, Meckler had two jobs, and it was everything he could do to get the sketch going. It was a simple riff on a law banning nude dancing in Abel's hometown of Erie, Pennsylvania.

There could still be exotic dancing, just that the girls had to wear G-strings and pasties at all times. Meckler didn't see a problem there. It was better they didn't take everything off, leaving something to the imagination, plus it was more hygienic. But no, that wasn't Abel's style. And why did Abel have to mock Pennsylvanians over their beliefs, of all things? Again, as a Christian, Meckler certainly did take offence, and he was pretty sure God was going to get Abel for this. Still, Meckler's job was to do it and like it, so he did it, telling himself he wouldn't be yoked with nonbelievers, even if he had to do their editing.

Oh Lord and Savior, they were so far behind, everyone looking at Meckler until he had Abel sitting on his ass on set two, legs spread, proud of his silver open-toe heels, garters, and stockings. Holding a bouquet of glitter roses in front of his crotch, a rhinestone-encrusted cross rested between his fake cleavage, a white feather boa draped over his shoulders.

Abel was getting into this method-acting thing. He knew his globby eyeliner was right, trashy blonde wig, too. Now, he really was Tammy Faye Bakker on an Amoral Crusade.

"Say Hallelujah," he told the studio audience, "because Erie legislators love my lingerie so much they want to pass a bylaw making it required."

"Hallelujah," they responded, roughly in unison.

The impressive thing was that they were standing, throwing their arms in the air, and honoring a God that dared to mix sex and religion. In that moment Abel really thought he was the first, at least on cable, wishing he had a gaudy ring for everyone back home to kiss. Yeah, Abel knew he might be getting ahead of himself. But even the people who were anti-pasties-and-G-strings, they'd be happy just to be put on the map. Or, at least they ought to be.

Whatever they said, Abel just wanted them to say something while everyone jumped aboard his Amoral Crusade. It was all he needed, one schtick. A gag with legs that could extract a reaction. Something they could peg a movie to—T-shirts, dolls, collector cards.

Behind schedule? Who cared? This was ground-breaking teletheater.

***

Nathan and Claire agreed to disagree on the Cyrus thing, breaking together around six. With Abel and some of the other players working through supper, they found a table off in the corner, away from a half dozen or so low-level staffers. Tonight, it was Alberta sliced tenderloin with truffled mashed potatoes.

"You ever put out a spread like this?" Nathan asked. "Domestically?"

"Not likely," Claire said. "And I thought you said you don't mind I can't cook."

"Actually, I stood mute by reason of I was on my best behavior, trying to get some cho-cho." Nathan put his elbows on the table. "Mean you don't cook at all?"

"Was trying to be sexy, is all I was doing." Claire wiped her mouth with a white cotton napkin, leaving a lipstick smudge. "Of course I cook, some—chili, pesto, steaks, fishes, things you do with the top of the stove, fewer dishes. Plus, there's this rice dish I make with mushroom soup, Campbells, yum. But I don't, you know, use the inside, the oven. I don't bake. And I don't know a truffled mashed potato from that green shit caused the PEI potato famine, 1962."

"Green *merde* caused the PEI famine?" Nathan shifted in his seat. "Really?"

"No." She looked up, deadening her eyes. "Not really."

Thinking he could love her, *stupide*, biting the inside of his cheek.

"There wasn't even a PEI famine," she said. "History—shame on you."

Nathan leaned in. "University-educated white girl knows her history, huh?"

Again with this. "I went to community college, alright, St. Clair."

"Same thing."

"Not the same thing." Claire picked up her tray, standing. "I took Law and Security Admin, hands on. You—you make it sound like I'm some sort of women's studies yahoo."

There, she thought, walking.

On the way out, they made a fuss over Toledo Marseilles. Nathan said the spuds were beautiful. Claire asked for the recipe. Toledo looked around the room, whispering. "For you, I will make the exception. I will photocopy. But you are to share this with no one, copyrighted material."

He seemed shocked when she kissed him, trying to brush a black current smudge off his cheek with her thumb, leaving traces.

Nathan bounded downstairs muttering something about copyrighted material and how Toledo was going to get money every time people made spuds his way. *Tabernac*, it was that kind of thinking that caused famines, not green *merde*.

Following, Claire joined Nathan at craft services where they used the machine to make cappuccinos. Nathan told Claire she ought to attend a workshop on workplace behavior. Kissing the chef—that was appropriate? She said Nathan was jealous, and a little too PC. He said she was wrong a lot, mostly because she was only PC when it suited her. She demanded to know what he meant about her being wrong so much. He tried to convince her it was a compliment of sorts, almost endearing. She rolled her eyes, said she was going to the ladies, that she'd see him outside. He said yeah, okay, bummed one of her lady cigarettes to have with his coffee.

***

To the frustration of Dan Meckler, Abel was still tinkering with his Amoral Crusade, reworking it here and there, improvising, going back to his room to check his make-up, he said, and doing the skit over and over. The studio audience didn't mind. They were laughing, going along with it. Bunch of eaters and poopers, Meckler thought, getting off on seeing a B-lister dressed as religious whore, so God was probably going to get them, too.

Behind camera one, Meckler couldn't help but think how much he hated shooting on videotape, poor quality, and next it seemed that they were going digital. It didn't matter that the examples Meckler had seen to date devolved into pixelated fog. Everyone was declaring digital the next big medium, when Meckler knew damn well that if something was worth shooting, you had to film it. But what the hell? Tape's all Abel's worth, disposable, Meckler thought, looking into his monitor, watching Abel caress the mic like a dick. Even through the harsh make-up job caricaturing Tammy Faye Bakker, Meckler could see something wrong, but what?

Turning his head, narrowing his lens into a close-up, Meckler crossed his left arm, resting his right elbow on it, holding his chin. What was this now? What the fuck was this? Dropping his arms and backing away, he said cut right at the part where Abel, as Tammy, was on about how much Erie legislatures love his lingerie.

Abel, shielding his eyes from the lights, said, "Why cut, Danny?"

Meckler waved at himself. "Abel, come here."

"No, Danny." Smiling as though something occurred, Abel looked out to his people in the bleachers. "You can share it with everyone."

Meckler reached for his megaphone, bellowed, "We're taking five. Abel, get here."

Abel's smile trembled as he awkwardly stepped off stage in his heels, clipping a wire, falling to one knee. Struggling to hold his expression as he pushed himself up, he carefully shuffled over. "We were going good, Danny."

"Go to your room, Abel, and look in the mirror."

"Why, Danny?" Abel held his hands out, desperate. "Why couldn't you save everyone the time and tell me what you see from across the room?"

"It's your nose."

"What's wrong with it?" Abel went cross-eyed. "Too shiny?"

Meckler pointed in the direction of Abel's dressing room, putting a hand on his shoulder, pushing. "You need to look in the mirror and see what I see. Then you need to sharpen the fuck up before God gets all of us."

Abel was pissed, thinking Meckler was pretty much there to say action and cut, so who the hell was he to tell Abel Otto to sharpen up? And God was going to get us? Please. At this point, Abel had to assume the rumors were true, that Meckler had been sending money to the PTL Club before the Jessica Hahn thing broke, so he was probably just mad that a German Jew was sending up his kind of Christians. "What's your obsession with my nose, Danny? If there's something off with my make-up, say it. We can fix it right here."

"It's not your make up, Abel."

"What is it then?"

Meckler sighed. This was unbelievable. "It starts with C and rhymes with ocaine."

"What?"

"You heard me. What's happening is you're too stunned to believe I'd actually call you on your coke, and now you're buying time to process while you're raging on a heavy stimulant." Meckler gave Abel another push. "Go wipe your nose. The rest of us are at work."

Abel was about to say something, turning when his heel clipped another wire, stumbling, falling. While the studio audience couldn't hear the conversation, they thought it was part of the show. Everyone was standing, howling at Abel on his hands and knees, skirt riding high.

"Hallelujah."

Meckler gave the eaters and poopers a thumbs-up, mock satisfaction, speaking into his megaphone. "This is what we're here for, people—the glorious future of American cable."

Then, as if on cue, they stood, cheering, someone shouting, "Bravo!"

15

Outside, Nathan stood next to the charred evergreen, smoking a cigarette with his cappuccino, wondering what had the audience going inside. "That's actual laughter, people cheering," he said to Claire as she joined him. "It's not just the flashing signs telling them, laugh. I can tell."

"It's Abel." Claire licked her pinky, smoothing a cowlick on Nathan's right brow, pasting it down. "I peeked inside on my way from the ladies. He's dressed like a woman, drag."

"That's a very secure man." Nathan gently pushed Claire away. "Takes courage, a man wears panties on cable TV."

"You empathizing?"

"I guess." Nathan didn't see anything wrong with it. "So?"

"Trying to tell me something?"

"About what?"

"Panties," Claire said. "You trying to tell me to dress you up in my love?"

No, Nathan had to be the top by reason of him being a bottom at work. In turn, that's why Claire was the bottom. She was a top at work, needed a break from her responsibilities. Given that, it was best if she continued wearing the panties in the relationship.

"Relationship, huh?" She looked around, planting a stolen kiss on his cheek. Next, she tried to wipe away another black currant smudge with her thumb. Licked her index when that didn't work, Nathan pushing her away a little more roughly this time.

"You my grandma? Putting spit on, wiping me. It's the work-place. What are you doing?"

Claire bit her bottom lip. "Just lovin'."

"Not lovin', just buggin'. Harassment, some would call it, wiping spit on me. Assault an officer, if it was the other way around."

"Assault by bodily fluids, is what it's called." She was trying to kiss him again when Veronica walked out, Nathan caging his face with his elbows high by reason of he thought Claire was angling some new way of wiping him with saliva.

"Another delivery," Veronica said, pulling an envelope out of her inside jacket pocket, handing it to Claire.

She studied it, then Veronica. "Same type of envelope the tip about Cyrus was delivered in, security features. Called a security envelope."

"Call it a favor," Veronica said.

"What's in it?"

"Your love note shredded, plus the part on the other side about the Chuck Barris robbery. Your handwriting. The girly loops give you away." Claire looked inside, saw blue pen marks on the paper slivers, shot Nathan a look. He put his hands up, said he didn't do anything.

"I found it." Veronica stopped, dangling it out there. "In the green room. It must have fallen out of Nathan's pants while they were down around his ankles."

Nathan looked at Claire, down. "I just—"

"You just, you just—what?"

"It's not his fault." Veronica brushed her curly bangs back, letting Claire see her scarred brow. "At least he didn't put anything in writing."

Claire tried to avoid saying anything else that might incriminate her, waiting to see if she was fired, again. Is that where Little Arlene was going?

"Don't be threatened," Veronica said. "I think you might have something here. You're right, it is do-able." She waited a few seconds. "I mean, if they can do it on a Chuck Barris set, hell, with Arlene's security, it should be a walk on the beach."

Claire let that go, looking at the envelope, focusing. It really was the same kind of envelope the tip about Cyrus came in. White on the outside with squiggly blue patterns on the inside to camouflage the contents. "Nathan was right, that wasn't random. You set Cyrus up, orchestrated it. Worked us all like puppets."

Whoa, Nathan never said all that, but since Claire mentioned the similar envelopes, yes, he was asking. "So did you?"

"Not here." Veronica turned on the pavement, stumbling, looking around. "Thursday is our dark day, if we're on schedule. Meet at my house for a barby, pending the sked, us three."

"Why do you want to do this?" Claire said. "Is this a trap, you want to catch us saying something out of class?"

"The only thing bothering me, if you really are planning something, is that I'm left out. Better, I've got a plan. Do you have a plan?"

Claire looked at Nathan. No, they didn't have a plan.

"I didn't think so," Veronica said. "Fine then, Thursday?"

Nathan took a breath, said, "Thursday." Claire looked at him, suspicious, like he'd done something else wrong. "We're just going to listen, so I don't know why you're sucking your mouth into a little asshole like that." Only Claire kept looking at him that way.

Thursday then. It was settled. Veronica would get directions to them. "Also, I came to give you an Attila alert. Arlene just left her Queen Street office. She's on her way."

"How long does it take her?" Nathan said.

"I never know." Veronica scanned the street. "Could be 20 minutes if she hits a line at Tim Hortons. Any time if she wants me to make her a Traditional. Usually, she wants me to make her tea." Rolling her eyes. "Imported from Philadelphia."

But Arlene was coming, and she was on the warpath about this Cyrus thing. It wasn't the petty cash so much as Heathcliffe Wilson. He wanted to make an example of Cyrus, an example of Arlene Marion and Associates.

"He's just mad because Abel made fun of him," Veronica said. "Main thing is it keeps Arlene occupied."

"Occupied," Claire said. "You're so terrified of her, you can't just stand up to her like a grown woman. Why do you work for her?"

Veronica glanced at her Swatch, past seven. "Why do you?"

Claire ignored the question. "They call you Little Arlene."

"And they call you Angie Dickinson," Nathan said.

Claire shot Nathan a look for making the name up in the first place. Cute at first, but now it was kind of grating the way he was using it against her. "Better than Little Arlene. At least Angie Dickinson's hot. That's what you said. Now you think Little Arlene is hot?"

"What?" Nathan smiled at Veronica. "It's okay for big girls to be hot but short ones not?"

Prick, Claire thought. "Midget sex is hot, is what you're saying?"

Nathan didn't bother, watching her remove a cigarette from her pack.

"And you don't want to be smoking when she gets here." Veronica pointed at Claire. "It's one of her things, at least when she's like this."

Claire bit down, jaw protruding below her ears. "Why?"

"One of the things she most hates about herself, like it's dirty. She'll go for months without. She's not even what I would call a social smoker. But every once in a while she just has to have one. Says it relaxes her." Veronica looked up and down Cherry Street, heading toward the door. "Remember, the job for now is to look alert, busy. Play your parts."

"Yeah, I'll be laying low, focusing on my role," Nathan said, walking towards his kiosk, pointing to Claire's cigarette. "And you best put that back in the pack."

Claire looked to Nathan. "You're scared of her, too."

He broke stride, stopping. "And you're just looking for trouble, fighting every battle."

Claire accidentally blew out a match as she tried to light up, reloading. "At least I fight."

"You," Nathan said, grinding his index at her like a slow drill bit. "Waste your fights like an animal. Means you're in no position to fight when it counts. Just as my adoptive mother says, and, like I told you, she's a game warden."

"Game warden, what does a game warden know about people?"

"That people are *animale*, behave impulsively."

Here we go, Claire thought. "And this applies to me how?"

Nathan thought on it, said, "Let's say you have a cottage and you're the outdoorsy type likes to tinkle on your land, nourishment. Next day, there's coon cucca everywhere, plants dug up, trouble by reason of you attracted their attention, so they acted irrational, war. Same thing with you and Arlene. Every time she drops an itty-bitty *merde*, you become aggressive without thinking. I mean, maybe she's tripping today and we don't want to wake her. But you see her—no, if you even hear her coming—your *animale* function kicks in. Like the raccoon, you're so mad you can't even think about how to best position yourself to raid her garden later on."

"Some interesting beastial trivia there, Ranger Collins." Claire took a drag, exhaled. "But the way you're talking—disciplined, calculated—you're thinking now maybe it can be done?"

Nathan cast his eyes at the building. "If that girl's in, I'm thinking maybe, theoretically."

At that, he shuffled to his kiosk, saying he wanted to get back to his reading.

Claire broke the other way, heading to the main entrance. Mom's a game warden, how nice. Feeling a bit reddened by the sun, a bit reddened by Nathan's condescending *animale* BS, she thought screw him, letting himself be walked on like that.

Finishing her cigarette, flicking it into the container holding the charred evergreen, Claire's mood brightened when a police van popped in to collect Heathcliffe Wilson's compressor. In fact, she was diplomatic, professional, even helpful, at least until the van left. Then she lit another cigarette, exhaling as Arlene's Jeep pulled even with Nathan. He looked up from his book, a woman with hands bound above her head on the cover.

"What are you reading?"

"*One Lonely Night*," Nathan said. "Just at the part where Mike Hammer's whipping the commie spy by reason of she's a commie. Hammer says it has to be that way by reason of her father never beat the communism out of her."

Arlene looked at the book. "You don't think that's exploitative?"

"No, *Madame*, by reason of as conservative as Mickey Spillane is, at least he makes big girls sexy, which is more than I can say for this here *Otto Show*." Nathan held the book out. "Asides, by whipping the commie he saves her from getting shot by fellow comrades."

Okay, okay, saying it was close enough to literature, Arlene told Nathan to keep the cover down so people would not think he was looking at hardcore bondage porn. Also, she told him to drop the *Madame* malarkey and speak English unless someone addressed him in French, then gave the gas a nudge, pulling into her spot, number two.

Not quite sure of where her right side was, she left a gap of seven feet between her and the next car. Shitty little Yugo 45, she was not going to park near that. Anyone who drove a car like that was a communist, and communists did not care what their vehicles looked like, so why should she have to park next to a communist? Fishhooks, she should not have to. And what was a Yugo 45 doing in spot number three anyway?

Nathan tried to ignore that she took so much space. Seeing as how he was now half-fixing, theoretically, to rob the lady, he tried to separate himself from the situation. Thinking that he couldn't do anything about where she parked, out of his control, he marked his page with a matchbook, powering on the 6in1 Radio Lantern, picking up the baseball game. Toronto at Oakland, no score in the third. Junior Felix, just up from Syracuse, at bat.

Claire, she was blowing smoke rings, figuring Arlene had been something special in her time. That's why she talked to them the way she did, because she wasn't special anymore.

"That is going to kill you." Arlene approached the canopy, pointing a Tim Hortons to-go cup. "You know that, right? Sooner or later, it will kill you, dead."

"Helps keep my girlish figure, meantime." Claire put the cigarette in her mouth, looking Arlene up and down. "Might make a body think about taking it up."

"I do not smoke myself, so I do not care for it on my set. Moreover, I do not like riff-raff hanging around with coffin nails dangling from their lips. It does not look good for important people, TV people. That is why hardly no one else on set smokes."

Claire motioned to the concrete, butts everywhere. "Who do you think these belong to?"

"They are mostly yours, one way or another. You are always out here, smoking, giving people who do not usually smoke a cigarette, which makes you an enabler."

"I'll thank you to know my cigarettes are brown." Claire held up her package of Mores, flipping it open, pointing at the container holding the singed evergreen. "Aside from that, I put mine in there." Then pointing at the pavement. "You see that, none of those butts are brown. I don't do that to the people I work with. I'm a peace officer, ma'am." She bent down to pick up a roach, holding it in Arlene's face. "As such, I thank you to know that I don't smoke dope—jeez."

"Enough with the protesting," Arlene said. "Just understand this: Security guards and ex-cops have much common ground. You saw what happened to Cyrus. Never forget that everyone is replaceable, so dummy up." Walking away, laughing, thinking how she always wanted to say that. She was telling Claire to shut up, right? At least that's what Arlene hoped TV cops meant.

Inside Cherry Beach Studios, grabbing a handful of green grapes at craft services, Arlene bit a few off at the stems and dropped the rest in the trash, walking into the studio, seeing Abel parading onstage in drag, declaring himself a G-string Christian in the fight of his life with Pennsylvania legislators. Somehow, as Tammy Faye Bakker, he was going to get constitutional protection extended to nude dancing as a form of free expression.

"This is a non-profit cause, almost," Abel said. "About paying homage to how we, as American Christians, say Hallelujah."

"Hallelujah," the audience responded.

Searching, Arlene saw Veronica behind camera two, watching until their eyes met.

"Goddamn you." Arlene mouthed the words, leaving the studio and ducking into the washroom. She removed an amber bottle from her purse, shaking out a pill, washing it down with a gulp of Tim Hortons' version of Traditional.

How was she going to explain this? *The Otto Show* was something The Comedy Channel wanted to run against *The Seinfeld Chronicles*, or whatever the frick NBC was calling it. Even though the pilot hadn't aired, The Comedy Channel seemed sure that Jerry had been green-lit. That's why they were creating content to run against him. Arlene, she was familiar with Jerry's work, and she knew he wouldn't be prancing around in ladies funderwear. On top of that, The Comedy Channel wanted the flexibility to re-run *The Otto Show* at all hours. As a new channel, it would be thin on content, so they might want to run Abel, say, in the afternoon. Afternoon—if they ran this sketch at 4 am, Evangelicals would sacrifice themselves in the streets.

Deciding to problem-solve this later, Arlene headed for the door. Outside, she appeared from beneath the canopy, made a beeline for Claire, said, "I am sorry about before. Please, can you spare a smoke?"

Claire figured this had to be a trick, extending her pack anyway. "Really?"

"I have not had one since rehab, believed I had to give up everything." Arlene selected a cigarette, put it in her mouth, taking a light, thanks, then a hit, closing her eyes. "Feels good, soothing. You know, I think I gave up too much."

Softening, Claire said, "You remember the honeymoon?"

Arlene took another drag, as good as the first, head rush. "Honeymoon?"

Claire's eyes blurred to happier times, a gun at her hip. "You know, when you first started flirting with self-destructive activities, before anything was a habit, when it was still fun. You could do anything you wanted all day and all night, then not do it for months."

Honeymoon. Arlene exhaled, thinking, no, no, she couldn't remember that part. But at least she wasn't giving Lawn Boy the stankie in the green room.

16

June 25, 26, 27, 28, 29

Sunday featured a skit about Joan Jett's love life, peccadilloes in women's music. Monday had Abel as a Pakistani, Russian, and Mexican, adopting their accents to sing one-note songs. Those bits didn't fly, mostly because Abel hadn't written any jokes, like it'd be funny enough to mimic. He seemed to make up for it Tuesday with a routine revolving around Fred "Rerun" Berry as former Black Panther Patrick Critton using dance to teach inmates how to hijack airplanes.

Abel wrote in an Andy Rooney riff Wednesday, babbling about it becoming acceptable to wear G-strings above the waistline, juicy, when Janet Boroski walked in, bending over to pick up a dollar bill on a string. This way, Andy could pull the string every time Janet reached for the bill, repeatedly showcasing her ass cleavage, and everyone seemed to get a kick out of that. In addition to her usual duties, that meant Janet was an extra, so she'd be paid twice for the day.

Putting his beliefs on the shelf, Meckler was hustling, Abel was working hard, and shooting was back on schedule—ending with Zsa Zsa Gabor drinking, driving, and slapping an actual cop playing a cop, Mike Bullard, Abel in drag again. That meant Thursday was in fact a dark day for most everyone. Along with Arlene, however, Veronica spent a few hours at the studio, brewing tea, dealing with paperwork, and returning phone calls until Arlene's landline rang.

"I would thank you to get that," she said.

Veronica picked up, said hello, just a minute, holding the phone out. "It's Cyrus."

"Pardon my Greek, but tell him to give suck to my hard *phallus*." Arlene sipped her Traditional, pulled a face, sour. "Tell him a man who makes $300 a day is irreplaceable until he wants more. And then, tell him a man who wants more is milking a boy cow. Do it. Tell him."

Veronica spoke into the mouthpiece. "Arlene says you can give suck to—"

Cyrus stopped her, saying just tell Arlene the rent-a-cop and the parking attendant had something to do with the petty cash thing. Cyrus had racked his brain, and the only time he was out all day was over that bird caper. When did he have time to take the money? He truly didn't.

Veronica relayed the message, Arlene's lips curling. "Ask him if he subscribes to the lone-gunman theory. See what he says." Waiting. "Go ahead, ask."

"This is a lot you want me to do, taunt him." Veronica cupped the mouthpiece with both hands. "All I need is Cyrus raging at me because he's raging at you."

"I would thank you to do what I say. That is your job, no?"

"Look, people say he collects dead guy photos. He thinks Billy Idol was present when John Belushi OD'd, that *The American Journal of Medicine*'s patient zero study was a hoax, that Milli Vanilli lipsynchs. I mean, he probably collects different editions of *Catcher in the Rye*."

Arlene ignored all that, saying just ask, does he subscribe? Veronica reluctantly took her hand off the mouthpiece, repeating the question. Cyrus said the lone-gunman theory was flawed. And didn't they see in *Variety* that Kevin Costner was about to settle this? Then Cyrus apologized, saying this had nothing to do with Veronica while she relayed his message.

Really? Costner claims more than one gunman? Again, Arlene said Cyrus was milking a bull, to tell him he was fired, turfed, blackballed, done. Also, tell him Arlene knew about the gingham Ralph Lauren sofa from the Corky and the Juice Pigs special. Veronica bit her lip, hanging up as Cyrus outlined a four-part question truly pointing to a conspiracy of grunts. Arlene locked her desk, sliding some things into a snakeskin briefcase, throwing a burgundy sports jacket over her blue T, saying, "I want you in at five tomorrow."

"Five? Nobody's here at five."

Fishhooks, Nathan's relief was there all night, and from now on they had to have at least two people on set by 5 am for insurance purposes. Seeing as Veronica was being contrary, she would take the first turn. If her behavior improved, perhaps a little something could be done for her. With that, Arlene headed for the door then she was gone.

Veronica killed time manicuring her nails, filing, making sure Arlene wasn't returning. Satisfied at 2:10, she went in the kitchen, put a pair of mint-green dish gloves, using a key she'd marked with a white band to unlock Arlene's desk, searching without disturbing until she found an amber bottle beneath some spec scripts and publicity shots.

Removing eight tablets, she slid them into a small Tylenol cylinder, dropped it in her purse. She was about to leave when she figured that she, too, was entitled to a melt-in-your-mouth massage, going back to Arlene's desk, taking two—one for now, another for later. Closing the bottle, it looked almost as full as before, so she re-opened it and tapped out more than she counted, putting everything back in place.

A glass of water later, she floated out of there and into traffic. She'd taken a crew rental, sliding a CD compilation that came with the vehicle into the player, *The Dodge Caravan Swings!* Forwarding to track 10, mouthing words with Bobby Darin, she called herself irresponsible, irresistible. Somewhere in her head, she saw herself with pretty things in her hair, wearing her slip dress and shaking her martini shaker. Hands of men and women reached out, holding triangle glasses with olives, everyone calling her irreplaceable, too.

***

Waiting in his cruiser for the light at Lake Shore intersecting with Queen's Quay, Morton McNab was pining for another ciggy, just one more and that'd be it for today, when he saw the Caravan. The way it was coming on, really going, he knew it was going to run the red, sending his eyes eastbound to a Cutlass skidding sideways, colliding with the guardrail.

"Gonna bust your ass, you leaving-the-scene motherfucker." Morton flicked on his cherries, pulling into traffic, hearing the sound of metal against metal. In all the excitement, he hadn't looked, either, cutting off a blue Honda Accord, sideswiping it, both cars careening over the curb, coming to a stop under the Gardiner overpass.

Muttering a string of F-sharps, Morton hammered the steering wheel, got out of his car, circling it, calculating damage, then walked over to the Accord. He looked inside, seeing a teenage boy, another next to him, both dressed in dark suits.

"You guys okay?"

The kids looked at each other, back to Morton, yeah.

"Good," Morton said, feeling himself wind up. "Because so far, I need to just g'head and get a new bumper and a quarter-panel for my 1988 Chevy Caprice, and I'm not even a mechanic. Your daddy, can he pay for all this? This accident you caused."

The driver looked up, eyes so full of blood Morton was sure he was on the moon, shaking like he was going to snap, say something.

"I know what that look means, captain, no question, and you don't want to be giving it to me at this particular time. Now I said, can your daddy pay?"

"My dad's dead. Just came back from the funeral. He died three nights ago, heart attack. You still want him to pay?"

Shit, Morton put his hands on his hips, throwing his head back and looking into the sky. If he wasn't feeling bad about smoking, what he'd done with his life, or Claire's predicament, he was smacking into some kid who just buried his father, trying to make the dead dad responsible. The guilt, it was with him, eating away whenever he made a bad decision. On the upshot, nobody could call him on that dinged front quarter panel now.

***

Veronica felt she was walking on pillows on her way into the Thursday open-air market on Queen's Quay. She shopped, picked up some things for her barbecue from the vendor known as Mademoiselle Madeline's Gourmet. Mostly, Veronica drank a latte with chocolate shavings from Johnny Jetfuel's booth, lost in the Spanish guitar serenading shoppers from a ramshackle stage on Lake Ontario with a song she didn't know, words she didn't understand. Wondering if she would ever hear the song again, she entertained thoughts of asking the musician about it between sets, then thought she should leave well enough alone and take in the moment, the peace, without worrying about how she might replicate it later.

Fifteen minutes of that and other procrastinations, she was still floating, past the Spanish guitar player, dropping a fiver into his case, then through small crowds to the minivan, loading her groceries, climbing inside, hitting the ignition, and backing out. She bumped a concrete reinforcement, then, realizing it wasn't her vehicle, had a slightly scared giggle before hitting the gas, cranking the volume, taking a couple lefts and heading east on Queen's Quay.

Touching her face, nice, smooth, supple, doing an understated cha-cha with Peggy Lee in her seat as the boy from Ipanema went walking, she caught the advance green at Parliament, hooking another left across Lake Shore. A cop was at the side of the road, that McNab, the guy Claire brought in, running out and shaking a fist, yelling.

Behind him, Veronica saw the cruiser and a Honda banged up on the far side of the curb. She tilted her head to compensate for the low angle of the sideview mirror as she passed, thinking something must have happened because there seemed to be yet another accident, cars everywhere. But who was McNab yelling at? Her? Why would he be yelling at her? She hadn't done anything. It was probably eyewitnesses he was looking for. And Veronica was just a rubbernecker, so it wasn't like she was leaving the scene.

The rest of the drive was a blur. Other than hearing Wayne Newton, Dinah Washington, and was that Sarah Vaughan? Veronica couldn't remember much else about the trip, or even the exact route she'd taken, clearly on automatic pilot, back to her townhouse south of Riverdale Farms, idling in her driveway while Tony Bennett sang about what plenty of money could do. And for the first time, she began to understand what might have hooked Arlene.

The pills made Veronica feel nice, sure, calm. But Veronica felt too nice, dreamy, like who would want to abstain and see the world for what it was? So, on a certain level, she understood how someone might not have the inspiration to detox. Plus, there was the power of the unguarded moment, white space in her brain, room to think freely without running her thoughts, as Robert Smith would say, through something else's train.

So, yes, Veronica could empathize, and empathizing helped her understand Arlene, which was important. That was the thing people didn't grasp about going after a person in power. If you're going to kill the king, or, in this case, the queen, you'd better get it done right the first time. Otherwise, if you let them up with that knowledge, they were going to sic their considerable war machine on you, and who wanted that?

Not Veronica. She didn't see the percentages in out-and-out hating Arlene. That would only serve to make Veronica less objective. No, in order to take over, she needed to understand Arlene to fully exploit any weaknesses. So sure, Arlene's technical addiction was to the pills, absolutely, but the pills were a byproduct of her addiction to power, the ability to free up one's mind while one is regularly in a state of crisis. Maybe that meant the pills were indeed medicaments to help her deal with the psychological violence of both attaining and maintaining power. Veronica figured it had more to do with the maintenance part, just getting through the everyday fuckery among people who's livelihoods depended on tax credits, grants, trade agreements, and every little whim of America.

17

Cyrus' pledge to go cold turkey on weed lasted six days. At 6:48 pm, according to his digital Timex, he used his cordless to page Hollis, punching in his digits. And right on, she called from a pay-phone within minutes.

"Cyrus?"

"Yeah, me." Cyrus was in no mood for pleasantries, but seeing as he wanted something, fast, he figured he should go through the motions. "How're things, Hollis?"

"Good. You?"

"Mint," Cyrus said. "Just fucking mint. Listen, I was wondering if you could drop by."

There was a moment of dead air. "For what?"

"What do you usually drop by for?"

Hollis said, "I was just there last week."

"Well, I need you to drop by again, the sooner the better. Can do?"

Hollis thought about it, said can do. She'd be right over.

Cyrus said bye, hanging up, cupping his hands over his nose and mouth when the phone rang again. He figured it was Hollis, already calling in a late excuse, and picked up, hello. Following a pause, he found himself listening to a recorded message from Mary's Ministry asking if he was in need of urgent prayer. He hung up, thinking that was kind of ominous.

∗∗∗

Veronica stole two hours of sleep, almost, wrapped the fish in foil, showered, shaved, brewed a pot of Nabob, picking herself up with one cup, black with sugar, then another, before getting the barbe-cue started. Sitting in the living room, pulling her hair back with a half cap, she looked blankly into a JVC TV mounted in her en-tertainment center. Aiming the clicker, checking on the new chan-nels that came with her pirate cable—homes and gardens, music, sports . . .

Eventually, she settled on the western channel, watching *The Lone Ranger* long enough to figure out that Tonto was conning a cowboy into admitting his crimes by reading out documented proof from a blank sheet of paper. Flicking the unit off, she drifted, staring at an overwrought oil-painting of a girl with corkscrew hair, poetry scrawled over the foreground in backhand slant, waves crashing against hope, and could someone please take her hand?

As agreed, Nathan and Claire arrived around seven, seeing Veronica through the window as they stepped onto the porch. Nathan didn't want to ring at first, watching her sitting on a backless couch. She seemed serene, and he hadn't seen that side of her. An orange longhaired cat with its fur cut to resemble a tiny lion played at her feet with a sports-sock toy.

Precious, Claire whispered, wondering aloud what the cat had been through to attain the look. Poor thing, it was probably trying to think of what it did wrong.

"So this cat's Christian?" Nathan said. "Can feel guilt?"

Claire went on, saying sure, it was okay now, but what about winter? If this year was anything like last, it was probably thinking it would need a whole new coat by fall.

"Cat thinks a lot," Nathan said. "Lot of issues, cerebral, planning ahead."

Looking at Claire, he asked what she had gone through for her polka-dot dress. Was it a game? A toy? And what was Molly Ringwald going to say? Her outfit was supposed to be an exclusive, right? Sure looked like one-of-a-kind.

Claire forced a smile, pushing Veronica's doorbell. The first bars of "Für Elise," Beethoven, meant big, strange people, the miniature lion jumping, landing spread-eagled. Looking all about, it ran low to the ground, down the hall for cover.

"Must feel in the wrong about something." Nathan pointed. "You see it go?"

Veronica greeted them, walked them through the house, pointing out the washroom, then steered them out back, the barbeque smoking. Her yard faced west, making the space a virtual hotplate. That's why she made sure to have them arrive just as the sun was setting. The clouds were a polluted pink-orange, Claire getting chippy right away. "So what'd you get for us, girly?"

"Antipasto, catfish, and chicken," Veronica said. "Everything from the same booth at the Thursday open-air market on Queen's Quay, Mademoiselle Madeline's."

Claire raised the right side of her upper lip, held it, saying catfish and chicken was going to be like eating chicken and chicken. She seemed different in the late sun. Maybe it was the drinking catching up, or maybe it was the heat, but Nathan thought her eyes looked too close together, probably because she was over-plucking, and it was apparent that she was compensating with cosmetics to give her thin lips contrast, just like Angie Dickinson before she got cancelled. She was motioning to the picnic table now, saying catfish tastes like chicken because of the feed at the fish farms.

"Catfish eat chickens?" Veronica asked, turning it back.

"They feed catfish grain," Claire said, "same as chicken. In other words, you're feeding us chicken along with something that's going to taste like chicken, is what I'm saying."

"Lay off." Nathan handed Veronica a brown paper bag. Now there was a woman, natural, the way she didn't bother covering that scar running through her brow. The rest of the TV trash, Nathan knew they'd run to the nearest plastic surgeon over a mosquito bite. "We brought burgers. Makes for nice variety with the catfish and *poulet*. Besides, catfish, that's a delicacy I haven't had since the USF&G Classic in New Orleans, 1986. Lemon pepper."

Veronica smiled, relieved, tilting her head. "Lemon pepper."

Lemon pepper, Claire thought, studying Veronica's profile. Same stupid, dainty nose as Arlene—and was that what Nathan wanted? He goes to The Big Easy and orders lemon pepper?

***

Cyrus sat on the couch holding himself, rocking, waiting. When the phone went off, he picked it up halfway through the first ring, hello?

"Hey, it's Hollis. Running late, sorry. I was just on my way, Spadina and Queen. Then I got paged to pick up this thing on the Danforth, so I had to go and—"

Glancing at his watch, 7:20, Cyrus said, "You're supposed to be here like a half-hour ago, said you'd be right over."

"I know, I know," she said over a horn, breathing slightly heavy. "But you've got to understand I'm a courier first."

"Courier first my ass—it's Thursday night."

"Thursday night can get busy in my business, people trying to get a jump on the other guy before he gets to work Friday, everyone with one last chance to get something done before they kick back and party. Anyway, what I'm saying is, I'm almost there. Five minutes away."

"Five?"

"Five, 10 at the most."

"Okay, 10 at the most. I've got to be somewhere." Hanging up, Cyrus held his head, thinking he was going to do some biblical shit to whoever put him in this hole. At first, he'd been sure it was those burnouts working the lot, but how could they hate him enough? Arlene was probably right. They didn't have the initiative. Still, whoever did this, Cyrus was going to drive to Cherry Beach Studios and kill everyone if he didn't get his hands on a bag of dope. It wasn't bad enough they seized his Billy Idol bootlegs and photos. No, they had to take his pot. Who did that? And how would Arlene feel if someone seized her medicine?

***

By the time everybody ate, there was still enough left for another party, too much food. Nathan saw it wasting, gathering it up, telling Veronica to sit down. "And Claire, hey Claire how about little help? A little help by reason of you haven't done a damn thing."

Nathan attributed his courage to the two Löwenbräu in him, cracking open another after he and Claire brought the leftovers inside. She'd already downed three spritzers, Veronica two white wines, so they were easing up, talking about the new Indiana Jones movie until Claire pushed her glass forward on the picnic table, brass tacks.

"Thanks for your hospitality, but time has come to tell us why you're jerking chains." She had her eyes on Veronica, cynical. "I'm happy as anyone you arsed Cyrus, and I want to get to that. But you leveraged me." Nodding to Nathan. "Leveraged him, us."

Veronica looked to Nathan. He said, "Due respect, you used some big words the other day, making it sound like we're supposed to listen to something you have to say about that thing Claire and I agree can't be done." Opening his hand. "So please."

Veronica nodded. "Okay, I did you a favor shredding that note, right?"

"You leveraged it," Claire said. "That alone is suspicious, seven years police experience says. How do we know you didn't photocopy it? And you're still leveraging, like we owe you."

"If I was leveraging, you would never know," Veronica said. "I worked two years as a researcher for the Liberals, so I know how to deliver a plain brown envelope, thanks. A photocopy wouldn't stand up anyway. You could have written, 'It has been done. It's do-able.' on a Hallmark, and then I could have cut and pasted it to the news story, photocopied it, used white-out on the edges, photocopied it again. A photocopy doesn't mean anything."

"Unlikely you'd go through the bother, would be the judiciary's take." Claire rubbed her thigh. "Like Cyrus, his conspiracies, your conspiracies."

"You haven't done anything," Veronica said. "I've nothing on you. I just want in."

Claire said that would make it a three-person split. She didn't know if it was worth the risk, felonious repercussions considered, you made this a three-person split. "Law of diminishing returns, know what I mean, Little Arlene?"

Veronica laughed that off, hands pointing at her townhouse and the things around it—the marble birdbath, Jackie the lion cat, now courageous enough to sniff the wild flowers. "You can have the money. It would be too risky for me to have it."

"Fine, you got all this." Claire leaned closer. "I'm impressed, very impressed. But then why risk it running a whim-wham on your boss?"

"Whim-wham," Nathan said, thinking Claire could kiss his vaguely ethnic ass. "Just ask what's in it for her? Why she's doing this free, is all that's needed to be said."

Diplomatic little prick. Claire was exercising due diligence, is all she was doing, so why did he go after her like that? "I wish to know what we're getting into and why she's onside?" There. She could be diplomatic, too. "All I'm asking."

It was a simple question, a good one. But Nathan was diverting Claire, talking about how Veronica brought him in during the Babylon sheet-metal fire, saving him from the *toxines*, when Veronica put a hand up, saying it was okay. That she was next in line. That Arlene didn't own the company anymore, not a controlling part anyway.

"Bullshit," Claire said. "Her name's on the building. That, and she hates your scrawny ass. She's not going to help you. Why would she help you?"

Veronica said Claire was half right. Arlene owned it, past tense, but she needed investors to be competitive in the Hollywood North era, that free trade turned the industry on its head. A year ago, everyone was competing for grants, and they still were. But now, with the American profit motive and star machine, everyone was also competing to get big productions here, and that took money, lots of money.

So, there was that, then grant money from a project that went tits up had already been spent on other things. Arlene had to pay it back, financial trouble. By the time the investors bailed her out, again, she was hiding in rehab. She told the investors she got hooked after the slip-and-fall at the film fest, but by then she had wiped out the buffet table at Wong's and taken out a waitress at the Russian Tea Room. Investors find out about that sort of thing, especially these investors, and they didn't like it. That's why they sent Veronica in—to keep an eye on their interests until they eased Arlene out. Veronica just wanted to give them the reason they needed.

"Next in line—why be in such a hurry?" Claire said. "Why not just let it happen?"

"She's the executive producer, I'm director of development." Veronica stopped, took a breath, choosing her next words carefully. "I'm good to go with that. I could wait patiently and learn until the changing of the guard. She's done most every job, so I'm the first to admit that she has some things to teach me. That's how I came to her, with guarded respect. But you see what she does, treats me like she treats you. I'm the DD, and I don't even have an office at AMA. I have a cubicle. I make her tea. Tomorrow, I have to be in at five—five. I can't do this with her."

"Punished again." Nathan was almost convinced, just one thing. "So how does us stealing Kiwi's stipend help you? Looks bad on you, too, doesn't it? Kiwi's stipend gets boosted."

Again, Veronica was sent in to watch Arlene—not do her job, not get in her way—just watch, report back. In short, Veronica was to do what she was told and let everyone else play their roles. As for Arlene, all the investors were going to see was a prescription opium addict blacking out and losing their money.

18

Cyrus paced, swearing he was going to source a book on hydroponics and grow his own. It was just, he floated Hollis, what, 60 bucks every two weeks? And he referred people to her, industry people who knew other industry people, creative people with money. In all, Cyrus was probably worth $500 a month to Hollis, rent. Still, he had been waiting on her for almost an hour, and that was after she said she'd be right over.

Didn't matter. Every dealer pulled the same stunts. First few scores, they'd be on time, respectful. As soon as they came to understand themselves as Cyrus' guy, the amounts would dwindle, and they'd be late. The Velvet Underground had a song about it, "I'm Waiting for the Man," and like the song, Hollis was never early. Sometimes, Cyrus needed to get high just to get over the stress of waiting for her. Mostly, he needed to get high to forget himself.

Looking for a distraction, he flicked the radio on, some raved-out shit with enough repetition to put him into a mild trance, and it would have, if only the raved-out shit wasn't fading into a station ID, CKLN 88.1 FM Toronto, when it was too early for a station ID. A small group of people came on after that. They were pissed off about pornography. Like, seriously. Cyrus thought it was funny, they were so mad, until one recommended a therapy for porn users. Oh God, she was telling listeners to superimpose images of their mothers over the faces of those acting in the porn. And Cyrus, he couldn't possibly see how putting mom's face on Tex Anthony while he's taking eight inches would make the world a better place. Thinking, no, that'd only make the world a more fucked up place, Cyrus killed the power, wondering where the station manager was, letting people go off like this, playing the station ID at the wrong time, when the phone rang. Figuring it was Hollis with another lame excuse for being even later, Cyrus picked up, hello.

"Mott?"

"No."

"May I please speak to Mott?"

"Nobody here by that name," Cyrus said. "Wrong number."

"Oh," the caller said. "Mott told me to call him here, wrote it out and everything."

"Read the number to me."

When the caller read the digits back, Cyrus confirmed them. But again, there was no Mott. Then the guy asked Cyrus, sweet as pie, if he could leave a message, just in case Mott showed. Cyrus laughed and said sure, remembering his name, Ian, who said Mott would have the number.

***

Nathan was satisfied, theoretically. But the girls went on for a good while; Claire grilling Veronica over motive, Veronica calmly explaining her interests, then Claire with another good question. "Cash. Why are we getting paid in cash?"

Veronica took a breath, thinking what the hell? She'd taken it this far, what would a little more insider info hurt? It couldn't, and she needed to share something to build trust and pull Claire onside. "To the investors, it's a shell corporation, a company that's not going to make real money. At this point, AMA exists to clean their money by paying it out in wages and petty cash. They don't care about it as a profit business, per se. They allow for the possibility of losses on productions like *The Otto Show*. Even if they get less back, it's clean. This should be an easy gig for her, no pressure to produce a hit. But you don't get three chances."

Claire snapped her fingers. "So Arlene is Smurfing." When the other two didn't understand, Claire unpacked it. "Smurfing: Taking a large mass of dirty currency and reducing it into increasingly smaller amounts until it's not worth Revenue Canada's while to go through the rigmarole of hunting it down. People who perform the function of reduction are called Smurfs, makes Arlene a Smurf."

Veronica looked at Claire, smiling oddly, getting only part of it. Yes, she'd heard it called Smurfing, but she never understood why.

Smurfs multiply faster than rabbits, Claire explained. Hence Smurfing. While committers were also called straws, straw men, and scarecrows, Claire said they were now by and large known as Smurfs because their play involved a myriad of miniature deposits—or, in this case, payment of wages—to break bigger chunks of dirty currency down. Crime societies, bikers for example, make miscellaneous modest deposits of a much larger mass to multiple accounts, Smurfing. Paying more than two dozen employees cash—that could also be Smurfing.

Veronica liked that, smiling, learning something. "Smurfing—anyway, yes. That is the angle, the reason you are getting paid cash. Arlene is Smurfing."

"So then, what are you going to do for us?" Claire looked around the yard, behind her. "Like, I'm not saying, I'm just saying."

"Theoretically," Nathan added.

Veronica picked a strawberry out of her fruit salad, biting it in half. "Just that I am in a unique position to run interference so that you won't be seen. I can guide you, point you."

"And how much will we not be seen getting away with?" Claire said. "Theoretically?"

Veronica swallowed, looked away. "In total, if no one else quits or gets fired, just about $64,000, according to my calculations."

"Your calculations. Just about."

"Look Claire, if you don't believe me, look at the crew list of people getting paid cash for 18 days work. Add in all casual staff, a few no-show jobs, and petty cash, and I bet you come up with a number that looks like 64,000, all in one place at one time without out a camera or a guard in sight. It could have been more except Arlene's not hiring a replacement for Cyrus this season."

Claire nodded, thinking okay, maybe it was do-able. "Give us a few?"

Veronica said she'd go inside, turn on the stereo and create some privacy noise. "Just a sec. I want to get a CD from the van."

***

Next to Cyrus on the couch, the green dial phone rang quickly three times, meaning Hollis was in the vestibule downstairs, finally. Cyrus, making for the push-button cordless in the kitchen, buzzed her up. He walked to the door, waiting for footsteps, opening before she knocked. As soon as she was inside, he said, "Thought you were going to be like five, 10 minutes."

"What was I—11, 12?"

"More like 40." Cyrus dropped three twenties on his Deco table, bare metal. "Which makes you an hour-plus late in total. I called at 6:48 and look-it." Holding out his watch. "Almost eight. I know I'm one of your best customers, yet you treat me worse than the Bell Canada guy treats me, truly, making me wait."

"Yeah." Hollis shook her hair out her grey helmet. "But I'm better looking."

Cyrus looked her up and down, said right.

"Besides, what happened to the bag you bought last week?"

"Confiscated."

"Busted? You didn't say my name, I hope."

"No, nothing like that. It would be against code anyway."

"What happened?"

"Let's just say that's why I need more." Cyrus slapped the air, ending it.

"Drag." Hollis scooped up the money, replacing it with a Ziplock, a quarter. "Hey, I've been on the road all day. I'm hot. Who does a girl have to blow to get a drink around here?"

Cyrus took a breath. "Gatorade okay?" When she said alright, he started off to the fridge. "Made some this morning, orange, already cold."

"Awesome. Original's grody, no taste, and did you hear they're coming out with Gatorade flavors beyond orange and lemon-lime?"

"I did not hear that." Cyrus stopped, turned back. "And you know how?"

"'I'm a courier, need to be concerned about electrolytes." Hollis looked at her watch, 7:59. "Do you get that new western channel with your pirate cable?"

"Yeah, why?"

"Quick." Hollis took off her yellow windbreaker. "*The Rifleman*'s starting."

Cyrus came back carrying two glasses. "Didn't I tell you I have to be somewhere?"

"C'mon." She went into her knapsack, pulling out a geometry-set tin. "I'll smoke you some of mine, special, Maui Wowie."

"That mean you're selling me remnants? Holding out?"

Hollis looked disgusted. "No."

"Well, how come mine doesn't have a way-out brand name?"

"Because you don't put enough twenties on your table for way-out. You want Maui Wowie, Maui Wowie commands you to put another twenty."

***

Sitting next to Nathan at the picnic table, Claire put her arm around him, pulling him near. "Okay," she said. "But do you know why you're doing it?"

Nathan's eyes widened. "You kidding?"

"No, you do something like this, you have to ask yourself—felonious repercussions considered—why? So I'm asking."

Spitting inside, thinking felonious repercussions, Nathan wiggled away, standing. "I'm an ethnic *homme*, don't know where I came from, 37, run out of things I can be without marketable skills, education, or ambition, works in parking, has a bad back caused by carrying golf clubs. Advising white folks with excellent hand-eye coordination on club selection, pacing yardage, reading putts, walking the course early for pin placements—that's my calling, only I can't do it anymore by reason of scoliosis. Asides, I'm getting calls from my sublet landlord. Maybe he's coming home, no mention of when or what I paid. See, it's not money as much as it's security. This buys me time to go wander on my own private pursuit of happiness, a rest from the business of living. Plus Arlene calls me Lawn Boy behind my back. I should jack her just for that." He held his forehead. "And if she tells me to speak English one more time, when I'm just being respectful, I swear I'll kidnap the labor minister. See what she has to say then."

Claire laughed, said what the fuck good would kidnapping the labor minister do? Nathan allowed himself to crack a smile, said he wasn't sure, now that Claire was being so detail-oriented, but that they could probably figure out a way to monetize it, ransom, if nothing else.

There, that was good enough for Claire, and fun. But it stung, too. Again with his private pursuit of happiness, like his plans didn't include her, another three-week date. Great, she thought, blaming '80s feminists for whatever they did to do to their generation of men, turning them into little man-boys who wanted to find themselves, one-hand commanders. And try as she might, she never could coax mom's nipple out of their mouths.

"Look." Claire held her hands like a scale portraying balance. "I know it's all good and fun now, just don't get out of touch with the seriousness of the situation. Like, you could commit yourself, work your way up in this industry. I see lots of minorities on set doing well."

"They're all comedians," Nathan said. "Executives and the workers, except for Toledo and I, are white. All of them."

Claire crinkled her nose. "Think that's intentional?"

"It's institutional," Nathan said. "Like it's okay for the Huxtables to entertain, but the system doesn't want them making decisions. And me, I'm not an entertainer."

***

In her room, Veronica slipped out of her jeans and T-shirt, into the black slip dress she saw herself wearing on the way to the open-air market. Fighting out of the half cap—damn thing was pulling, killing her buzz—she pushed her hair to the side, pinned it in place with yellow, red, and green berets. Then she put the CD from the crew van on, bumping it to Peggy Lee again.

Moving onto the kitchen, singing the boy's like a samba, she found the martini shaker in a cupboard above her fridge, pouring vermouth inside. Just a kiss, she told herself, not bothering with measurement. Then she looked out the window, watching them talk it through.

***

Nathan sat back down, reaching under Claire's chin, lifting it. "So why are you doing it? Angie Dickinson herself, *policière* doing a payroll heist—that's the $64,000 question."

Claire closed one eye. "You just solved your own mystery."

Nathan withdrew his hand. "How?"

"They're not going to let me back, then what?" Claire looked at the neighbor's yard, gnomes holding samples of harvest. "I can't pick up and work for another force. Fired cop, everyone knows. Even rural forces—Chatham, Peterborough, Glencoe—they don't hire fired cops, and all that makes me one ex-cop with a lifestyle to support." Thumbing her chest. "I'm not ending up in a sublet bachelor. I'm in a basement as it is. That's where it stops. I need."

Although she'd taken a jab, Nathan felt for her. Just a poor university-educated white girl drinking all the time—how many spritzers was that now?—trying to hang onto her life. Being a cop must've disheartening enough, in touch with bad customers all day, but think about being an ex-cop, having everything taken away. Same time, she had computer skills and a good healthy back, sturdy. Only 31, she could still be anything, because, eventually, her nudie shoot would be excused, if not lionized. She just needed to evolve.

"Need," he said, "how about you freelance like Thomas Magnum. He had a good deal at the Masters estate. And Jim Rockford, he lived in a trailer, but he was happy. You could tell."

Tom Selleck, James Garner—Claire didn't think he was that stupid. Or was he drunk? No, it was just the poor guy had already worked on the fringes of the business long enough that he was running out of real-life reference points.

Dropping a red-black paisley napkin into her lap, leaning back, she couldn't believe she had to explain this. But, save for a handful, established, being a dick was a high-risk, low-paying gig, and she didn't want to end up chasing pervs, adulterers, and insurance frauds. She wanted to be a police officer, a regular cop. That was her calling, and if she couldn't, she still had to eat. Like, she was on leave without pay so she could use 32-K-plus tax-free, her security.

"But that little rich girl," Claire added. "We want to get involved in a whim-wham with someone that uptight? Someone with that much to lose?"

"Whim-wham," Nathan said, wishing right away he hadn't repeated her cop-talk. She knew by now that he didn't like it, and throwing it back only emboldened her. That was the non-verbal fuck-you he was picking up anyway. "Veronica's fine because she has the most to lose." Looking up, he saw her in the window, pretty berets in her hair, hearing the disc switch over to Wayne Newton, "Strangers in the Night." She was standing in what looked to be a slip, shaking a martini shaker. "Asides." Waving her back into the yard. "She seems to be loosening up some."

Claire slapped his arm with the back of her hand. "You think she's hot?"

Nathan rubbed the hit spot, said she's pleasing. Claire demanded to know what that meant, pleasing. Veronica's attractive, Nathan said. Why? Was Claire jealous? No. Good, by reason of Veronica was out of Nathan's league. Claire slapped him again, asked what that made her? Nathan said Claire was also out of his league, or at least she would've been during the Victorian-era. Claire asked what the Victorians had to do with it. Nathan said they liked their woman fed, that having a fed woman was a status symbol. Slap. Was he saying Claire was fat? Nathan leaned away. He was just saying, as someone educated on the history of beauty, that Claire's ideal cultural window would have been the late 1830s to the turn of the century.

"Turn of the century?" she said, keeping her right up, ready. "And how is it you know so much about the history of beauty? You have a PhD in pussy?"

Nathan looked at her, astonished. "By reason of I read, every day."

Claire leaned like she was coming in with that backhand right again, only to sweep wide left and pop him on the ear. Equality and all, Nathan thought about giving her a shot back, and Claire knew. She told him, go ahead, that she was looking for an excuse to bring him into line.

Bring him into line? *Merde*, now that Nathan thought on it, he wondered if he could handle her, if push came to shove. Not only were they roughly the same size, but Claire was in shape, mean, trained to make people submit. But Nathan wasn't going to cry uncle. Nah. He just pointed at her and said, "You keep lashing out, I'll lash back."

Yeah, Claire said, it'd be easier if Nathan learned to fly right. And in case he was threatening, she was fixing to pop him again when Veronica walked into the yard saying, "There's no hitting."

19

"What's with all the dead guys?" Hollis pointed to an autographed picture, eyes so sad and loopy and fucked up it made her eyes feel like watering. It was inscribed:

> For who is Chester?
> What has he got?
> When he finds out he cannot
> Best, Sid Vicious

"Hobby," Cyrus said. "Collecting."

"But like—Janis Joplin, Jimi Hendrix, Ian Curtis, Cliff Burton—they're dead, all of them. Where do you get them? I mean, they're all signed."

"I have sources who have sources who have sources," Cyrus said.

"How do you know they're real?"

"Reputable dealers, certificates of authenticity. Besides, if, say, the Vicious was a fake, it wouldn't be inscribed for Chester. Unless your name is Chester, that only devalues it. If they told me they could get one for Cyrus, I would be suspicious. But no one's going to forge one for Chester, then try to sell it to me, Cyrus."

Hollis wiggled, said it made sense.

Made sense—Cyrus was trying not to rip her head off and punt it out the window. First, baby dyke's an hour-plus late, then she wants Gatorade while she watches *The Rifleman*. Okay, so she was sitting on his couch and watching his TV, but now she was bogarting when the whole point of this operation was to get Cyrus stoned on that Maui Wowie before he started acting out the violent shit in his head.

"You know." She took another slow draw, nodding at the screen as she let it out. "Chuck Connors played for the Cubs, baseball."

Cyrus didn't know, didn't care.

"Yeah, also played basketball, NBA, for Boston." Hollis took another hit, talking through her teeth as she handed the Maui Wowie to Cyrus. "He's like 6'5". Did you know that, that he played basketball as well as baseball, both professionally?"

"Yeah, I mean, no." Cyrus took a hit, feeling better knowing the THC was in him. "How do you know? I mean, why do you know? You're like 23."

"Western channel's epic bio series." Hollis pointed at the screen, kicking out of her bike shoes. "And I'm 24 next month."

"I don't know much about him, personally." Cyrus took another toke, watching. It was an early episode, the Connors character, Lucas, having just bought this ranch and some men in black were setting it on fire. "But would you believe I've had his gun in my hands?"

"Get out." Hollis looked at Cyrus, the screen, back. "You mean you've held the same kind of gun, same make?"

***

Careful not to look Veronica below the neck, Claire thought nice slip, bitch, firing questions until all three agreed, theoretically. Now, in practical terms, how were they going to do it without being seen? Veronica said just a sec, running up the porch, inside, returning with a pad of yellow paper and a pencil. Sitting across from Nathan and Claire, handing the pad to them, she smiled at her sunflowers. She'd managed to get a few of the blood-red variety and they were blooming, hopped up on egg shells and coffee grounds.

"This isn't written in stone, just what I propose, a way it can be done without being seen," she said, refocusing. "A simple plan based on the three-legged stool of political planning."

Something else you learned at Liberal Party campaign school, Nathan thought. Tilting his head to Claire, her hair brushing his lobe, hand on his thigh like she didn't just smack him three, four times. She smelled like cocoa butter today.

As they read, Veronica pitched the three-legged stool like a script. Act one called for her to steal three walkies from set, good ones with transparent earplugs. Nathan said people were wearing all sorts of ear gear on the street—Walkmans, radio headsets, hearing aids—so an itty-bitty earplug with an itty-bitty wire wasn't going to attract attention by reason of . . .

Veronica watched him go on, Nathan staring past her, a grave-yard far in the distance, the buzz of animals at Riverdale Farms. One pissed off rooster was rising above the rest when Nathan wrapped his monologue about how those *petite* wires were going to be so incognito. Veronica nodded, explaining that they would use some obscure sub channel—36, perhaps—on pay day. Better yet, that part was already done, the walkies in hand.

"Kiwi was talking about that my first night, that three walkies were missing," Claire said. "That he was going to have to pay for them. Those our walkies?"

"Yes."

"So, you been planning something for a while. Orchestrating."

"Just gathering resources," Veronica said, "until of course I came across your note."

Claire stiffened, pointing her hand like a gun. "Don't you lever-age me."

Veronica raised her hands in mock surrender, showcasing per-fectly shaved armpits. Moving on, she outlined Act two, which called for her to acquire some Percs to spike Arlene's tea with early on pay day, put her to sleep. Of course, she'd already acquired said medicaments, but didn't want to say anything else that might leave Claire feeling leveraged, the nasty cunt. And why was she slapping Nathan like that when Veronica was inside? Were they playing?

"That's the important part," Veronica said. "Once Arlene starts losing consciousness, I excuse myself, grab a double-double down the street, as per routine."

"What about the desk phone?" Claire said.

"I'll unplug it."

"See that you do."

Right, Veronica said. Now for Act three: Nathan, upon receiv-ing Veronica's signal, would enter the building to find Arlene face-down in her tea. If, for whatever reason, Arlene brought in her own tea, the whole thing would be called off with the code word "licorice." That, however, would be an unlikely aberration of Arlene's morning routine of being served. So, unless Nathan heard something about corkscrew candy, he could expect to find the money on Veronica's desk, which is where Arlene would be, out. He might have to move her head to the side, but Nathan's job was simply to scoop the money, stuff it in a knapsack, then be gone.

And oh yeah, he would have to get the mint-green dish gloves from the kitchen, wash out Arlene's tea cup so that no traces of Percodan were found. It had to look as if she knowingly took the drugs, like she'd mistakenly double-dosed.

All the while, Claire would be watching Nathan's tail out on the street. Aside from driving, her job was to radio in if someone came in after him. Worst case, Claire could say licorice, abort. Unless licorice was said, nobody else was due in the office until 10, so they'd be hitting Arlene when she was vulnerable, no one to catch her fall.

"The way I see it." Veronica closed her eyes, using a visualization technique she'd read about in a magazine put out by the screenwriter's guild. "We hit at 8:30-ish while she still has all the cash, before anyone other than her and I are due. I put her out, you take the money, simple."

"So they're going to think she drugged herself," Claire said. "She wakes up saying, 'Where's the money? I blacked out.'"

"Never trust a junkie." Veronica rolled her shoulders. "And all that."

They were all shaking their heads when Claire took a closer look at the plan on paper. "Cameras, duty guards—you sure there isn't something? Having 64-thou on hand and all."

"Nothing," Veronica said. "Arlene says she's waiting for digital tech to evolve, but she's just cheap, like Cherry Beach. All AMA has is a lock alarm, and get this, her code is 007. Thinks she's so cool."

Nathan thought it would've been cooler if she'd picked an obscure spook's ID, like the vacuum salesman from *Our Man in Havana*—59200/5. "But we're unlikely to need it by reason of we won't be breaking in, right?"

"Since we're taking every precaution, you should know it. But no, I can't see how you'd need it. Arlene will open shop, let us through the front door." Veronica stopped. "I just need to know, do either of you have criminal records?" Looking at Claire. "Aside from the porn."

Claire bit down, shaking her head, no, adding that porn was not illegal.

Nathan said he hadn't been busted for anything other than a speeding ticket he couldn't talk his way out of on his way to the Bank of Boston Classic in '85.

Veronica looked back and forth, satisfied. "Good, no suspect pasts, so?"

Nathan, thinking of the curvature of his spine getting worse, reached for his martini glass, raising it. "To robbing Attila the Hen on pay day."

Claire and Veronica did likewise, everyone drinking to it.

"We should talk regularly between now and then, fine-toothing it." Veronica took the pad. "Learn it, make it second nature. It's simple, really, but we don't want paperwork lying around. Either of you want to read this again before I burn it?"

Nathan and Claire looked at each other. No, they caught the gist.

Ripping the top page out, Veronica dropped the pad on the table, walking to the barbecue. She crunched the plan into a ball, firing up the burner, standing with her back to Claire, who pulled the pad to herself, coughing and ripping the next sheet out at the same time, folding it twice like a letter. Lifting the left side of her dress, slipping it into her lipstick-garter, smoothing herself.

Okay now, maybe Nathan hadn't been to law-and-order school, but he'd seen everyone from Columbo to that chick played Sheba Baby make the same move. Thing was, they were gathering evidence, so what was Claire up to? *Tabernac*, Nathan was starting to believe maybe it could be done, and here was Claire, testing the trust. Kind of like Disco Dick in Houston, trying to hit a ball out of a creek when there was a chance in ten of pulling it off. And how much was Dick's whiff worth? Somewhere around $64,000, if Nathan's memory served.

***

Hollis was barefoot, down to her black Body Glove, logo in orange. On screen, the fire at the Lucas ranch was spreading.

"I'm telling you I'm talking about that very gun." Cyrus pointed at the TV. "I've held it in my hands a few times now."

She whispered warm in his ear, c'mon.

Cyrus gave her a double-take, sighed. Watching the bad guys dragging away Connors by horse, trying to break him. "You know what I do."

"Time to pass the Dutchie." Hollis waved at herself. "You're in movies, TV."

"Set design." Cyrus took another toke, palming off. "I get things for movies, TV."

Hollis reached for the joint, looked around his sparse apartment. Other than dead people, the art wouldn't be missed, especially A Girl with a Broom, Rembrandt's poor chimney sweeper. "Kind of depressing for a designer's pad, don't you think?"

"Yeah, well that's what I do, and I'm telling you I've had to get the Rifleman's rifle. Latin guy in Toronto—our gun wrangler—rents it out."

"Cool." When Cyrus didn't say anything, she hit the joint and started feathering his hair. "People say how the gun was the real star, the way he pumped it."

Cyrus looked sideways at her. "You know I'm into guys, right?"

"Yeah."

"Well then, why is your hand in my hair, moving?"

She pulled away. "Thought you were sending me subliminals last time, saying you're bi."

"Bi-polar, I told you. That's why I smoke pot, evens me out. I'm a medicinal user."

"Medicinal?" Hollis snorted out a laugh. "So, what, you have like a prescription?"

"Don't laugh. New Mexico recognized medicinal marijuana in 1978. We'll catch up."

"Meantime." Hollis leaned back in, whispering in his ear. "Why don't we get fucked up and fuck each other's brains out."

Cyrus pushed her away, saying no means no.

Hollis reached for her socks, working one on. "Mean you never think about it?"

Cyrus held a hand to the TV. "Yeah." Connors was free and had his gun now. "And I think I could do it, get hard, have sex with a woman, get off, maybe even enjoy it."

Hollis stopped working her sock. "But?"

"It'd truly be against code."

"Code, there's a code says we can't help each other out?"

"Unwritten," Cyrus said. "Wouldn't stand well. Deviant, the community would say."

"Thanks." Hollis started pulling her sock up again. "Deviant, thanks a lot."

Connors was pumping the Winchester, one of the earlier automatic weapons. Somewhere in the mix was a moral lesson. The more Cyrus thought, herb soothing, Lucas seemed to be saying don't let people fuck with you on your own turf.

***

Veronica had her back to the table, sticking a barbecue fork through the grill, making sure to turn every part of that yellow sheet of paper into ash.

"So how'd you do Cyrus?" Claire said.

Covering a smile, Veronica didn't want to appear smug, so she kept her back to them, saying she'd been thinking about it, then did it kind of impromptu. Cyrus' keys were on his desk, so she took the opportunity, grabbing them when she saw Claire go to the green room. After that, she ran up to Arlene's office, opening the locked drawer then the safe inside with keys she'd copied from Arlene's chain while using the Cherokee during rehearsals, grabbing the cash.

There was no one out in the lot—other than Sundance smoking up behind the kiosk, singing "Fast Car" with Tracy Chapman, should've heard him—when Veronica put the cash in Cyrus' trunk, Cyrus' keys back on his desk. In all, it took about your average commercial break before she was back in the studio, standing behind Meckler like she'd never left.

"How about the naked Billy Idol pictures?" Claire said. "You plant those, too? Because if you planted those, I know what it's like to have unauthorized photos made public, and I know—"

Veronica stopped Claire, facing her to say she saw the envelope in the trunk, but didn't open it, that she didn't have time. And well, she wouldn't know how to procure naked pictures of Billy Idol, which was probably a good thing. She planted the cash, yes, but that was it.

"You do that for us, too?" Claire said. "Another favor."

"I did it for myself," Veronica said. "Cyrus was the last person left on Arlene's side, a classic divide and conquer thing. That's why I wanted to draw the police in while the bird was there. Get your cop friend in the building without a warrant so he could hopefully find the damn bird and keep them both occupied. I knew she'd want police in for the stolen petty cash."

"So it worked," Claire said.

"Better than I could've hoped. Arlene will be dealing with this for the rest of the shoot, meaning nobody will be watching me."

Nathan said, "So who was the courier came and ruined my book?"

"Just a courier." Veronica shrugged. "Guy I know from a cafe here in Cabbagetown."

Claire motioned to Nathan. "Means you kind of set us up, too. Used us as a diversion."

"One of those MacGuffins, Hitchcock would call it," Nathan added.

Veronica stepped one foot under the table, sat down. "I gave you both an alibi."

Alibi, huh? Between all these favors—two pretty white girls doing right by Nathan—he decided maybe the situation did have some markings of entrapment. Course, both women had their reasons, but he felt out on a branch, thinking it best to have his own paper. Speaking to Veronica, he said, "You prepare the lemon-pepper catfish yourself?"

"Yes." Veronica looked at him, the way he avoided her eyes. "Why?"

"May I please have the recipe?" Nathan pushed the yellow pad of paper to her. "Lemon pepper catfish *à la* Veronica."

Veronica pulled the pencil from behind her ear, said sure, writing it out.

Again with the lemon pepper, Claire thought. Well, if he wanted lemon pepper, she wasn't his kind of girl and that's all there was to it. Like maybe that bitch could use the inside of the stove and bake him muffins every day, too, fatten his skinny ass up.

20

Friday, June 30

Nathan arrived on set about three hours after Veronica, before eight, going through his breakfast routine—nuts and twigs and stuff, blueberry yogurt, OJ, and a peanut butter granola bar—then he went out to the lot, adjusting pylons and taking his place.

In his kiosk, he noticed the brick's indicator, another message from Larry Something saying he might have a flight. Waiting for a return number, getting none, Nathan disconnected and powered up the 6in1 Radio Lantern, pulling a face when the DJ promised spiritually conscious rhymes as if Nathan was going to be saved by Christian rap. Man, he wanted background music, instrumentals, so he turned the dial, picking up BBC News on the part-time jazz station. Didn't CJRT have enough volunteers to run programming? No, they had to run free content like this just to stay on the air. And *tabernac*, Nathan couldn't believe what he was hearing. Some wonk, with the snobbiest little accent, was reporting a claim, deadpan, by China's defense ministry, stating that no one had been killed at Tiananmen Square, not a single person.

Ever since initial reports almost four weeks ago now, Nathan had been zoning out on the details. Not that it mattered, the way BBC eggheads were droning on about intellectuals, dissidents, and democracy. In short, people were massacred for reading the wrong books, singing the wrong songs, thinking the wrong thoughts, and saying the wrong things. That was the point Nathan kept coming back to while the BBC used flowery language to describe a body count now ranging from zero, apparently, to thousands upon thousands upon thousands.

When another voice came in, Nathan turned the static off. He felt shame for figuratively looking away, thinking he should know, that everybody should. But around Cherry Beach Studios, nobody seemed interested in the front section of the papers delivered every day. So long as sports and entertainment didn't go missing, everyone was, like, you know, awesome. China? Sudan? Those places seemed worlds away, only rating for a mention if Abel thought he could dumb down their cultures enough to turn them into the butt of a joke.

Thinking how life here seemed to go on and on and on, despite it all, Nathan decided to have a go at *The Toronto Star* crossword. He was chewing on his pencil, trying to come up with a five-letter word for tropical resin when a familiar evergreen MGB needing a paint job pulled up. Dan Meckler was inside, UB40 seeping from the speakers, "Red Red Wine."

"It's Najam, is it?"

"Nathan, sir."

"Sorry, I know a parking spot is like the New Jerusalem around here, so I had an idea."

"An idea, sir?" Nathan frowned, thinking at least the guy shaved today. Smelled good, too, lemony yet antiseptic, like Pledge. "For the parking?"

"That's right, for the parking." Meckler was careful to talk slowly and evenly so this Najam could follow. "If you simply change the direction of all the pylons and have everyone park north-south as opposed to east-west, I bet you could add as many as a dozen spots."

"That a fact?" Nathan scanned the lot. Yeah, this was a good idea. "Many as a dozen?"

"That's right, all you need to do is have everyone park north-south. Can you do that, Najam? Can you do that for me?"

"Mr. Meckler?" Nathan could barely ignore it, Meckler referring to him as Najam again, the prick. "You are *Monsieur* Meckler, right?"

Meckler nodded, yeah, he was Meckler, impatient.

"Well," Nathan said, checking out the bondo-and-primer spots on Meckler's B. "I'm thinking maybe it'd be best if you stuck to the directing—helluva job, as I understand it, lots of personalities, disorders—and I stuck to the parking. Keep everyone focused on their respective tasks at hand, their specialties."

Christ almighty, Meckler said Najam just didn't want to re-arrange the pylons, lazy, and that he'd talk to Arlene. That she was Najam's superior, yes, but he, Meckler, was also Najam's superior. Then he slapped his ride into drive and said God was going to get Najam for this.

***

Ever since Cyrus smoked a little dope last night and chilled, he was glad he hadn't gone postal. Why bugger up his own life any worse? No, his revenge would be following Oscar Wilde's advice and living well, finding something better. Once Cyrus came around to that way of thinking, he began to appreciate the idea of starting fresh on a Friday, like Hollis said, getting business done while the slackers were winding down. Yeah, he'd get his own spin out there while Arlene and her busy bodies were scrambling to replace an irreplaceable man.

Thumbing through his index cards, he called Takeaway Films. Denny Duguay wasn't in, which was just a well. Cyrus was hearing static on the cordless, so he didn't want to leave a message, a bad impression. Instead, he hung up, made a mental note to catch up with Denny.

Moving to the living room, he sat on the gingham Ralph Lauren sofa that fell off one of Arlene's trucks when she was in rehab, allowing himself a laugh. Fuck sakes, when did he last have a laugh? In hindsight, maybe this whole thing was just as well, he thought. Picking up a green dial phone—it was going to be vintage soon, almost—he tried Mick Grier at Roundhouse Productions. Grier was in a meeting, so Cyrus left a message. Same with Joey Ryan at Guardrail Films, as well as Kira Paige at Citizen, Dean, and Associates.

Cyrus said cocksucker out loud when he got an automated message at The Gary Orange Project. Looks like everyone's winding down for the weekend, he thought. Switching to the cordless, hitting 231, Orange's extension, waiting though the personal greeting—today's date, how Toronto's high was going to 31 but with the humidex it was going to feel more like 35. It was the long way, Cyrus thought, of Orange saying he was screening his calls.

"Hi Gary, it's Cyrus. Listen, I was remembering what you said a while back and thought maybe a change would be truly good. If you could give me a shout, here, that'd be great. Let me give you my number . . ."

***

The green room was said to be ready when Sundance waved from the van, delivering Vanity from Cherry Beach Sound, just around the corner. She hadn't had a hit since "Pretty Mess," and her last LP, *Skin on Skin*, failed to chart, so she was putting down demos and trying to score another record deal. That's why she was available to *The Otto Show*. That's also why she was 45 minutes late for a bit on underwear models pushing cigarettes. She had one line— "You think Joe Camel knows what to do with this?"—and nailed every take. Nonetheless, for the next hour she posed in a gold chain-edged bikini, repeating herself and sharing cigarettes with Abel. He was dressed as the Marlboro Man, rubbing his tan chaps against her from behind, blowing smoke.

Outside, it had to be a hundred degrees, whatever that came to in metric. Nathan didn't know by reason of the golf world still worked under the old system, but there was a smog alert, too. Despite the battery-operated fan, he was cranky by reason of he'd drank too much yesterday, thick tongue. The dull pains in his head made it difficult to tolerate the little things, like background performer JD Heyman waiting for his bit out in the lot, always in motion.

First Heyman was telling Nathan about his girl problems, a dispute over credit card bills. Going into intimate details—her full name, Nancy Something, how she always smelled like celery— when Nathan said he didn't want to hear it. After that, Heyman had his shirt off, his torso a perfectly sculpted mass of electrolyzed flesh. Throwing punches at an imaginary speed bag, bobbing, making deep, guttural man noises like he really was hitting somebody.

Nathan looked away, turning the battery-operated fan up, fiddling with the radio until he couldn't take it anymore. "Hey skins." Pointing to his headset. "They got a bet on the two-way."

Heyman stopped, waiting for the rest.

"They're trying to figure out who you're coming on to, feinting and jabbing like that," Nathan said. "Me, the cop, or the head lady in charge?"

"Talent doesn't sell." Heyman chin-pointed at the building. "They want me this way."

"Tragic flaw. A waste of your skill by reason of they can't see it, you looking so good."

Back to the part-time jazz station, Nathan caught a BBC item revolving around "the winds of change" being fanned by Mikhail Gorbachev's *glasnost.* Apparently, in a speech on Soviet Central TV, Gorby declared that his economic transformations would go hand in hand with freedom of expression and democratic elections, among other rights.

For a moment, the Cyrus situation, coupled with the BBC report, inspired Nathan to dream up a skit in which former president Ronald Reagan was handing over a file to the new president, George Bush, containing naked pictures of a young Gorbachev, thus guaranteeing his complicity in destroying the USSR and ending the Cold War.

Nathan giggled at his topical funny, making a mental note to pitch it to Abel. Then, glancing at Heyman, Nathan thought better of it, telling himself to just be the parking guy. That getting these assholes to park between the pylons was job enough. Along with AIDS and the *menace nucléaire* everyone learned to live with, it did indeed seem that people here were detached from the rest of the world and rapidly losing interest. They just wanted to be reassured that things were getting better, that the Americans were on it, and well, Nathan figured, at best, Abel would dumb it down into something else entirely to avoid sharing credit, so why bother?

Switching the radio off, Nathan turned his attention to the introduction of Ian Adams' *S: Portrait of a Spy.* It was the second Virgo edition, updated with shattering new material:

Did the KGB infiltrate the RCMP?

Did the CIA know? And who is S anyway?

It was all very fascinating. Still, Nathan couldn't help but think he would've been more into it, if only the book had a big-boned

Mountie girl shooting off her *pistolet* on the cover. Someone to back up this S fellow, Nathan thought, deciding to give his other book a try, a James Dark novel, which did have a hot chick on the cover, promising explosive results, when his brick went off. Plucking it off the ledge, he hit talk, hello.

"How about I come over tonight?" It was Claire, waving a cigarette from the far end of lot, holding her phone in the other hand. "Your turn to entertain, cook."

"*Oui.*" He wondered why she didn't walk over and ask. "Only let's make it tomorrow."

"Why, you got a date? Plans?"

"Just let's make it tomorrow," Nathan said, distracted by another alpha car coming at him. "Have to go, have a customer."

When the 1971 Galaxie 500 pulled up, he looked at the man inside, big hands turning the steering wheel into a plate. He had a prematurely grey Princeton cut, dark flecks. "Heathcliffe Wilson," he said, leaning through the window, blinking stardust eyes. "For Arlene Marion."

Nathan nodded once. "The Heathcliffe Wilson?"

"The Heathcliffe Wilson. Bet you thought I was black."

"No sir. Used to be a big CFL fan."

"Oh yeah? Who won the Grey Cup last year?"

Nathan said he didn't know, emphasizing that he used to be a fan, a Montreal Concordes booster, but that he hadn't really followed the CFL since the team folded. That when the Montreal team came back under the old name—the new Alouettes, they were calling them—he didn't want to invest in something that might not last.

"It's okay," Heathcliffe said. "Everyone thinks I'm black. Just admit you thought it because of my name. That, and the fried chicken. That's how everyone knows me—the chicken."

Nathan looked off, Heyman back to bobbing and jabbing. "I saw you play, sir."

"That a fact? When? Where?"

"Olympic Stadium, 1983. Saw you miss four field goals against Saskatchewan. That's when I knew."

Heathcliffe said, "Knew what?"

Tabernac, Nathan was trying to be diplomatic, but what the hell? Heathcliffe Wilson was asking an honest question, albeit by reason of which Nathan didn't know, so he was going to get an honest answer. At least that's what Nathan was going to tell Arlene if Heathcliffe complained. "That's when I knew no self-respecting black man would miss four field goals in one game, not that I'd heard. You ever heard of a brother missing four straight?"

"No," Wilson said, "but that doesn't mean it hasn't happened."

"Just not that either of us are aware of."

Shit, shit, shit—Heathcliffe wasn't in yet and he was already kicking around the parking guy, only he, Heathcliffe, was getting the boot. Speaking stiffly, he said, again, he was here to see Arlene Marion, that they had a 12:30.

Nathan pressed his talk button. "Nathan for *Madame* Marion."

He heard a click in his ear, then, "Go for Arlene, and speak English."

And there it was, again. Thinking it was no wonder the pepsies back home were dreaming up militant French-only sign laws, Nathan said, "It's not on the sked, but the Heathcliffe Wilson is here, says you two have a 12:30."

Fishhooks, Arlene forgot. She told Nathan to get Heathcliffe that nice spot near the doors. She would be right down.

***

Cyrus finished off a corned beef sandwich, wiping away a dab of mustard when his phone finally rang. Looking at the cordless, he thought about making for the real phone in the living room, washing down his last bite with some water, expecting the phone to ring again. When it didn't, he grabbed the cordless instead, hit talk, hello.

Nothing.

"Gary?" Cyrus said. "Hello?" Banging the phone on his kitchen table, putting it to his ear. "Hello?" Banging some more, banging until he noticed the mouthpiece swirling around his feet on the sheen black and white tiles. He said no, quietly at first, then shouted it, NO.

***

By the time Heathcliffe Wilson pulled into spot five, Arlene was pep-stepping over, telling JD Heyman to put his shirt on and stop punching. He looked like the boy next door to those guys who strip to their tuxedo cuffs. Is that what he was going for? Before JD could say Chippendales, Arlene was greeting Heathcliffe, ushering him inside, telling him Vanity was in the building, that he might get lucky and meet her. First, they went upstairs for a one-on-one Mexican lunch in the dining room where Toledo Marseilles was serving tacos, taco salads, handmade tortilla chips, salsa. Two Löwenbräu—a bottle and a can—had been set next to pint glass, special.

"Thing about Mexican cuisine is it's all the same," Heathcliffe said, digging in, food already in his mouth. "You have your lettuce, tomatoes, refried beans, cheeses, and meats with papery bread or a hard shell for a wrap, then something hot and cold for dipping." Toledo tempered himself, turning away as Heathcliffe selected the green bottle over the can, tilting it, reading the aqua and gold label. "And why Löwenbräu?"

"Your car." Arlene looked at him, tugging at her side curls, flirty. "A man who drives a Galaxie 500 has to be a Löwenbräu man."

"Very nice." Heathcliffe took a pull on the bottle. "Anyway, we're both busy, so how about we settle this matter about the birds and get back to the things we do. Business, for me."

Arlene picked up on it. The sonofabitch said birds, plural. Taking a breath, she said she was operating on the understanding that everything had been returned, and she wanted to say, personally, how sorry and embarrassed everybody at AMA was over—

Heathcliffe cut her off. "Compressor came back broke and the bird has a hole the size of one of those Gremlin heads. Not the gay Gremlin, I mean the one voiced by Howie Mandel."

Arlene bit down, thinking the Gremlins' craniums were the same size, and she couldn't recall their sexualities being an issue. But fine, she'd buy a new bird, get him out of here. "If you say it, I believe it." She brought her veined hands together. "You are a man of honor, a football legend, and we at AMA will gladly pay to have your bird replaced."

A legend, Heathcliffe thought. She was already blowing ultra-violet up his ass, so he tapped on the table. "This is the third bird, plus compressor, stolen from one of my shops. Your boy was caught, and I want restitution times three. Give me restitution times three, I drop the charges."

"The set man has been fired," Arlene said. "Out of respect to you. He was resourceful. He could get things, but he was a $300-a-day thief. He stole from you, my business neighbor, and that is why he was fired. It is the same thing as stealing from me, if he steals from you."

Heartfelt as that was, Heathcliffe understood Cyrus was rip-ping-off Arlene as well. Bottom line, Heathcliffe was out three birds, not one, noting that the last was taken by a fox from Arlene's den, and did she understand the ramifications? This was someone working on her behalf. Legally, Heathcliffe said that made Arlene an agent of sorts to Cyrus. After that, Arlene, knowing the bird was stolen, stood by while it was made part of a sketch in this here comedy show she was profiting from.

Arlene said, "Why do you even think you know all that?"

Heathcliffe remembered what his brother-in-law told him about keeping his name out of it, something about conflict-of-interest. "Doesn't matter how, just that I do. I also know that I can have that sketch with my bird killed in one phone call."

"Killed?" Arlene dug in. The prick didn't know who he was dealing with. "Mr. Wilson, I am a reasonable woman negotiating in good faith. But you are threatening me with things you cannot back up. That is not good faith. That is extortion."

21

After his initial outburst, Cyrus tried waiting patiently. He figured the lost call was for sure Gary Orange getting back, that Gary was the type of guy who worked Fridays, that someone walked in while Gary was calling and put him off. Cyrus, not wanting to seem desperate, knew he ought to keep waiting, but he couldn't stop himself. If that really was Gary, it was the closest thing to a callback—a truly good prospect—and Cyrus needed a new gig as much as the re-affirmations.

Cyrus dialed on his good phone, saying piss when he got the switchboard's recorded message. Waiting through every option before being routed to the operator as a dial customer. Establishing human contact, finally, asking for 231, Cyrus was patched through, hearing another ring, then the voice. "Gary Orange."

"Gary, it's Cyrus."

"Cyrus who?"

Cyrus who? For Pete's sake, Gary. "Cyrus Dagan."

"Oh, Cyrus. I was just going to call again. Called you a few minutes ago, then Pam came in and things got hairy, sorry. What's up? I mean, isn't *The Otto Show* shooting?"

"Long story. I wanted to talk to you about that thing that you mentioned."

"Let me get this straight—you quit AMA?"

"It truly is more complicated, a crucial difference of opinion." There, Cyrus hadn't managed to trap himself in a lie, ass covered.

"Yeah," Gary said tentatively, voice falling. "The lady likes her pastels, I hear you. But that thing we talked about, I hired someone. Obviously, I had to move on that."

"Oh."

Then Gary picked up, hope in his voice. "But we have a little action from TVO, some money to do something on historic dwellings, *Original Homes of Ontario*."

"Oh." Cyrus said, feeling optimistic himself.

The dilemma with *Original Homes of Ontario*, Gary said, was that while the *nouveau riche* could meet the expenses of one, their furnishings rarely jived, and, in fact, were often gauche. Which was why Gary could use a guy like Cyrus, someone to dress the original homes up properly, originally. "You want?"

"I want," Cyrus said, leveling out. "Would be a nice change, truly."

"Just one thing. It's publicly funded, so it's not the same pay, $180 a day."

Cyrus thought about it. Okay, he'd do it special for Gary, but it would be more next time.

"Also, we're going to have to do something with your title. Government's sure to question why we need a set director for historic dwelling segments. We'll have to call you a location scout, something like that."

Cyrus closed his eyes. "I thought you said there was just one thing, Gary."

***

"Extortion?" Finally, Heathcliffe was in control, enjoying himself, leaning back, crossing his legs, and challenging Arlene to, legally, frame this as such. "Go on."

"You are telling me you can have the sketch killed," she said. "You are a powerful man, and I respect your power. But you know you cannot do that."

"Laws, likely retroactive, are coming so you can't profit from crime—entertainment-wise, movies, books." Heathcliffe took a pull on his Löwenbräu, swallowed. "In fact, civil courts are anticipating these laws, taking a dim view of people making crime pay, and providing restitution for victims via existing libel law."

Arlene moved her lower jaw back and forth, the guy talking more legalese. If he wanted to go there, fine, this was her wheel well. "Not that this is my crime, but what about the hippie junkie from the Stopwatch Gang? The bank robber, he wrote a book a few years ago, an autobiography, and got around all this, some said, by calling it a novel, fiction."

"Great read." Heathcliffe rubbed behind his ear. "*Jackrabbit Parole* by Stephen Reid. I tore through it in two sittings, always a good sign. Now, autobiographical as it may be—"

"I read it." Arlene jabbed herself with an index. "And I am telling you it is his life story, a few things changed to make himself, a hardcore drug addict and career criminal, look good."

Heathcliffe said that was his exact point. Reid wouldn't be able to write that book today. If he did, nobody would publish it. See, his book was published before legislators, courts, and lawyers got their hooks in, meaning criminals profiting from crime by creating content around it were in for a rough ride going forward. And in case Arlene hadn't noticed, Reid hadn't written a book since. Even the one he had written was mysteriously difficult to find. Heathcliffe had to order his copy special through This Ain't The Rosedale Library, which carried anything, including a manual on how to safely electrocute one's nipples during watersports.

"See, politicians got involved because Clifford Olson threatened to write about killing those kids," Heathcliffe said, recalling his lawyer's points. "Buy some groceries for his fam, Cliff said. Now, until some of this gets through Ottawa and Queen's Park— it could take years—civil courts are stepping in, de-facto-style, to prevent criminals, Cyrus, in this case, and their agents, you, from making crime pay by selling their stories or making videos. Doubly, courts are ensuring that offenders and agents can't profit from mocking victims. That's my lawyer's interpretation of the present civil climate. And you're mocking me, dammit, saying my chicken's rubber, gets girls fat, neither of which pass a libel sniff test. If you were in America, the First Amendment might protect you. But you're not in Kansas, Arlene, no free speech here."

Heathcliffe's lawyer was itching to argue—technically, he had precedents, co-comparators—and was waiting on Heathcliffe's say so. So far, Heathcliffe wasn't saying so. In fact, he was holding back, telling Arlene it didn't have to come to court. But if she didn't pay for three birds and compressors, he was going to let his lawyer loose, hire an investigator. Maybe he'd find something supporting new claims against Arlene, her company. If there were other victims, he'd look into making it a class-action thing, bury Arlene in costs, take her out to sea.

Personally, Arlene said she fought against using Heathcliffe's bird, tried to protect him, and she had witnesses to that effect.

Thanks, but as Heathcliffe understood, Arlene was in charge of Cyrus, responsible, and paid cash. Maybe he'd have his investigator dig into that, too. People paying cash, that's the kind of people had something to hide. Either way, Heathcliffe was going to get his restitution.

"Well I don't think you—"

"Don't underestimate me," Heathcliffe said. "How do you think it got this far? Your boy is charged with all kinds of things— theft, assaulting a cop."

Arlene rubbed her temples. "You cannot reasonably expect me to pay for three."

"I'm three rubber birds short and three hot air compressors. If you don't give me money for three of each, I make this a personal project, understand?" Heathcliffe waved his hand across the table. "Bugger up your whole episode, force you to shoot something else."

Thinking he watched too much *Matlock*, Arlene said, "What do you want?"

Heathcliffe said 25K would cover his birds, compressors, time, and loss of enjoyment.

Arlene considered arguing, then said, "I am making you a take-it-or-leave-it offer of 20K, payable the day after we finish shooting, July 7th. A judge, I promise, would find that more than commensurate for a man who can prove our staff took a single bird. But please understand that my offer carries stipulations."

Here we go, Heathcliffe thought. "What's the catch?"

"This is all under the table, cash, and I want your word that (A) this is the end of it, civilly, and (B) you are going to stick by the criminal charges against Cyrus, testify."

"Sure," Heathcliffe said. "Just because it's criminal, it doesn't have to be civil, but why?"

"Just see that you support his prosecution."

Okay, if she was deep-sixing Cyrus, Heathcliffe would cooperate. He wanted a pound of flesh, too, and who was to say Cyrus didn't steal all three? If he stole all three, he probably got away with a raft of unrelated atrocities. Doubly, if Arlene paid under the table, Heathcliffe could charge the insurance, make some real money, all tax-free, and what was so wrong with that?

"Twenty thousand, cash," he said, extending his right hand. "July 7th."

***

No one else was phoning back—lots of backed up business, it seemed, a Friday, or maybe everyone really was winding down—but Cyrus was okay with that. He was taking the rest of the day off himself, lounging on the couch. Even the fact that he couldn't find a pack of rolling papers didn't set him off.

"Improvise," he told himself.

Pulling a pad of yellow sticky notes off the mantel, rolling a joint with one, lighting up, he drew hard, surprised the bleached paper didn't cause increased irritation. Fuck, he was a resourceful guy. That's why he was landing on his feet, and so what if it wasn't a rich gig? He'd be back working, renewing lapsed contacts. He was thinking this whole mess would barely graze him when the phone rang. Grabbing the dial phone at his feet, he laid back, staring at the stucco ceiling. Of all the places he'd had, each one had the same ceiling. "Hello," he said, half-expecting to hear Gary Orange with further details. Instead, a more officious voice replied.

"Hello, Mr. Dagan. Orest F. Jefferies here."

"Yes, sir." Sitting up on the couch, Cyrus held the phone with both hands. "Good news?"

"Afraid not, son. Arlene Marion wants to revoke your bail. You know what that means?"

"No. I didn't even know she could do that."

"Means you've got to come up with $10,000 or go to jail and wait to appear."

Cyrus thought about it. That would leave him with like six-grand, and how long was he supposed to make that last? Goddammit, why had he put so much into the car? "By when?"

"July 7th, pay day. Arlene still owes you a little something. She'll take that off, plus you have to give her another eight or so, thereabouts. All entirely legal, paperwork, everything. Or, you can wait until she revokes and post yourself. But it's simpler to just pay her the difference."

"Fine," said Cyrus. "In the meantime, what do I do for a lawyer?"

"Oh, I'm still your lawyer on the criminal matter—no conflict there—so long as you and Arlene part amicably. But if you're down to what it sounds like, I don't think you can pay. If that's the case, I can arrange for a court-appointed—"

"I already have a new gig," Cyrus said.

"Collateral?"

Cyrus took a deep breath. "My Impala."

"Year?"

"1960."

"Condition?"

"Pristine, just back from its summer makeover, new paint, the chrome re-chromed, everything touched up. I finally found the matching ashtray, too, original."

Jefferies said just a moment, Cyrus listening as Arlene's big-shot lawyer flipped through pages, the 1989 *Kelley Blue Book*, most likely. A minute or two later, Jefferies said, "Bring it to AMA on the 7th, 10:45 am sharp. We'll work out the paperwork."

"Fine."

"And Cyrus?"

"Yeah?"

"I'm a good lawyer, so don't worry. This is going to work itself out. Just a question."

"Go ahead."

"Where did you say that cop faked the assault an officer?"

Cyrus paused, said, "Behind an abandoned gas station, the old Total station, why?"

"Never mind. Just where, exactly, did you say McNab hit him-self?"

"The old commie, I told you. McNab pounded his head against the old commie's face."

Orest didn't say anything for a few seconds, reading his notes.

"Look Cyrus, I thought you said he hit himself on the wall and then said dammit. Your story is changing."

"I'm telling you the commie guy's face was on the wall, graffiti—a stencil job. DAMMIT! was the artist's tag. That's exactly where McNab hit himself, and that's exactly what I told you."

***

After shaking Arlene's hand, Heathcliffe bit into another taco, dripping onto his lap. "This is why I don't wear $1,200 suits."

Twelve-hundred-dollar suits—Arlene checked out his golf shirt. The zipper leading up to his collar would have made it kind of bitchin'. As it was, with the cartoon chicken logo and taco stains, it looked he was due back at the deep-fryer. "Why is that?"

"Bad investment." Heathcliffe pushed the rest of his meal away. "One sloppy taco, one drippy drumstick, you're out $1,200. Makes it a bad investment for a man works in food."

Wiping his mouth, he said he had some important restaurant business to attend to. Happy to be rid of him, Arlene took him by the hand, flirty again, pulling at her side curls, leading. They passed the green room on the way. A pissed-off woman was inside, speaking sharply, loud and clear, complaining about a used condom behind the beer fridge. Heathcliffe pointed at the door. "The voice, is that Vanity?"

Arlene held her breath, nodding.

Narrowing his eyes, Heathcliffe said, "What's she doing looking behind the fridge? We get people at the restaurants saying they found something nasty behind a radiator, trying to get free wings. I say, 'Do you look behind your radiator at home?' They say no—stupid. I say, 'Well, don't do it here. And why would you do something in my house you don't do at home?'"

Arlene nodded again, thinking she was lucky to get rid of the loon this cheap. "When you leave, could you please tell the parking man he can take lunch. I will send someone to cover."

Yeah, for 20-thou, cash, Heathcliffe would do that, too. Noticing a zip in his step on the way to the Galaxie, he keyed his ignition and listened to that baby purr like it was 1971. With a flick, he had the radio on, National Velvet's "Flesh Under Skin." The song had been in rotation for months, but Heathcliffe didn't make much of it until he saw the video on MuchMusic, this goth, Maria del Mar, close-ups of her mouth singing about the conflict of sin. Healthcliffe remembered her as a cigarette girl in the clubs, and he'd been interested in her music ever since connecting the dots, her subtle widow's peak, of all things, making him crazy, hot.

He recalled enough lyrics to keep up, singing along as he backed out. Putting the Galaxie into drive, the song faded, DJ saying National Velvet would play Edgefest tomorrow. Heathcliffe considered making the trek to Barrie, then decided to catch her at an intimate venue here in town, somewhere he might have a chance to chat her up, lowering the volume as he pulled up to the kiosk. The sight of the parking guy brought Heathcliffe back to that terrible day at Olympic Stadium, 1983. "Guess everyone else's eaten," he said.

Nathan blinked. "Why do you guess that?"

Heathcliffe looked at the book the guy was reading, *The Bamboo Bomb*, Asian sexpot on the cover. Hello, Heathcliffe was right there, and the creep wasn't even covering that he had the porn. "Your boss says it's your turn to eat." Heathcliffe thought back, the fans mocking him, chanting shit *la merde*. "That someone will cover." Leaning to the passenger side, he flipped open his glove compartment, producing a coupon, handing it to Nathan. "Two for one chicken and ribs until Labor Day. Bring your girlfriend. You do have a girlfriend, right?"

Nathan took the coupon, looking at it. "I'm not really sure."

"What does that mean?" Healthcliffe said. "You're not really sure."

"Not sure means I'm not really sure."

"Are you unsure of yourself?"

Nathan thought on it, said, "Maybe. Kind of like when you missed four straight field goals. Bet you were pretty unsure of yourself that day, huh?"

22

Nathan took the night off from Claire to nurse his hangover. It wasn't that he didn't want to see her. Just that they'd been together most nights since their first, and he was due time alone at whatever he was calling home these days. Along with the 11-inch Candle TV rendered useless, this Larry had hundreds of LPs stacked around the room at various heights, good standard stuff—John Lee Hooker, Oscar Peterson, Stan Getz—but the record player was spinning faster than 33 1/3 rotations per minute. That left Nathan listening to the part-time jazz station with the stones to spin Perry Como, the DJ saying send money soon or there won't be any "Paper Moon."

At least this Larry had an interesting little library. Nailed crookedly to the wall, painted tomato-red, were the corkboard remains of a kitchen cabinet, swinging open to reveal Larry's pride, four rows of rare and out-of-print spy paperbacks, each individually sealed in plastic.

As much as the James Bond covers had pretty girls, Nathan didn't get excited by reason of he'd seen the movies. Opting for the next best thing, he was into today's back-up book, a bit obscure, James Dark's *Bamboo Bomb*. The poor man's 007 was stiffing some knock-out for dinner in Singapore when Nathan heard three quick knocks, a pause, then two slow knocks.

"Police, open up."

Biting the inside of his cheek, marking his page with a Big Slice napkin, Nathan placed the book on the coffee table as he crossed the room. Opening up to find Claire in maroon gym shorts *avec* white piping, a matching top with Volleyball '89 stenciled across her chest, nice.

"What?" Her green-brown eyes were dull, a sheen of perspiration across her cheeks. "You going to let me in?"

Smelling beer, Nathan stepped aside, motioning Claire into the one-room unit. She stepped out of her PJ Flyers, toes squishy on the brown shag. Musty, she said, figuring that a light hue of blue paint had turned grey. Half-dead plants all over the place, a golf club next to the door, probably that Pittsburgh Persimmon he was on about. "So now I get it." Looking past the balcony into a Green P parking lot. "You didn't want me to see your place, the shame."

"It's not that bad."

"It's a dump, not even an interesting dump." She sniffed. "Just a dump smells like crackhead pets, rats, probably roaches, and other vermin, topped off with a dollop of curry."

Nathan thought she really was his grandma. "Not the kind of pad you take a girl you want to impress, no."

"How about a drink? Offer a girl a cold drink on a hot night, that's sure to impress."

"I have both kinds, cans and bottles." Nathan nodded to the antiquated fridge, big chrome handle. "Get one for me while you're in there."

She made for the fridge, opening it, makeshift rows of Löwenbräu, looking back at Nathan. "I drink one of these, it makes me accessory after the fact."

"What?"

"What—you're stealing from Arlene already."

"Busted," Nathan said. "Unless you want to become an accessory after the fact."

Sure enough, she did, opening two Löwenbräu. On her way to the couch, BBC News chimed in. However many died at Tiananmen, Claire said it was depressing, that there was nothing they could do. As for the Soviet situation, she figured that was resolving itself, that the wall would fall like The Gipper said. And yes, they had to talk about the hundred-thousand Americans living with AIDS, of course, but what were they supposed to do? Stop fucking? Stop living? Like, why couldn't they just dial into CHUM 104.5 FM and get down to life?

Nathan thought his girl was right, that he should let go, listen to something fun, so he turned the tuner where she wanted it, and Goddammit if they didn't get lucky.

"I know this one," he said, finding a grove on the plodding beat. "Fine Young Cannibals."

"'Good Thing.'" Claire jumped up to join him, Löwenbräu in hand. "New number one in the U.S. Means it's also number one here, or that it will be, probably."

"Second best number one this year, behind Elvis Costello." Nathan grabbed Claire's beer, took a slug, handed it back. "These guys are all black, right, the musicians."

No, Claire told him, just the singer. And hey, why would Nathan go right to black?

They laughed, put their arms around each other, and danced.

"Good Thing" faded into the new soundtrack anthem, "Batdance." Nathan thought it had range for a pop tune, more of a funk jam actually, so he had to do some improvisation, the way Prince kept changing beats and styles. Along with Jack Nicholson, Claire shouted "This town needs an enema." They caught their breath during a PSA—Corey Hart counselling youth to butt-out—then kind of lost it, throwing it down after the DJ came back with "You Shook Me All Night Long." And when Brian Johnson got to the refrain, Claire started shaking her *seins* like Nathan had never seen a natural-walking woman shake her *seins*. Working double time, she pushed his face into those 36Cs, mine all mine, when someone pounded on the floor from below. At that, Nathan dialed down the volume and they fell into the couch.

By two, seven Löwenbräu were scattered on the coffee table pushed up against the wall. The Berber couch was folded out, Claire sitting on the edge, fighting out of her Volleyball '89 tank top. Below, Nathan was on his knees, pulling down her matching shorts when they heard someone playing with the lock.

"Expecting company?" Claire whispered.

"Not even."

Pulling her shorts up, she made a shush sign, grabbing the Pittsburgh Persimmon, standing next to the door when it opened. A tired-looking kid with curly brown hair—so curly it looked like pubic hair—stood in the frame with a big backpack on his shoulder. Stoned, Claire thought, and looking for something to steal so he could sell it and get stoned again.

First, he got the Pittsburgh Persimmon to what Claire called the groinal region—oof. He sort of doubled over, but was still on his feet when Claire came up with a right to his jaw. That knocked him upright, back, stumbling into the hall, falling over. Neighbors peeking, she was standing over him in her maroon bra and matching gym shorts, poised with the Pittsburgh Persimmon when Nathan said stop—that's Larry.

"Larry?" Claire said. "Larry's why you don't want me to visit? You some kind of sissy?"

"My sublet landlord, Larry Something, I told you. And you're not too PC about it now." Nathan turned to Larry. "The fuck're you doing breaking in late like a clumsy cat burglar? You're not due, nobody said."

"I found what I was looking for."

"And what was that?"

"A standby flight, cheap."

"Whatever, you rented out the place to me."

"That's why I'm here, need it back. Did you get my messages? And hey." Larry pointed at his naked copy of *The Bamboo Bomb* on the coffee table. "I told you those are off-limits."

Nathan waved that away. "Don't even. I got four messages saying you might be coming back some time, no mention of money."

Claire looked at Nathan. "You got paperwork says you sublet?"

"Of course, I hand over $1,700, I get something tangible, a receipt."

Back at Larry, Claire said, "You heard him, he's got the place, see you in a few weeks."

Larry reached into his pocket, pulling out a bankroll. If Nathan left now, Larry would give him $425. Claire took it, told him to stand in the hall, they'd talk about it. Outside? Like, this was Larry's lodge. Not yet, Claire said. Okay, but could Larry have his money until it was settled? Nope, Claire was trained as an impartial third-person party and she would hold it as part of the dispute-resolution-mechanism-process-thingy.

As Larry shuffled into the hall, Claire pulled her Volleyball top over her head and sat on the edge of the hide-a-bed, adjusting herself. "Look, I don't want you to take this the wrong way. I've known you what, a week?"

"And?"

And, well listen. While Claire cared for Nathan in that still-getting-to-know-each-other way, she was just saying this was a good excuse for him to get out of here, out of St. Jamestown.

"I mean, it's musty."

Musty? If only the girl could go down on herself the morning after. Same time, Nathan had a tendency to get ripe this time of year and she never said anything about that. But was he reading her right? This wasn't some way of telling him she'd drop off him at the welfare hotel. "So it's kind of like that song, England John and Dan Ford?"

Claire shook her head. She didn't know it.

Nathan said she wasn't talking about him moving in, didn't want to change their lives. Picking up the beat, she leaned in and kissed him, warm wind blowing, holding it until Larry hammered on the door.

"Do we have a deal?"

Claire looked over her shoulder, shouting just a sec. Turning to Nathan. "Wanna?"

"Just temporary?"

"Until you can arrange something, put a little money away."

"Okay," Nathan said, "but no hitting."

That sort of pissed Claire off, Veronica putting that in his head. But fine, whatever Claire had to say, she'd say it. "Just fucking around," she said, hands up. "But I get it, no hitting."

Once it was decided for real, it took a few minutes for Nathan to gather his belongings into matching army surplus bags. Then he went to the off-kilter cabinet, opening it, removing some books, choosy. Claire took the books away, replacing them on the shelf.

"What?" Nathan said. "He has the first 007 Pan printing, can't find that anymore, worth some dough. Same with one of his Spillanes. Then he has all three from the James Dark series, Signet firsts. Plus some Russian translations—"

"What, Russian spy novels?"

"Yeah."

"Didn't even know there was such a thing, likely propaganda."

"Same as what we have, I expect." Nathan opened his arms. "Just another point of view."

"Yeah, pro-communism."

"Well, commies have to win sometimes." Nathan let his arms fall. "Anyway, it's stuff I want to try. Four-twenty-five is less than what he'd owe, and that's not accounting for inconvenience." Pointing to the kitchen. "Plus I'm leaving $30 of Arlene's beer in his fridge."

"I know, did the math." Claire stepped in front of him. "So why not take all the books?"

Nathan thought about it, smiling by the time he said alright. Watching Claire work her left fingers between the wall and the cabinet, same thing with her right, then pull until the nails gave. "Just want you to have someplace to put them, keep my place tidy while you're there."

Hoisting the unit over her head, she told Nathan to pocket the cash, grab his bags and get the door, passing Larry watching his collection walk away. Yeah, maybe Nathan could love her after all. Even Abbie Hoffman would've been delighted, the way she was boosting those books.

"Hey," Larry said. "Hey, you can't take those."

"Can, and she is." Nathan handed the keys over, adjusting the army bags on his shoulders. "By reason of not only the cable's out and the record player runs fast, false advertising, you walked right on in, killed my *joie*."

"But." Larry put a hand on Nathan's forearm. "Those books are priceless."

"I know what you have." Nathan hefted the Pittsburgh Persimmon in his right hand. "You need to understand this is condition-sensitive stuff, and a lot of it has stamps, names of previous owners. It's those kinds of things devalue a book. As it is, collection's worth two, three hundred max. More or less, that's what you still owe me, plus penalties for evicting a man—by reason of what?—

just as he's about to have relations with his girlfriend."

Girlfriend, huh? Claire liked that. She put the cabinet down near the elevator, starting back. "Hey Larry, that's your name right, Larry Something?"

"Yeah."

"Well Larry Something, I'd get my hand off my boyfriend, I was you."

23

July 1 to 6

Saturday had Abel playing an unshaven, uncombed professional Aries building his social life through telephone personals. Sunday, he was Tommy Lee, waxing funny about the porning of Heather Locklear. Shooting stopped early that night when the extra playing Heather OD'd. Instead of calling an ambulance, too public, Arlene automagically brought in Dr. Platt to administer the adrenalin shot. There was some disagreement about who would pay his fee until it was revealed that the extra OD'd on Abel's coke, so Arlene made some promises, had her sign some papers, and peeled off some cash.

Later, Meckler and Arlene held an intervention. Abel claimed Cyrus gave him the coke, and that the extra's near death was all the intervention he needed. That didn't sit right with Meckler. Nope. He said Cyrus had been outwardly terrified of coke since Len Bias OD'd in '86. But if Abel had the nerve to lie about that, God was for sure going to get him, so Meckler was happy to leave Abel in his Lord and Savior's capable hands. God? Abel said God hated homos, so why was Meckler sticking up for Cyrus, of all people? Love the sinner, Meckler said, hate the sin. Upon witnessing their exchange, Arlene understood exactly why she was fricked on drugs and called it a day so she could go home and get higher than the CN Tower.

Monday—like Sunday never happened—Abel was the Rolling Stone no one remembered trying to buy a drink. Tuesday, he was wearing a white-shirt-and-tie combo with a dark suit, Monty Hall making a deal in a brothel. Wednesday, Abel was slated to play Tank Boy—the missing activist who bravely halted tanks at Tiananmen Square—but Meckler convinced him it was too soon. In reality, Meckler didn't think Abel could handle the content. Instead, Abel played Ayatollah Khomeini having a heart attack while chasing Salman Rushdie through the dessert, because, like, that wasn't going to upset anybody.

It was Thursday July 6 now, the last day of shooting, which was probably why Arlene eased up and gave Nathan permission to take an hour to sit inside and watch former Montreal Expo Rusty Staub spoof baseball in Canada.

Rusty was the Expos first star in the '60s, going to the trouble of learning French before being traded to New York and bouncing around the majors. Still, he held a special love for Montreal where they knew him as *Le Grande Orange*. These days, he was something of a baseball ambassador and was slated to join a host of former Expos and Blue Jays tonight for a celebration of Canadian baseball at SkyDome. The Jays had just moved in, and it seemed every game was also a celebration of this, that, or the other—something to fill seats. Knowing this in advance, Abel had called his agent who called Rusty's agent who called Rusty.

It was agreed that Rusty would play himself in a bit revolving around declining attendance at ballgames in Montreal. Within 48 hours, they had an approved script. If nothing else, Abel assured Rusty, it would light fires under the asses of Canadian baseball fans, the message being to use it or lose it. Sticking to that spirit, the Expos had a size 50 uniform made up with Rusty's old number 10, sending along socks and rubber cleats. Rusty, he was just delighted everything fit comfortably as he waited for his cue, watching Meckler behind camera one.

Until now, Abel saw Rusty as a company motherfucker, happy to have been there, somebody who never said anything bad about anyone. That's why this sketch was going to feel good, Abel promised, real, serving as neighborly payback for Montreal trading Rusty just when he was getting comfortable with his new language. Besides, Rusty was pretty much Canadian now, half anyway, so why shouldn't he make fun of them? The Americans were going to love it, too, especially the Yankees. They never wanted baseball in Canada. And with the dollar the way it was—the Canadian Peso, Abel called it—baseball probably wasn't going to be in Montreal much longer.

After a lead-in lamenting lack of Montreal support for America's game, Abel became upbeat, saying the Expos were acting aggressively to get fans out with unheard-of deals.

"For instance, what's this weekend's ticket promotion, Rusty?" Abel asked, saying it like he'd heard the American announcers. "In Montreal, *K-bec*."

"Buy two tickets to Sunday's game, get two more free." Rusty waited, fighting his smile. "Buy four, you get four more free."

"And what if you buy, let's say, eight?" Slow now, Abel told himself, don't get too grabby. "What happens when you buy eight tickets?"

"*Sacrébleu!*" Rusty waited another second, straight-faced. "You buy eight tickets to a ballgame in Montreal, they let you pitch."

Meckler decided to do it again because *Sacrébleu* might be deemed a cuss in America, depending on time of day, censored because *The Otto Show* promised to be profanity-free. Rusty argued that real French people didn't even say *Sacrébleu*, that the word itself was a cartoon, so it shouldn't count. No way, Meckler said, this was the real world, TV, and *Sacrébleu* counted, so they did six more takes, the laughs dwindling. Meckler, Rusty, and Abel eventually agreed to go back to the original take and massage it, maybe even bleep *Sacrébleu*. Not that any of them knew the exact translation, only that it somehow fractured the third commandment.

***

Sitting in her usual spot high atop the bleachers, Arlene felt calmer despite Rusty's blaspheme. Sure, there had been trouble, a hell of a lot of trouble, but somehow season one was almost in the can, on schedule. She'd even stopped the bleeding on the Cyrus situation, saving money by having Meckler do both jobs, money she would put down as owing to Heathcliffe Wilson. She was breathing easier, knowing she had met all commitments, meaning they would be back shooting season two a week from now.

Wondering who she would tap as her new set designer, she was making a short list in her head when her brick went off. Reaching, hitting the talk button, she said hello, finding herself talking to Gary Orange. Fishhooks, if Orange was in front of her, she would slap his little pink face. She had seen him the night she went down at Uptown Theatre, and some people said he had been carrying around a little instamatic. But what really made Arlene suspicious was that Orange was among a few industry people to come off well in that satirical rag that took the piss out of her, *Frank*, likely their Hollywood North mole.

"How you doing, Arlene?" Gary said. "You okay?"

Feeling the familiar tension, flashbacks, she decided to stand the prick up. "What is that supposed to mean? Am I okay?"

"Nothing. What I mean is, 'Hi, how are you?'"

"Fine," Arlene held her breath, waiting.

"Me, too . . . Arlene?"

"Yes, Gary."

"I need to talk, off-the-record-like."

Arlene paused, thinking what the hell? Orange would not be going off the record if he had a tape recorder running. That would be illegal, no? "Go ahead, Gary."

"I need to know, what happened between you and Cyrus Dagan? I need to be sure, this was a personal thing, right? A crucial difference of opinion?"

***

Funny, the fact that Nathan was bilingual was in the plus column big time when he was interviewed. But all this time on set, through a whole season, and Rusty Staub was the first guest Nathan had a chance to *parlez vous* with, so he took it. Following Rusty out, asking questions in French about the old days and getting the man's autograph on an envelope from Arlene's office. Rusty was still in uniform, wearing it to his next appearance. Shifting from foot to foot, he listened as Nathan went on about 1979, Rusty's second go-around with the Expos. In particular, Nathan recalled Rusty's grounder during a late-season game that took a wild bounce off the plastic grass at the Big O, scoring everyone and sending the pennant race into chaos. He said it was a shame you guys had to run into the Pirates, that the Expos would've been the best team in baseball that year if hadn't been for Pittsburgh.

Rusty asked if Nathan ever read *Old Man and the Sea*. When Nathan nodded, yes, it was the first real book he read, Rusty switched to English, mostly, and said, "Always fear the Pirates of Pittsburgh, especially Kent Tekulve's sidearm-underhand *fromage.*" Climbing into an awaiting minivan. "That's what Hemingway should've written."

As Sundance drove Rusty away, Nathan started to his kiosk, waving, thinking how he didn't go to ballgames anymore. That baseball didn't make him feel the same way. But maybe it was time to try again. Maybe he'd get home when the Expos were in town, take mom—if he could get her out of the deep woods—like the old days. He was worrying that he'd seen the Expos for the last time when a K-car pulled up. Soon, he was explaining that there was no audience parking available at the studio, sorry.

"But I see spots available," the driver said, pointing all over. "More than a dozen."

"Could be empty, sir. But all this is reserved for cast, crew, important people from TV."

The man reached into his messy wheat hair, grabbing a few locks, tugging. "Helluva way to treat customers. Helluva way. I'm a customer, and you're treating me like an inmate. Being a prick about it, too. I bet you think you're pretty important in there, in your booth."

"It's a kiosk, sir, and sweet as you talk, there still isn't any audience parking."

***

Facing south in a spare cruiser, alignment off-kilter, Morton McNab waited on the light at Cherry and Lake Shore. He was tempted to smile when he saw the metallic Dodge Caravan stop for the red, pulling a piece of paper out of his pocket, a partial plate match.

Morton didn't switch his flashers on until the light turned, watching the vehicle head west on Lake Shore. He was careful this time, nosing out into traffic. A block later, he had Sundance pulled over, connecting him to *The Otto Show* right away. Telling him he ran a red on Thursday, causing an accident with a police cruiser. Apprising the stupid surfer kid of all the charges he was facing—leaving the scene, among others—until Sundance put his hand up.

"Officer?"

Morton held on, biting the inside of his lip. "G'head."

"I work for a production company, means a dozen people drive this van."

"I saw you," Morton said. In reality, he didn't get a good look at the driver, seeing only enough to know it was a mousy blond person, so he wanted to test the kid, bluff him into a confession.

"Officer, Thursday was a dark day for all of us."

Morton had heard enough already, told the kid not to get smartass with disingenuous empathy.

"I think you're taking this the wrong way," Sundance said. "Dark day means we don't shoot. Everyone on set had the day off, almost, means I didn't have access to the van that day. I don't drive this on my own time, so it couldn't have been me."

"You hear that, T.J. Hooker?" Rusty Staub leaned over, looking up from the passenger side. "It couldn't have been him. Now if you don't mind, I have to get to CityTV for an interview with Jim McKenny. May we please carry on?"

"T.J. Hooker? Really?" Morton leaned in, looking over. "And who are you there, on your way to CityTV? Captain Kirk?"

"You don't know who I am?"

Morton, shook his head, no.

"I'm Rusty Staub, *merci beaucoup*."

"What are you? Some sort of comedian? An actor?"

"It's baseball." Rusty pointed at the SkyDome. "I'm in baseball."

Morton looked at the Dome, back to Rusty, a man of size, 40-something, in a uniform, shocks of orange sticking out from under his cap. "You're too old to be in baseball, too tubby."

"Tubby?" Rusty showed teeth. "Are you calling me fat?"

"Are you denying it?" When Rusty said he was big-boned, Morton said, "Just kindly step out of the vehicle, and let's find out who you really are, as opposed to the part you're playing."

"What? Why?"

Morton waved at himself. "Just get out of the van there, big boy."

Rusty reluctantly did as he was told, stepping out onto the shoulder. "Now what?"

Morton, rounding the van to meet him, said, "Lay some ID on me."

Rusty patted his back pocket, nothing. "I'm in uniform." He turned, showing his last name, STAUB, above number 10 on his back. "That's all the ID you need right there, T.J."

***

Back in the lot at Cherry Beach Studios, the K-car driver, backpedaling now, extended his arm, pushing a fiver. "Look, I'm sorry. Here, take this."

"No, sir." Nathan pulled further into his kiosk. "It's not a matter of whether I like it. Hell, it was up to me, I'd let everyone park. Just doing what I'm told. Last the head lady said there's no audience parking." Stopping to check out the guy's ride. "And if she sees an '81 Reliant screaming uh-oh, better get Maaco, she's going to be asking after it."

"This is the car that saved Chrysler. Anyone should be proud to park next to it." When that failed to move Nathan, the guy tried something else. "I received a piece of paper in the mail said free audience parking."

Nathan felt impatient, the guy grinding. But okay, fine, what else did Nathan have to do? Nothing, except maybe worry about the Expos, so he'd be diplomatic, play ball. "That piece of paper. May I see it? You have a piece of paper says you can park, that's a different matter entirely."

The man made a production of checking under his seat, between visors, the glove box.

"I bet you don't happen to have it handy," Nathan said. "That piece of paper."

24

Revisiting religion, again, Abel was decked-out in a robe, wearing a bald skullcap and peddling Pope-on-a-Rope for $10.99. All folks watching from home had to do was call 1-800-THE-POPE and have their credit cards ready. At $21.99, there was *The Pope* VHS. A cassette/VHS combo called *The Pope Does '80s Ladies* was $39.99, and state-of-the-art Christians could add $10 for the CD, something that would last as long as their love of Christ—forever.

Abel, as John Paul II, started the medley with the Whitney Houston from Colby's. She did a solid "I Wanna Dance with Somebody." After that, it was "She Bop" with a Cyndi Lauper from the Tuft Agency. Vanity was slated to play herself. But she was saying she wouldn't be back because of the used condom in the green room. Without approval, Abel reached out to the Whitney Houston. She knew a Vanity from the Boom Boom Room who happily made a "Pretty Mess." The Vanity, in turn, knew a Madonna from Komrads, so "Like a Prayer" made sense. Better, the Madonna was friends with a Cher from La Cage aux Folles on Yonge Street, and yes, she had the new hit down, so Abel recruited her, too. Now she was lipsynching to "If I Could Turn Back Time."

If there was ever a thread, Arlene figured it had been lost on one of Abel's trips. See? She did know where they were coming from. But surely, what with John Paul II dancing and singing with actual drag queens, the line into oblivion had been crossed. Watching from the back row of metal bleachers, Arlene hit the talk button on her walkie. "Arlene for Veronica."

"Go for Veronica."

"Go to 10."

After they both did like so, Arlene said she couldn't believe Veronica green-lit this. Making fun of Tammy Faye Bakker was one thing. With the downfall of PTL, Tammy didn't have a reputation to defame. So, fine, fair game, even if Abel took it one toke over the line. But *The Pope Does '80s Ladies*? Really? Was Veronica all there? Abel was on stage dressed like the Pope, dancing and singing about female masturbation and male ejaculate with chicks with dicks. Did Veronica understand the connotations, the ramifications? This wasn't just sacrilege. This was drug behavior. Everyone on stage was clearly on drugs. Whoever wrote it, also on drugs. And talk about HIV, everyone up there was plausibly positive as well. Abel, too, the way he was cavorting with crossdressers, none of which was funny.

"Better than that fat joke you wrote in," Veronica said. "What percentage of the States did CNN say was obese?"

This, Arlene said, pointing down from up above, was not palatable. It was cultural pornography, shock-jock excrement. Advertisers would see this as a slap in the face to innocent AIDS victims like Ryan White and put their money behind Jerry Seinfeld, someone who could represent. And did Veronica see Jerry's pilot last night? No? Well, she should have, because there was something to be learned. Even if it was rough, it was palatable.

As a creative person herself, a writer who graduated at the top of her class, Arlene said she wanted to make dramas. Something edgy, a thriller, or perhaps a production of the script she wrote during her graduating year, an A- about the human condition. Thing was, even when they made these projects in Canada, they almost always used American prodcos. Comedy—that was pretty much all Hollywood North was trusted with for now. So long as that was the state of things, it was never a good idea to defecate where one feasted.

But look at the audience, Veronica said. They were loving it, probably a little turned on.

Oh, they loved it, sure. Arlene closed her eyes, saying of course they loved it, that they were toque-wearing hosers who only went to things because they were free. They probably laughed at their own belches, discussing flavors—oh, that one is ketchupy. What did Meckler call them? Oh yes, eaters-and-poopers.

"That is why they are in our audience, laughing on cue. They do not have jobs, money, or even a plan. Frick the audience, it is crap like this that gets you admonished, banned."

"Banned," Veronica said, mocking. "You should be so lucky, so brave. If you even dared to offend, to be admonished, none of us would ever have to work again."

"How do you figure?"

"Repackage it as a VHS, wrap a publicist's hook around it. At worst, we dine out on a banned, straight-to-video comedy for a year. After that, some maverick network would pick it up. Make it a cool taboo thing, like Pepsi did with Madonna. Pepsi knew she was going to kiss the black saint's feet, that everybody would be outraged, that everybody would make money."

Madonna? Abel Otto was no Madonna, and Pepsi was facing a boycott. On top of that, Abel had just cut every Roman Catholic viewer out of *The Otto Show*'s universe. Did Veronica even know what that meant? To cut out so many people right off the bat. Blast it, some of the investors wore transparent socks. That meant they were RC.

Sorry, Veronica said. She'd be more careful next time Arlene went to rehab. Otherwise, the only thing anyone said was that it had to be profanity-free. They might have to deal with Rusty Staub's French curse later, sure. But Abel was supposed to have free reign. Didn't Arlene get the memo? Other than the swearing, The Comedy Channel gave Abel complete control. That's why he agreed to shoot *The Otto Show* in Canada.

"Yeah," Arlene said, "but do they know their lead is up here tooting with trannies?"

Veronica said she wasn't sure, but Arlene probably wasn't the person to broach that.

***

Cyrus wore black house shorts, Michael Jordan's, doing chin-ups on a bar he'd mounted in the living room. Telling himself, okay, he'd been fired, was facing some legal problems, but there was no point in worrying about shit before it happened. Telling himself at least he had a new gig when the green dial phone rang, he picked up, hello.

"Cyrus, Gary Orange here."

"Gary." Cyrus sat on the sofa. "How are—"

"Listen Cyrus, there's a problem."

Fuck, there was only supposed to be one problem. First the

money, then the job title. Okay, so he was going to pull down $180 a day as a location scout for *Original Homes of Ontario*. How much worse could it get? "What sort of problem, Gary?"

"What sort? Problem, Cyrus, is you lied to me. Crucial difference of opinion? Was it a crucial difference of opinion made you steal Arlene's petty cash? What are you, on crack?"

"Gary, that's what I was trying to explain before, that it's truly complicated. It's—"

"You're facing charges, man. Theft, stealing props. You've also got assault an officer. Or is it assault-ing?"

"The cop did it to himself." Cyrus held his forehead. "I've got my lawyer taking DNA samples at the scene. But yeah, I think it's assault an officer, not assault-ing."

"Either way, this is government money, we just can't. You were fired, man. Difference of opinion—my mole says you stole 10-grand."

"Did Arlene say that? It was only $4,800."

"Only 48-hundred, huh? So, what are you saying is you stole from her, but not as much as my mole said? And what's this about naked pictures of a very young Billy Idol?"

"I swear," Cryus said. "He's at least 21 in those shots."

"Yeah, well, I heard he's very young."

"Goddamn you, Gary. If you'd let me finish."

"You sitting down, Cyrus?"

"Yeah."

"Well, are you by any chance sitting on a gingham Ralph Lauren sofa from the Corky and the Juice Pigs special?"

Cyrus automatically copped a feel of the cushion, said yeah.

"See ya, Cyrus."

***

Shooting on season one should've finished early, near six. But now Abel had the cameras out in the lot, celebrating the luxuries of time. Wasting outtakes, impromptu style, he was looking for one more story or sketch.

Nathan looked up from Mickey Spillane's *Delta Factor*—the movie tie-in, Mickey's ex-wife Sherri holding hands with Christopher George on the cover—to see seven or eight cronies standing there.

Next to Abel was a balding ginger Nathan recognized from Second City print ads. Nathan couldn't remember the ginger's name, only that he was supposed to be the next great improv jester. A camera and boom mics were set up behind them.

"Why did the skunk cross the road?" When no one answered, Abel said, "Because he had a beer can stuck on his head."

Other than the guy from Second City, everyone was too tired to laugh. But indeed, a poor skunk was stumbling all over Cherry Street wearing a split Löwenbräu tin.

Abel looked at the ginger. "You got anything?"

He opened his mouth like he was about to speak, then shook his head, no.

"But you're the imrov guy," Abel said. "That's why we brought you in, to improvise."

While the ginger stood silently, bowed, Abel turned to Nathan and pointed at the skunk. "That thing going to shoot stink at us?"

"I don't think so," Nathan said. "Not so long as you don't go poking him."

"Any way we can get it off, the can?"

"I know how." Nathan pointed at Arlene's Jeep. "But you'll need a blanket."

Abel's eyes lit up. "Is it open?"

"Keys in the ignition."

"Okay, go get it. Do it for me."

Nathan looked Abel up and down. "You can get away with it, star of the show. But me, I do it and there goes my *emploi*, bye-bye."

Abel looked at Arlene's Jeep, double taking, then ran to it like a kid chasing a kitten. Inside, he rooted around, appearing with a red, black, and blue flannel blanket. Abel wasn't sure what was happening or how it was going to turn out. But he felt that he could manufacture something here—even if the local improv guy was stunned—and go along with the moment like Francis Ford Coppola in *Apocalypse Now*, shooting Marlon Brando's gobbledegook, hoping for something that could make sense to the story without knowing what it might be. "Now what?"

"We drape the blanket over the animal," Nathan said, "then I work the can off."

"We?"

"I need help to cover it, then you hold it."

"It'll shoot."

"Not if we cover it first."

"How do you know?"

Nathan took a step back, indignant. "My adoptive mother's a game warden, taught me."

"Game warden? I thought you were from Montreal. There's no hunting in the city."

"She commutes to this place 90-plus minutes away, back," Nathan said, visualizing mom's cottage near Lanaudière, not far from Mastigouche Wildlife Reserve, deciding he didn't want to get specific. "Has a shack deep in the woods, stays there three, four nights a week. Game warden."

"So it's definitely not going to shoot? Mom's a deep-woods game warden, you know?"

"Worst case, it'll shoot into Arlene's blanket, and you answer to that. Remember, I'm just following your orders, star of the show."

Abel liked that, claiming responsibility on camera. Yeah, he'd take the fall.

In for good, he took two corners of the flannel, following Nathan, covering the skunk. Through the cloth, Abel held the animal around its haunches while Nathan worked the can off.

"When I count to three, run." Nathan hadn't hit two before Abel bolted, following him.

The skunk peeked out from under the blanket, scampering into the field across the street.

Abel called for Kiwi's work gloves. He gladly contributed, smiling, proud to be part of it. Abel pulled Kiwi's gloves on, then got caught red-handed putting the blanket back in the Jeep. Arlene was out of the building, having heard it on her walkie. Somebody had their talk button stuck—it must have been the Kiwi, he was coming in strongest—and she heard everything.

Abel couldn't figure how she heard everything, but it was all good, even if some of what she was saying had to be bleeped. The important thing was that he'd improvised—without the help of the redhead, the tool—to tell one last story. Yeah, whatever happened next, Abel had made the most of his time. Sure, he'd made mistakes, but good things were happening, too. As for the rest, it was out of his hands now. Time to relax. Time to enjoy himself.

25

For the next half-hour, everyone hung around the lot smoking, drinking, and gossiping about Arlene, Hollywood North, the Americans, and tomorrow's release of *Lethal Weapon 2*.

Abel asked whether anybody caught Jerry Seinfeld's pilot last night. Most people made faces, said Jerry who? But Gene Gene the audio machine saw the intro and he said the music was busting over that Jerry guy's voice. Yep, Meckler said it started poorly, in a laundromat of all places. Imagine, Jerry has a show set in the apple and he opens in a washateria? That's why, Meckler said, it lagged, that it eventually came together, kind of, when they worked a woman in. By then, it was too little too late, which explained the weak ratings.

Ratings didn't matter, Abel said. His agent heard that NBC passed before the pilot aired. Fox, too. That test audiences hated the characters. And well, as much as Abel liked Jerry personally— he was a nice guy, decent—Abel couldn't figure how a show about nothing made it to the pilot stage.

When Freak wondered aloud what the '90s would be like, Janet Boroski hiked her G-string, saying she was anxious to leave the me decade behind, that the '90s would be community minded and Seattle would provide the soundtrack. Had anyone heard an album, just new in the shops, by a band called Nirvana? No? Well, *Bleach* was the title, and no wonder they hadn't heard it. Janet said Nirvana was only getting play on CKLN. Just give commercial radio time to catch up. Nirvana was going to rule the world.

"And when," asked Meckler, "will it become acceptable for women to wear G-strings so high on their midriffs?"

That would come later, Janet said. For now, women were clinging to their granny panties.

About 60 feet away, inside his kiosk, Nathan was still on the job, back into *The Delta Factor*, just at the part where Morgan the Raider is being framed and drafted into service by the CIA. All he has to do is marry this wholesome girl operative and pose as a major drug dealer so he can free a scientist held hostage on a

Caribbean island prone to hurricanes. Cuba, mayhaps?

Thinking he was going to make mud if he had any more of that fancy coffee from craft services, Nathan pushed the Styrofoam cup aside, hearing Billy Idol shout more, more, more. Looking, Nathan made the Impala revving up a block away. It headed towards his kiosk with a jump, growing larger like a blue-assed fly, again.

Tabernac, if Claire wanted to make a whole $125 more a day, she could earn it, deal with Cyrus. First, Nathan hit the flasher on his 6in1 Radio Lantern, then he set off the built-in audio alarm, producing an urgent, irritating horn that was immediately intensified for anyone on channel eight when he pressed the talk-button. "Nathan for Claire."

Near the canopy, Claire grabbed her headphones—her ears—saying, "What the fuck?"

"That's the audio alarm on my 6in1 Radio Lantern. Means *sécurité, sécurité, sécurité*."

"In English," Claire said.

"Means help me. We have a situation, your specialty. Cyrus is coming, playing the Billy Idol too loud, and oh Christ *de calice de tabernacle*! He's giving it the gas. Help me."

Claire was running at the drop of Cyrus' name, ordering Nathan to turn the alarm off. Nathan figured he had every reason. But fine, if Claire wanted to kick Cyrus' ass, he'd kill the horn. Doing so, he looked up to find her blocking the Impala as it approached. The car lurched, screeching to a stop. Nathan didn't think her body block was a good idea. Then again, this was her specialty, he thought, watching Cyrus stick his head out the window to say, "Are you truly sure you want to put yourself on the line here?"

Claire stood with her feet as wide as her shoulders, hands dangling as if she had something to draw. "I'd like to see you try something, give me a reason."

"I need to see Arlene," Cyrus said. "Housekeeping."

"Write a letter. I have orders to keep you off the set. You know how it is."

"Oh yes." Cyrus stomped on the brake then the gas, making the Impala buck. "I know how it is, truly. Get her down here. I don't even want to go inside, on advice of counsel."

Again, Claire told Cyrus she'd been directed to keep him out. That she was going against orders by not reporting him immediately, now. In other words, she was trying to do Cyrus a favor, so why didn't he stop playing with his ding-a-ling and beat a hasty retreat instead?

"Fine." Cyrus pointed at the building. "Just you tell Arlene to bring my Billy Idol ephemera to her office tomorrow. I want it all back."

Hands on her hips, Claire said she'd pass it on, but Cyrus needed to depart now—not now, but right now—in order to avoid another wood shampoo.

His eyes were a bit heavy as he ducked inside. Putting the Impala in reverse, he backed up then punched into drive, pulling beside Claire. "You know what you did?"

"What?"

"You turned a man who makes $300 a day into a man who has nothing to lose. A truly dangerous situation in any business."

"Means what?" Claire said. "You using weasel words to threaten a paid-duty officer?"

"Weasel words." Cyrus threw his head back. "You see Zoë Tamerlis in *Ms .45?*"

Claire shook her head, no.

"Well, in terms of clarity, let's just say I'm Zoë and I'm coming for you." Then Cyrus stomped on the gas and tore out, his back-end clipping a tree as he turned onto Cherry Street.

Everybody came running over to make sure Claire was okay. Satisfied, Sundance said Cyrus would never work in the business again. Kiwi scoffed, saying Cyrus would never bloody well work again, period. Freak said that was probably for sure, what with the naked pictures of a very young Billy Idol, and that was on top of the *Ms .45* reference. Had anyone seen *Ms .45?* Well, Freak had, and if Cyrus saw himself as the Zoë Tamerlis character, like, he was going to shoot every one of them, at least the men.

Janet Boroski generated some talk around calling the cops for real, but Kiwi didn't bloody well want that, no reason, neither did Abel, and so everyone carried on.

Officially, set finally shut down around 7:30, before Sundance started across the lot holding an envelope up to the falling sun.

"Veronica says you can get out of your cage in 10 minutes," he said, dangling the letter in front of Nathan. "And you're either still spanking the rent-a-cop or she's mad at you. Not to mention, if she's mad at you, chances are you're still spanking her."

Nathan leaned half his body out of the kiosk, holding on with his right and snatching the envelope with his left. The two looked at each other, Nathan motioning to the space behind him. "Go ahead, smoke your joint, *garçon.*"

"Okay, Lawn Boy."

"Hey, *garçon,*" Nathan said. "You don't call me Lawn Boy."

"Then stop calling me *garçon* already and read your love letter. Like, do you shit on me cause everyone else shits on you? Is that it?"

"*Oui, garçon. C'est dommage.*"

"Keep it up," Sundance said. Hiding behind the shack, sparking up as Nathan read.

> Nathan,
>
> I could use some help after the party, that'd be good. AC is on the fritz, landlord's man won't be in this week. Means I can't do more than sit still in front of some fans wearing my new orange triangle bikini with wood beads and O-ring details and get sweaty. You know a man knows something about air conditioners?
>
> Love, Claire

Nathan didn't know why she was putting anything in writing at this point. The capital-L Love part gave him a twinge, too, like she was talking about more than moving in. But the rest sounded pretty alright. He could see her in her silly new outfit on the screen of his mind, perspiring, a little loopy, when he heard a familiar whine in his ears. "Arlene for Nathan."

Nathan, hitting his talk button, said, "Go for Nathan."

"I heard Cyrus was here."

"Yes, he wanted to talk to you. Before Angie Dickinson here ran him off, he told her to tell you to bring his Billy Idol items to your office, that he wants them. Also, he said for Claire to think of him as the Zoë Tamerlis character in *Ms .45*, then he peeled off, hit his car on a tree."

"Fishhooks, I am going to need a restraining order. Anyway, have you seen Sundance?"

Nathan opened his back door. "Attila's asking after you."

Sundance giggled. "Hide me." Taking another toke, cracking up. "That's right, garcarooni. Do it."

Pressing the button, Nathan said, "Can you come again, *Madame*? Some great big truck just went by and I couldn't make out *une crisse de chose*."

"Stop cursing on the air," Arlene said. "And why do you insist on using French with me when I keep telling you, speak English?"

Nathan thought on it, said, "I guess I'm practicing so that I don't lose it."

"And why's that important?" Arlene wanted to know.

Closing his eyes, hesitating, Nathan said, "Because it's the only part of me I'm sure of."

Arlene thanked Nathan for sharing, said that was heartfelt, sincerely, that it gave her a better idea of where he was coming from. But just so they were clear, this was not cultural development day. This was work. And so long as Nathan was working for AMA, he was to address French people only in French. Otherwise, he was to speak English, and was that clear?

"Yes, Ms. Marion."

"Okay then, what is Sundance's twenty?"

Nathan hesitated, said to Sundance, "You gonna give me some of that boo to go?"

Sundance took a second or two to deem the request reasonable—Nathan had hid him quite a bit—then nodded, yes.

"You mean Jeffery Brewer?" Nathan asked Arlene. Trying hard

by reason he felt bad for calling Sundance *garçon*. Poor kid hadn't done anything.

"Call him Sundance," Arlene said. "He is not here to be a PA, no. The only thing he wants is to be a background performer. 'Can I have a small part in this? I'm already here, why call Tuft? I can do it.' The point is I need him for his real job, a clean-up in the green room. You would not believe what the drag queens did in there, especially the Cher. So give him to me."

"Sundance, yes I last saw him a while ago hauling bags of trash across the lot in the hot sun," Nathan said. "Maybe someone sent him out on a run after, something like that."

"That kid does not do anything unless you stand on him."

"Oh, I think you got the wrong boy, Arlene. Blond kid, 21 or so, nice big teeth rounded like pearls. Tan, splattered in freckles, surfer type?"

"That is the one."

"He's a hard-working kid, Arlene, motivated. Maybe you're catching him on breaks."

"Like I told you before. You are a bad liar, Nathan. Just make sure that he gets his behind to my office. Until then, I will be watching you. I can see you from here."

Nathan waved. "Copy that."

Also, Arlene did not want Abel around her Jeep under any circumstances. He said he pulled rank on Nathan, fair enough. But did Nathan know how that made Arlene feel?

"No." Nathan looked out on the lake, wishing he was on one of those tiny boats. "How?"

"Do you get that western channel with your pirate cable?"

Nathan hit his talk button, no.

"Well then, did you ever watch *The Lone Ranger*?"

Some, Nathan said, in his youth.

"Good, because there is an episode when Tonto stops abruptly, saying there are Apache to the east, so they head west until Tonto decides the Apache are that way as well. They ride north, more Apache. When they head south, you guessed it, even more

Apache. That is when the Lone Ranger turns to Tonto and says what do we do? Did you know what Tonto said?"

By now, Nathan recognized this as an old Tonto joke, as opposed to an actual scene. Still, instead of correcting Arlene—not worth the fight—he hit the talk button, played along, said no.

"Tonto said, what you mean we, white man?"

"So you're feeling surrounded? That what you're telling me?"

"That is the feeling that I get, yes," Arlene said. "It also means, if you let Abel in my vehicle again, you will be fired for disloyalty."

"Job's over, Arlene. You're going to fire me, now?"

"I thought you were interested in sticking with AMA for the second block?"

Surprised she was leaving the option open, Nathan said, "That's right."

"Then keep Abel away from my Jeep and we will do a little something for you," Arlene said. "It has been a trying time, and you have done alright, despite a couple, shall we say, glitches. On the other hand, if Abel gets in my Jeep, you will be docked for cleaning charges, if nothing else—fined." Pausing. "And another thing."

Nathan sighed, hit the talk button. "Yes."

"No more stankie in the green room."

26

Cyrus sat on the alley curb behind his three-floor wartime brown box north of Dundas on Jarvis, inspecting the Impala's damaged back quarter panel. Locking his hands behind his head, he told himself the heap was worthless now. Well, maybe worthless was overwrought, but Cyrus had just put how many thousand into the car and it wasn't mint. It wasn't near-mint or even excellent. It was simply very good, and, in the collecting world, very good meant, unless it was a bargain, to keep looking. That being the case, would Orest F. Jefferies want it? Unlocking his hands, Cyrus didn't think so. The car wasn't a collector's item anymore. It was a project. As such, Cyrus didn't see as how he had anything to offer Jefferies in terms of collateral.

Thinking that was that, he pushed himself into a standing position, giving the Impala another glance, and headed for his building where the new heterosexual yum-yum from one was holding the door. Saying thanks neighbor, checking out his cakes in those tight jeans, juicy, Cyrus jogged upstairs wondering how it all got away so quickly. Or had it been quick? Maybe it started years ago, stealing little things—boots, a mirror, drapes. It would've been fine, he thought, keying his lock, if only he hadn't started stealing big things, like that gingham Ralph Lauren sofa from the Corky and the Juice Pigs special. Stupid, he said, stepping inside, dropping into the same couch when the phone rang. Sighing, sitting up, he reached for it, hello.

"Just calling to pick up me messages."

The caller had an odd accent, UK-English, but off. Rather than escalate yet another situation, Cyrus told the guy he had the wrong number, that this wasn't an answering service.

"Just tell me, did Ian call?"

Cyrus thought about it, said as a matter of fact, he received a call from Ian for Mott this time last week, Thursday. Ian said for Mott to call him, that Mott would have the number, and was this Mott?

"That's right," the voice said. "Mott the Hoople."

Hearing someone crack-up in the background, Cyrus said Mott the Hoople was a band, asshole, not a guy, and that this matter would be referred to Bell Canada, bye. Then Cyrus gently placed the phone on its cradle, wondering who hated him enough to carry out a seven-day crank.

***

Below the parking lot lights, Abel held a Löwenbräu in one hand, teriyaki burger in the other, hugging Arlene without his hands. "Arlene Marion is fucking back," he said. Pulling away, putting his beer down on the cement, standing upright, raising her hand like a fight champ. "Fucking back." Turning to her. "Of course, working with you is a little like pissing in the wind." Letting her hand drop. "And as a person, I think I liked you better when you were on painkillers. Speaking of which, do you have any leftovers?" Waiting a beat. "Just kidding." Oh man, Abel loved giving her the old slap-and-tickle. "But you are fucking back."

Arlene watched Abel retrieve his beer, Abel making her the punch line again. He had all of them, bona fide industry trash, thinking they could do better, that they had a better idea of funny. And the things they said. She knew they were calling her Attila the Hen. She heard it when Kiwi's walkie was stuck on talk. Now here was Abel, right to her face, saying he preferred her on painkillers, diminishing her.

Fishhooks, Arlene really was back on those Percs, so a part of her wanted to make Abel wrong. If only she didn't have to hurt herself in the process. Maybe that's what Abel was up to, drawing her out, exposing her, and that only increased Arlene's desire for something to slow her down, mentally, while Abel was jacked up, going faster. The more she thought, this is what happened when you had a role player for a lead. Would anyone remember Rex Smith driving a 300-mile-an-hour motorcycle? Arlene did not think so. This time next year it would be the same for Abel—back to bit parts in *Cannonball Run 4* or whatever they were calling the next instalment of that insidious franchise.

"Stick to the first part," she told Abel. Stupid prick couldn't just drop a compliment. Always had to be some kind of bite, like the whole lot of them, darkly sarcastic bastards, all. "I'm fucking back. Leave it at that."

Dinner had been held over to accommodate Abel's whims, giving way to a staid tailgate motif. Vegetarians gnawed on wild corn barbecued with husks and garnished with blackened twigs Toledo Marseilles insisted were supposed to look that way. The rest ate meat—perfectly grilled steaks, boneless chicken breasts, burgers, and lamb shish kabobs. They washed it down with beer and wine, everything free, as always.

Toledo claimed to be wearing nothing under an apron with a Grizzly on the front, the caption below reading BEAR NAKED CHEF. Up top he wore a Gilligan hat. Smiling, pointing his flipper at Claire, trying to get her to eat something else. Perhaps a steak, a small one wrapped in peppery bacon, filet mignon.

"He best be wearing something under that apron," Nathan whispered in her ear. "Can't be cooking in Canada, serving food, *sans* pants."

While Claire begged off Toledo's offerings, she gratefully accepted a photocopy of his truffled potatoes recipe. Wondering where Toledo had been keeping the recipe if he wasn't wearing pants, yuck, Nathan checked out little notes attached to the cheeses, one identifying as aged Quebec cheddar. "Eight years old. Jeez, Toledo, why not break out the fresh stuff?

In a nutshell, Toledo explained the aging process; the older the cheese, the sharper. Nathan said that he was from Quebec, where the cheese came from, so he was pulling Toledo's leg, thanks, and maybe he should put on some pants. About that time Abel slid in to chat Claire up. Abel had heard who she was, and he had that strong German beer in him. So, you know, he was kind of wondering what it'd be like to make it with a cop who posed for a skin rag, whether there was a spot for something like that next season. Did Claire still have the outfit? Yes, well, had she ever thought about making it with someone famous?

She raised a brow, said that when she was younger she used to get off to posters of Nick Nolte. Then she heard that creative people tended to not shower regularly, smelled, especially Nick.

Sean Penn was said to be as stinky. That was Madonna's problem with him, Claire said, that he didn't bathe regularly.

"How about you, Abel?" She looked him over. "Do you bathe regularly?"

Oh yeah, Abel's head shook, yes, clean. Not only that, he'd take another shower to make sure he was fresh. Dammit, Abel didn't feel right unless he had a shower after every shit, but that didn't mean Claire had to shower. Abel liked his women sweaty, natural scents, their tacos zesty.

Claire leaned forward, lips moving softly on his lobe. "How'd you like to fuck me with your girlfriend on speaker phone from Chicago?"

Abel jammed his hands into his pockets. No, he didn't want to do that. Besides, he didn't have a speaker phone. What about something else? Had Claire ever heard of the unicorn? No, well what he really wanted was for her to give him a rimmer while jacking him off—the unicorn. Oh yeah, Claire said, that sounded hot, and for Abel to call when he became famous.

***

Cyrus poured over a list of authentic weaponry he'd leased for one set or another. A crossbow, circa 1839, seemed poetic, but how could he work it? What was it going to take, a minute a shot? No way. As for guns, there were certainly more powerful practical options, but Cyrus figured Chuck Connors' rifle was the least obvious to be suspected for contemporary killing purposes.

The weapon in question was an 1892 .44-40 Winchester carbine, souped-up into a crude machine gun. Cyrus thought it would look kind of cool, vintage. That's why he was into a small plastic box filled with cue cards, a source list of names and available guns—among other props and gadgets—cross-referenced in alpha by subject matter. On the front and back of each card were tiny notations. Pulling one, he picked up his green phone and dialed the digits, relieved when he found himself speaking to Albert Diaz after the third ring.

"How's it going, Albert?"

"Cyrus, what?"

"I was hoping you have the Winchester Chuck Connors used in *The Rifleman*, hoping it's available. Need it yesterday, so I was also hoping to swing by and pick it up tonight."

"Yeah," Diaz said. "Only how 'bout first thing in the morning?"

"Sorry, truly." Fuck, Cyrus hated groveling for Diaz. "First thing's too late. It's sort of an add-on—a bonus for the VHS edition, if nothing else—so we'll be shooting by first thing. It's a Chuck Connors skit."

"How're they playing Chuck? He the butt of some joke? They doing a legend like that?"

Impatient, Cyrus said, "I don't know. That's not my end. All I know is that Abel Otto must have that gun in particular. He just laid it on me."

Diaz paused. Something didn't make sense. "I thought *The Otto Show* wrapped today."

"Was supposed to. Officially, it did. But like I said, Abel wants to try this one thing. Says it might even turn out to be his signature gag, if it works. They have Cherry Beach leased for another day. Abel, he's aggressive, the kind of guy that likes to do something with every second he has. Obsessive compulsive, if you ask me, truly."

"Okay, okay," Diaz said. "Come and get it, 10:45 sharp, only I want double."

Cyrus didn't see any reason to haggle—it was all going on Arlene's tab—but thought it might be suspicious if he didn't. "I'll give you time-and-a-half, Albert."

"Double."

"Why double?"

"Two reasons, Cyrus: One, I'm already giving you a break, because, technically, I'm supposed to be with the guns, all times. You know how much that'd cost if I went by the book, how much that'd hold up production? And two, having some guy I don't know so well come 'round my house at night looking for a gun fires eight shots in less than three seconds gives me the willies. I've got children. This time of night, that's what it's worth, double."

"Alright, double. When can I pick it up?"

Wasn't Cyrus listening? Diaz already told him 10:45, sharp. That he didn't want Cyrus early or late. And what about his Smith & Wesson 629 Trail Boss with the Hogue grip? That was due back today.

Cyrus thought it weird that the underlings hadn't looked into returning it. It was a gun, after all, proof that the whole thing was going to hell without him. "Abel still wants it," he found himself saying, "for tomorrow's skit."

"Nobody told me. You understand how I get edgy, equipment isn't returned. That's my thing, remember? I'm on time, you're on time. Or at least make a call, give me a reason."

"Yes, my fault, truly," Cyrus said. Thinking all the business he threw Diaz, and he still treated Cyrus this way. "I'll tell you all about it, 10:45, damndest thing."

***

Veronica, Claire, and Nathan broke away from the herd, hiding by the loading dock. At worst, Claire said it'd look like they were sharing a spliff. And well, everyone else seemed to be quietly taking tokes or doing discrete lines whether Arlene cared for it or not.

The DJ segued from "Dancing on the Berlin Wall" by Rational Youth to "Planet Claire" by the B-52s. Claire liked that, dancing as you'd expect a cop to dance to a new wave song that was all about her, stiff, like someone might say she's from Mars, but happy. Her interest waned when the DJ mixed in "99 Luftballons" by Nena, prompting Nathan to get up to get down.

"Seriously," Claire said, "you like this?"

Nathan, clapping his hands, bopping, said the unnatural, obese baseline was already aging poorly, but it was the happiest song about Armageddon he ever did hear. Sure, it was happy, Claire said, probably because the Bulgarians were nuking the shit out of us. And how did a song by a Bulgarian girl with hairy armpits chart here? Nathan said Nena was German, the song anti-war. Bulgarian or German, Claire said both were commies, and how did Nathan know the song was anti-war? Did he speak commie? Nathan told her there was an English version, but he preferred the original German take.

"Whatever makes you whole," Claire said, hesitating. "Pretentious prick—is that what's in your wank archive, hirsute honeys singing like they're spitting, because that ain't me."

Nathan shot her a look, said it was common for European girls to have hairy pits, and, not that Nena was offering, but he wouldn't kick her out of bed for leaving her razor in Stuttgart. Besides, Claire didn't seem to mind Mitsou singing in French. That's because French was a Canadian language, Claire said. Also, Mitsou shaved.

Nathan was happy when the DJ changed the subject, flawlessly connecting beats with "Kiss Off" by the Violent Femmes, Gordon Gano warning all that this will go down on your permanent record. Then, when Gordon got to his list, Claire killed Nathan's *joie* completely, complaining about lyrics she understood this time.

"'I forget what eight was for,' stupid. This guy, he doesn't even know his own words and they put the record out like that?"

That did it. Nathan stopped dancing, telling Claire she wasn't qualified to critique Gordon Gano's very literary songwriting. Whoa, Claire said it was her right to free speech, and she thought this Gano sucked horse cock. Nathan's eyes got wide. He said there'd been a fair bit of objectively bad music released over the past 10 years—Starship's "We Built This City" topping out—and here Claire was shitting on one of the few organic specimens. Oh, she said, it was a specimen alright, and that she should kick Nathan's skinny ass just for liking it.

In that moment, with Gordon Gano singing you all can just kiss off into the air, Nathan knew he should've been putting the kibosh on this whole deal, for he was thinking aloud, saying he should break up with Claire just for that, plus the hitting. But he was going to be a good *homme* and give her one last chance, asking if she knew who Joe Strummer was when Veronica brought them back to here and now.

"You'll be happy to know the job's richer than originally thought," she told them. "Twenty-thousand richer."

"Seems the Gods of mathematics are multiplying at just the

right time." Nathan scratched his chin, thinking yet another university-educated-white-girl favor. "By reason of what, exactly?"

Veronica caught it, the way he said exactly, mouth tight. "Just a little addition," she said, mimicking, "by reason of Arlene's paying Heathcliffe Wilson 20K to make the rubber bird issue go away. He wants money to replace all three birds, plus his compressors, or else. Just look for an envelope marked Miscellaneous Liabilities. That's Heathcliffe's restitution."

"Quite the stack to catch," Claire said, the barbed opening guitar riff of "Never Say Never" by Romeo Void prompting the DJ to adjust levels abruptly. "What does that change?"

"It changes your take, that's all," Veronica said. "Should now be $84,000 plus whatever she has kicking around in petty cash, close to 90-thou total. Now, let's go over this one last time. My job is first. Crush up the Percs, dissolve them into Arlene's tea. If that fails to happen, or if anything else goes wrong, any one of us can call it off by saying the word licorice."

"Where'd you get the things anyway?" Claire said. "The Percs?"

That was the best part. Arlene really was back on the shit. Meaning Veronica was able to take the pills right out of Arlene's desk, her own stash.

"Perfect," Nathan said. "Only how do you know how much to give her?"

"I looked it up at the reference library, and the consensus, after cross-referencing, seems to be that six should put her down without causing permanent damage."

"You sure?"

"She can have up to eight, so I'm even allowing for the possibility of her dropping a couple on her own." Veronica kept things moving, turning to Claire. "Okay, so you're driving?"

"Affirmative."

"Good, so long as you don't hear licorice, it's a go for Nathan."

Picking up the beat, Nathan said, "You radio us on sub-channel 36, confirm you're going for coffee. When I see you cross the street, I enter the building. Arlene should be down. I take the money out from under her, leave. You come back, find her like that, then call the investors. They probably don't want 911 involved by reason of the kind of money it is, probably advise you to bring in Dr. Platt on the dub, like when the extra playing Heather Locklear OD'd."

Veronica looked at Claire like there was something else. "Where do you stash the cash?"

"Thought you didn't want it," Claire said, "the money."

Veronica said she didn't need them to get caught, either. That was bad business for her. She just needed to know that they had a plan, for peace of mind.

"Don't worry about our plan for the money." Claire saw herself in a glossy photo she'd carefully torn out of *Vogue*, taped to her bathroom wall, rolling around on hundred-dollar bills. "We have one and we'll be sticking to it, so rest your mind."

Veronica nodded tentatively. "Can I at least ask whether you have worked out an escape route? I do not need to know what it is, just that you have one."

"You do your job and we'll do ours," Claire said. "In fact, giving you that information would be dangerous if you should get caught up in misadventure, bad business for us."

Even though Claire would be doing the driving, Nathan went over the route in his head. From Queen East head west to Parliament, hang a left, then a right on King to Dufferin, back to Claire's. After, he and Claire would catch a cab back to AMA like they were on their way to get paid, simple. But he didn't think Veronica needed to know either the route or that they were planning to hide the money in Claire's diversion safes, either. "So, are we done then?"

Claire and Veronica looked at each other, back at him.

"I guess," Veronica said, the DJ pivoting to "Fascination Street" by The Cure.

"Why?" Claire said. "Somewhere you have to be?"

"Need to borrow some items from set." Nathan looked at the unguarded door, then Claire. "Get myself a suit while I'm at it. Think I'm the same size as Abel. I saw him wearing that nice suit when he played Larry King."

Veronica took a sip of wine. "I wish you wouldn't do that."

"Don't worry, it's chaos in there since Cyrus got severed, *merde* everywhere. Asides, if I see anybody, I'll just tell 'em you okay'd it." Nathan held a hand to Claire. "Keys, please."

"You're going to steal, put stolen goods in my car? No thanks, not after everything."

"I need tools, you want me to fix your AC."

Claire shook her head, no.

"C'mon. I'll pick you out something nice. What size are you, 12?"

Yeah, 12, nice of him to be so detail-attentive, she said, handing her keys over. Only she wanted a whole outfit—shoes, size 10, accessories. He knew what she liked.

27

Cyrus pulled up in front of a bungalow and put the Impala in park. Even at night, he could see that the lawn needed to be sprayed, the way Hector Diaz seemed to be cultivating dandelions. Maybe he doesn't want to use pesticides, Cyrus thought, checking his Timex digital, 10:39 pm. Good, he was six minutes early. Whatever happened next, there was no way he was going to do anything in the punctuality genre to send Diaz into a pout.

Looking up and down the street, clear, Cyrus thought about sliding a bootleg into the player, Generation X live in Osaka, 1979, then remembered the boots had been seized. And well, the studio recordings were a little rote, given Billy Idol hadn't put out a decent record for six years. Why had Arlene taken it that far anyway? There was no reason. Cyrus was a collector, a musicologist. As such, he had a right to listen. And please, there was nothing wrong with those pictures. Billy was clearly of age there, as Cyrus had noted. And if naked pictures of Billy as a legal adult existed, Cyrus had a right to see, for, in addition to a musicologist, he was a cultural anthropologist. What was Arlene going to do now, turn them over to Billy?

At first, Cyrus didn't think she would go to such lengths, like it should've been enough to fire him. But now that she'd submarined his new gig with Gary Orange, it looked like she was trying to bury him, truly, so why should Cyrus expect mercy? He shouldn't.

As Cyrus checked his watch again, 10:41, he asked himself what Billy Idol would do in a situation like this. If Cyrus wanted the most literal answer, it could be found in the lyrics to "Don't Need a Gun," one of few bright spots on *Whiplash Smile*, and what did Billy say there? Well, while Cyrus didn't know that one lyric-for-lyric—like, it wasn't Cyrus' style to memorize substandard LPs—Billy clearly sang along the lines of you don't need a gun when the other guy doesn't have one. Same time, Cyrus had it from quality sources that Billy was smoking a fair amount of crack during the *Whiplash Smile* era—that's probably why the album was only okay—so why should Cyrus seek wisdom from Billy's crack period? Again, he shouldn't.

After all, it was Billy's poor judgement to underuse guitarist Steve Stevens on *Whiplash Smile*—likely another decision made under the influence of, you guessed it, crack—that caused the rift between them, the synth, the keyboards, or whatever the credits said, overwhelming the guitar to the point where all songs truly needed to be re-recorded live on the floor of a biker bar to get Stevens' guitar right. But now, with Stevens moving on to greener pastures—the *Top Gun* soundtrack, Michael Jackson, and his own outfit, The Atomic Playboys—that seemed unlikely, and what was Billy going to do?

Cyrus had read all about the new guitarist, Mark Younger-Smith. He was supposed to be a blues rocker capable of gnarly riffage, and while that alone seemed promising, who the fuck was Mark Younger-Smith?

The writing was on the wall. It was going to be like when Mick Ronson left Bowie. *Diamond Dogs* aside, Bowie was never that good again. So, Cyrus thought, checking his watch, 10:43, if Bowie was never that good after losing Ronson, Billy Idol was clearly, as Arlene had said, on the decline as well. That being the case, who was Billy to say whether Cyrus needed a gun? Billy probably had butch guys around with butch guns at all times, guys in the shadows. It was easy for Billy to say he didn't need a gun, sure, but where did he get off being preachy about it to others who didn't have the same level of protection? Guys like Cyrus who were on their own, up against the world, up against straight society. Figuring he was Goddamn right to arm himself, Cyrus checked his watch one last time, 10:44, and stepped out.

***

Nathan thought Claire's *seins* looked more substantial in the orange triangle bikini with wood beads and O-ring details. He even had a joke at the ready about how many of those you could get by the kilo, but again, was none too sure of his metric and didn't wish to insult the lady. She was sitting in the middle of her couch, open palms on either cushion, posing in front of the fan, as promised.

In her head, she was fretting over Veronica's question about the money. Initially, Claire felt guilty, like her suspicions had everything to do with her own insecurities. Then, giving herself a shake, she figured she ought to be thinking like a cop in case she had to be one again. What kind of stunt were they pulling anyway? Did they even do payroll heists anymore?

Up and off the couch, she crossed the room, opening her walnut desk, removing the folded sheet of blue-lined yellow paper she'd taken from Veronica's on the dark day.

"Been meaning to ask," Nathan said. "I saw you, was sitting right there at the picnic table. Why are you collecting evidence? Shouldn't be collecting evidence, should be getting rid of evidence. We're going over to the other side, bad. You know that, right?"

Claire held the paper up. "This is the sheet beneath the sheet Veronica wrote the plan on."

True, but Nathan knew what it was. He wanted to know why she'd taken it, to what end?

"Well." Claire rooted around in her drawer, producing an HB pencil with an eraser. "You take your pencil, run dull lead sideways over the page like a charcoal sketch, and there's the entire plan in Veronica's handwriting, only reverse. Wherever she made indentations in the paper, her handwriting will show up in yellow."

Okay, it was official: Claire wasn't answering the question, so Nathan protested further, figuring she could be talked into destroying the evidence. "Being evasive is impolite."

"What?"

"What—I asked why, Claire? Why did you take that?"

"Insurance." She held the page to the light. Yeah, it was all there. "Insurance in case Veronica even thinks about arsing us."

"All that is is insurance to arse all of us. Best insurance is burn that, flush the remains by reason of Angela Lansbury knows a *homme* has some kind of cop equipment can read ashes."

"There's no such thing—Hollywood." Claire ran her eyes across the indentations. "As for this, I'm protecting me, protecting you. Shows her conspiring, leverage in a worst-case scenario."

Nathan was about to say something when the phone rang, Claire picking up, hello.

It was Morton, telling her the deputy chief was pleased about the rubber chicken collar, no question. And yes, as a matter of fact, Morton was gassed up at The Cruiser, new gay cop hangout, secret location. Only gay cops knew about it. That's why they called it The Cruiser, two meanings, and did Claire get it? Yeah, Claire said, clever. Morton said it was awesome, glory holes in the men's room. Like, they were both men's rooms here. Claire told Morton to just be safe. He said, of course, hand jobs, then congratulated Claire on the petty cash bust.

"Great caper, Malik. Good intensity, no question. Show's initiative, teamwork."

"Thanks." Claire folded the yellow paper twice, putting it in her top desk drawer. "Nice of you to say." Turning, looking back at Nathan, she saw him lying on the floor, hands over his rib cage, staring at the ceiling. "But it's no big deal."

"Is a big deal, Malik." Morton was excited, accentuating the positive. "Was talking to the association lawyer, Marty Clemson. He says this's going to put the screws to those dinosaurs on the police board. Says a cop like you ought to be on the case. And you know Deputy Chief Walsh's beating the bongos for you, no question. Saw him today, told him the rubber chicken bust was all your doing, half anyway. You can't believe how happy he is to get Heathcliffe Wilson off his back. Know what that's worth, Malik?"

"A lot, and nice of you to mention, Morton." Feeling Nathan's eyes on her, Claire made sure to give him something to watch, a jiggle. "You smoking?" she said into the mouthpiece.

"What?"

"I said, you smoking?"

"N . . . Yeah, I've had one or two. Same as not smoking, this city."

"Good for you, Mort. But listen, you're drunk, I'm drunk—"

"Seeing as we're both drunk, we should party. They let women in here."

"Thanks." Claire looked at Nathan, giving her hips a shake this time. "Nice offer, but it's not a good time to talk shop."

She sat on her desk, one hand on the corner, other on the phone. And Goddammit if she wasn't a talking 976-ad, call her. Sure, Nathan thought, Calvert coerced her into posing. How'd Cal get the pics in *Gallery* without her sig? Big magazine, Nathan figured they'd have contracts. And of course, he remembered Madonna making like she fought publication of those black-and-whites, *avec* armpit hair, in *Playboy* and *Penthouse*, until they dug up some papers Madge signed in the '70s.

"That guy from the set," Morton said to Claire. "That French guy, Nathan. He there?"

"Yeah." Claire looked at Nathan, blew him a kiss. "But he's not really French, just from there, Montreal."

"Good for you," Morton said. Thinking she's serving *poutine* to the parking guy, bottoming out. "About time. He know how to drive the pork truck into salmon city?"

Claire giggled. "Yeah, he knows."

Knows what? Like, they were talking about Nathan, and hello, he was right there. What did he know? *Tabernac*, if she was telling Morton about tomorrow, that was entrapment.

"Listen," Morton said. "I need to ask. Jeffery Brewer, the kid you call Sundance, did he say anything about Rusty Staub and I?"

Claire snapped her fingers at Nathan. "Sundance say anything about Rusty?" Nathan shook his head, no. Claire relayed the message to Morton. "No, to either of us. Why?"

"No, no, that's good. I told him not to."

"Why, Morton? Why did you tell him that?" She waited. "Morton?"

"Look, it's just I'm in trouble already. That's why I was talking to Marty Clemson."

"What kind of trouble?"

"Cyrus' lawyer is trying to get counter charges filed, false arrest, brutality."

"False arrest—they know he took the bird, the money."

"Yeah Claire, but it's the assault an officer they're after. They asked how come my blood was on the wall where Cyrus said it would be."

"What'd you tell 'em?"

"I said that's where the assault an officer took place."

"And is it?"

"Yeah."

"Okay, so what's the problem?"

Morton sighed. "Now they want to know why I drove Cyrus behind an abandoned Total station."

***

As per instructions, Cyrus met Hector Diaz in the garage at the side of his house the moment it struck 10:45. Diaz was inside, cleaning the rifle, oiling it. Cyrus tapped gently on the side door, let himself in, talking. "Did you know Chuck Connors played for the Cubs?"

That's right, Diaz said, a little impressed. Did Cyrus know Connors also played professional basketball? Cyrus said yeah, Connors was 6'5". Played for the Celtics, right? Six-six, Diaz said, but yeah, Boston.

Encouraged, Cyrus pressed. "Do you also know, the U.S., being diplomatic, offered to acquaint Brezhnev with any United Statesian, and Brezhnev wanted to meet the Rifleman."

Diaz, polishing the gun, looked at Cyrus skeptically. "How'd you know that?"

"New western channel comes with my pirate cable, epic bio series."

Shaking his head, Diaz smiled. Even on a layman's level, someone was respecting his guns, their history, their people, so he let himself get into it, saying how Brezhnev and Connors posed for pictures together. That Connors made so many trips to Moscow some people smeared him as a red. He wasn't red, just buddies with a red, and there was a difference. Ideology aside, it was two disconnected people connecting. Diaz thought that was a beautiful thing.

"I truly did not know that," said Cyrus, thinking of that Lenin mural McNab assaulted himself on. "About the communism. Anyway, you got cartridges for this, right?" There, he said it, dropped it into the middle of all that nostalgia, casual.

"Cost you extra." Diaz waited for an explanation. Getting none, he said, "And you didn't get 'em from me. I'm only authorized to give you guys blanks. Why do you need cartridges?"

"What do you care?"

"I care because I'm giving a guy a gun shoots eight shots in three seconds. He's supposed to be shooting blanks, law says, only now he wants live ammo, so I'm asking—why?"

"Sorry." Cyrus stepped back with his hands up, someone else to blame. "It's late and I'm doing Abel Otto's bidding when you and I should both be snug in our beds. He wants to do this target-practice bit behind the studio, middle of nowhere, wants live bullets. They're for him. I truly don't know what it's about. All I know is that he said he wants the Chuck Connors rifle and I told him you were a can-do guy. Now are you going to be a can-do guy?"

Yeah, Diaz would be a can-do guy, if it was worth his while. "Fine, can do. But cartridges are going to be 50 bucks each, and you didn't get 'em from me."

Cyrus thought about bargaining, making it look good, then figured he might as well get it done. "Fine—double, plus 50 bucks a cartridge. Add it to the AMA bill." Reaching for the rifle on the workbench. "Just so I know, how do you safely load this? Abel's going to ask."

"Simple." Diaz took the gun, worked it open, deposited the cartridges. "Make sure the round side is facing down. So long as you don't fuck that up, you won't shoot yourself."

"Okay, now take them out and let me do it, just so I know, for Abel."

Diaz unloaded the gun, handed it back to Cyrus along with the shells. Remembering the drill, he kept the points down, closing it, then pumping it. "That how you do it?"

Diaz looked at Cyrus, the way he was holding the gun, pointing it, and why did he pump it? God, if he knew how to pump it, he had a pretty good idea how to load it, so what was he trying to pull here? And to what end? "Before, on the phone, you said there was something you were going to tell me."

"How's that?" Cyrus said.

"I asked you how come the Smith & Wesson 629 Trail Boss with the Hogue grip hadn't been returned. You said you'd tell me all about it at 10:45 sharp, damndest thing."

"Right." Cyrus nodded. "Damndest thing."

Hector Diaz knew the habits of greenhorn shooters. Looking directly into the barrel now, he realized he was going to die once he confirmed that the gun had been safely loaded. "Trouble at work, man? You wanna talk about it?" He was trying to stall, buy himself a few more seconds. "Say, you're probably not old enough, but did you know *The Rifleman* was often criticized as too violent?"

"Yes." Cyrus looked at Diaz through the crosshairs. "But it was also arguably the best western TV series of its era."

Hands high, Diaz wasn't arguing, just stating a fact, and how did Cyrus rate *The Rifleman* against *The Lone Ranger*? Tough to compare, Cyrus said. The Ranger was capable of mercy, even when putting you in the shithouse. Chuck Connors as Lucas, not so much.

28

Claire wasn't kidding about the air conditioner. Damn thing was out, and the fans weren't doing much to cool down the place. Nathan made it worse on himself by going along with her repairman gag, wearing a huge pair of insulated painter's pants, toolbelt making the drawers hang halfway down his skinny ass. He'd stolen the get-up from wardrobe, a few other things from set, including a toolbox. And he was right. There'd been virtually no supervision back there since Cyrus got severed.

"You're sure?" he said, looking at Claire. "Morton pepper-sprayed Rusty Staub? Is that what you're telling me?"

Claire nodded, looking up as she remembered the rest. "Rusty got lippy, called Morton T.J. Hooker, saying he was in baseball, that he had to be somewhere. Morton didn't know who he was, thought he was too old for baseball, too tubby, and that set Rusty off. One thing led to another. Morton called Rusty Captain Kirk. Told him to step out. Rusty turned his back on Morton, disrespect, so Morton turned Rusty about face and gave him the spice."

"Well then, how come Rusty's not trying to press charges, like Cyrus?"

"Morton doesn't pursue assault an officer charges so long as Sundance and Rusty don't talk. It never happened. Best deal for all sides."

"Seems every time it doesn't go a cop's way it's assault an officer, plan B." Nathan stopped, put a finger to his lips. "And let's back things up."

"You mean, roll it back?"

"Right," Nathan said. "Roll it back, roll it back. Don't take this wrong, but I know what?"

Claire squinted, shook her head. She didn't get it.

Nathan pointed at the phone. When Claire still didn't clue in, he said, "While you were gabbing with Morton about my language skills, where I'm from, you said, 'Yeah, he knows.' Now I want to know what you and Morton were talking about, the thing it is I know."

Claire looked up, ahh. "That you know how to drive the pork truck into salmon city."

Nathan winced, said there were better ways of saying it, *romantique.* Why was McNab even asking, let alone putting it like that? Did they go to the gym together, too, take saunas?

Pointing back and forth at the phone and Nathan, Claire said, "He was loopy, asked do you know how? I said, yeah, you know, trash talk. Why, what'd you think I was telling him?"

Nathan said it should be obvious, opening Claire's cooling unit, diagnosing the problem. "Needs a new filter and energy-saver chamber." He didn't know an energy-saver chamber from a BTU, but it sounded good, so he pressed his luck, told her it would be $90 to fix, parts and labor.

"As it is, there's a run on air conditioners by reason of heat, so you probably want to pay me and be done with it until spring," he said. "I can get you through. Next year, buy a new one."

"Well, to tell you the truth, *monsieur,* I'm kind of in a spot." She laid sideways on the couch, a hand slung over the curve of her ass, playing along. "You may have heard of me, girl in trouble, broke." Pulling on a beer. "Can't we negotiate for your share of rent, services rendered?"

Now he was supposed to work off his rent, huh? Impressed that she knew a little French—any French at all—Nathan dropped his drawers, stepping out of them. Said he'd moonlight for the low, low price of $70. That he was quoting 1987 rates, and she couldn't reasonably expect better for his bacon buggy, or whatever cops called it.

"Pork truck." Claire reached into her purse, slapping a fifty and twenty on a crate doubling as her coffee table. "And there'll be a tip if you do it like I say, rough. Understand, Lawn Boy?"

Oh yeah, he understood alright. Right away, he was up and on her, saying bend over. Pushing her down, pawing at the orange triangle bikini with wood beads and O-ring details, fingers digging into her ass cheeks. She said hey, trying to turn around when he hauled back and gave her a nice spank, another. "Lawn Boy, huh? Isn't this how you said to do it?" He pulled on her top until the seams gave, making a tearing sound. "Rough?"

"Hey, I also said."

Somewhere inside, she thought he was really going to fix the AC.

"Hey means what?" Nathan said, little wood beads and O-ring details flying everywhere. "You said do it rough." Pushing himself inside, she felt scratchy against him, and he was thinking that was the downside of a shaved *minou*. Eventually, it turned coarse.

***

Cyrus walked briskly out of Hector Diaz' garage, breaking into a jog when he saw lights coming on at the other houses. As he opened the Impala's driver-side door, a woman in a white night-gown walked onto her porch, raising her voice, hey!

Waving, saying hey back, casual, Cyrus ducked into his car, hit the ignition. He stopped himself from flicking on the lights because they would illuminate his plates, and he didn't need to leave his digits and letters with the girl in the white nightie. It was bad enough that he was in a vintage car, something unique, unforgettable. And now what in the actual fuck? She was running across her lawn, onto the street, standing in front of the Impala, screaming help, gunshots.

Right there, in that moment, Cyrus thought about shooting the intrusive busy body walking into the middle of all this without bothering to put on any clothes. Yeah, he could've stepped out and put a bullet into her, blam, end of story. But then what did he want to waste a bullet for when he could stomp on the gas and run her down?

Look at her, he thought, deciding to flick the lights on after all, blasting her with the brights. In a way, he admired her courage, sort of like the underground Russian cartoon character Octobriana tattooed on Billy Idol's left bicep. Whereas Octobriana fought Soviet and American oppression, this woman was taking on Cyrus and whatever hell he brought to her community. She could be inside her house, hiding in the dark. Instead, she was right there, defiantly pointing and yelling to anyone, call the cops. Shouting something about gunshots at Hector's when Cyrus stomped on the gas, running her over, ka-chunk.

He told himself not to look back, barreling past a handful of houses, bringing the Impala to a stop, looking into the rearview anyway, and Heavens to Betsy, the chick was wobbling, trying to stand upright. Cryus threw the Impala into reverse and gave it the gas, running her down again, ka-chunk. Then he slapped it into drive, ka-chunk, peeling out of there.

He slowed at the stop sign, taking a right and glancing in the rearview. Nothing looked like it was coming for him, so he eased up, wondering what Billy would say about this, parking in a metered space. Hearing sirens, he thought he should be getting out of there as he flicked on the radio, and then, fuck, the first bars of "Eyes Without a Face" came on, Billy all out of hope.

As much as Cyrus strongly endorsed the *Rebel Yell* LP, he did not care for "Eyes Without a Face," and spoke publicly of it as a nonsense peppermint punk radio single. He even had his own satirical lyrics, singing them over Billy.

Guy without a brain
Such a human shame
You got a guy without a brain

Funny, but the reality was the song cut a little too deep, reminding Cyrus of someone, someone he wanted to be with, someone from school who dropped out, someone Cyrus never saw again. Seeing sirens come at him from the opposite direction, then pass, turning onto Diaz' street, Cyrus thought how the song was about disappearing on someone like him, and he really didn't like Billy's songs about lying and deception. Sometimes, like now, it was as if Billy was singing to Cyrus, and only to Cyrus.

***

Claire stepped out of the shower and wrapped herself in a towel with *I Love Lucy* characters. Peeking through a gap in her blinds, Blundstones facing Birkenstocks at head level, she muttered "drugs" and walked dripping into the living room. Beneath her cleavage, Ricky Ricardo wore a pork pie hat, driving his convertible. Fred was in the back wearing his own pork pie. When Claire turned, Nathan could see the passenger side, Lucy and Ethel, laughing.

Nathan was figuring they were on their way to Club Babalu for the hottest mambo act when Claire started complaining about an in-your-face drug deal right outside. She'd seen it through the bathroom window. Two-bit Barnes Man doing business in front of a cop's residence, she said, off-guard when Nathan sparked up a joint. "And where'd you get that?"

"That in-your-face drug deal." He exhaled a sticky-sweet plume. "You couldn't make me? Some cop you are. Can't even make your own boyfriend."

Claire didn't recall Nathan's footwear outside the window, but boyfriend? Even though he'd said things about dates and a relationship, they hadn't really defined themselves. There was a race thing they'd have to deal with, whatever he was, and she was already cracking jokes to relieve the tension, but boyfriend? Fuck yeah, so long as he shut-up about his private pursuit of happiness, maybe he really could be the boyfriend. She popped him with an open hand, tracing her curves with her free index. "Boyfriend? Think you're entitled to this? Exclusive? Regular?"

"Regular anyway." Nathan rubbed his right ear. "And where's that billy club. Give you a wood shampoo myself, see how you like it. I told you, no hitting."

"Okay." Claire put her right hand up, stop. "I know where you're getting that, and I'm telling you, I don't want Veronica in our relationship."

"She's not," Nathan said. "I'm just saying, no hitting."

"Yeah, well I bet you wouldn't be saying that if she didn't put it in your head. And, probably, you wouldn't be crying like a *grande dame* if you thought you could take me."

"Take you?" Nathan was still rubbing his ear. "You hurt me, Goddammit, why?"

"Ripping my handmade orange triangle bikini." Claire pointed at the floor. "Wood beads and O-ring details everywhere."

"Should've heard those fly off the elastic. They go fling, fling,

fling . . . Asides, do it rough, you said. Plus, you, calling me Lawn Boy, inciting me to do it more like you said, rough."

"And then I said no."

Nathan took a hit off the joint, holding his breath as he spoke. "You said hey."

"I didn't say rip my clothes, and anyway, you're smoking drugs in my apartment." She looked at him, wet bangs dangling. "Where'd you really get it, the pot? My fridge?"

Nathan let the smoke go. "Sundance gave it to me by way of thanks I always hide him."

"You know." She stopped, closing her eyes, remembering what Morton said. "He just sat there, didn't say anything about who Rusty Staub was before Mort pepper-sprayed him."

"What's Sundance supposed to say? 'Hey cop, no calling Rusty fat, no use of force on *Le Grande Orange.*' Not his fault you people are wound so tight."

"You people? And Sundance is dealing? That's probably why he didn't say anything."

"He gave me a joint," Nathan said. "No dealing, gave, free."

"He bartered, paid you with dope in exchange for services rendered."

"You make it sound like I polished his putter." Nathan took another hit. "Asides, his dad owns the biggest stereo chain in town, Brewer's Beats." Exhaling. "He doesn't need to deal."

"You mean he owns one of them. Like when an individual owns a Tim Hortons."

"No, I mean he owns the whole little chain, like Heathcliffe Wilson owns Heathcliffe Wilson's Fried Chicken. Brewer's daddy, Mr. Brewer, owns the franchise, all the stores."

"So why do they make him work on set?"

"Daddy's one of the investors. Ask me, papa got him the job to learn the work ethic."

She readjusted the towel, said, "Little fucker's up against the stem."

Nathan didn't know what to do with that. "Up against the stem?"

"Means he's a marijuana addict."

Nathan plopped a hand on his head, saying Sundance smokes a plant that grows in the ground, making him the same kind of addict that eats too much cilantro. Claire said don't kid yourself, that Sundance was prone to bouts of paranoia. Good-looking kid like that wants to be hidden, means he's up against the stem, a pothead.

"And you wonder why I call you Angie Dickinson, all war on drugs."

"Who cares?" Claire said. "Let me smoke on that."

"Maybe you're up against your own stem." Nathan handed the joint over, going down the hall. Taking the first left, he sat on the bowl so she wouldn't hear him tinkle, noticing his reflection in the glossy Cuervo ad. Claire had pulled it from a magazine and taped it to the opposite wall. The picture had a Spanish-looking woman wearing a towel with *I Love Lucy* characters, just like Claire. She held a deck of cash, money all over the bed she was lying on. A fit, unkempt *homme* leaned in holding a shot of tequila. It was smug, and Nathan didn't like it.

Bad enough Claire had been collecting evidence. Now she was getting ahead of herself, and who knew what she was really telling Morton? She was a cop, and those people tended to have strong bonds. Take *Hill Street Blues*. As hardnosed as Buntz was on Chief Daniels, punching him, deep down Nathan knew Buntz loved the Chief, but not like a bitch.

29

Cyrus parked the Impala in the alley behind his building. Reaching into the back, he brought the rifle up front and wrapped it loosely, so as not to give away the shape, in craft paper, taping it. Done, he stepped out to examine the front bumper, and dammit, there was another good ding, probably from that woman's head, the Impala devalued again. There was blood, too. Not a lot, but enough that Cyrus had better take care of it. He was wondering how to wipe it off when he noticed the white nightie hanging from the underside of the bumper, torn off Diaz' nosey neighbor. Oh why oh why couldn't Cyrus have just driven around her?

This was not good.

Bad enough Cyrus had run her down. But if he had her nightie, clearly, he'd left her naked on the road back there. So now it wasn't just going to be a psycho thing. It was going to be a sex psycho thing. And not just a sex psycho thing. No. By this time tomorrow, Cyrus figured there'd be stories about him being a closeted heterosexual psycho.

As if that would explain everything, he thought, wiping the woman's blood off with the last stitch of clothing she ever would wear.

Taking a step back, he noticed that he missed a spot and touched it up, then rounded the vehicle to find—yep, Cyrus knew it—another ding on the back bumper, more blood. Wiping it down, deeming the Impala a jalopy, he headed for the stairs, meeting the wisp of a girl with yellow hair from the second floor halfway. Hi, Cyrus said. Slowing as she looked away, the yellow-haired girl said hi back, passing and picking up pace, sort of crab-walking sideways, bolting, the pitter-patter of her little Dr. Martens fading until she made the door.

Jesus, she could already see it on him, something doomed. Of course, Cyrus thought, it could also be that the yellow-haired girl noticed him carrying a blood-stained nightgown. Truly, they were going to make him out to be a sex psycho het for sure.

Climbing another flight and a half, opening the EXIT door, he was relieved to see no one in the hall on three, heading for his place at the end. Soon as he let himself in, he dropped the nightie in the trash, then rolled a nice fat one, lighting up that Maui Wowie and drawing deep, an old song seeping upstairs, Joey Ramone asking why is it always this way?

One by one, Cyrus went through old friends in a little vinyl book he'd bought at a dollar store years ago. It was baby blue with a tiny gold phone on the face, creased. Cyrus opened it, bending it back, realizing he didn't have a friend in the world until the letter E, Jimmy Erskine, so he phoned, left a message saying he was just thinking of Jimmy, good times in the schoolyard. And well, Cyrus wanted to say so. See you on the other side. Long distance, Cyrus got a hold of Marc Freeman, relaying roughly the same sentiment, this time about college, Interior Design at Ryerson. Freeman said thanks, but he had company, bye.

Cyrus thought about making another attempt, then lost his taste for it. Already, he was saying cryptic crap, giving himself away to anyone who knew better, at least in hindsight, and he truly didn't want them blaming themselves, thinking they could have stopped him.

"Can't," he said on his way into the washroom for a quick whore's bath. Water pressure poor, he ran both taps wide open, looking in the mirror. And Jesus, Diaz' blood had sprayed Cyrus' tan bowling shirt, back-blow, so much it looked like Cyrus had been wounded.

Upon closer inspection he saw rust-red specs encrusted across his nose, so he killed the sink taps and stripped. Setting the water just right in the white tub with black feet, he turned the shower on, stepping in and drawing the see-through curtain when he saw pink water running off his body and down the drain. No wonder the yellow-haired girl was afraid of him.

***

Back from the head to the living room, Nathan saw two bottles sitting in front of Claire. "Nice towel, I meant to say."

"Thanks," she said. "But listen, I'm nervous, jumpy about tomorrow. Thought we'd have something to take the edge off. Cuervo light for darky and dark for me."

"No, no." Nathan shook his head. "I hit limit. But go ahead, you think you can handle it."

"Say yes. Do it with me."

"No, I'm telling you."

"Damn you, I bought this special for us. Humor a girl."

He almost gave her another no. Then smiling, opening his bottle, he said alright. Heading to the kitchen, he ran the faucet, pouring out the contents, replacing Cuervo Light with water. He carried the same bottle when he returned with glasses of water between his forearm and rib cage. In his free hand, he had a knife, lemon, and salt shaker. "Help me."

She laughed, taking the knife and lemon, cutting wedges while Nathan licked his hand. He went to shake salt on it, then looked at Claire when something made a cha-cha sound inside the salt shaker, tossing it on the couch. "How many decoy safes you have?"

Instead of answering, she tracked down the real salt shaker, a ceramic Yorkshire Terrier Nathan thought looked more like a bookend. Like the salt's priceless, right?

First, they toasted Attila the Hen—Claire chasing it with stolen Löwenbräu—then to ripping off Attila tomorrow, a third to Kiwi for giving Arlene the nickname, a fourth to Abel for stuffing that skunk blanket in Arlene's Jeep. It became a blur of shots, shots for no reason, and Claire was tilting her head, hair falling forward.

Nathan thought of her first note, the clipping about the heist at Chuck Barris' prodco on the back. With Claire loopy, Nathan figured this would be a good time to test her truth, so he asked where she got the article. She looked straight ahead, slurring, saying she hoofed it to the library that morning, cabbed it to her car at the bar, drove to work. Then she raised a slow index. "Why you asking when I'm sauced?" Looking at Nathan. "You don't look sauced."

Nathan hesitated, said, "It's just we discussed robbing the place the night before, spent that night together. Next day, I start work an hour before you, then boom, you roll in and already have the situation researched, *avec* printed materials. Didn't that take time?"

No. Claire wasted more time hailing a fuckin' cab than she did searching the library computer for payroll heists at production companies.

"So what? You just type 'payroll heist' and 'production company' in the computer, articles pop up on the screen, then you press print?"

"Pretty..." Claire hiccupped. "Much."

"They can do all that, that fast?"

"Oh," Claire said, eyes fluttering, "they can do more. Just . . . you . . . wait."

Again, Nathan prayed for death before he had to learn computer. He wondered where the world was going, whether this was a good thing, all this information out there. Certainly, if old news was so accessible, personal info would follow, if it hadn't already. And how would that be a good thing, the whole world able to find out about Nathan? If Claire could call up ancient shit up about Chuck Barris in a heartbeat, anyone could as easily read about Nathan walking out on Disco Dick at the Phoenix Open. So how was Nathan ever going to live that down? Didn't matter, caddying was over, he told himself, looking at Claire trying to stay with him.

Her green-brown eyes were dull, puffy, and Nathan didn't think it was so sexy anymore. Not like the first time. She was sloppy now, soaked in her own sweat.

He leaned her back on the couch, undoing the towel from above her breasts, pulling it open. Then he reached for his bottle, unscrewing it, pouring a shot of water into her belly button and sucking it out. When he looked up, her hip bones were poking out a bit, a hand draped over her forehead. She was peaceful, eyes closed, mumbling gently, something about Chuck Barris.

Nathan dipped his fingers in Claire's glass of water, splashing her face. She didn't flinch, so he did it again. Nothing. He slipped a pillow behind her head. Nudging her a few more times, he grabbed her keys off the coffee table, taking the toolbox he'd stolen from set.

Selecting the oddest key on her chain, something that looked like a drill bit, he inserted it into a tiny hole on the spine of Shakespeare's works, opening the book to find the middle cut out and framed into a box. Seeing her gun, he confirmed the model, a perfect match. Briefly, he looked over his shoulder at Claire, still out, then went to work, emptying the six bullets from her gun, laying them on the floor, removing the top level of the toolbox, retrieving the gun from set. He breathed easier when her bullets fit.

Same *pistolet*, he reasoned. Means bullets from one Smith & Wesson 629 Trail Boss ought to work in another Smith & Wesson 629 Trail Boss, both with the same Hogue grip. Same *pistolet* needs the same parts, right? Just like a 1960 Impala needs 1960 Impala parts.

Replacing Claire's empty gun in the book, locking it, putting it back on the shelf, he slid the gun from set into his toolbox. When Claire stirred, he froze. He wanted to get everything else done, but figured he'd have one more chance and crossed the room. He stepped out of his boxers, kneeling at the foot of the couch, nudging Claire. She didn't respond, so he carefully picked her up, forgetting she weighed about the same as him. He'd made it past the doorway when his knees buckled, hearing her groan as he dropped her a foot above the bed.

***

Cyrus dried off with one towel, hung it, wrapped another around his waist, killing the lights and walking to his living room where he laid on the sofa. He would've put another towel behind his head to guard against mold, but what did it matter? Whatever was about to happen, he was resigned to it, and that brought about a sense of relief, even if he was taking others with him.

The sound of sirens gave him a start, getting closer, then passing. He figured it would take the better part of tomorrow for the cops to catch up to him, and by then, it would be too late.

Closing his eyes, he willed his heart rate down, calming himself, thinking he might get at least a little sleep when the phone rang. He decided against answering, assuming it was someone he called earlier. And well, he'd already deemed that a bad idea, so he didn't think talking to them now was any smarter. When the machine clicked over to his outgoing message, he was nonetheless curious about who was calling, but they hung up. Outside, he heard an argument, somebody cheating on somebody, then the phone rang again. Cyrus waited out three rings, his outgoing message, and the click. This time someone was speaking sternly.

"Hello, Cyrus. This is Emma Banks. I'm a Chrysalis Records rep here in Mississauga. Sorry to be calling late, but some unauthorized materials I am told were in your possession have come to me, and I've just now learned how to contact you. I'm afraid this is an emergency for us, as the copyright holder of materials published by unauthorized publishers . . ."

A copyright emergency—this was another crank. Cyrus knew it. Somebody from *The Otto Show* was drinking and dialing, maybe that rent-a-cop changing her voice, so Cyrus picked up, sweet as ever, saying, "Hello, Emma. Are you friends with Mott the Hoople?"

The stern voice stumbled, saying she didn't rep Mott the Hoople, sorry. Okay, but just so she knew, Bell Canada had this line under surveillance. Fine, Emma said. What with the materials that landed on her desk, she was cutting to the chase. She needed to know where Cyrus acquired the naked pictures of Billy Idol, as well as the bootleg recordings.

Cyrus looked at his watch. "Do you truly expect me to believe someone from Chrysalis is phoning me at the midnight hour about a few bootleg Billy Idol cassettes?"

"This represents an actual emergency for us," Emma said. "With digitization and the internet now a reality, we need to cap sources before this stuff gets out there, forever. Unauthorized material seems fun to fans, but this is going to be the industry's fight for the '90s, and you have a line a lot of bootleg materials licensed to Chrysalis."

"Oh yeah," Cyrus said. "If it's so serious, how come it's not Bill Aucoin phoning me?"

Emma paused, said Aucoin hadn't repped Billy Idol since '86.

Cyrus knew this to be true. Hard as it was to believe, Billy fired Aucoin for being a cokehead himself. In a way, Cyrus thought it would be like The Pogues firing Shane MacGowan for drinking too much, like that was going to happen. Same time, Aucoin was the money man who was supposed to keep shit in a pile while Billy snorted, smoked, and fornicated his way to oblivion, so the firing made sense on some absurd level. More importantly, the common poser didn't know who Aucoin was or when Billy fired him, so the call appeared legit, maybe. Okay, Cyrus was listening while Emma was being so knowledgeable, and what could he do for her?

"We want the people who sell these items," she said. "Generation X live in Osaka, 1979, Billy solo from someplace in Illinois I've never heard of, 1984, and more. Plus, the naked photos could easily be monetized by someone other than the copyright holder if the internet goes the way we expect. This doesn't have to affect you. Just tell us where we can find your bootleggers."

"And if I won't?"

"Then Chrysalis will come after you, legally."

"For sure, Billy Idol is going to sue me."

"Billy has no choice in the matter," Emma said. "Chrysalis is effectively the copyright holder. Mind you, we already know you're the guy who gave Billy hell at Sam the Record Man during the *Vital Idol* promo tour, so I doubt he wants to stop us."

Cyrus let out a frustrated laugh. Now Billy really was after him, at least Billy's peeps.

Ah, Cyrus thought about the punk rock girl in front of *La Maison Du Croissant* selling fake Rolexes, rare concert tapes on the side. What was her name again? Oh yeah, Annabelle. Then there was Benjamin, who Cyrus bargained with at Times Square Books for the dreamy pics.

"Cyrus, you there?"

"Yeah, here."

"So are you going to name names?"

Cyrus thought it was all so far beyond this, so why did he

want to sic Billy Idol's peeps on Annabelle and Benjamin? "No," he finally said. "I'm not going to do that."

"Why? Why not?"

"Because that would truly be against code."

"Code?" Emma said. "What code?"

"Code that says you don't pinch your peeps, even when someone says they did wrong."

30

Friday, July 7

Claire was still a bit tipsy the first time she woke. Had to piss so she went and did it, lighting one of her Mores and sitting on her throne. She looked at the girl wearing the Lucy towel in the glossy magazine page on her wall, torn edge down the left side of the page, then to the same towel now slung over her rack.

It had been all good, the camaraderie, back when they were just saying, theoretically. The fun had been the chase, kind of like the lead-up to getting laid. But now it was happening, today, and she was whispering "licorice," practicing, telling herself bailing was still an option.

The toilet finished its cycle as she sat on the living room couch, smoking her cigarette in front of one of her fans, stubbing it in a Canadian Club ashtray. Her head was on the verge of pounding. She'd been here too many times—the pain, the dryness, the urgency—so she had two more quick shots of Cuervo Gold. Bought herself an hour, then what?

Feeling warmth inside, she noticed Nathan's wallet sticking out of his painter's pants on the floor. Glancing to the bedroom, she heard his relaxed, steady breathing. Back to the floor, she lifted his pocketbook, finding an envelope with Rusty Staub's autograph. Inside was Veronica's catfish marinade recipe. Lemon pepper, Claire thought bitterly, withdrawing the fifty and the twenty. Taking her money—he had to be kidding. The money was a prop, and he took it like Claire was a girl who had to pay for it. She didn't think so. Opening the top drawer of her desk, she checked that her folded yellow sheet of paper was still there, placing the bills on top, then a little chapbook, *Community Policing in Canada*, over the bills and shutting the drawer.

She lit another cigarette, put it in the ashtray, her last butt still smoldering. Leafing through Nathan's ID, making the odd mental note—his middle name was Jason, a member of the Professional Caddy Association, a true pro. Thinking how she hadn't caught him in a lie yet, then who was she to talk? How many times had she spun things so he'd think better of her?

Sliding the wallet back into his pants, hitting her cigarette, she thought maybe she shouldn't have had all those tequilas. She'd seen the copy of her *Gallery* contract. Couldn't remember signing it, but that was her handwriting, her girly loops. And again, here she was, drinking, re-opening the drawer, pulling out the chapbook, the money, then the yellow paper. Unfolding it, she re-read the three-point plan. It was difficult to follow the indentations, but it was all there. Claire remembered how smug Veronica had been about the Chuck Barris note. Stupid bitch should have burned her whole pad.

Just like she told Nathan, that yellow paper was an insurance policy. Our insurance policy, she thought, carefully folding it twice. Placing it inside the drawer, Nathan's cash on top, then the community policing chapbook.

Yeah, this was do-able. She just couldn't remember why she was doing it anymore.

***

Cyrus was operating on two hours sleep, up moments before his alarm went off at 4:59, showering, shaving, rubbing lotion on his face. Then he closed the bathroom door, looking at himself in the antique full-length mirror he'd lifted from that butch cop drama, *Night Heat*, the younger Dale sister checking herself out.

Briefly, Cyrus regretted that he hadn't put himself on the Stanozolol program. Always had a feeling, but if he'd known it would come to this so soon, he would've increased muscle mass and size, enhancing his fat metabolism in the process, just like Ben Johnson. Sure, Stanozolol was for racehorses, but it would've made Cyrus stronger, more effective, for this day. Same time, he looked good. Natural, no ink or piercings, pure.

He was glad he had the foresight to buy a new jock, Bike brand. Was a bit pissed that he had to buy an XL. He wasn't XL in anything, except shirts because of his height. It's just that they made those jocks so tight, and, well, he needed support as much as comfort.

Out in the kitchen, he prepped a cup of fair-trade coffee he'd set to brew automatically. That was his failsafe. In case the alarm didn't go off, the sounds and smells would've been his secondary. He was thinking ahead, smart, nailing details, ahead of schedule.

Making a big breakfast—bananas, pecans, pancakes—he pep-talked himself. Saying how boys like him never lasted. How they had to live for a defining moment. What was it he'd heard about the brightest candles? Oh yeah, just like his dad, Dwight Dagan, Cyrus was going to burn twice as bright.

He was all of seven when the old man fell off the TD Tower washing windows at 41. And his father's father, 37 when they found him with ligature wounds around his throat in the vicinity of what came to be Regent Park, Cabbagetown traditional, just a few blocks from here.

All the way through the bloodline men died young. Women, too. Ava, Cyrus' mom, had a heart attack at 49. Cyrus thought it was more like a broken heart, and they were developing science on that. But whatever the cause, Cyrus would also burn half as long.

He'd have a few minutes at best, so he prepared like an athlete on game day. His song, "Untouchables," was on the record player, Billy Idol singing about their mutual passion to escape days that go by, their desire.

Patronizing a secret salon, Cyrus thought Billy would've done himself a favor by escaping a few days earlier, quite a few. Man, 1981, why couldn't it have stayed 1981 forever? Back then, there were still real self-made stars, people who turned culture upside down. Now they had a star system, a pecking order, and soon, they were going to have contests to determine the stars. Unscripted programming, it was being called—look ma, no writers—and every major network already had something in development. Young Billy would've never stood for that.

Anyway, 1981 was also the year Cyrus bought "Don't Stop," Idol's four-song EP. "Untouchables" was kind of a throw-in, an after-thought, a B-side, and even a retread. But that song always did it for Cyrus, filling him with sweet melancholy.

It stuck in Cyrus' craw that the Kevin Costner film didn't use Billy's song, but then Costner would've had to admit he'd lifted the title. And hey, how did Emma find out that Cyrus was the same guy giving it to Billy at the record store? Cyrus was still trying to forget that.

It was September of '87, almost two years ago, when Cyrus found himself face to face with (his) Idol at Sam the Record Man. Billy was appearing in support of *Vital Idol*, a greatest hits package of extended mixes. The end was nigh, and Cyrus was mad the end was nigh, borrowing phrases from songs to frame questions. What happened to promises, promises, Billy? Thought you'd never sell out like they did, Billy. Why couldn't you die on the blue highway, Billy? The incident made the wire services, becoming a four-inch international news item, Cyrus speaking on behalf of disenchanted fans who didn't have a voice.

Ah, maybe that was the problem.

Never sell out like they did.

Do you remember promises, promises?

There was a time when Cyrus truly believed all that. To a certain extent, he was still living his life on the basis of codes, slogans, and beliefs, which was why he never got over *Whiplash Smile*. Like, Billy should've tried punching air a bit more. That've been good.

All said, Cyrus had to admit that "Untouchables" would forever carry, taking him back to those years when punk's prettiest boy was still his own guy, pissing off everybody. And, oh how Cyrus wished it had been different, that his own Elvis could have been up there waiting for Cyrus, along with rest of his dumb-dumb club.

James Dean and Jimi Hendrix were framed on the wall along with Joy Division singer Ian Curtis—*Love Will Tear Us Apart (Again)*—who hanged himself. Sid Vicious and John Belushi were mounted on either side of Len Bias. The latest addition was a hockey card of Pelle Lindbergh, an NHL goalie who ran his Porsche into a wall in '85, his name scribbled in black Sharpie, his DNA present, according to the certificate of authenticity.

***

Waking up dry well before six, Nathan looked at Claire snoring lightly, out again. Slowly rolling out of bed, naked, he walked gingerly to the kitchen, letting the tap out low into a juice glass. Back to the bedroom, sipping, he stopped at the door, listening. Claire was definitely sleeping, so he reached into his pants on the floor, removing his wallet. Right away, he noticed the cash missing. Seeing the envelope with Rusty Staub's signature, he flipped the top, removed the yellow sheet of paper, walking over to Claire's desk, sitting down to read it.

Lemon-Pepper Catfish à la *Veronica*
- *Place fillets in foil*
- *Coat both sides with olive oil, lemon juice, Worcestershire, lemon-pepper*
- *Refrigerate 12 hours*
- *Barbecue until fillet turns white*

How did Claire say it again? Oh yeah, roll it back, by reason of there was no way Veronica had time to refrigerate for 12 hours. She'd worked well into that afternoon on the dark day, now that Nathan thought of it. And he was acquainted with that Thursday open-air market, excellent prices. As he recalled, Mademoiselle Madeline offered only two choices of catfish—lemon pepper and Cajun—meaning you couldn't get it from her plain and do it yourself.

Nathan decided it wasn't a particularly good lie or even a big one, but Veronica was lying about something, so she was probably lying about something else. Still, he didn't see how having evidence lying around was good for any of them.

Opening Claire's desk drawer, flinching when it squeaked, *tabernac*, he stopped himself. Hearing her gentle snore, he went to work, finding the HB pencil, turning it upside down and rubbing out Veronica's recipe, blowing erasure shavings off the page.

Satisfied any noticeable trace of the recipe was gone, he re-folded the page like a letter, removing the *Community Policing in Canada* chapbook. Seeing the cash Claire had given him on top of her yellow paper, he took the money and made the switch, swapping in his now-blank yellow paper for Claire's, placing the chapbook on top, closing the drawer.

Listening for Claire, still snoring, he retrieved his wallet and tucked the cash back in along with Claire's yellow sheet of paper, which went into the envelope signed by Rusty Staub. He then took a quick shower, dressed quietly in Abel's Larry King suit and sat down at Claire's desk, writing out a note on the back of her phone bill.

***

"Eat 'em up," Cyrus told himself. "Carbs—eat 'em up, eat 'em up . . ."

Flipping the flapjacks, he put down the spatula and carried his quiet chant into the living room where he put the needle back on the record. In less extreme light, he looked at himself in another mirror, heavy brows and dark eyes. Thinking his face looked like an old-style newspaper photo shaded for contrast, he pulled on a pair of beat-up 501s and a Levi's shirt, tying a navy handkerchief around his throat. Thought about wearing the ostrich cowboy boots, except would they be good for running? Instead he slipped into the Fluevog Angels—12-hole, traditional, with a white stitch swirl, trying to remember which wardrobe he stole them from. Of course, the Fluevogs came from Jeanne Beker's Fashion Television program, and was she truly the diva for that duty? Cyrus didn't think so. What was she, from Scarborough? Just another one of Moses Znaimer's *savants* in too deep.

Whatever, seeing himself in the full-length mirror, he told his reflection that he looked good, authentic, like a young Burt Lancaster, only updated. Yeah, kind of like Matt Dillon in *Drug Store Cowboy* meets Lancaster in *Criss Cross*. No, no. *Criss Cross* was a payroll heist. How about Dillon in *Drug Store . . .* meets Lancaster in *The Kentuckian*? Yes, Cyrus thought that was impressive on its own, more appropriate, too. The important part was that he could still get things. Right up until the end, that's what they were going to say. He could still get things, even naked pictures of Billy Idol.

Yeah, now that it was all going sideways, Cyrus was proud of that, too.

He sang with Billy in a whisper about time setting them free. Looking at himself, Cyrus didn't like the Fluevogs, thought they spoiled the outfit, too flashy, so he went back to the ostrich boots, checking himself out all over again, better. Yes sir, he was going to shoot as many of them as he could with the seven bullets. Maybe he'd try to conserve bullets, figure out ways to kill two with one. Dammit, why didn't he find the rest of his bullets before he shot Diaz? It would've taken another minute, max. Also, if he had more bullets, he could've practiced, learned to use the weapon properly. And fucking hell, now the flapjacks were burning. He could smell them.

31

Second time Claire woke she was screaming at Veronica in a dream. Coming out of it, determining whether it was real or Memorex, she recalled watching Veronica bring Nathan muffins at work, letting him choose when that new Elvis Costello song came on that stupid lantern radio thingy, all of them singing how they knew a carefree girl with a mind of her own. They laughed and danced and ate muffins. Even though Nathan kept an appropriate distance, it was enough to bring Claire around, and she saw herself walk to them. When Veronica offered a morning glory, Claire batted it out her hand and said thanks for fluffing Nathan, then Nathan started swearing in French, everyone yelling until Kiwi ran out shouting that one of them had their talk button on, stuck.

Alright, Claire thought, that didn't actually happen, good. But why was she having nightmares about Veronica baking Nathan muffins? Thinking it must mean something, that she shouldn't ignore it, and hey, why was Nathan asking about that Chuck Barris clipping last night? He was suspicious, sizing her up, but that's probably because he was so afraid of computers he didn't know how fast they worked. At least that's what she hoped.

She looked at the clock, past 6:30. Her head was pounding and she had a shitty taste, dry, prompting a fantasy about turning the Smith & Wesson 629 Trail Boss on herself. Beside her, the note from Nathan made it worse. Saying how he woke up early. That he went for coffee at that pretentious pothead cafe up the street, every one of them up against the stem.

At least he didn't steal the car. Can't drive stick, she told herself, dragging her feet to the washroom, turning the shower on and blasting herself with cold water until she couldn't take it. While the jolt made her feel slightly better—clean again, fresh—she was still desperately hungover when she walked into the living room, wrapping the *I Love Lucy* towel around herself and flicking on the tuner. She sat on the couch hearing all about China blaming their now ousted leader for winding up intellectuals at Tiananmen Square. Claire was trying to wrap her lips around the ousted leader's name—Zhao Ziyang—as the Q107 news reader next reported on a coup in Sudan. And really, they were sending even more suicide bombers into Israel now?

It was all a little much. Like, Claire genuinely felt for people getting fucked over everywhere. While it was more subtle here, she felt that she was getting fucked over, too. Now that she was about to do something about it, she didn't have room for the Chinese, the Sudanese, or the Israelis. It was going to be everything she could do to get through the morning, so she tried to push it all aside, and was doing a decent job until she asked herself if, maybe, she was a posterchild for the decade. The drama, the porn, the policing—it always seemed to be about her, so, naturally she figured it had to be Cyrus when they turned to local news. Something about how police were looking for the driver of a blue vintage car after two murders on a residential street last night. Closing her eyes, convincing herself it was a coincidence, she felt relief when the newsreader dovetailed into something mindless, sports, only now they were talking about the Dubin Inquiry into drugs in amateur sport. That just depressed her, thinking about how Ben Johnson ran his 9.79 then had to return the Gold. Onto baseball, they reported Rusty Staub missing after failing to show for a scheduled appearance at SkyDome last night. That freaked Claire out, having the inside scoop. She felt herself calming as they reported on the actual game, something normal, the Blue Jays beating Baltimore 4-1, Todd Stottlemyre picking up the win.

After some wittier *répartie* about Phillies slugger Mike Schmidt retiring, the host played that fucking Elvis Costello song she'd just been dreaming about, so she killed the volume, wondering when she was last carefree.

Eyeballing her Cuervo Gold, hair of the dog, she made for the coffee table. Reaching quickly for the bottle, too quickly, knocking it on the hardwood floor, spilling it out, she held an index finger to her head like a gun saying kill me now.

Nathan's flask of Cuervo Light was on the other end of the table. She thought of a lecture back at the academy, told herself to focus, cutting a lemon wedge, licking her hand, pouring salt on it, then a shot. Throwing it back, spitting it out just as quickly.

"Water," she shouted, pounding her feet. "No." Louder now, screaming no, no, no until someone stomped on the floor up above.

Then, thinking of her gun again, snatching her keys off the coffee table, she opened *The Collected Works of William Shakespeare*. The Smith & Wesson 629 Trail Boss was still there, but why was that dark-skinned bastard drinking water out of her bellybutton last night?

Carrying the gun under her arm, she went into the kitchen, grabbing a cold Löwenbräu, heading back to the living room. One hand on the can, other on her forehead, she thought about the yellow sheet of paper from Veronica's, where was it? She remembered as she saw her desk, opening the top drawer, pulling out the chapbook, *Community Policing in Canada*. She remembered the cash, too. The $70 was gone. Fuck around, he actually took it. But then she'd been stupid enough to offer so that was probably her fault, except, wait a minute. She looked around, listening. That son of a whore took the money and didn't fix the air conditioner. Just thank Christ he hadn't taken the yellow paper, their insurance, their trust.

***

Nathan walked into the Mary's Beanery making a peace sign, ordered two Americanos to fly, asked where's the facilities? The hipster redhead girl wearing a black Talking Heads T pointed him to the back, downstairs. He said *merci*, took the route, passed the no-smoking sign next to the men's room door, opened it, getting a whiff of stale pot and cigarettes, then locked himself into a cubicle where he pulled the yellow piece of paper out of his wallet, a pack of matches from his front pocket. Getting a flame on the second strike, he held match to the paper. Before the upper right corner took, a voice two stalls over said, "Hey, it's no smoking in the washroom."

"That's right." Nathan dashed the match, the flame leaving a soot stain. "No smoking."

The guy flushed, leaving the stall and washing his hands, drying them as he faced Nathan's stall. "You saw the sign, and I know who you are. Recognize you by your shoes."

Nathan looked down at his shiny black brogues. It was the first time he'd worn these kicks, so he thought about taking the *homme* to task, asking, oh yeah, then who am I? Abel Otto? The show wasn't even on TV, yet the *homme* was saying he'd seen these shoes in particular. Then, thinking back to one of his own windy lectures, Nathan decided this wasn't a fight worth fighting. "*Pardon, monsieur*," he said. "Won't happen again."

"Better not. I know you saw the sign, Frenchie—*ne pas fumer*—and I know you know . . ."

Biting down, Nathan thought how he'd apologized, promised to do as the guy wished, and that was on top of the smell. It was so obvious people had been smoking grass in here, cigarettes as well. Yet the guy—probably pissed because his wife's giving him no cho-cho—was still going on when Nathan had already conceded. Asking, did Frenchie know what the fine was for smoking in a no-smoking area in the province of Ontario? If the guy said one more thing, Nathan was going to threaten to spark up one of those Cohibas, same as Castro, see how his little pink lungs liked that. Same time, Nathan couldn't help but think that maybe this intrusion was happening for a reason, that the Gods of golf were telling him to back off and think twice about burning that yellow paper.

***

Noticing erasure shavings on her desk, Claire went from worried to gravely concerned. She couldn't remember erasing anything, then figured she had more important things to obsess over. Who knew what she was up to when she blacked out anyway? Way back, in a tequila rage, she'd allegedly pushed some poor girl down the stairs for flirting with Calvert—no memory of it whatsoever. She'd woken up just last year in a lobby across the street wearing a tank top and matching boxers, hibiscus everywhere. In between, there'd been other incidents, so her being tight and working an eraser didn't seem like a stretch. Except what the hell had she been erasing?

Back to her room, she hid the gun in her panty drawer, re-trieved the Canadian Club ashtray, lit a cigarette, and fell in bed with her beer, pulling the towel to her chin, worrying whether Nathan was coming home, whether she'd made one off-color joke too many. God, she was trying to break the ice, to, you know, con-front the race thing playfully. He couldn't be that sensitive, but she knew she had to stop it with the hitting, that it was pissing him off. Still, why was he fake-drinking with her? Fuck around, she was go-ing to get to that right quick.

Hearing the door, she placed the beer on her bedside table and butted her cigarette, quietly waiting until Nathan came walking into her room and then flinging the Canadian Club ashtray at him, missing, shattering it behind him. He didn't say a word, didn't flinch, just stood there holding the Americanos, waiting for an explanation.

"First," Claire said, "I want to know what you did with your tequila?"

"Poured it out," he told her, deadpan.

"Why?" She jammed a hand between her pillows, reached for the Löwenbräu with the other, held it to her crotch. "The tequila was a gift to you, and you arsed me. Got me drunk, asked skill-testing questions."

"Look." Nathan let his head fall. "I told you I didn't want to drink anymore. Don't know how many times I said it—we can argue that—but you wouldn't take a no."

"Kind of like you when I said 'no, don't tear my bathing suit.'"

"Different matter entirely. Asides, you didn't say don't tear it until after I'd already done did it—rough, like you said. Plus, you calling me Lawn Boy, inciting me."

"Also said no."

"We talked about this." Nathan placed both coffees on the dresser and rubbed his eyes. "You said 'hey.' Otherwise, I didn't want to upset you over the tequila, so I didn't tell you, okay? Just keeping the peace." Raising his voice. "Now look at you, feel like *merde*, not thinking clearly, still drinking when you have to drive.

Is that professional? No, not helping with your punctuality or diplomacy, either."

"Okay, okay," Claire put the beer down, massaged her temples. "I started to get scared, like this was the part of the movie where you gave me the arse."

"Nice. You're the one stealing, I found out. Accuse me of arsing, and you're in my wallet, taking my hard-earned money."

Claire thought about arguing how the $70 was a prop, that he didn't fix the AC, then just held her head in hands as he went on until, finally, he said something that caught her interest. And check this out. He even got Claire an outfit for today. Outfits for both of them, so they could do this thing incognito. Getting a complete Cher outfit, would she call that being arsed?

After she said no, he reached under the bed, pulling out a suit bag, tossing it to her. She opened it, finding a pair of silver platforms, bell-bottom jeans with rhinestones, faux crocodile belt, chartreuse halter with a crossover neckline, and a Cher wig. She tried to say something, but her voice cracked and she stopped herself, cradling the clothes in her arms. "Size 12?"

"*Oui*," Nathan said, "by reason of it had to fit the Cher drag queen."

"Drag queen?"

Nathan sat next to her, said, "It's just a size, as in you're the same size as that person."

"Yeah, and that person has a penis."

"Fussing over a number." Nathan caressed her forehead. "Also, you're experiencing post-alcoholic-something-something." He remembered her on day one—taking down Cyrus, giving Arlene hell. Now here she was, a hot mess, tears welling in her bloodshot eyes. "It'll all be over soon, so let's us pull it together. The both of us, punctual, professional, and diplomatic, okay?"

"Yeah, pros."

And as she clutched her new clothes in the throws of post-alcoholic-something-something, she realized that she really didn't want to be a cop so much as it was the chocolate that made her peanut butter complete. Nathan was right. All these years, and it was about a good look for her body type, sturdy. Oh God, she'd clearly been out of touch for some time. Still, she was going to rock that Cher outfit, so she did her best to move forward, standing, dropping the towel, opening her top drawer and looking for panties that wouldn't show lines.

"Pick it up," Nathan said. "We've got to get going, traffic."

"Okay." She turned, pointing a pink thong at him. "Just, before we do, promise that you won't let Veronica bake you muffins—ever."

Nathan looked at her wide-eyed. "Did I miss something after the commercial break?"

"Promise me."

"That I won't let Veronica bake muffins for me? Why, Claire? Why?"

"Because it sure seems you want a girl can use the inside of the stove, a baker."

"Are you kidding?"

"Fuck around." She was shaking the panties, serious. "Prove your love. Say it."

"Okay, okay. Veronica ever offers to bake me muffins, I promise to say no thanks."

"Just no," Claire said. "No 'no thanks.' Just 'no.'"

"Okay. No muffins. Now could you kindly pick it the fuck up?"

32

Arlene re-read Dan Aykroyd's inscription, the prick giving everyone ideas. She then raised the cup with her name on it, heavy, looking to Veronica. "You put something in my Traditional."

"What makes you think that?"

"Because I've been low on pills," Arlene said, thinking how she tried to get off the Percs, tried to be nice. She did it once in a while, too. Aside from letting Lawn Boy slide after getting the stankie from the rent-a-cop in the green room, she looked for little ways to bond with them, breaking down, sharing a smoke, Lone Ranger stories. She paid them for the dark day, all of them. She didn't have to do that. Yet more and more, even the lowest of the grunts were doing little things to humiliate her. Buy her a douche bag—everyone from the rent-a-cop all the way up to Abel—any time she showed a shred of humanity, they viewed it as weakness, an opportunity. How the frick was she supposed to be nice when they were always looking to hurt her?

Even just a few minutes ago, she tried to say sorry to Veronica, so this sort of proved she was right about the calculating bitch all along. It also proved Arlene was right to have been so hard on her and the rest, if only she could have sustained that posture.

Looking at the clock on Veronica's desk, Arlene noted that it was 8:27 am, that she was slurring, repeating herself. Saying when you are scared, that is when you get caught.

Veronica, seeing Arlene's eyes move slower, jaundice taking hold, decided it would be okay to start taunting now. However it turned out, she said the investors were going to think Arlene did it to herself. If she lived to blame Veronica, fine. They'd think Arlene was deranged on top of the drugs, saying anything to save herself. Never trust a junkie, and all that.

Arlene looked at her tea cup. "Just tell me how many things you gave me."

"Eight," Veronica said.

Eight? Arlene thought it possible for eight to do the job, but young Veronica should have done her research. Eight was dangerous, sure. But the maximum daily dose was 12. While no one ever said take eight at once, Arlene figured she had a chance as long as she stayed awake.

"You do not know what you are doing. Eight, I have had eight for breakfast."

"And then I gave you another eight in your second tea, cup with your name on it."

Arlene looked down at her near empty cup. "Another eight?"

"That's right, eight for every cup. Think of it, you would have lived to tell if you only asked once. It would not have helped, but I was still willing to give you that if you only took what you needed. You, you tried to take everything—take, take, take. Telling me be in at five, pick the kidney beans out of your chili, make your tea . . ."

Veronica was still talking about taking, but Arlene was busy worrying about the warning signs—the shallow, labored breathing—and her hands. First they were just blotchy—no huge change—but now her palms were bluish, needles and pins. Arlene could still see them through the slits of her eyes, another sign that she was going down.

"Goddamn 16," she said. "Too many."

"Plus however many you took on your own this morning."

Arlene thought about it, two more, 18, mustering enough strength to reach for Veronica's desk phone, the unplugged chord dangling.

***

Claire pulled her Daytona into an empty spot near Arlene's production office, looked at Nathan on the passenger side. "Something I've been meaning to talk to you about."

Nathan took a breath. "Okay?"

"We didn't use a condom last night," Claire said, sipping her beer.

"You didn't say use a condom last night."

"Well, we're supposed to use one each time, every time."

"It's okay," Nathan said. "I pulled out."

"It's not okay. How do I know you're not sucking dick on the side, unsafe?"

"They say you don't get it from sucking dick."

"They say—so you're sucking on dick, but I shouldn't worry?"

Nathan was just saying that wasn't how you generally get it, that sucking dick was only what they called a theoretical risk. Claire wanted to know how he knew that. Again, Nathan said he knew that by reason of he reads, every day, that Claire should try it. Still, he assured her they'd use a condom each time, every time going forward. She was right. It didn't make sense to use one some of the time. Claire thought on it, said no, that sometimes she wanted to feel all of him, but she better not find out he was sucking on dick. Nathan promised he wasn't, but just so they could square up, why was Claire on about all this? First the muffins, now the dick-sucking.

Claire gave it some thought, took another sip of beer and said, "I think I'm compartmentalizing. Like if I'm worried about Veronica baking you muffins and you sucking on dick, I don't have room left to worry about we're doing a payroll heist. Like, now."

"Okay," Nathan said, pointing at Claire's Löwenbräu. "What's with the drinking?"

"I decided I'm a functioning alcoholic," she said. "Today, this is how much I'm functioning. You know someone willing to do this is functioning better, call them."

Nathan didn't know what to say to that, inserting his transparent ear plug, tuning into channel 36, telling Claire to do likewise.

***

Morton McNab sat in his squad car in front of Heathcliffe Wilson's Fried Chicken. He wasn't exactly staking the place out, just establishing an hour of police presence, as per Deputy Chief Walsh's instructions. Thinking how he'd been wrong all along, that he'd keep getting shitty cases as fast as he could solve them. And when they had to, when they really, really had to, they'd get around to assigning him a new partner, somebody to watch him, report back.

What'd they mean leaving him all alone? At least he'd been learning from Claire. She'd been seven years on the force, and Morton hadn't logged half that time. Experience—he didn't need to be out here with no one to hold him back, no one to take his mind off the smoking.

It had been five weeks now. Averaging a bummed ciggy or three a day, there had been times when he felt he'd beaten the physical addiction, until last night, and now it was there in his head. Dustin Hoffman's post-coital smoke in *The Graduate*. Coo-coo-ca-choo, yourself, Dustin—Morton couldn't stop thinking how good one would be right now. Realizing that he'd been going through withdrawal when he had the accidents, that he would've been more fluid if he'd been smoking, that he wouldn't have jumped on the poor kid burying his dad. And what was he thinking pepper spraying Rusty Staub? Same with Cyrus. Morton already had him, so why did he fake the assault an officer? Theft over a thousand was bad enough. But no, Morton had to frame Cyrus, make it worse. Now look at how many people were fucked-up, Morton included.

It was withdrawal, yes, but along with the withdrawal came guilt for everything he'd become. Why couldn't he have found a nice girl like Claire? Maybe things were changing in the outside world, but a gay cop? What was he thinking? Morton had been kicking himself over the smoking, drinking, and hand jobs for so long that he was mad at himself, loathing, and everyone was getting a taste. Even Claire, asking her where she was during the petty cash thing, then she goes and solves the case.

Claire, there was a cop's cop. She backed Morton every time, even when he rolled what he thought was a drunk, only it turned out to be a guy had the Alzheimer's, couldn't hold his head straight. No wonder they hadn't given Morton a partner yet. Sure, some days he'd ride with Salsky or Leroux, but they were probably just keeping an eye on him. That, and they'd probably made him on account of the white hankies. Also, he was the only uniform in 51 Division who didn't know who Rusty Staub was. That alone made Morton minty, their eyes.

Looking for a diversion, a way out from under his skin, he flipped channels on the police radio, then the sub-channels. Stopping when he picked up chatter through the static on 36.

"I am now leaving the building," a woman said.

"How's Attila the Hen?" A man's voice this time, vaguely familiar.

"Going, going, and gone." The woman again. "She was fighting off the nods for a while there. Lots of heart, but by the time I left she was facedown, out."

"Copy that."

"Is it safe for him?"

That was a third voice, Morton told himself, another woman, familiar.

"If she's not completely out, she won't remember a thing by the time he gets up there."

"So, is she out or not?"

That voice. Either Morton knew it, or he should just g'head and trade his lungs for sanity. Yeah, that's what he was going to do, grab a deck of smokes, get some perspective. And Attila the Hen? What could Margaret Thatcher possibly have to do with any of this?

"She's supposed to be out before he goes in."

What the fuck? Morton knew that voice, but who was it? Oh, to hell with it. One ciggy, just one ciggy would straighten Morton right out.

***

Outside AMA, Veronica passed the girl sparing for change with the ferret on her shoulders. Seeing Claire, Veronica winked on her way by the Dodge Daytona, hitting the talk button, singing a few bars of Cher's new song . . . If she could turn back time.

Veronica was four or five doors down when Nathan stepped out, passing the hippie girl, dropping a mess of nickels, dimes, and quarters into her basket, thinking his donation might rate for good karma as he entered the building, then the elevator.

"I'm in the box, rising," he said a few seconds later. "How does it look out there?"

"Clear," Claire said. "Clear as the best part of the day."

***

Clear? Clear as the best part of the day? That voice, Morton thought, Claire? No, it wasn't Claire, just someone who sounded like Claire and talked like Claire. Someone else singing that new Cher song. Jesus H. Christ, Morton needed a ciggy, and a drink. Man, why did he have to stay at The Cruiser so late? That's how they'd found out he was queer. Had to be some flunky there, taking names.

Drive, he told himself, chase the signal, but he didn't know which way to go. He looked in the rearview, as if some telltale sign of activity might've left a trail of popcorn—nothing. Eyes up front, the only thing of note he did see was through the window of Heathcliffe Wilson's Fried Chicken—the ex-Concorde himself, drinking something, reading a coffee-table book with a football player on the cover. He was at a corner table, sitting below an artist's rendering of himself in his prime, looking up, making sure Morton did his full hour of police presence. Next to the driveway, the changeable sign read, "Yes, Heathcliffe Wilson now serves breakfast!"

***

The elevator doors opened directly into the AMA offices. Nathan walked in wearing Abel's three-button navy Valentino with fat mustard pinstripes. Looking in all directions, he made for Veronica's cubicle. Smiling, wondering where his own private pursuit of happiness was going to take him next, maybe Havana . . . Everyone was talking about Havana, cheap flights out of Pearson . . . Then he saw Arlene clutching the unplugged phone. Trying to sit upright, fighting it.

"Little Arlene." Her pupils were pinheads. "Put 16 things in my tea."

Like her hands, her face was turning a bit blue. Nathan figured she was about to fall headfirst. But she just crossed her arms, wavering, mumbling something about being surrounded like the Lone Ranger, then put her head down on her desk, breathing slower.

Nathan took a moment to fret about being seen, then figured she was either too drugged to remember or too drugged to be believed. Even if she did recall him, she sure looked like someone back on the shit, so he went ahead, gathering pay envelopes into his blue knapsack.

Satisfied he had all but one, he had to nudge Arlene a few inches away, looking through the top drawer until he found a plain brown envelope where Veronica said it would be, feeling a thick stack inside. Miscellaneous Liabilities had been neatly printed on the outside in marker. Nathan packed that one away as well, turning to Arlene, placing his knapsack on the green filing cabinet, looking at her. Putting his hand on her neck.

***

Veronica sipped her double-double, thinking it was taking longer than planned to get out of the dry cleaners, but she didn't care. Kinky-haired redhead kid in front was trying to claim a powder blue tuxedo he'd dropped off late in '88. He finally had an occasion to wear it. An awards ceremony, something to do with the university, and now he needed his suit. Clearly, Veronica thought, the kid wanted someone to ask what award he was getting, but nobody bothered.

Instead, all three staffers assigned themselves to the job and someone managed to find the garment. That settled, Veronica placed Arlene's ticket in front of the cashier, trading cash for a sports coat—and yes, they were able to get the stain out—plus two pairs of designer jeans.

Outside, starting back, she slid the transparent earpiece out of her collar, reinserting it, picking up Nathan's voice. "I said she's cold, *froid.*"

33

Heathcliffe Wilson had read all the relevant parts of a book entitled *Official Canadian Football League Records and Facts*, and still couldn't find a black, or anyone else, who missed four field goals in a row. Had to be someone, but it wasn't like Heathcliffe could call the league office and say please give him a list of blacks who missed four straight three-pointers. He was thinking of how he might put it another way when he noticed Morton McNab pull away before he was done his full hour of police presence. Up from his table, Heathcliffe run-walked out of his restaurant carrying a cup of coffee. Cursing, looking at his Bulova with the Concordes logo, 8:43 am.

***

Morton headed east on Queen. Noticing the signal on sub-channel 36 weaken, he pulled a U-ie, bouncing off the far curb, telling himself he ought to g'head, have that smoke before he killed someone. Killed someone? Shit, son of a bitch, whoever was on the radio, they were definitely saying someone was cold. Talking French, too—*froid*. What was that, code for dead? And whoa, what was that again about Attila the Hen? It had been in the news for months, stories about Margaret Thatcher losing her grip, so was that what they were on about? Couldn't be on account of none of them sounded like limeys. Must've been code for something else. Same with the Cher song. More code.

***

Heathcliffe jogged to the street, muttering how he was due one full hour of police presence and this schizophrenic Morton McNab hadn't put in 40 minutes. Skittish uniform, Heathcliffe said, dumping out his cup on the asphalt. He was going to call his brother-in-law this afternoon, later. That's it, get his 20-grand cash money first, call Walsh later. Prioritize, just like in '85, when he retired moments after kicking that three-pointer to beat Edmonton on the last day of the season.

The CFL didn't pay kickers shit, didn't pay anyone shit—except for maybe quarterbacks—and the Concordes were about to fold. Yes, it was time for business, financial recognition. Time for Heathcliffe to go out on a high note. He knew everyone would tear him down all over again if he tried out for the second coming of the Alouettes, especially that reporter from *The Globe and Mail*, fucking slope. What did a Chinaman know about Canadian football?

Massaging the back of his neck, Healthcliffe walked to his Galaxie 500, getting inside, hitting the ignition. The radio came on mid-song, Blondie. Turning out of his lot, he sang along—I'm gonna get ya', get ya', get ya'—heading west towards Arlene's office. Thinking yes, Heathcliffe was going to see her early and get his restitution, now. Thinking how Debbie Harry got her restitution through song after that Bundy tried to get her. And then how he, Heathcliffe Wilson, was getting his restitution in cash. Tax-free, $20,000 was more like $30,000. And that wasn't counting what the insurance was going to pay, even more restitution.

First, Heathcliffe had to get some gum. His mouth tasted like ass, so he pulled up to Stephenson's Variety. Everything had an order to it—gum, money, then he'd catch up with his brother-in-law about that Morton McNab who didn't give his full hour of police presence.

***

Less than a half-mile ahead, Morton's adrenaline pumped as the signal grew stronger. Passing the street girl, he wondered how many laws she was breaking, and that was before he even considered her vermin. McNab had read that three-quarters of all urban rodents were rabid, so there ought to be a law against that, too—no rats for pets.

***

Cyrus pulled the Impala into a metered spot down the block from Arlene's office, keeping his head low when he noticed the squad car passing from the other direction. And fuck if it wasn't that cop who faked the assault an officer, that Morton McNab. What was he doing here?

***

Walking slowly towards the office, Veronica broke into a smile. She had taken it to the next level and it was all coming together. She saw Claire get out of her car, pouring a can of Löwenbräu into the gutter, the alky, hocking up a loogie, spitting as she ran into the building. That wasn't part of the plan. Even so, it was just as well, Veronica thought. Let Claire go inside and see it, scare them both. Really make them part of it, all of it, ensure their silence.

For a few moments, Veronica caught herself wondering how long the investors would respectfully wait to put her name on the shingle. She could see it now, Veronica Williams and Associates (VWA). She would have savored the internal sight, but behind Claire's Daytona, a hundred yards or so, she saw the Impala, parked. Cyrus jumped out in his cowboy get-up, a big old gun down low to his side like a perfect plastic action figure as he, too, ran into the building.

Cyrus wasn't due in until 10:45, Orest S. Jefferies the same time. Veronica had half-expected Cyrus to pull something, but this was supposed to be over well before he arrived. And what on earth did he have a gun for? Unable to properly process, she threw her double-double on the sidewalk and fell into a panicky jog, hitting the talk button before deciding what to say next. "Cyrus is on the way in there dressed as a cowboy with a great big gun. He followed you in, Claire." Shit, she'd been too fast, dropping names.

***

"Cyrus—Cyrus fucking Dagan," Morton said to himself. "And Claire, it is her."

Sensing the signal weakening, again, he pulled another U-ie, thinking about calling for back-up, trying to put it in a nutshell. He didn't know how many times he was going to have to tell them, but it sounded like someone was cold, as in dead, on sub-channel 36, Queen East area between Parliament and Heathcliffe Wilson's Fried Chicken. Somewhere around here, they were talking on walkies, sprinkling in some French, probably code, singing the new Cher song, more code. And oh yeah, Morton was hearing Claire Malik's voice, so she was somehow involved, as was, apparently, Margaret Thatcher. Unless, of course, that was all even more code.

That'd be great, turning in his former partner. Whatever she had herself into, it would be like turning in any other officer. This time tomorrow, they'd be addressing Morton as Serpico. That chicken-stealing guy—Cyrus Dagan—he was in the mix, too, and that was a problem. Morton had specifically been told to steer clear of Dagan, pending Internal's investigation.

Morton didn't know how many assault-an-officers that Dagan guy was guilty of, but, on sub-channel 36, they were saying he was armed, dressed as a cowboy... Dressed as a cowboy—back in the radio room they'd deem that proof Morton was queer. The hell was he supposed to say? That something was going down around here somewhere and he couldn't decipher all these fucking codes?

Queer—they wouldn't just say Morton was queer, they'd haul him in for a sample, then what was he going to tell them? That he'd been in a room where other people were smoking it? And who would speak for Morton? The union? Morton didn't think so.

***

Heathcliffe was chewing on a stale stick of Big Red outside Stephenson's Variety when his car phone rang. Walking to the Galaxie, lowering himself in, he answered, hello, speaking to his brother-in-law at headquarters.

"Listen," said Walsh. "Is that cop still out in front, that McNab?"

"No," Heathcliffe said. "Matter of fact, I was going to follow up with you because he didn't give his full-hour of police presence."

"Yeah, he's in some kind of trouble over the guy stole your bird. Trying to get in touch with him, give him a head's up, but he's not on the radio, not on the right channel anyway."

"What kind of trouble?"

Walsh sighed. "Now don't you go saying anything, Heathcliffe, but Internal wants him. Looks like he really did fake the assault an officer, being brought up on charges."

"So he's probably suspended."

"Likely suspended, pending."

"He get paid?"

"Too early to tell."

"Okay," Heathcliffe said. "But then who's going to do my full hour of police presence?"

34

Cyrus bypassed the elevator for the stairs, stopping on the second floor, looking out the window to see if he'd been followed. Watching Veronica run in after him, he held his breath, listening to her panting, letting go when she took the elevator. Dammit, why did she have to be here? Then again, he had to leave someone so it didn't look like he was a complete het psycho. It had to appear as though he'd put some thought into it, if nothing else. If he spared Veronica, it would be clear that he'd only gone after the baddies. Same thing when Chuck Connors, as Lucas, did those dudes who torched his ranch. Like, there was a reason Cyrus was killing people. Seriously.

**

Three floors of Muzak, "Silly Love Songs"—I-I-I love you—and the doors opened into the AMA offices. Right away, Veronica saw Claire training a gun on Nathan. She was standing beside Arlene, who was facedown on the desk, the top of her head exposed. Claire was telling Nathan she was sorry, but she was not connected to this anymore. Murder becomes part of the equation, gives her two choices: She cleans this up a little, spins it, solves it, and she's back on the force. She doesn't, and she's in the broth with Nathan and Veronica, jail.

"Doesn't give me a choice anymore, murder being part of the equation. A cop, particularly a female cop, in jail, no way."

Veronica waved her hands, hello, didn't they hear her on the walkie? Cyrus was in the building, armed, probably underneath them.

Claire ignored her, thinking it was a diversion tactic, that Veronica had probably been baking Nathan muffins on the side all along. That they meant to kill Arlene, cut Claire out, and buy a house in the suburbs with a great big muffin oven. How wonderful for them. Besides, if Cyrus was in the building with a gun, why hadn't he clipped Veronica? Cyrus with a gun, ha. If Cyrus ever got his hands on a gun, he'd kill everyone, the psycho.

Nathan thought Veronica was up to something, too. He just couldn't figure what side she was on. Probably her own, he decided, opening his suit jacket, telling Claire to looky-see.

"Dumb, I told you not to bring a toy gun, dumb and stupid." Claire watched his right hand. "Take it out slowly, drop it on the floor, kick it to me."

Nathan pulled his jacket open a little further, reaching. "You turning on me?" Nodding to Veronica. "Been thinking maybe you'd turn on her, but me, your own boyfriend?"

"I'm sorry." Claire wiped at the perspiration on her face. "But I let you go, I have to cover for you, makes them figure I'm involved, murder. Now the gun. Drop it on the carpet, kick it to me. Just the way it turned, is all, sorry."

"Why don't you just go ahead, shoot me? Twenty years is just as bad."

"Damn you Nathan, you know I will. Now put the gun down."

"You first."

"PUT THAT FUCKING GUN DOWN."

"Shoot me."

"I'LL PUT IT BETWEEN YOUR EYES."

Nathan looked like he was about to spit, then did. "So you keep telling me."

Claire screamed something about being sorrier than a Maple Leafs fan when her gun failed to report—click. She went to fire twice more—click, click. It looked like she swallowed a mouthful of Comet, Nathan said, pointing the other Smith & Wesson 629 Trail Boss at her.

She might've thought he was freaking—whatever, fine—but Nathan wanted to prove a point. A millisecond after this *pistolet* went off, he said Claire's miniscule, philistine, Gordon Gano hating brain would mercifully stop running. Toy gun—fuck her. This was a Smith & Wesson 629 Trail Boss. Same as Claire, only he had her bullets. Some pro, she hadn't checked.

"Mine?" Claire studied her Trail Boss. Hefting it, she noticed it light for the first time, turning it sideways, looking back at Nathan. "You don't want to shoot a cop with my bullets. Fuck around, you're pointing a whole lot of gun at me, loaded with dumb-dumbs."

"Dumb-dumbs?"

"Dumb-dumbs. Hollow-pointed bullets. Explode on impact, rip me inside."

"Thought those were illegal."

Claire nodded. "They are."

"Ought to use them on you just for that. Bet this *pistolet* isn't even registered."

***

Cyrus sparked up a joint and hit it, holding the smoke, looking up at the red-on-black EXIT sign as he exhaled. Taking another draw, he heard voices on the other side. He couldn't make out who was saying what, only that they were arguing. The main thing was that he had a good idea who was trapped in there. By now they must have figured out that he had come for them. And so what if a tear was running down his face? He was ready, on, singing in a deep whisper about how he'd be with the untouchables tonight.

***

Careful not to beg, Veronica tried to calmly re-emphasize that Cyrus was in the building, with a gun larger than anything she saw here. And she was thinking they had to assume he had real bullets. They could say what they wanted, but Cyrus knew how to get things.

The more she went on, Nathan started to think Veronica really was trying to divert him, but from what? The money? Fuck it, he had enough to worry about with a live *pistolet* on Claire. Hands over her head, cowering when Veronica spoke again.

"Don't do it. If there's a gunshot here, murder really does become part of the equation, like Claire says. If murder becomes part of the equation, we all lose. Right now, we do not necessarily have a problem, if we re-group."

Re-group, what were they supposed to do with Claire? Pointing the gun at her in stabs, Nathan said she turned on him, that she turned on Veronica, too. He told Veronica to ask Claire about that yellow paper.

"Paper?" Veronica waved that off, no time. "As Arlene says, when you are scared, that is when you get caught, and now everyone, including me, is making little mistakes. Let's just slow this down, talk it through. We get out of here in the next few minutes and this is still just some old TV flunky with a history of drug problems who OD'd."

"Nonetheless." Nathan shook the gun at Claire. "She turned."

Claire said, "You turned on me stealing my bullets."

"And it's a good thing I did by reason of you were going to shoot me with those bullets, kill me. Sort of cancels what I did out, saving my own life and all."

"Nobody's turning," Veronica said. "We are all walking out together while we've still got time to work out our problems, later."

Nathan sniffed, said he smelled pot moments before the EXIT door exploded open. Cyrus pointed the Rifleman's gun in their general direction, his mouth gaping open at Arlene facedown on her desk. Pink-eyed, he looked at them one at a time, finishing with Veronica. "It's been you and them all along, truly part of the conspiracy of grunts. A divide-and-conquer play over how Arlene was in love with my shit."

Nathan reacted slowly. Even though Veronica had warned them, he still didn't quite get it, the way Cyrus let them get a real good look at his cowboy togs. Telling Veronica he planned to spare her, but now Cyrus was going to do her first, stepping forward as he fired off a couple shots. Both times, the Winchester bounced in his novice hands. Too much gun, he missed Veronica, the second blast blowing part of Arlene's scalp off, a red splash over the pictures on the wall behind her. The force of the blow briefly jolted her into a proper sitting position, slumping forward again, a red puddle expanding on the desk.

Nathan had the *pistolet* on Cyrus by then, shooting, catching him near his right eye, Cyrus falling against the wall. Fucking hollow points really did explode on contact, a third of Cyrus' face gone, just gone.

"Huh." Nathan was half-surprised his shot connected. He

looked at Cyrus' stains, blood on the wall, a little gathering on the floor. Said "huh" again.

Veronica looked at him. "Huh, what?

"May be dressed up like a cowboy, but I guess he had a little Indian in his ethnicity."

"How do you figure?"

Nathan, waving his gun at Arlene, said, "By reason of he basically scalped her."

Turning, he asked Veronica what were they supposed to do now, murder times two being the equation? Two times murder, and Nathan hadn't even capped Claire yet. So, in other words, by the time they got out of there, it was going to be three times murder. What did they do then, when the equation became three times murder?

"I keep saying, you're not going to shoot her," Veronica said. "We need her."

"Need—I'm about already as mad as Scott Hoch when he missed that 18-inch putt to win the Masters, and then she puts a *pistolet* on me, her boyfriend, when this was her idea in the first place. The trust is gone, man—gone."

35

If Morton McNab hadn't manned up and called some of this in yet, it was because he could still hear them in dispatch, laughing, making jokes about *War of the Worlds*. Besides, he couldn't hear a thing on sub channel 36 anymore, dead air.

Yeah, he was starting to think maybe the job was making him batshit—everybody lying—until he spotted Claire's Daytona. Slowing, he gave her car the once-over as he passed it, empty, steering four or five car lengths ahead, parking short of the girl with the ferret.

Stepping out, Morton put his hands on his belt and looked to the space around him. To the gutter, spotting a partially smoked ciggy, he picked it up, brushing it off, straightening it, putting it in his mouth. He thought there was so much goodness left, patting himself down for a light he didn't have. Bitching about how they'd taken lighters out of the squad cars—politically correct again—he looked up, raising his voice. "Hey, street kid." The girl with the rodent looked at him, yeah? Then he said, "Got a light?"

"No."

"What do you mean, no?"

The girl, unsure of what part he was having trouble with, said, "No, as in, no, I don't have a light, officer. I don't smoke."

Morton crossed his arms, thinking how he'd better not say it out loud, no question. Just the same, he was sure he'd managed to find the only street kid in Toronto who didn't smoke. That's when he noticed the old-style Impala parked well behind Claire's ride, Goddamn Cyrus Dagan. He was here. But where was everybody?

***

Upstairs, Nathan still had the gun on Claire. "Now give me your *pistolet*."

"That's great, taking a cop's gun." Claire shook her head. "Think about it, Nathan. Taking a cop's gun, serious shit."

Nathan told Claire to get real, that she wasn't a cop anymore. Asides, it was already some serious *merde*. Two dead, when was the last time it got this street for Claire? Giving her time to argue, he waited, saying he didn't think so, now her *pistolet*, please.

She made a sour face, on the verge of making a production out of it when Nathan took her gun, emptying out four bullets from the Smith & Wesson Trail Boss from props into her piece. Leaving a single slug in the gun from set, he untucked the front of his shirt and wiped it down. Then he used a Kleenex to carefully put the gun from set in Arlene's right hand, getting her prints all over it. Resting it on the desk, he stepped back, pointing Claire's gun at Claire. "Got a job for you." Nodding to Claire, then Arlene. "Read about something like this in a paperback, *Briarpatch*. See, there's one bullet left in that *pistolet* from set and I want to you to guide Arlene's limp hand to aim it at Cyrus. Don't touch it. Use Arlene's fingers and shoot him again."

Veronica saw where this was going, asking isn't there a *Miami Vice* scene like this? Nathan said he didn't watch *Miami Vice* by reason of the coppers dressed like sixth and seventh members of Duran Duran, unbelievable, at least until Nathan met Angie Dickinson here. But whatever Don Johnson and the other guy were trying to pull, Ross Thomas used said device first in 1984, winning an Edgar for *Briarpatch*, and that anyone who used it thereafter needed to buy Mr. Thomas a drink. Then he turned to Claire, said, "Now I want to see you do it, use the *Briarpatch* device."

Claire looked at him, asked why? Two reasons, Nathan said. One, he wanted to make Claire part of it just in case anything else went wrong, give her an opportunity to win back some trust. She asked what the second reason was. Nathan said he wanted to make it look like Arlene and Cyrus shot each other, give them all an out now that murder was two-times the equation. Again, he told her, just pick up Arlene's dead hand and shoot Cyrus.

Nathan still had the piece on Claire as she wrapped her hand in Kleenex, carefully picking up Arlene's hand, using it to fire a shot into the wall above Cyrus.

"She missed," Veronica said.

Didn't matter. Nathan said the important thing was to get

residue—but not prints on the *pistolet*, if she did it right—on Claire's hands in case she turned again, leverage. Now all three of them had something to lose. Looking to Claire, he asked what was she going to say? That yes, she did fire a shot, but hers was the one that missed? Asshole.

She bit down, resting Arlene's right, gun in hand, onto the desk.

"Okay," Veronica said. "Now we clear out."

Not quite. Nathan told Veronica to plug the desk phone back into the outlet. That done, he sent Veronica to the kitchen to slap on the mint-green gloves and rinse out Arlene's tea cup. Apologizing by reason it was supposed to be his job, but she had to do it while he was busy training the *pistolet* on Claire. Who could trust her after she missed? In fact, Nathan said he ought to shoot her just for that. He gave her a chance to win back the trust, at least some, and she fucked up again. *Tabernac*, why did she try to shoot him?

***

For a moment, Morton thought he'd heard a shot, somewhere, but what the hell? Jonesing as he was, who knew what Morton was hearing? He looked up and down the street for someone smoking, pissed he couldn't see anyone. Glancing at the street kid, he felt relief when he caught a longhair in a leather drop an envelope into a Canada Post box then light up. Looking both ways on Queen East, clear, Morton briskly crossed, cutting the guy off as he headed west.

"Hey. Hey, can you please help me out there, captain longhair? I need a light."

The guy watched as Morton put the half-smoked butt in his mouth, said, "I'm in a hurry officer." Picking up his pace. "Have to be somewhere."

Morton stepped in front of the guy, putting a hand on his arm, telling him everyone had to be somewhere. The guy looked at Morton's hand on him, back at Morton's face, asked if he was under arrest. Morton strengthened his grip, telling the guy that if he didn't come up with some flame for this half-smoked ciggy, he,

Morton was going to pepper-spray the guy, take his smokeables, as well as his lighter, charge him with assault an officer, then put him in jail where they'd cut off all his beautiful long hair. So how about it? Could a cop having a nic-fit have a light? That's all Morton was asking for—a fucking light.

By the time the guy produced a Zippo with the Honeymoon Suite logo, Morton had enough and confiscated it, slapping the guy's face, telling him to hand over his pack. The guy stood there, stunned. Morton double-slapped him, front and back hand. At that, the guy handed over a pack of Player's Light flip top. Morton snatched the deck, told the guy to screw-off.

Watching him round the corner, Morton opened the pack, three-quarter's full, extracting a fresh king, putting it in his mouth. The Zippo caught on the first try, Morton lighting up, closing the flash, swish, and looking up at the clear blue sky as he took his first real hit, head rush. Yeah, Morton was a smoker. Alright, he thought, heading back to his car, where was Claire? What was she up to? And was that a shot few minutes ago or not?

***

The elevator opened as soon as Veronica hit the button. Through three floors of Muzak, "Just a Gigolo"—looking at themselves in the mirrors singing along in their heads about how they ain't got nobody—until the doors opened, leading to another set of doors framed in brass. Out in the street, they saw the cruiser, though none of them made Morton McNab personally. He was in his car, frustrated by dead air on sub-channel 36, fiddling with settings as a smoldering cigarette dangled from his lips.

"Just a cop in a car, busy," Veronica said. "Let's have an everyday conversation while we pass, something silly about clothes, background noise."

Picking up her beat, Nathan said they needed to stop by Chinatown. He wanted their opinions on a second fitting for this hand-tailored Armani. It was *très bien*, soft, set-in sleeve, slight ripple in the lapel, something Nathan could wear for business just as easily as a bar on the wrong side of the tracks, St. Jamestown.

Sounds nice, Veronica said, professional. Also diplomatic, Nathan, told her. Only thing, he was a little nervous by reason of he couldn't decide on the sleeves. Veronica forced out a laugh, asked what's the problem? It was the *tailleur*, Nathan told her, the *tailleur* thought shorter sleeves made a statement about a man's commitment.

"What do you think?" Veronica said.

Nathan paused, seeing himself standing in a three-way mirror, some old dude with a tape measure at his feet. "That they're too damn short."

Morton made Claire after picking up Nathan's French, the parking guy in a suit he couldn't possibly afford. And why was Claire decked out like the Cher drag queen from La Cage aux Folles? Taking a moment to be sure he was matching both back to the walkies, *The Otto Show*, Morton pulled his .38 Smith and Wesson Special, letting all three get further ahead before stepping out from behind. Identifying himself, telling them freeze—he'd heard them on sub-channel 36—and to turn slowly or they were going to be wearing their ass cheeks as beanies. Then he took a pull on his ciggy, said, why Claire? Morton didn't know all she was into, but it sounded bad, someone cold, dead. Why, when she was so close to being exonerated. And was that a shot a little earlier? If so, like, who shot who?

Catching Morton hyper-focused on Claire and his cigarette, Nathan drew in one fluid motion, firing wildly, sending Morton running for cover in a zigzag pattern, hiding behind a city garbage container, the three of them making for Claire's Daytona.

Nathan pointed the *pistolet* at Claire, grabbing her keys, letting himself in behind the wheel. Stretching awkwardly, he opened the passenger side, Veronica jumping into the back, Claire in front. Morton was up in a cloud of smoke with the cigarette in his mouth, grazing the roof with a shot, then back behind the container.

"Go, go, go." It was Veronica, screaming.

Nathan slammed closed fists down on the steering wheel. "I can't."

"Why?"

Nathan couldn't quite believe it himself. "I don't drive stick."

"But you're the parking guy," Veronica shouted. "Even I can drive standard."

"Fuck around." Claire backhanded him. "Gimme my gun and you two do a Chinese fire drill."

Nathan looked at Veronica. She said, "Do it, talk about it later."

Handing Claire the *pistolet*, Nathan said she had three bullets, use 'em selectively, that they didn't want to find themselves in a spot with no bullets. She looked at him, said did he think she needed to jack off? She was a cop, seven-years experience. She knew when to aim and shoot.

Opening the door, crouching behind it, she fired a warning shot past her former partner—Claire could see him peaking around the city container, still smoking—as Nathan rounded the car. He was strangely fascinated at the hippie girl struggling with her ferret. Poor animal's in shock, he thought, realizing that she'd remember every one of them, even if they did get away.

Veronica was still crawling over the gearshift when Nathan slid into the back, turning, seeing that the hippie girl couldn't handle the ferret. It was scratching, cutting her, and screaming horrible, kicking. Freeing itself, running like a confused animal runs. Starting low to the ground, stopping, standing on its hind legs, starting again.

Claire reminded herself of how much ammo she had on Morton, thinking it was her or him, no way around it. And when he showed himself, she took aim and pumped the second last bullet into her former partners's throat, seeing his hand go to his neck. Twisting, stumbling, free arm flailing, the other still trying to stem the gash, he tripped over a sewer grate, falling onto the sidewalk, losing his cigarette.

Stunned, Claire's hands dropped to her sides. She was wondering where one went from here when she heard Nathan shouting, "C'mon now." He was waiting in the back, leaving room for Claire in the front, by reason of he didn't know, helping her.

As she jumped in, Veronica hit the ignition, looking up, seeing a flat-black Galaxie 500 coming too fast from the east. She waited for it to pass, thinking Claire was right, that she, Veronica, should have just let it happen, that she should have been patient, sucked it up and taken the abuse until Arlene did it to herself.

All three of them looked on as the ferret shot out into the street. Instinctively, the driver of the Galaxie swerved right then left around the rodent, losing control, barreling full on into the Daytona's driver-side door. Plowing the car up onto the sidewalk like street snow, pinning it crookedly against Arlene's building on an angle.

36

Veronica was screaming about her leg, how bad it hurt, while Nathan watched Heathcliffe Wilson feeling for blood through his spider-webbed windshield. Nathan looked to the end of the street, back to the front seat. The impact had crushed Veronica's side, pushing her up against Claire and the passenger door, which was jammed on a bad angle against the bricks. Both had cuts and abrasions on their faces, but they looked stunned more than anything. Claire was coming out of it, turning, looking back. "The knapsack, the money—where is it?"

Nathan's eyes opened wide. He started talking about all the excitement, how Claire turned on him. Feeling around the space next to him as if the blue knapsack might appear, he saw it in the screen of his mind, sitting on top of the green filing cabinet in Veronica's cubicle.

"Fuck around, all this BS about being punctual, professional, and . . . And . . ."

"Diplomatic?" Nathan said.

"And you're telling me that you forgot? You know what this means?" Claire dislodged her left hand from beneath Veronica, reaching for Nathan's face. "Means we haven't had a chance since we left that office."

Nathan looked all about, behind him, seeing Morton writhing in a trail of his blood on the pavement, gurgling, reaching for his cigarette. Claire started to say something else, but Nathan shushed her, listening for sirens. Hearing none, he watched the hippie lower herself to the pavement, looking under a black pickup, reaching. She was up a few seconds later, the ferret skittish, holding on around her shoulders again. When their eyes met briefly, Nathan said, "We haven't had a chance ever since that particular hippie girl decided to spare for change in that particular spot on this particular day."

"How's that?" Claire was still pawing at him.

"You used to be a *policière*, figure it out, the sequence." Looking back through the window again, seeing Heathcliffe Wilson,

Nathan slid a hand over his mouth. "Scratch that. Assuming your McNab doesn't live to tell—like, aren't you supposed to aim for the legs?—the only reason we still have a chance is by reason of I left the money upstairs. See, we have no motive, so kiss my vaguely ethnic ass."

There, he said it out loud this time.

Claire, watching Heathcliffe Wilson examining his teeth and gums in the Galaxie's rearview, said, "What do you mean we have a chance? We can't get out, trapped, no money."

"Your *pistolet*." Nathan was fast now, alert. "I asked before. It's not registered, is it?"

Claire's mouth opened, but she said nothing, wondering how he was angling to use it against her.

"Just tell me."

"No, it's not registered, okay?"

"Good," Nathan said. "Now we have one bullet left, according to my count, right?"

"Yeah."

"Then gimme."

"You going to shoot me?"

Veronica jammed her elbow into Claire's ribs. "If he was going to shoot you, you'd be dead. Give him the gun, see what he can do. I don't hear anyone else saying we have a chance." Turning away. "And gag me—you stink like Löwenbräu."

Seeing Heathcliffe Wilson step out of the Galaxie, Nathan pushed Claire's head from behind. "I've got a plan, the start of one anyway. You got a plan?" When she didn't answer, he said, "Just give me the *pistolet*, then grab at it when I hand it to Heathcliffe Wilson."

"What? I don't think—"

"Don't think, no time. Just follow instructions. Do what I say this one time. Grab at the gun when I hand it to Heathcliffe, but don't take it. Just get your hands on it."

She still didn't quite get it but handed over the Smith & Wesson 629 Trail Boss anyway as Heathcliffe rounded the bumper. Walking into the angled space between the car and AMA bricks, he bent his lanky frame, looking in, seeing Claire and Veronica borderline okay in the front. Hearing Morton McNab grunt, Heathcliffe stood upright, saying "Jesus" when he saw the cop trailing blood, consciousness almost gone. If he'd only done his full hour of police presence, Heathcliffe thought, bending at the knees, recognizing Nathan in the back.

"No time," Nathan said. "It's a crazy sniper shooting at everybody." Handing the Smith & Wesson 629 Trail Boss over, butt forward. "Stay down and take this."

Heathcliffe held his arms up, said, hey, hey. What happened here? Why did this dude from the studio lot have a gun? And why did he want Heathcliffe to have it?

"Take it," Nathan said, "and get down. You're our only chance."

Each man thinking he was his own only chance, Heathcliffe crouched when a car backfired in the distance. He looked around, picturing himself in some twisted fucker's crosshairs as he scanned the space around him, tall buildings, thousands of windows.

Listening for sirens, he heard none, so he reached, thinking sniper, maybe he'd better have a gun at that. Putting his right hand on the butt, left on the shaft. Noticing Claire's hand in the mix. Then the parking guy's thumb hooked around the trigger, the gun going off in their hands.

Feeling the kickback, holding the Trail Boss himself now, Heathcliffe heard the hum of city, then the first siren. He couldn't see a cruiser, but the sound was getting closer when he bent down again, looking into the back. Nathan was holding his bloodied right shoulder with his left hand, his feet running on spot against the far wall, grimacing like he'd taken it in the ass.

"You did that on purpose," Heathcliffe said. "I saw you, your thumb."

Nathan nodded, still holding his shoulder, making a noise, guttural, the first cruiser approaching. "That's right," he said, holding himself tight as he could, more kicking. He figured things might line-up better if Heathcliffe knew exactly what he was supposed to deny in advance. That way, he'd end up denying it before he was interrogated. And well, he was going to deny it anyway, so what the hell? It would also allow everyone in the car to get their stories straight. "We're going to say you caused this by reason of you're strung so tight, mad about your rubber chickens, your pride, restitution."

"Restitution? I'm supposed to get paid today, 20-thou. That's my restitution right there."

"Cash? Probably part of some hushed-up deal, no paperwork?"

"Right." Heathcliffe's eyes twitched. "But I can't see Arlene denying it."

"Yeah, only I think she's *décédé*, Mr. Wilson."

"*Décédé?*" Heathcliffee took a moment to self-translate. "You mean dead?"

"That's right."

Heathcliffe did a double-take at the building, back to Nathan. "How do you know?"

"I'm going to say you told me while you were threatening to blow my head off with your hollow points, that we heard shots, took cover before you hit us with your car, pinned us in, then you ran upstairs, more shots. After that, I'm saying you came back down, shot the cop and came for us. Why? I don't know. You're mad at Cyrus. Cyrus and Arlene are mad at each other, and it sure seems like everyone from you to Rusty Staub had misadventures with Morton McNab." Tallying all that up, Nathan stopped. For some reason, Claire's claptrap about a boat of poo, that New Order song, flashed in his brain and the rest came to him. "Beyond that, I'm just telling the cops to be cops, to figure out the bizarre revenge triangle out for themselves, and to get me a doctor."

Heathcliffe looked at the gun, raising it to Nathan's head, pulling the trigger, getting that sharp clicking sound. He repeated the drill twice, same thing—click, click. Then there were voices saying drop it, and he did. Reaching in with his bare hands, trying to get them around Nathan's throat, Heathcliffe was screaming about his restitution when they brought him down from behind. That's right, just you keep singing from that book, Nathan thought, holding himself, retracing footsteps in his head, brushing them out just as fast.

The girl with the ferret was gone. Unlikely to come back by reason of who would want to get involved? Even if she did, she was a street kid, so who would believe her? No one by reason she was already a considered criminal just by being a street kid, probably on drugs, a questionable truth-teller as such. And Morton McNab, he had to be dead, a trail of red-black blood longer than that putt Disco Dick made for eagle at the Panasonic Las Vegas Invitational back in '84.

Upstairs, it was all very sloppy, but Nathan didn't have to explain that.

He wasn't up there, officially, so it was best to let the coppers put that together for themselves, what with Heathcliffe denying everything before being asked. As for the money, that was just as well forgotten, too, on Veronica's filing cabinet. So long as the money was in the vicinity of where it was supposed to be, Nathan saw a window of opportunity. They just had to get their stories straight, now, before emergency pried them out and separated them.

Bad as the pain was—and man, his arm burned—Nathan had the wherewithal to tell Veronica to give Claire some gum, that she smelled like *merde*. Watching Veronica go for her purse and hand Claire some Chiclets, he silently fine-toothed his account in his head. Yes, even with a bullet, he could talk his way out of anything. He was going to tell them he was with Claire and Veronica on the sidewalk, prancing about in goofy clothes from set, celebrating end of season, pay day, when they heard shots upstairs. After they jumped in Claire's car to get out of there, Heathcliffe Wilson came lumbering in, took a run at them in his Galaxie, then ran upstairs himself, some kind of bizarre revenge triangle, additional gunplay.

Heathcliffe was up there for all of a minute while they were pinned inside. On the way out, he got into a gunfight with Morton McNab, shot him. That's when he came back for Nathan, Claire, and Veronica, jamming the *pistolet* inside the Daytona, yammering on about his restitution. And but of course, both Nathan and Claire grabbed at the *pistolet* before it went off, explaining residue on their hands. You bet they went for the *pistolet* when that crazy Heathcliffe Wilson shoved it through the window. He was still trying to shoot them when the police got there. Cops saw that much.

Nathan just about had the whole thing written down in his head when two uniforms looked in on him bloodied in the back. "You alright?" the closest said.

"Got me in the shoulder." Nathan felt the warmth run down his torso. "Need medical attention, as you can see, a doctor."

The one doing the talking said the cavalry was on the way, hold on. Then, looking at Morton McNab, he said, "The fuck happened here?"

Nathan kicked the back of Claire's seat to make sure she was listening, saying he was just the parking guy came to get paid. Claire, too.

"Paid-duty officer," she told them, chewing, smelling fruity now. "Claire Malik."

The two cops connected the face to the name, looking at each other. Turning to the brass sign on the building behind them, back. "You work for AMA, Production Company?"

"That's right," Nathan said. Thinking at least he still had his spy books, a 6in1 Radio Lantern, and something better than all that money. "Under the table."

37

Thursday, July 13

It was after nine, day one of season two. Unable to come up with a five-letter word starting with F for garden tool, Nathan slipped the pencil behind his ear. The hot sun wouldn't climb over Cherry Beach Studios for another hour, but Nathan was already having a time taking care of himself. His right arm was in a sling, which had him reaching with his left for the bottle of generic Tylenol 3s on his ledge. Awkwardly holding it between his knees, he struggled with the childproof cap until the bottle popped out, rattling onto the floor. Cursing, reaching for the talk button with his good arm, he said, "Nathan for Sundance."

"Go for Sundance."

"I dropped my medicine and can't pick it up."

"And?"

"Means a little help, please," Nathan said. "A little help for the man had six hours surgery pulling Heathcliffe Wilson's bullet bits—hollow points, illegal—out of my shoulder."

"Just waiting for you to ask, say please."

Nathan was about to say move faster, you can do better, when he saw the kid on his way. Rounding the kiosk, Sundance opened the back. His headphones were hung around his neck and he was sniffing, rank. "Get out. It's too small for both of us."

"Sundance, I got a sling on my arm."

"Got a sling on your arse?"

"No. No sling on my *derrière*."

"Then get out. It's your wound, stinks so bad."

Nathan said it wasn't the wound. He had to keep the wound clean by reason of he didn't want gangrene or that nasty new flesh-eating business. The stink was from the skunk came back in between seasons one and two. Nathan gets a beer tin off Pepé Le Pew's head, he returns to the scene, sprays the kiosk—must've been frightened—and drops the deuce. How's that for thanks?

"Just get out, man." Sundance waved his hand back and forth. "It's too small a space, whatever the source of the stink."

Nathan extended his good arm. Sundance made a face, taking Nathan's hand, helping him up. Soon as Nathan was out, Sundance stepped inside, bending, picking up the plastic bottle and tossing it underhand to Nathan in the doorway. He tried to catch it with his bad arm, reflexes, getting caught up in his walkie-talkie wire and hurting his sore spot. "Hand them to me," he said, caressing the right shoulder with his left hand.

Sundance came out of the kiosk and picked the bottle up. Nathan took it, hesitating, then held it out. "Open them."

Although he thought about arguing, Sundance took the bottle back and figured out the cap's child-proof features. "Now what?"

"Take three out."

Sundance tapped a few into his left palm. "Okay."

"Now put 'em in my mouth." There it was. Sure, Nathan had been shot, came a pubic hair from going to jail, but he could still lay it out there, deadpan, like James Dark when he stiffed that Singapore lady at supper in *The Bamboo Bomb*.

"Put your dick in your mouth," Sundance said.

"Okay." Nathan raised his good hand, pointing. "Put three on my ledge, then close it, the bottle."

"You sure it's three?"

"Three."

Sundance read the label. "Says here two at a time. With everyone getting killed, drugs involved, cops, I'm not giving you more than it says—two."

Nathan glanced at Sundance, then the bottle. "How many does it say give a man got shot with a bullet explodes?"

Sundance looked at the label again. "Doesn't."

"Yeah, well his doctor says give him three."

"Dr. Says You, maybe. I'm giving you two." Sundance replaced one pill in the bottle. "If I can't smoke dope—and I can't, cops, like I said—you only get what the label says, two." He closed the bottle, putting it on the ledge along with the two loose tablets, heading out, he said, to do other things Nathan couldn't do for himself, pylons for now. Putting his headset back in place, ears on, he heard a series of clicks, then "Kiwi to Sundance, Kiwi to Sundance . . ."

"Go for Sundance."

"Tell Nathan his bloody talk button is on already, stuck."

Sundance scowled at Nathan. "Your talk button's on, stuck."

Nathan looked at himself, squirmed around in his sling, untangling the chord, ensuring he was off-air, looking up. "I fixed it, what?"

"Everyone's getting shot. I'm talking about pot, drugs, cops, and you've got me bugged." Sundance stormed off, talking over his shoulder. "Thanks. Thanks a lot, Lawn Boy."

**

Inside Cherry Beach Studios, Dan Meckler thought he'd better be jumping for Veronica, even if she didn't have the decency to be here. That's why he had Abel ahead of schedule on day one of season two, shooting just a little before 9:30 am.

Meckler had thought about starting with a skit portraying Abel as Joe DiMaggio with a case of the shakes at Marilyn Monroe's grave—her headstone telling him to cut out caffeine—but that was going to be easy, so he convinced Abel to save it for a rainy day. Instead, they decided to impress everybody and get the tricky stuff out of the way, the Christmas special.

That meant Abel was in drag for a change, complete with heels, a G-string with fur details visible through the open Santa coat, blonde wig beneath a Santa hat.

"At Christmas, Mrs. Claus likes to dress sexy, without looking skanky," Abel said in his best falsetto. "I like to give Mr. Claus a reward, something for him to look forward to when he comes home every year, something extra, something—"

"Cut," Meckler shouted.

"Cut?" Abel couldn't believe it. "You kidding? I was sprinting. Why cut, Danny?"

Meckler looked away. "Because you're not and the folks at home don't need to know."

Abel shielded his eyes from the lights. "I'm not what?"

Meckler ran a hand over his face. "Abel, you're not circumcised, right?"

"Right. My *Zaida* had to pass as an uncircumcised Greek, so that's how we Ottos roll, natural." Abel opened his arms. "And?"

"And," Meckler said, lowering his eyes to Abel's crotch. "I know that how?"

Abel looked down at himself, pulling the Mrs. Santa coat together, walking off stage. His right knee buckled when his heel clipped a cable. "You didn't have to tell me like that, Danny."

Ding, dong, the queen was gone, and Meckler was happy again. Thinking maybe he could get away with leaking Abel's out-takes onto that new internet deal that was about to destroy the world. See what everyone in Erie, Pennsylvania thought of Abel then. "Don't worry about it, Abel. Just tape that thing down. Just a little tape, that's all you need."

And the poor people in the bleachers were laughing again, without prompts.

***

Back in his kiosk, Nathan crunched pills with his teeth, swallowing chalky bits dry. He pursed, bitter, as he flicked on the 6in1 Radio Lantern, the part-time jazz station coming in. Something from the new Dewey Redman album faded, making way for BBC News to lead with another angle on Tiananmen Square. Apparently, the Chinese government had released a most-wanted list naming, blaming, and shaming 21 student leaders for sparking last month's confrontation. Hearing that one had already been turned in by his sister, Nathan couldn't help but figuratively look away, again, the sheer betrayal.

He reached for the dial, switching to CFRB 1010 AM where he might catch up on domestic matters. First, there was a meandering bit on Prime Minister Brian Mulroney lobbying the provinces to ratify a new constitution. Next item featured an interview with Ontario Attorney General Ian Scott discussing illegal donations made to his own party. Nathan had heard about the scandal. They'd been calling it the Patti Starr Affair, and while Nathan didn't entirely grasp the fine print, it was clear that the Liberals were up to something sketchy in terms of selling influence, even if they were way ahead in the polls. Thinking about holding his nose and registering a protest vote for the NDP—they were safe, unelectable—Nathan was about to dial surf when the radio started telling a story he already knew, mostly.

"Constable Claire Malik—suspended when her porn past turned up in an American skin rag—has been quietly reinstated after saving two Hollywood North workers from a mad gunman late last week.

"Malik's former partner, Constable Morton McNab, was killed after a gunfight allegedly involving Hollywood North producer Arlene Marion, her former set designer Cyrus Dagan, and a surviving man charged in connection with what police are calling a bizarre revenge triangle."

Allegedly, the radio said, Marion and Dagan shot each other after falling out over work-related matters. The killings appeared to be connected to a simultaneous incident in which a local restaurateur rammed his vehicle into another where Malik and two of Marion's employees were taking cover from the gunplay.

"After engaging with Marion and Dagan, then allegedly shooting McNab, the man is said to have approached Malik's vehicle and pointed a gun inside. Due to her swift action, a casual employee received only a flesh wound to his shoulder before officers arrived.

"Charged with one count of homicide as well as attempted homicide, aggravated assault, and assault an officer is Heathcliffe Wilson, a former kicker with the now-defunct Montreal Concordes and current owner and operator of the Heathcliffe Wilson's Fried Chicken chain. Sources say conspiracy charges are also pending."

Ironically, the radio said, McNab was the arresting officer when Dagan was charged in connection to the theft of a large rubber chicken from Wilson's restaurant last month. Now police were alleging that Dagan was also the gunman responsible for the death of Hector Diaz. In a related incident being considered as a sex crime, police claim that Dagan stripped one of Diaz' neighbors naked before chasing her in his vehicle and running her down multiple times.

Nathan didn't know this Diaz, but the radio said he was a firearms expert who leased rare weapons to Hollywood North sets, so that answered a few other questions, namely how Cyrus got a hold of that souped-up rifle.

As for Claire, after providing an eye-witness account of McNab's assassination as well as Wilson's feud with the production company, the radio said she would receive full back pay.

Minding the sling, thinking good for her, Nathan shifted on his perch, breathing easy when he heard that contrary evidence provided by a panhandler had been dismissed as unreliable. Also, police were investigating how a large dose of prescription opiates got into Arlene's system, but by reason of what? Radio didn't say, beyond mentioning her recent stint in rehab, conventional logic surely following that she couldn't stop popping those pills like Tic Tacs, perfect.

Once the newsreader started talking about Cyrus being found in possession of unauthorized nudes of a very young Billy Idol, Nathan switched signals again, returning to the part-time jazz station, which was back to jazz, thankfully. "Idaho" by Count Basie and his Orchestra, just the right amount of pep for the hour.

Fiddling with the antenna, then the tuner, getting reception right as rain, Nathan sat back and watched Sundance out in the lot, dropping pylons all over the place. He was trying to help, just cranky by reason of maybe he really was the way Claire said. How had she put it? Oh yeah, up against the stem.

38

By 10, a new paid-duty officer patrolled the lot in search of a comfort zone. Compared to Claire, she was a sweet *petite*, younger, and her crests were intact. She looked like she'd come off the night shift, tired and bored. Whatever, Nathan fiddled with his radio when he experienced interference, likely a weather pattern, until the part-time jazz station came back clear. Hearing a greasy horn he couldn't place, he looked down the street, watching Arlene's Jeep float to him like a ghost. Veronica waved on her way by, parking in spot number two. She looked thin getting out, wobbling on her cane, walking slowly to Nathan's kiosk.

No matter how many times they were asked, Veronica and Claire dutifully repeated Nathan's bizarre revenge triangle until the truthmakers deemed it fact. Veronica doubly did her part, keeping a straight face through the funeral, only who's idea was it to have Mike Bullard give the eulogy? Over and over, he looked around, saying how Arlene would have loved it here. Loved it—Veronica thought it was a miracle the old lady didn't rise up and slap Bullard.

"Thanks," she said, approaching, looking up at Nathan. "Thank you."

Nathan nodded, pointing an index out of his sling. "So the investor's own Arlene's ride?"

"Company car, tax purposes." Veronica smiled without showing teeth, gracious. "And don't be envious. It still smells of skunk."

"Got my booth, too." Nathan took a breath. "Let me ask you something." Waiting a beat. "You mean to execute Arlene, or did someone just get over-enthusiastic, make a mistake?"

Veronica faced the studio, the rent-a-cop out of earshot. "They think Cyrus killed her, that she killed him. They also think Heathcliffe Wilson fired shots up there before he came out and shot Morton. You read, right?"

Did Nathan read? Yes, and he was pretty sure Arlene was dead before Cyrus shot her. Again, Nathan felt her when he went up for the money, *froid*. Now, how much of that Percodan did Veronica give Arlene? That was the $64,000 question.

"I gave her enough to put her to sleep, six things."

"She said you gave her 16 just before she went down for good." Nathan looked off. "Same amount, more or less, I expect as what they're saying in the news, metric."

"She had already taken some without my knowing, even told me so, okay?"

"Right." Nathan watched a gang of gulls swoop down on Lake Ontario. He figured Veronica was lying, again. Same time, it was done, and he had to attend to the here and now. "Seems like everyone got what they wanted."

"Seems like it."

Tabernac, none of this was Nathan's idea, but he was the one who fixed it. Talked all their ways out of everything. Made a *policière* of Claire again, a producer of Veronica. A producer—no, she was the executive producer now. But Nathan was still out in lot, and Veronica was making him ask. "Seems like it worked out so well I'm also due a little consideration."

Veronica brought her voice down. "You do not want money. Money goes missing, people start asking where it went. Right now, it is a bizarre revenge triangle, complicated yet simple."

Complicated yet simple, huh? Did Veronica hear CFRB? No, well they were trying to figure how so many things got into Arlene. Knowing full well, Nathan thought that alone ought to be worth cash-money.

Tugging her hair, Veronica said, "Licorice already."

"Heathcliffe Wilson, did he get his cash-money restitution?"

Peeking left through her round translucent shades—Sundance adjusting his headphones, making googly eyes, the pothead—Veronica said, "You know he did not."

"Well, where did his 20-thou go?"

"I have it." Veronica patted her Coach purse. "It is due back in the kitty, accounting."

"Yeah, well it's due in my kitty, is where it's due."

Veronica slid the sunglasses to the top of her head. "Look, I will make sure you are taken care of, do a little something for you. It is different now."

Nathan thought a lot of things were different. Veronica had traded her wishy-washy sports jacket for a brown chevron-paneled blouse, unbuttoned to her *décolletage*. Below, she wore a low-waist skirt. Her hair was straightened, but her face, there was something about her face.

"You put cover-up on your scar." He reached, touching his own right brow.

Mirroring him, she unconsciously touched her brow, catching herself, jerking away. "What does that have to do with anything?"

"It's just I always thought that was the most beautiful thing about you, the thing that kept you above the fray. How did you get it anyway?"

Veronica said he wouldn't find it very intriguing. Nathan said try me. Okay, on prom night she was at the beach, trying to open a beer bottle with a jackknife, stabbing at the bottle cap when the knife bounced up and she stabbed herself in the face. Nathan thought it was kind of intriguing, looking at her purse. "Just get me Heathcliffe Wilson's restitution envelope, 20K."

"And if I cannot?"

That was it. He didn't want to do it this way, but she wasn't going to pay him just because it was right. Reaching into his pocket, he winced when his shoulder hit the wall, holding his wallet and removing the envelope with Rusty Staub's autograph, producing a folded piece of yellow paper from inside. Veronica felt the hook, her mind running over the three-legged stool. She committed it to yellow paper, but she burned it. Yes, yes—she was sure, even if she had been tripping that day.

"Nathan, is that supposed to be something incriminating?"

"That's right, incriminating."

Veronica's arms were crossed, one swinging out to the piece of yellow paper with what appeared to be a soot stain. "Show me."

Unfolding it, he showed her both sides.

"Blank," she said.

Removing the pencil from behind his ear, Nathan held the paper in his bad hand, explaining that this was the piece of yellow paper beneath the one Veronica wrote her plan on. All Nathan had to do was cover most of the page in sideways pencil and Veronica's directives would scream out in reverse. Stealing the walkies, spiking Arlene's tea, going for a Tim Hortons long enough for payroll to be poached—it would all be right there in Veronica's hand.

"You took that from my house? A guest, and you stole something to use against me?"

Nathan said he liberated it from Claire who stole it by reason of she didn't trust Veronica, didn't like her. Asides, Claire was a *policière* again. No telling what she'd do with it to, so Veronica should be thanking Nathan, again. He just wanted to get paid, please and thank you.

"Who would you give it to? That incriminates you as well as me. Claire, too."

Nathan said that should tell Veronica how desperate he'd become to get out of the lot.

Hands in her hair, she said, "Why would you even think you would need something against me, blackmail?"

"Isn't blackmail." He looked at the slow flow of cars on the expressway, everyone pressing. "Claire called it insurance. I call it I-think-it's-worth-your-piece-of-mind-to-have-this-piece-of-paper-destroyed. I say it's worth 20-thou today. Tomorrow, maybe I decide the same amount as when the Gods of mathematics were multiplying."

The way he put it, so easy, the boast didn't seem out of line. But then she looked into him, her pupils tiny dots. "Know how I know you are bluffing?"

This was gonna be good, the girl calling crap while she was high. "How's that?"

"Do you get the new western channel with your pirate cable?"

Nathan sighed. "No lady, I don't even have a TV. That's the problem. I'm living at St. Leonard Hotel, back in St. Jamestown, $150 a week. I share facilities, no TV."

"Ever watch *The Lone Ranger?*"

Here we go, but okay, he'd play along. "Some, in my youth."

"How about the time Tonto draws a confession out of someone

by pretending to read out evidence against him, except his piece of paper is blank?"

Nathan scratched his chin. "Didn't see that one, but how does it apply here? I showed you mine was blank." Tapping the page. "It's the indentations gonna get you, different play entirely."

"Oh, it is the same play." Veronica pointed at the yellow paper. "Take your pencil and show me—show me my plan to rob the place, in my own hand."

Humming along to a Wes Montgomery riff, Nathan took his HB pencil and shaded the page, admiring his work before holding it up like this was arts and crafts time. "*Voilà.* You, in your own hand, charting out how you're going to drug Arlene so as we can pull a payroll heist."

Jesus, that was Veronica's beautiful penmanship, writing out a pre-emptive confession. She heard herself shout-whispering that they were on the same side. Why did Nathan have to do this? She was going to do a little something for him.

"A little something, *merci.*"

"That's right." She held out her right palm. "A little something."

"What? You were going to make me grip? Say, 'Hey Nathan, c'mon over and grip this.'"

"I was going to make you something, and you had to make it personal, why?"

"Had to be that way by reason of you're turning on me right now."

"How?" Both of Veronica's hands were out, arms spread. "How am I turning on you?"

"By talking to me as you are." Nathan looked off—Sundance confused, holding a pylon, looking at Nathan as if to say where do I put it? "By making it complicated. By having me walk into a situation where I had to shoot Cyrus, kill him. Then, after all that, by talking to me just like you are, like her."

"Claire?" Veronica said. "You're comparing me to Claire?"

"It's Arlene you've become. Drugged up. Not using contractions, talking about Tonto, moral lessons, when I'm not even First Nations, probably. Then you dangle a little something for Nathan so long as he's good, after how much I did for you—Arlene all over again."

Near the set door, Nathan saw Kiwi, watching, cupping hands to his headset. Next to him, Freak was tugging at the collar of his powder blue T-shirt that said WINK, I'LL DO THE REST. Janet Boroski walked out, hiking a lemon-lime G-string above her hip-hugger jeans when Nathan did a double take. "Why are they all looking at us?"

Watching the rent-a-cop adjust her headset then jot something in a notebook, Veronica found herself turning, like her body understood what her head was processing, noticing the wire tangled in Nathan's sling. He held up his left hand, what?

"Your talk button." Veronica closed her eyes. "It is on, stuck."

"Huh." He looked down at himself, seeing his own private pursuit of happiness becoming the leading cause of unhappiness for so many. "This is all hearsay, right?"

"Goddamn you." She stepped forward, pawing at his sling. "They can still hear us."

First came throbs of fear, confusion—how was he going to explain this while he's on Tylenol 3s? A fast-forward reel of plausibilities ran over an old movie like subliminal text in the theater of his mind. He was thinking about blowing off the conversation to a skit they were working out, something they'd pitch to Abel. Then, hearing the first bars of Shadowy Men on a Shadowy Planet doing "Summer Wind"—the part-time jazz station logging it as Canadian content—something inside gave. No way he was going to talk his way out of this, not the way Brian Connelly's guitar wailed so hardass and melancholy and bittersweet over the summer wind lingering there. Maybe it was the realization that it was over, but Nathan felt slightly better once he accepted Frank Sinatra's concept of two summer sweethearts, content over duration.

Worrying what his momma was going to think, seeing her adopted son in the news, Nathan asked Veronica if Claire turned in her brick yet. Told no, he reached for his, holding it with his right, punching digits with his left. He heard the connection patching through, ringing, wondering how he found Claire in this shitty parking lot. Inside, he could see her, the way she was when they first hooked up, looking through her bangs. Then the image was gone, her tentative voice replacing it.

Yes, he told her, watching the rent-a-cop start towards him, he knew they were supposed to be incommunicado. Never mind for now. Did Claire have a change of clothes? She carried a spare, right? Hearing her say yes, it was going to be cool, he tried to picture her in a Pho-Pa after she spelled it out. When he couldn't conjure an image by reason of he didn't know a Pho-Pa from a *faux pas*, he said whatever, she needed to get in her car and drive. What? And why—why was he saying this?

"Run," he told her, the rent-a-cop closing in. "Don't think about it. Just run, Claire, run."

The rent-a-cop was behind Veronica now, telling Nathan to come on out of his kiosk. He held up an index through his sling, just a sec.

"Hope you know, that's your phone call. The fuck're you talking to anyway?"

"It's his girlfriend." Veronica looked to the lake, the breeze hitting her. "His girlfriend."

Saying *au revoir*, maybe for once and always, Nathan dropped his brick, thinking about the great caddies—Angelo Argea who carried for Jack Nicklaus, Gary Player's man Rabbit Dyer, and Lee Trevino's looper Herman Mitchell, an excellent player in his own right. How many major championships between them, and Nathan couldn't even will his man into the winner's circle at the Canadian Open? *Tabernac*, all this meant was that Nathan was never going to reach his potential, ever.

He was wondering if they'd let him keep the 6in1 Radio Lantern in jail when Abel exploded through the doors in his Mrs. Santa suit, holding his cellular a foot from his face, shouting at it.

"How can you say that to me? We haven't even aired yet."

Abel held the phone close, listening, then yelling that Jerry Seinfeld had fuck all to do with it and throwing his brick up against the wall, shattering it.

Dan Meckler walked out, clearly concerned. "What the fuck, Abel?"

"*The Otto Show* is stillborn, cancelled."

Meckler, noting that Abel's mascara was running, said, "They say why?"

"NBC passed on Jerry so they don't need anything to go up against Jerry." Abel slowed, catching his breath. "They weren't wild about some of our religious connotations, especially the Pope-on-a-Rope. Also, they mentioned Rusty Staub saying *Sacrébleu.*"

"They know what it means?"

"Not really, just that it takes the Lord's name in vain, somehow. They were sore that I tried to slip something foreign past them. But it was mostly about Jerry—Jerry, Jerry, Jerry."

"Bullshit." Meckler looked at Abel all tarted up and shook his head, nope. "I not only told you what was going to happen, I told you who'd be calling the shots."

"What, Danny? What did you tell me? Are you saying you know who pulled the string?"

Meckler nodded once and said, "I told you." Pointing an index to the sky, then directly at Abel. "That God was going to get you."

Abel lit up with a second round of emotion, charging Meckler, pushing him against the wall, buckling him with a right. Meckler checked for blood, yeah, smiling, taunting Abel about standing on his head in three-feet of shit for an eternity. Abel reached back, removing one of his stilettos, using the heel to beat on Meckler. He wasn't smiling anymore.

The rent-a-cop watched the scene unfold—Abel really giving it to Dan—back to Nathan. "Stay here," she told him, withdrawing her billy club and breaking into a run.

Veronica hobbled in the same direction, appearing to follow, then climbed into the Jeep, hitting the ignition, pulling out, and stopping in front of Nathan's kiosk.

"Get in."

Nathan watched members of the studio audience pour outside, some of them ignoring Rupert the audience coordinator and jumping into the fray, taking sides.

"Come on."

Waving his good hand, Nathan said, "No *más.*"

"No *más.* What does that mean, no *más?*"

"Means no more. Means I've got nothing, like Roberto up against Sugar Ray. No *más.*"

Veronica looked at the fight—she couldn't see the rent-a-cop anymore, so many people involved—and told Nathan for the third and final time to get in.

"How far do you think we'd get?" he said, avoiding eye contact. "And for how long?"

"I have an envelope with $20,000 and a full tank of gas, almost. Should get us through dinner."

"You going to bake me muffins?" He looked at her. "Every day?"

Veronica closed her eyes, nodding, yes, fine, okay, sure. She'd bake him muffins. Every day. Now get in.

Seeing the rent-a-cop cuffing Abel, Nathan stood, pocketing his pills, the yellow paper, then stepping out. He reached through the window when he remembered the 6in1 Radio Lantern, grabbing it, before rounding the bumper and climbing in. Veronica hit the gas and hung a right on Cherry Street. Nathan locked his door, turning to see the rent-a-cop controlling Abel, looking around. It just seemed to just be occurring to her that Nathan and Veronica were gone.

"Where should we go?" Veronica said. "Where could we go?"

Nathan pointed forward. "Take Lake Shore to the DVP. Get to the 401, head east, rural Quebec. I know a place deep in the woods where you can bake those muffins."

"Every day." Veronica looked at him. "And what the fuck?" Back to the street. "I don't mind baking, especially if we're wanted felons and you know a place deep in the Quebec woods. But why is that even an issue at this point, muffins?"

"I don't hardly know myself," Nathan said, "except Claire was on about it, made me promise not to let you bake me muffins. Until then, it hadn't occurred to me that you baked, or that you doing so for me would be desirable. Now that I don't have anything—other than my Tylenol 3s, the 6in1 Radio Lantern, this yellow piece of paper, and half of Heathcliffe's restitution—I just can't stop thinking how badly Claire didn't want you baking muffins for me, so I figure there's something to it, that women know about *merde* like that." He glanced in the sideview, the rent-a-cop a spec in the road. "Plus, I think it's important to have something to look forward to, every day, until they come for us."

"Claire." Veronica held out her brick to Nathan. "You want to call her again?"

"No." Nathan reached for the phone anyway, grabbed it. "Not after what she said about Gordon Gano. And that's on top of the hitting, plus she tried to shoot me." Throwing the phone out the window.

"Hey—hey, what did you do that for?"

"Computers," Nathan said. "The way this is going, they probably have a way to use computers to track us through our cellular telephones. That's why I didn't bring mine."

Veronica made the light at Lake Shore, turning, telling Nathan he was paranoid. As they blended into mid-morning traffic, he looked about, eyes in every car, and said, "I am now."

Vern Smith is a former production assistant who spent almost 10 years on the fringes of the film and television industry as a writer and copy editor for *Canadian Screenwriter* magazine. He has also worked as a newspaper reporter, political advisor, radio DJ, and caddy. His first novel, *The Green Ghetto* (Run Amok Books, 2019), was deemed "a model for modern westerns" by *Broken Pencil*. His novelette, *The Gimmick*—a finalist for Canada's highest crime-writing honor, the Arthur Ellis Award—is the title track of his second collection of fiction, *The Gimmick: novelettes, stories, and sketches* (Run Amok Books, 2020). A Windsor, Ontario native and longtime Toronto resident, he now lives on the wild blue yonder of the Illinois prairie.